Here's the Score

Here's the Score

*The Story of a Rural Colorado
School's Rise to Basketball Fame*

Ronald James Newton

To order additional copies of this book, contact:
Xlibris
1-888-795-4274
www.Xlibris.com
Orders@Xlibris.com
763435

CONTENTS

Utopia ix
Acknowledgments xi

Chapter 1   Born to Play 1
Chapter 2   Early Learning 7
Chapter 3   First Competition 19
Chapter 4   Child's Play 25
Chapter 5   The Gym 36
Chapter 6   Touch of a Teacher 46
Chapter 7   Difficulty in the Fifth 53
Chapter 8   Inspiration and Support 59
Chapter 9   Coach Clark 64
Chapter 10 New Hoop 72
Chapter 11 Middle School 81
Chapter 12 Basketball Saturday 90
Chapter 13 Devastating Defeat 103
Chapter 14 Sophomore Entrée 111
Chapter 15 Dual Playtime 117
Chapter 16 Off Court 125
Chapter 17 Sophomore Seasoning 133
Chapter 18 Brothers 143
Chapter 19 Brothers Court 151
Chapter 20 Coach Adams 160
Chapter 21 Discipline 172
Chapter 22 A New Beginning 178
Chapter 23 Marching Onward 187
Chapter 24 Tournament Time 197
Chapter 25 Misstep 205

Chapter 26 Prom...211
Chapter 27 Award...216
Chapter 28 Summer...222
Chapter 29 Gridiron Success...227
Chapter 30 First...238
Chapter 31 Lesson Learned...243
Chapter 32 Midseason Woes...252
Chapter 33 Conference Champions..261
Chapter 34 District Drama..271
Chapter 35 State Tournament...281
Chapter 36 Championship..290
Chapter 37 Rejection...302
Chapter 38 School's End..308
Chapter 39 Dedicated Learner..314
Chapter 40 Last Days...325

Epilogue..337
Bibliography..347
Index..349

To brothers David, Roland, Richard, and
Gerald, my consummate teammates.

To all my brothers and sisters who inspired and supported
my dream to play basketball for Mead High School.

To Coach Jack Adams, who guided and
illuminated us with wisdom and integrity.

To my teachers who understood that who I was as a person
was more important than who I was as a basketball player.

To teammates Lyle Schaefer, Mike Eckel, Lanny Davis, George
Rademacher, Carl Hansen, and all the other players along the way
who helped my brothers and me in our quest for basketball success.

To schoolmates and community friends who encouraged
us with their presence and their voices.

Behold, how good and pleasant it is when brothers dwell in unity.

—Psalm 133:1

Utopia

Utopia, for me, has many meanings, such as a peaceful, hidden from the world; a secret treasury, and most of all, potential for perfection. The dictionary defines it as one that believes in the perfectibility of a human society. You take your choice or come up with your version, but it seems to always turn out to be something exceeding good. Let's go from there.

In 1955, I found my utopia—Mead, Colorado, a village of maybe two hundred residents nestled in a wonderful atmosphere. It had all the ingredients for beauty: green fields, small lakes, spectacular mountains in the background, and, most importantly, people with integrity who were certainly unspoiled.

I was a young twenty-five-year-old, just out of college, a veteran, newly married with a baby, looking for my first teaching position. My life to this point had been spent being a "jock," playing many sports with failures and successes, but it was always exciting, interesting, and challenging. Coaches and coaching in general caught my attention. The good techniques from great coaches were essential but not always exciting. However, poor coaches taught me a lot—how not to do it. Probably, a burning desire to teach positive enthusiasm exploded in my thinking. I think I ran my life in such a fashion as "So why not in coaching? Give it a try!"

I felt deeply that once you set your mind with enthusiasm and persistence, anything is possible. Now to find a teaching assignment for the test.

It happened. I was offered a job at Mead High School coaching three major sports, driving the athletic bus, teaching driver training, industrial arts, physical education—throw in a study hall, and yes, I was the new athletic director, a big assignment but well paid. I got the amazing sum of $2,900 with benefits for the year. I had a $300 car, paid rent at $30 a month, hauled my own water for the cistern, heated with coal, and thought I was lucky. Actually, even today I know I was much more than lucky. I was gifted an opportunity that few ever experience.

My student athletes centered around one family, which gave me a set of triplets, an elder brother, and a younger brother. I could have an entire starting basketball team from one family—the Newtons. But let's not forget the support group of Lyle, Mike, Lanny, George, Paul, Allen, and the entire study body. I had to sell the idea of practice with a purpose and make it fun and always positive. Hey, it worked. They bought in. The book tells of the success, but it probably misses the thought that a group of young students taught me how to lead. The thought has always been with me. The one downside is I was never able to grow up. Yes, I got older, but I am always looking for another chance to experience supreme success. I'm still enjoying working with kids even at the age of eighty-six. I want to thank Mead, the Newtons, and especially Ron. They all made my life worthwhile.

Coach Jack Adams

Acknowledgments

This story is factual as gleaned from memory of personal experiences and external oral and written sources. I thank my sister, Helen Newton Teter, who provided her own photos and those of others that she has assembled into the Newton family album. I'm indebted to classmate Irene Stotts, who provided yearbooks for photo sources and reference purposes. Grateful thanks also go to Patricia Newton French, Richard Newton, Roland Newton, Marcus Newton, Forrest (Frosty) Newton, friends, and classmates for the informed conversations we've had over the years that contributed to the content of this book. My sincere thanks are extended to my niece, Patricia Thornton Lewis, who scanned and digitized the family album photos and has designed the book cover; my photographer, Sheila Koenig, who has shot photos with black-and-white film of Mead and the school; and my editors, Lorraine Hale Robinson and Marcus Newton, who have critiqued and corrected my manuscript.

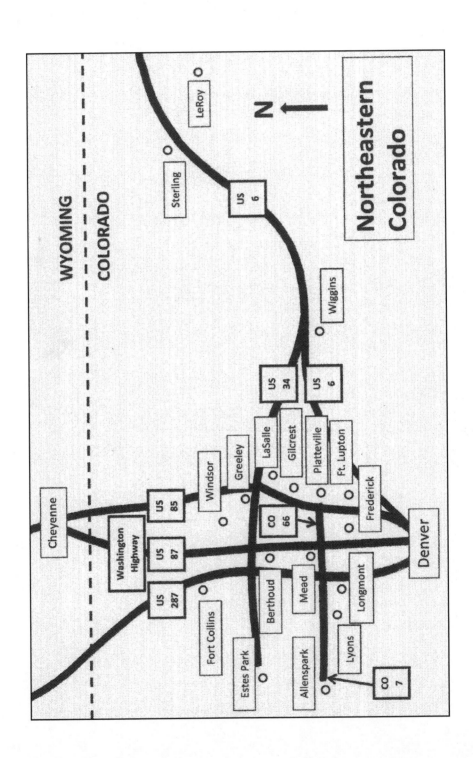

Northeastern Colorado

Mead Consolidated Schools Building, Mead CO. Circa 1950. *Mead High School Library.*

Chapter 1

Born to Play

It was September 1939, several months after James Elmer Newton and his wife, Laura, and their twelve children had been forced from the house they had rented for more than six years. Their landlord needed it for a new employee. With nothing else available, the Newtons moved into the abandoned Farmer's Union Town Hall on the south end of the small town of Mead, Colorado. Mead's population, at one time more than four hundred, had dwindled to half that as the Great Depression tightened its grip on the economy and forced many to leave and look for opportunities elsewhere. The bank, the hotel, the car dealership, the bowling alley, and the library closed. However, the pool hall, two gas stations, a drugstore, two grocery stores, a lumberyard, a blacksmith, an inn, a grain elevator, and two churches kept their doors open. The crown jewel of the community, the two-story red-brick Mead Consolidated Schools building, built in 1917, stood majestically on the south end of town.

Mead was founded as a result of the sugar beet industry that prospered in Weld County, one of the richest agricultural regions in the country. At the beginning of the twentieth century, there was need to build a railroad to transport beets to processing factories of the Great Western Sugar Co. that sprang up in the towns of Greeley, Windsor, Eaton, and Longmont. In 1901, Paul Mead, whose father had established the community of Highlandlake just a few miles northeast of Longmont, realized his lake community was to be bypassed by the Great Western Railway en route from Greeley to Longmont. The entrepreneurial Mead then converted a portion of his agricultural landholding to the development of a town plotted next to the railroad. Highlandlake buildings, townspeople, and businesses were relocated to the new town of Mead. Buyers of lots put up houses and stores spanning twenty blocks. By 1920, a thriving Mead was serving farmers from a radius of twenty miles and meeting the needs of the local populace. Besides beets, sugar, and molasses, the Great Western Railway also carried passengers. The tiny burg, situated on the Colorado Eastern Plains at an elevation of one mile and just twenty miles east of the Rocky Mountain foothills, provided residents a spectacular view of Longs Peak and Mount Meeker, both more than fourteen thousand feet high.

The large meeting room in the town hall where the Newtons lived had been transformed into a gym a decade earlier and had once been used by the high-school basketball team. But since a new gym had been completed as a Works Progress Administration (WPA) project next to the school, the hall was no longer needed, and town fathers loaned it to the Newtons at no charge.

Laura Dreier Newton, pregnant for the thirteenth time, had gained weight rapidly and suspected she was about to have her third set of twins. Now thirty-eight years of age and standing five-foot-eight, her slender frame was distorted only by her enlarged stomach. Although her hair had streaks of gray and her brow had furled, she was still as robust as a hired hand at harvest time. She could hoe a row of garden corn, pick a bucket of strawberries, milk a cow, and weed her flower patch. On her hands and knees, she scrubbed the kitchen floor and twice a week washed her family's clothes, wringing each item through rubber rollers she turned by hand.

James Elmer Newton was fifty years old. More than thirty years earlier, he had moved to Colorado from Kentucky as a single man. He hoped to establish himself as a farmer and take advantage of the prosperity promised to those who settled on the northeastern plains of the state. But alas, the Great Depression and his growing family prevented him from accumulating a nest egg needed to start a farm, and he remained a laborer, going from farm to farm, stacking hay, shucking wheat, herding sheep, topping sugar beets, planting trees, painting barns, and slaughtering livestock—doing whatever he could for an hourly wage.

James Elmer and Laura met in 1918 on the dryland wheat fields of Laura's widowed mother near LeRoy, Colorado, not far from the Nebraska border. They married in 1920. With the twelve-year difference in their ages and with James Elmer's Catholic background in sharp contrast to Laura's Evangelical Protestant upbringing, there were many in LeRoy who thought their marriage wouldn't last. But nearly two decades later, the two had stayed the course, surviving the ravages and setbacks of the nation's most severe economic downturn ever. The Newtons had suffered deeply through the Depression. Their one-year-old son Robert died of erysipelas, and Martha died at one week of age from a malformed intestinal tract. The five eldest—Orbin, Eunice, Raymond, Betty, and Rosemary—had lived three years in a Denver orphanage and finally were reunited with the rest of their family when James and Laura became eligible to receive $7 a child per month from the federal American Dependent Child Act of 1935. James had trouble finding work throughout most of the '30s but landed a steady job in 1938 when he began working on the gym construction project at the Mead school.

Late in the evening of September 28, 1939, when James left the hall and walked twenty yards to the pay telephone booth next to the drugstore. Laura was in labor, and he needed to contact Dr. Glen Jones, who practiced in nearby Berthoud. Three years earlier, Dr. Jones had delivered the Newtons' second set of twins, Maureen and Kathleen, and, the year before, delivered their fourteenth child, Gerald. James also called midwife Hulda Roman, who lived a quarter mile east of town; Hulda had assisted with the delivery of the twins and Gerald, and James knew he would need her help again.

Hulda arrived first, and she walked into the front of the converted gymnasium, where the Newtons' five boys were sleeping; they were separated by a curtain down the middle from Laura, who lay in bed on the other half of the court. Several chairs, a table, a small desk, wooden crates, a couch, and two sets of bureau drawers were scattered across the room, obscuring portions of the faded outlines of the keyhole and boundaries painted on the floor. Seven girls were asleep in the coatroom, and James had water boiling on the stove in the kitchen at the back of the hall. Prepared for the expected twosome, Laura had placed her twin daughters' baby baskets on the table next to her bed and had outfitted them with sheets and blankets.

At eleven o'clock, Dr. Jones arrived, and at eleven-thirty, the first child was born—a boy. Shortly past midnight, a second was born—also a boy. And surprisingly, at half-past midnight, Laura had a third boy, and Hulda placed him in the basket alongside another. There in the hall converted to a gym, a set of triplets, with basketball hoops hanging over their heads, was born. At the moment of their birth, the Newton triplets were destined to be basketball players. The next morning, their one-year old-brother, Gerald, held in the arms of James, peered into the two baskets holding three new brothers. Although too young to realize it, "Jerry" would one day play basketball with all three of them.

The triplets were named Richard John, Roland Joseph, and Ronald James—all with the acronym RJN. Right away, their brothers and sisters started calling them Ronnie, Richie, and Rollie. Rollie was the firstborn, weighing five and a half pounds. Ronnie was second—over seven pounds—and Richie was last at a little more than six pounds.

Thereafter, the triplets would walk in light of the community interest. They were the second set born in the state of Colorado and the first of the same sex. They became an instant sensation when their picture appeared in the *Greeley Tribune* for folks from all over Northeastern Colorado to see. More than two hundred visitors came to their door. This was the beginning of the constant scrutiny of a curious public the triplets would experience for the next eighteen years.

The Newton family did not remain in the hall for long. Their lives took a turn for the better when Laura and James borrowed $600 from Laura's mother to buy a nine-room house on the north end of town. The barn-like two-story stone structure had five small bedrooms, three upstairs and two downstairs. Living and dining rooms were also downstairs, along with a kitchen and pantry. Mead provided water to each household, but there was no sewer system. Waste water was deposited by pipe or bucketfuls on the ground outside, and each home had an outhouse. The seventeen members of the Newton household moved into the new home as the Great Depression ended and the second World War was about to begin. This became my home for the next eighteen years.

Shortly after we were born, World War II started, and my two eldest brothers, Orbin and Raymond, left home to fight the Japanese in the South Pacific. Our five eldest sisters still at home—Eunice, Betty, Rosemary, Helen, and Pat—were our surrogate mothers. They bathed and fed us, taught us our night prayers, read nursery rhymes and stories to us, made our beds, washed our clothes, and watched over us as we played. Eunice graduated and married in 1940, and Betty left home after graduation to enroll in beauty school in 1942.

Our brother David was born in 1941. He was our mother's eighteenth child. Dave, two years younger than us triplets, and Jerry, one year older than us, were both destined to join us on a future basketball team. At five years of age, we triplets made our first attempt at throwing a ball through the hoop of the basketball goal our fifteen-year-old brother Jack had erected in our backyard. With the ball in our hands, Jack held us above his head as we dropped it in the basket. Soon after, we stood below the hoop and attempted to throw a regulation size basketball into it on our own.

In 1944, our mother gave birth to her nineteenth child, our brother Marc, and in 1945, our sister Rosemary graduated and moved to Denver to take a job with the telephone company. As we triplets entered first grade in 1945, there were twelve siblings at home: four sisters and eight brothers. In 1946, our youngest brother Forrest was born. Forrest, nicknamed Frosty, was the twentieth and last child born to our mother. Inspired by their elder brothers, both Frosty and Marc would continue the basketball legacy established in the Newton family two decades before by our eldest brother Orbin.

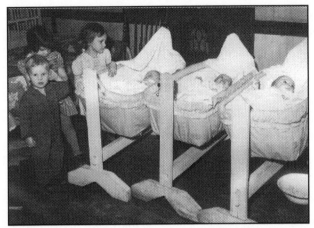

L-R: Jerry, Kathleen, Maureen, Ronnie, Richie and Rollie Newton, 1939.
Newton Family Album

L-R: Rollie, Richie, and Ronnie Newton, 1940. *Newton Family Album*

Mead Farmer's Union Town Hall, 2004. *Sheila Koenig*

Chapter 2

Early Learning

The Germans surrendered to the Allied Powers in May 1945, and in August 1945, the Japanese followed suit. By fall of '45, World War II, which lasted for more than four years, was officially over for the United States. Before entering the military, eldest brothers Orbin and Raymond had graduated from Mead High, and by the time the war ended in 1945, three eldest sisters—Eunice, Betty, and Rosemary—had also graduated. At war's end, seven siblings were attending Mead School, and three more were slated to begin in September '45.

We triplets, accompanied by brother Tom, walked five short blocks to enroll. Mom instructed Tom to make sure that we got to our first-grade classroom where the teacher, Mrs. Isabel Jepperson, was expecting us. It was almost eight-thirty when we walked up the steps and through the outer double doors into the foyer on the first floor. I detected the familiar odors of fresh paint and floor wax that custodian Marion Humphrey had recently applied. These smells signified beauty and cleanliness, and they reflected the pride that Mr. Humphrey had in caring for a building now nearly thirty years old. The foyer opened into a long wide hall with linoleum-treaded wooden staircases at each end, each leading to second-floor high-school classrooms, a study hall, and administrative offices.

We walked down a long hall divided by coat racks and lined with wainscoting of brown-stained pine. The upper plastered sidewalls contained George Washington's portrait and a picture of him in the *Battle of Valley Forge*. We passed classrooms with open doors of translucent chicken-wire safety glass and doorways topped with transparent glass transoms, all bordered with dark-grained pine. We could hear the boisterous and excited chatter of youngsters emanating from every room.

Tom paraded us into Mrs. Jepperson's class and walked us to her desk. Each of us wore bib overalls of white-and-blue striped denim, bought at Longmont's J. C. Penney, and strapped over new plaid sport shirts that Mom had sewn. Everything was new, including our high-topped brown shoes, our checkered socks, and our Penney's Foremost jockey shorts and strapped striatal-textured undershirts. Dad had cut our hair the Saturday before, and that morning, Tom combed it, placing neat parts on the left sides of our heads. We each carried a red-covered Big Chief tablet, a pencil, and a sack lunch of a peanut-butter sandwich and an oatmeal cookie. I held onto a box of Crayolas, which Mom said the three of us would have to share.

"Good morning, boys," said Mrs. Jepperson as we stood, while the eyes of twenty other students, sitting at their desks, stared at us. Mrs. Jepperson had been Tom's teacher, and she greeted him with "Good morning, Tommy. How are you today?"

"Just fine," said Tom. "My brothers and I are ready to start school."

"So these are your triplet brothers," she said admiringly. "I know their names are Richard, Roland, and Ronald, but tell me which one is which."

Tom put his hand on each of our shoulders and introduced us.

"Well, right now, it is difficult, but I know that after I get to know them, I will be able to tell them apart," she said.

Isabel Jepperson had looked forward to that day. She knew the enrollment of triplets in school was a special occasion, and she was happy to be their first teacher. This was her fifth year at Mead, but she had taught in other schools in Weld County. Like many single females who taught in rural communities and there met their future husbands,

Isabel married farmer Frank Jepperson, and they had two daughters—Ann, a freshman, and Susan, a sixth-grader. They lived on the northeast side of Highlandlake, a mile and a half from our house in Mead; Frank farmed acreage southwest of the lake.

Nearly forty, Mrs. Jepperson wore her black hair swept up into a circular band perched high and crown like around her head. Tall and slender, she usually dressed in a dark suit with a straight skirt and a matching top that covered a white blouse with a wide stand-up collar. Her narrow face was accented by a constant broad smile with lipstick-red lips, straight and radiantly white teeth, and arched, rouged cheeks. She was as kind and gentle as a grandmother at Christmas. When she talked to us, we each sensed we were just as important to her as her own daughters. Her warmth and respect were always evident, even when correcting errant behavior. She always addressed us as Richard, Roland, and Ronald, never by the nicknames to which we had grown accustomed.

Two walls of our classroom were covered with blackboards, bordered above with eighteen-inch bulletin boards upon which Mrs. Jepperson had pinned large letters of the alphabet, upper and lower case. She sat at her desk with one blackboard to her back and a third wall with two large windows with roll-up shades to her right. Columns of iron radiators covered in silver-like metallic paint were mounted on the floor beneath each window. The fourth wall had two bulletin boards, each completely covered with colored paper, upon which she had placed magazine cutouts of birds, children at play, and farmhouses.

Mrs. Jepperson escorted us to our desks, dispersed in different rows. Each desk had a pull-up seat and a stationary writing surface constructed of oak, supported by curved cast-iron legs ornamented with intricate curl designs and fastened to pinewood runners. Beneath the writing surface was a compartment for storing supplies and books. As we took our seats, Mrs. Jepperson gathered our lunch sacks and placed them on a small table in the back of the room.

Piled high on Mrs. Jepperson's desk were copies of the first pre-primer of the Elson-Gray Readers, *We Look and See*. She said to the class, "When you come back tomorrow, we'll start reading this book.

We'll read stories about a family with children named Dick, Jane, and Sally and their dog Spot and their cat Puff."

As we read Dick and Jane stories together, we learned words that went along with the pictures. "Tell me what Dick is doing in that picture," she said, encouraging us to express ourselves and perhaps use a word we had learned to recognize.

The differences between Dick's world and mine were like chocolate and vanilla. There were no references to the war just past or the Great Depression from which my family was still reeling. Dick's polo shirt and shorts were the clothes of a big-city boy, far removed from the patched overalls and flour-sack shirts I wore in my farm town. Like me, Dick worked around the house. He watered the lawn. Our yard was covered with weeds. Unlike me, he knew how to dial a telephone. We did not have one; we had to use a neighbor's. Dick's family was small and more wealthy than mine, and they owned a car. Of course, most of my classmate's families were small. Their parents drove cars, and many wore store-bought shirts or blouses. I found it strange and stiff when Dick and Jane referred to their parents as Mother and Father and their grandparents as Grandmother and Grandfather. Nevertheless, the Dick and Jane stories interested me, particularly those about their visits to their grandparents' farm, an experience my brothers and I had never had. The storybook dream world of Dick and Jane was one I hoped I would someday enter. Our family needed a car, and I wanted a bicycle!

At Christmas, Mrs. Jepperson asked us to sketch the Santa Claus face she had taped to the blackboard. Sketching was a favorite activity of mine, and drawing Santa was something I had been doing since I saw my first Santa illustration in the *Denver Post*. Mrs. Jepperson complimented me on my artistry. I had replicated Santa's face and had drawn Santa's whole body, complete with suit and boots, as well as a bag of toys over his shoulder. She pinned my drawing on the bulletin board for the whole class to see. Several days later, she gave it to me to take home to show Mom.

While we listened and learned from Mrs. Jepperson, our brother Jack, a high-school junior, was attending classes in the same building. Jack played guard for Mead High School's basketball team, but we triplets were never given the chance to see him play, nor did Mom and Dad attend his games. Jack and Mead High excelled on the basketball court. In league competition with Platteville, Windsor, Eaton, Johnstown, and Ault, and playing each team at home and away, Mead lost only to Eaton on its home floor. Mead avenged that loss with a victory over Eaton at Mead.

At breakfast that next morning, my sister Helen, a sophomore, described the win for us. "Last night was the biggest crowd we've ever had in the gym," Helen said. "We won. The final score was 21–20. Jack made nine points, and he made the final basket for Mead to go ahead."

Winning the league title, Mead entered the Weld County playoffs and defeated Grover, Eaton, and Wellington to qualify for the Class C state tournament. Jack and his team were defeated by Pleasant View in the first round but won the first game in the consolation bracket over Carbondale; Jack scored nine of Mead's twenty-five points. Then Mead beat Granada in the finals to win the consolation trophy. The winning team was photographed by a Longmont photographer, and Coach Edwin Spencer placed it next to the trophy in the case in the foyer of the gym. I could name every player in the photo; I saw them almost every day. From then on, every time I walked into the foyer surrounded with trophy cases, I looked for Jack's name on the consolation trophy.

School was enjoyable for us, and each September, we looked forward to it after a long summer vacation. Waiting for September's arrival also stirred further anticipation; it was the month of our birthdays as well as that of a classmate friend, Gary Olson. Gary had a birthday party after school and invited us. I felt we were very special guests since we were the only ones in our class invited. Gary lived on a farm two miles northeast of Mead, across the Washington Highway from where his grandparents farmed. His grandparents drove a new Buick sedan and resembled those in the Dick and Jane stories to a T, and Gary referred to them as Grandmother and Grandfather. Gary's grandparents had emigrated from Sweden and had earned ownership of their own farm and were able to help their two sons, Gilman (Gary's father) and Don (Gary's uncle), establish farms.

Margaret Baker Olson, brother of Mead's IGA grocer Dale Baker and Gary's mother, picked the three of us up in their new Chrysler and transported us to the Olson farm. We took turns riding Gary's horse and played basketball on the concrete driveway leading to the garage, where the hoop was attached. At suppertime, while eating hamburgers and drinking soda pop, we watched Gary open gifts of hard-backed books, comic books, and games from his parents and grandparents. Then we all had large pieces of a beautiful birthday cake that his mother had purchased at a Longmont bakery. Attending Gary Olson's birthday party was a ritual my brothers and I looked forward to every fall during our early grade-school years.

For us triplets' birthday celebration, our sister Helen made two different-sized sheet cakes and placed the smaller one on the other, covered them with chocolate icing, and mounted stand-up animal crackers on them to make Noah's Ark. The six candles were repeatedly lit so each of us could blow them out. I was pleased to receive the green plaid sport shirt Mom had made for me. Rollie got a maroon one, and Richie's was blue. With only family members present, we celebrated our sixth birthday during the evening supper meal. No outside guests had been invited, and no toys or games were received. How not "Dick and Jane"!

* * *

In fall '46, our second-grade school year started late. The dreaded disease poliomyelitis was spreading in towns and cities across Colorado. It became known that "polio" was transmitted orally and in fecal matter, so school authorities postponed bringing students together until after the viral incubation period waned. As polio was highly contagious, especially in the summer and early fall, Mead School did not open until the middle of October.

My sister Kathleen said, "Polio can be spread in water, so they've closed down the swimming pool in Longmont. It attacks the nerves in the spine and causes paralysis. It mostly affects young kids."

I was scared by what I heard about this disease and was afraid to go to sleep at night, worried that one morning I would be unable to get out of bed. I was frightened even more when Mom told us that classmate Frank Melchior "got polio" and that both his legs were paralyzed. Frank had dropped out of our first grade and did not come to school that fall; he was now using crutches, and he stayed at home for the year. His parents were hopeful that with rest, maybe he could overcome the debilitating menace. Research on the disease was financially supported by the March of Dimes, which had been encouraged by Pres. Franklin Delano Roosevelt, who was afflicted and confined to a wheelchair. Like children from all over the nation, we were asked to bring dimes to the school, where they were collected by teachers and forwarded to the March of Dimes. We collected dimes, many of which had the image of Roosevelt—a redesign of the coin—issued in '46 on the deceased president's birthday.

Shirley Abbott was our second-grade teacher. She had been raised on a farm near Keenesburg and had just finished two years of teacher training at Colorado State College of Education in Greeley. For the five-day work week, she boarded with Mrs. Effie Markham, who lived on Main Street and had been boarding Mead teachers for many years. On weekends, Ms. Abbott returned to her father's farm.

Ms. Abbott had long hair that curled and hung behind her shoulders to the small of her back, with her front hair rolled in a pompadour above her forehead. Stocky and compact, she wore full-length dresses with pendants attached. Her broad face was square jawed, and her eyebrows were dark. With her lips red with lipstick and a face smoothed with light makeup, Ms. Abbott's wide smile and gentle voice captivated my brothers and me, infatuating the three of us in a way we did not fully understand. While first-grade teacher Mrs. Jepperson affectionately related to us like a grandmother, Ms. Abbott connected with us as if she were a "girl-next-door" teenager—young, pretty, and vibrant.

One spring weekend, Ms. Abbott took us triplets home with her for a visit to the family farm. In a later conversation with my brother Marc, who recalled the discourse Mom had with Dad when he inquired about our whereabouts, "They went home with Ms. Abbott to her parents' farm," said Mom. "She wanted to show the boys off."

We understood that this was the case. We knew that Ms. Abbott considered us her special students. The opportunity for other students to visit her home would not be extended. That was a privilege provided only to us simply because of our multiple birth. I realized this and considered myself most fortunate. This was only one of many occasions where we triplets were singled out for recognition that others did not get. I knew it was not fair, and I knew it was not deserved. However, I was looking forward to going to another place and seeing a new environment, something we seldom got to do. This was the first time we "got off the reservation."

For this special occasion, Mom bought us blue T-shirts with frontal images of Red Ryder on his horse and aiming his rifle. Ms. Abbott proudly showed the shirts to her mother as we unpacked our single suitcase and placed them in a drawer of the dresser in the guest bedroom.

The next morning, we rode with Ms. Abbott's father in his truck as his son Gilbert shoveled ensilage into the feed trough of a cattle corral. We drove to the pasture to check on his cattle herd, and along the way, Mr. Abbott let us take turns steering his pickup truck. We fed chickens and gathered eggs, and on Saturday evening, Ms. Abbott and the three of us rode into town with her boyfriend, Bill Uhrich. He treated us to malts at the drugstore. That night, we each took a bath in a porcelain tub for the first time. We filled it half full with hot water from the faucet, something we had never done with the galvanized wash tub we had grown accustomed to using at home, where hot water was poured into it by the dipperful after another had bathed.

Knowing our Catholic background, Ms. Abbott had inquired about the times for mass on Sunday morning. In that discussion, I said, "Mom said it was okay for us to go to your church. She said we don't have to go the Catholic one."

With that permission, we triplets attended Keenesburg's First United Methodist Church with the Abbotts. By that time, I was feeling homesick, and the different nature of the service made it worse. Afterward, the three of us stood on the church steps, while Ms. Abbott "showed us" to her friends and other curious members of the congregation. Our identical Red Ryder T-shirts quickly revealed to them that they were seeing triplets.

"They are students in my second-grade class in Mead," said Ms. Abbott proudly. "Not only are they good students, but they are also good basketball players. Someday you're going to see them playing for Mead."

That afternoon, Ms. Abbott's brother Gilbert took the three of us to the Keenesburg ballpark. "I think there is a baseball game that is supposed to be played today," said Gilbert. We waited for ten or fifteen minutes, but nobody had showed up—then it began to rain. "Let's go get something to drink at the tavern while we wait for the rain to stop," said Gilbert.

The three of us sat on stools at the bar. I sat next to a middle-aged man who apparently had been there for several hours, drinking beer.

"Hey," he belted out to the bartender, "give these boys a Coke."

Drinking a Coke was a first-time experience for me, and I lifted the bottle quickly to my lips and took a big swallow. It effervesced into my nose, and I coughed and gasped. I wanted no more.

Sensing this, the jocular man asked me, "Do you like it?"

I shook my head, unable to speak.

"Here, let's do this," he said. "I'll show you what you can do with it. Grab the bottle and follow me."

I obediently descended the stool with the Coke in hand and followed him into the restroom. He pointed to the toilet and said, "Here, pour it in here."

I dumped it into the bowl, and he flushed it. It would be a long time before I drank another Coke. Thereafter, I would drink only orange soda.

Unlike me, Richie never showed any signs of anxiety or homesickness. On the Monday morning before we were ready to leave for Mead and go back to school, he sat on a horse, holding tightly to the waist of Ms. Abbott's brother Gene, galloping the horse over ditches and herding cattle into a pen to be fed. Richie was enjoying the moment and laughing uncontrollably as he bounced up and down and slammed back and forth with the abrupt stops and starts and leaps of the horse. I had no courage to get on a horse. I wanted no part of it. I was ready to go home.

First Grade. Front Row, L-R: Eddie Smith, Larry Heil, Richie Newton, Rollie New-
ton, Ronnie Newton, Larry Sterkel; Middle Row, L-R: Delores Leonard, Shirley
Smith, Vernon Benevidez, Johnnie Minch, unknown, Anita Jones, Shirley Hepp,
Patty Lamberson, Claudia Williams; Back Row, L-R: Voncille Boutcher, unknown,
Barbara Graham, Mary Helen Olson, Mrs. Isabel Jepperson, unknown, unknown,
Josephine Rademacher, Irene Stotts, 1946. *Mead Consolidated Schools Yearbook*

Second Grade. Front Row, L-R: Johnnie Minch, Voncille Boutcher, Richie New-
ton, Ronnie Newton, Rollie Newton, Anita Jones, Larry Nuss; Middle Row, L-R:
Shirley Smith, Patty Lamberson, Mary Helen Olson, Irene Stotts, Barbara Graham,
Josephine Rademacher, Shirley Hepp, Mrs. Shirley Abbott; Back Row, L-R: Larry
Heil, Gary Olson, Claudia Williams, Janice Frederiksen, Beverly Steving, Jim
Brunemier, Anita Jones, 1947. *Mead Consolidated Schools Yearbook*

Mead High School: Class C State Consolation Winners. L-Front Row, L-R: Donald Nygren, Robert Amen, Jack Newton, Louis Rademacher, Jim Markham, Howard Strickland, Coach Edwin Spencer; Back Row, L-R: Orville Markham, John Roberts, Charles Major, Walter Hansen, Howard Jones, Eddie Rosenoff. 1946.

Mead Consolidated Schools Yearbook

Chapter 3

First Competition

By the time our second school year ended, we triplets had become infatuated with Ms. Shirley Abbott, and we were devastated when she told us that she would be leaving Mead for good. She was going to marry her boyfriend Bill, and she would be teaching no more. We felt abandoned and sad we would not be seeing this wonderful lady again. However, our sadness was short-lived. Hazel Abbott, Shirley's sister, would be our third-grade teacher.

Hazel Abbott was just as pretty as her sister. She was thin, and her slender frame was accentuated by the fitted sweaters and straight skirts she wore. Her fingernails were painted a bright red, and her long hair curled at her shoulders. Her beauty was noticed by the high-school boys who stopped by during the noon hour to talk and flirt with her.

Her opened billfold on her desk one day revealed a picture of her and a male companion. Unabashed, I asked her, "Who's your boyfriend?"

She did not reply. She just smiled and blushed.

Our class was large, hovering between thirty-two and thirty-eight students during the year. Using our individual textbooks, Ms. Abbott taught reading, and she also divided us into groups to read books she had obtained from the Weld County Library bookmobile. Needless to say, arithmetic was the most challenging subject for most of us. Every Wednesday afternoon, we had a special play period where the boys played football in the fall, basketball in the winter, and softball in the spring. On Friday afternoons, Ms. Abbott left our class to teach art to the fourth grade, and fourth-grade teacher Ms. Elizabeth Crews reciprocated by teaching music to our class. As Ms. Abbott walked toward the door to leave with art supplies in her arms, she always turned her head to the right to acknowledge Richie sitting by the door by flashing her friendly smile at him. Richie always smiled back and lowered his head, hiding a blushing face. As with her sister Shirley, I sensed that we triplets were special people to Ms. Hazel Abbott, but Richie was her favorite.

By third grade, sports had become dominant in our lives. That year in 1947, we learned from our neighbor Ronald Weber that Jackie Robinson signed with the Brooklyn Dodgers as the first Negro to play major league baseball. And one fall Saturday, we got Mom and Dad's permission to watch a World Series game at the Mead Pool Hall. For the first time, they were being televised. Proprietor Grover Roberts had purchased a black-and-white television; we did not have one. That year, Rollie's favorite team, the Brooklyn Dodgers, lost to the New York Yankees.

Although we had an interest in many sports, basketball was our primary focus. Playing basketball at recess was random bedlam; there was one basketball shared by eight or nine boys, and at noon, there were even more players. There was no organized supervision, and the time was spent with one youngster shooting from outside the keyhole, while all the others waited underneath the basket to rebound. At first, I just remained on the periphery, hoping to get access to the ball as it glanced off the rim or backboard. Waiting patiently, I would occasionally get the ball and dribble beyond the group to shoot a set shot. Soon, it became clear to me that if I wanted to get my hands on the ball more frequently, I had to fight to establish "my ground" under the basket. I learned that going after the ball was a very physical endeavor, putting me in competition with my schoolmates and forcing me to use my innate quickness and experience in anticipating where the ball would end up as it caromed off the rim.

During the lunch hour in winter, with deep snow on the ground, the school playgrounds and the streets and sidewalks of Mead were not navigable, and elementary, middle, junior high, and high-school students assembled in the gym. Usually, students would play basketball or sit on the bleachers to eat their sack lunches and socialize. Sometimes there were organized activities, such as square dancing and volleyball for the older students, while the younger ones watched. For square dancing, music teacher Mrs. Lillian Spencer would "call out" the square commands in synchrony to the music from a Victrola on the stage. For volleyball matches, Mrs. Spencer stood on a bleacher, refereed, and kept score. For the lower grades, boys' basketball competitions between grades were played.

One winter afternoon Ms. Abbott announced, "Mr. Carlson [superintendent] said that you boys are going to have a basketball game with the fourth-graders during the lunch hour tomorrow."

The whole class shouted and clapped.

"So you boys make sure you have your tennis shoes here," said Ms. Abbott. "You know Mr. Humphrey [custodian] won't let you on the gym floor without 'em."

Besides Richie and Rollie and me, classmates Johnnie (Minch), the two Larrys (Nuss and Heil), the two Jims (Brunemeier and Landolt), and Denver Spencer rounded out the team. Gary Olson said he would keep score. We had no uniforms, but most of us boys wore J. C. Penney strapped undershirts; they would serve very well as basketball jerseys. It was understood that Ms. Abbott would depend on us triplets to organize the play of the team since we were the most accustomed to team sports and always took leadership roles when it came to organizing playground activities.

Heading out the door after being dismissed from school, I said to Richie and Rollie, "I think that Johnny should play first with us and that Denver [Spencer] should be our center, don't you?"

They nodded.

"Tonight I'm going to make numbers for everybody," I said. "We can pin them on our undershirts. My number is going to be 7—the same as Jack's. What numbers do you guys want?"

"I'll take 22," said Richie. "That's Charles Major's number [a star on Mead's varsity]. Which one do you want?" Richie asked Rollie.

"I want 42," said Rollie. "Ronnie Weber told me that is Jackie Robinson's number."

That night, I drew block-form numbers on a large piece of brown wrapping paper, colored them with a red crayon, and cut them out. I went to Mom's metal "pin can" and grabbed several bunches of pins and placed them in a used envelope.

The next morning, I put the numbers and pins into a paper sack and took them to school. The prospect of playing basketball in just a few hours made it difficult to concentrate on spelling and reading. I wanted to chat with anybody who would listen.

"You kids hush with your talking. You've got to work before you play. Get your work done now. The noon hour will come soon enough," said Ms. Abbott, empathizing with us.

At a quarter to twelve, Ms. Abbott said, "You boys who are playin' today need to eat your lunches now."

I quickly consumed my sandwich and cookie and went to the coatroom to put on my tennis shoes. As my teammates assembled, I gave them each a number and helped them pin it on the back of their undershirts. Denver Spencer pinned his to the straps of his bib overalls. When the noon bell rang, we were still not ready, and Ms. Abbott, seeing that game time was nearing and that students of all ages were rushing down the stairs and halls to the gym, came into the coatroom to help. When the last number was attached, we ran down the hall to the gym door close by. Johnny Minch, carrying our classroom basketball, descended the steps into the gym first.

Seeing the improvised uniforms on the tiny frames of us kids caused the large student crowd to howl with a loud collective whoop, which was only the beginning of the boisterous joy they would exude for the next thirty minutes. High-school basketball coach Edwin Spencer blew his whistle to start the center jump with Denver Spencer and the fourth-grade center Jerry Newton. Jerry leaped quickly to tip the ball to teammate Marvin Blazon, who skillfully dribbled the ball down court to score.

Thereafter, the ball would change hands from one team to another in rapid fashion. Each player would begin to dribble, only to have the ball taken away by an opponent. The ten of us players moved on the court like a flock of birds searching for food and shelter. As the momentum rapidly switched, the crowd yelled encouragement and clapped as the change in direction resulted in a basket. Soon, our third-grade team's excellent "dribbling and passing game" took over, and we dominated the scoring.

When the bell rang, signaling that the noon hour was over, our third-grade team was well ahead. This was the first game that my triplet brothers and I won on the basketball court. However, my excitement was dampened when I realized that I, acting as coach, had not substituted Larry Heil into the game. Also, our victory over the fourth-graders came at the expense of our brother Jerry, and this restrained my enthusiasm. I never enjoyed beating him, no matter the contest.

The sense of exhilaration by the student body and its enjoyable experience watching us play caused high-schooler Nadine Stotts to later stop me in the hall to ask, "When are you kids going to play again?" Before I could answer, she continued, "We'd rather watch you than the big boys."

I responded, "I don't know, but I hope it's real soon."

Three weeks later, our third-grade team was victorious over the fifth-graders, and I made sure that Larry Heil started the game. Our next-door neighbor and fifth-grade teacher Emily Newman was unable to watch us play, and she was astonished when hearing that youngsters two years younger had defeated her fifth-graders. Nodding in disbelief, she said, "Well, I declare."

The talent of us triplets and our brother Jerry soon became evident to all observers, students and teachers alike. Still, they did not realize they were watching a significant phenomenon with four brothers playing a game of basketball at the same time. In just a few years, there would be five of us on the court. Our brother David had entered first grade.

L-R: David, Ronnie, Richie, Rollie and Frosty Newton, 1947. *Newton Family Album*

Nadine Stotts, 1947.
Mead Consolidated Schools Yearbook

Hazel Abbott, 1947.
Mead Consolidated Schools Yearbook

Jerry Newton, 1947. *Newton Family Album*

Chapter 4

Child's Play

At an early age, we brothers had our own ritual of participating in the sport that was "in season." In the spring, it was track; in the summer, it was softball. We played football in the fall and basketball in the winter.

During track season, we used a vacant lot on the south side of our garden and across the street. No one in town seemed to know who owned it. Jerry, David, Richie, Rollie, and I put it to good use, where we set up our combined "high-jumping/pole-vaulting" pit. For a soft landing at the end of a jump or vault, we piled freshly dug moist soil to a height of eighteen or twenty inches. For uprights, we searched the neighborhood alleys to find suitable materials. We found a couple of eight-foot two-by-fours discarded by Mrs. Iva Stotts, who had just torn down an old shed. However, we still needed nails to be inserted every two inches along the length of the two-by-fours so we could adjust the crossbar to different heights. We scoured the alleyways, looking for discarded wood with nails we could remove. We also looked in the alley and in our backyard for nails, rusted with age. With the nails driven into the uprights with a stone, we inserted them into eighteen-inch-deep holes adjacent to the pit, each one extending six feet above ground.

From our silver poplar tree, we made a crossbar out of two branches bound together with string. Brother Tom taught us how to jump over the cross bar in a horizontal "barrel roll," leading with one leg over the bar, rolling the body around it, and kicking the second leg upward as the body turned and "barreled" over the bar. But Rollie preferred the "scissors" style, with his right leg kicking above the bar first, holding his torso upright as he moved above it, followed by a rapid kick over the bar once again with his left leg.

Finding a suitable pole with which to vault was a challenge. We found a lead pipe, but it was too heavy for us to carry as we ran toward the crossbar. A smaller-diameter aluminum pipe was too flexible and bent easily when we planted it into the ground to leverage ourselves over the bar. We discovered a narrow wood shaft that worked well but only for a while.

Our brother Jack, on his way home from work at the IGA Grocery, stopped to watch us vault and said, "Hey, let me try it." Jack, dressed in penny loafers and corduroy pants, grasped the pole and galloped toward the pit and crossbar. As he thrust the pole into the hole to lift himself upward, the pole shattered into several pieces, and he plummeted to the ground, landing on his back. Realizing what had happened, he lay there momentarily, laughing uncontrollably.

At first, I was not amused. "Doggone it, Jack. You broke our best pole," I said angrily. However, seeing him in that humbling state, I could not maintain my fury. I had to join in the laughter, and so did my brothers.

Each evening after supper, we jumped and vaulted in the dark with light from the nearby street light. Each was challenged as the crossbar was raised to the next level. We competed with one another until Mom called us in to get ready for bed. Early on, Rollie was demonstrating his superior physical strength and speed, and younger brother Dave was beginning to show that he could jump and vault as well as us triplets. It would not be long before he would jump and vault higher than all of us.

During earlier summer days, we played softball, and Ronald Weber and Loe Hernandez were our usual playmates. "Weber" moved to Mead as an eleven-year old in the summer of '45. His father Roy bought the house where the Yakel family lived, three doors south of our house. Roy Weber, a carpenter and handyman, repaired the house, gave it a badly needed exterior coat of paint, and shingled the roof. Despite the four-year difference in our ages, I felt a special bond with Weber; he and I had the same first names. He shared stories about baseball that had been told to him by his father and what he read in sports magazines. What we knew about the techniques and rules of softball, we learned from Weber.

Loe Hernandez was our other constant playmate. He lived with his mother and father, an elder sister, and two elder brothers. His father was a section-hand laborer with the Union Pacific Railroad. In '44, they moved into a tiny four-room house across from the town park, half a block from our house. Loe told us his original name was Leo, but in his early school days, he misspelled it, and the teachers kept calling him Loe. Loe, four years older than us triplets, was five and a half feet tall and weighed about one hundred and forty pounds; he was a good athlete, very, very quick. Loe's sister, Mary, had a good-paying job in Longmont, paid for his new clothes, and provided him spending money. "Lucky" Loe went to the movie at the Longmont Trojan Theater almost every Saturday night.

During our earlier years of softball, we made our own equipment. We constructed a softball by collecting string from as many sources as we could, from Mom's stored stash and from neighbors. We rolled the string around a small rubber jacks ball until the sphere was softball sized, and then we covered it with electric tape. We used a limb off our silver poplar tree in the front yard and cut it to the size of a bat and improvised a first-baseman's mitt out of an oilcloth that Mom discarded. We padded the mitt inside with cotton layers that Mom used for comforters, punched holes around the edge with a nail, and fastened the edges with string. We made bases by filling gunny sacks with dirt, and we sawed off the end of a one-by-twelve board into a pentagon for home plate.

I made a baseball cap from brother Raymond's old sailor caps by cutting off most of its outer perimeter, leaving enough to form a visor. In a box of clothes that someone dropped off for our family, I found some long knee-high socks and a sleek, shiny gold shirt with sleeves shortened below the elbow and trimmed in blue. It resembled a baseball jersey to a T. With long socks and jeans rolled up to just below the knee, and with my gold jersey and modified cap, I was a bona fide baseball player. Dave devised a similar uniform, wearing one of brother Tom's baseball caps. Weber taught me how to use a windmill wind-up, so I developed a softball fast-pitch delivery, with Rollie as my catcher.

With our sports equipment needs as a catalyst, we brothers earned money from several townspeople. Brother Richie pulled weeds from the gardens of the widowed Mary Johnson, and I did the same for United Brethren Church minister, the Reverend Burris. Red & White Grocery store owner Mr. Bunton paid me 40¢ an hour to weed his garden and mow his lawn. Brother Jerry earned 50¢ each time he mowed the Peppler lawn, and brother Rollie was paid 75¢ for a half-day's work weeding the garden of drugstore owner George Snider. Neighbors and townspeople would call Mom, asking if one of us could work for them; Mom would then send one of us to their house. We pooled our money, giving it to Mom for safekeeping, and then collectively decided how to spend our hard-earned cash.

When we had earned enough to purchase a softball, Mom bought one for us in Longmont, but we continued to use the silver-poplar branch until we had money to buy a bat. We started playing workup games among the five of us. Sometimes our sister, Kathleen, played, and so did Weber, Loe, and Herb Newman, our next-door neighbor and Kathleen and Maureen's classmate. When our distant neighbors Billy Amen and Vernon Widger came to play, we formed teams by choosing sides.

Our softball diamond was in our backyard, between the clothesline to the right of first base, and the chicken pen, to the left of third base. The infield was a combination of dirt and sand and low-level weeds. The outfield, lying in the alleyway, had tall ironweeds that obscured the ball on the ground from the fielder's view, sometimes resulting in a homerun before the ball could be found.

Bossie's cow corral was directly behind third base; if the ball was hit there, Weber told us it should be ruled a "ground-rule double," and the runner had to stop at second base. Immediately behind and to the left of second base was the coal shed. Between first and second base was a clear shot into the alley, behind which was Grover Roberts's horse corral. If the ball was hit into the corral, it too was a ground-rule double.

A ball going into the corrals was usually tainted with muck. With balls landing in Bossie's pen, the game was delayed while the fielder gingerly retrieved the ball, throwing it out for another to wash it under an outside water faucet.

One game time, we were in the cow pen so often, Weber suggested we not use the chain lock on the gate so we could enter easily. When the game was over, we forgot to lock the gate. When Dad came home to milk Bossie, he saw the gate was open, and she was nowhere to be seen. He found her in a vacant lot two blocks away, nibbling on alfalfa. Dad was not happy, and I'm sure he suspected it may have been one of us, but he said nothing. If he had, placing the blame on Weber would have been difficult. None of us wanted to tattle on a friend.

Although we mostly used our backyard softball diamond, we liked best to play in the town park, where there was a large expanse of bluegrass and where homeruns came only to the very strong. Mom let us play in the park only occasionally, and that was usually under the supervision of an elder brother or sister. Town marshal Wilse Lamberson kept the grass watered and mowed, and we could slide into bases on a smooth surface without removing skin from thighs and shins.

One afternoon, before Mom went to Longmont with Mrs. Newman to buy groceries, she commanded us triplets and Jerry to "clean up the yard." We had cluttered it with items of every sort: pieces of wood, tin cans, a shovel, papers, burlap sacks, a car tire, pieces of wire, a hammer, large rocks, and pieces of concrete. We were always building and playing with something but rarely got our materials back into their proper place when we finished. So every two or three weeks, the dictum rang out, "Clean up the yard." This time, Mom said to us, "Under no circumstance are you to leave this place. If you do, you'll certainly hear from me."

With four of us working, we quickly had the yard cleaned and learned our friends were playing softball in the park. Weber said, "We need you guys to play so we can have two teams." Naturally, we wanted to join them.

"Let's go. We got all our work done," I said to my brothers. "We'll only stay for a while."

"Yal," we can be home before she gets back," said Jerry.

Mom and Mrs. Newman finished shopping earlier than we expected, and they drove by the park. We immediately stopped our play and ran home. Mom and Mrs. Newman were carrying boxes and sacks into the house when Mom said, "You birds wait outside. I'll tend to you in just a minute." We all knew what was coming.

As Mrs. Newman drove out of the yard, Mom emerged with a butcher knife in her hand. She walked over to the elm tree in front of our house to cut four branches from it. She peeled the leaves off each branch, leaving a couple of small leaves at the tips. A mass switching of four disobedient children was about to take place.

I submitted to punishment first because I didn't want to watch my brothers withstanding the pain and knowing mine was coming next. Mom clasped our left arms with her left hand, holding on to us as she hit our bottoms and thighs several times with a downstroke of the switch. We danced and moved about with each whip, howling with pain, all except Rollie. He never made a sound and just stood there rigidly as Mom whipped him. Our next-door neighbor schoolmates, Sylvia and Virginia Gallegos, watched with grins on their faces and wondered what serious misdeed Mrs. Newton's boys could have done to deserve such punishment. In their minds and ours, there was no doubt that Mom was in charge.

Dad's form of punishment for our transgressions was more severe than Mom's. One midmorning before he went downtown, he said to me, "Fill up Bossie's water tank. It's about empty."

Weber and Loe had come to play softball, and we all wanted to start immediately. I dragged the garden hose across our backyard softball diamond and looped it over the fence and propped the open end into the tank. I turned on the water and went to play. Forgetting what I had done, the water continued to flow into the tank and over its sides for six hours until Dad came home to milk. Dad saw Bossie standing in her pen with water up to her hocks and her udder dipping into the pool.

Dad came looking for me. I was in the front yard playing with my brothers on our bag swing. I saw him come around the corner of the house. He had our cotton jump rope in his hands. He grabbed me and started to hit me with the rope. I yelled; the pain was the most I had ever endured from any whipping, including a switch or a belt.

I broke from his clutch and ran, bellowing like an abandoned, hungry calf. I ran out into our corn patch and sat down on a pile of cornstalks that we had cut and piled. I sat there sobbing with self-pity, thinking I had avoided further pain. Then suddenly, I looked up, and there was Dad standing in front of me.

"Don't you ever run away from me, young man!" he barked.

He grabbed two cornstalks and began to whip me again. This time, the pain was more severe, and his strokes were more forceful. I bellowed even more, hoping the whole town would hear me and come to my rescue. I remained in the corn patch for an hour, never even showing up for supper. I did not want to see Dad or anyone else. When I finally returned to the house, I went straight to bed.

Corporal punishment for my transgressions seemed to work. I didn't like the pain or the humiliation. Furthermore, Mom would compound the punishment by "grounding" and prohibiting participation in a favorite activity. Laura Dreier Newton was truly the mother hen in charge. She ruled the roost when it came to dealing with the misbehavior of her brood of seven young sons.

On another occasion I fouled off a softball one evening, and it landed smack on the windshield of Ted Rademacher's truck that Dad brought home after stacking hay and had parked next to our backyard softball diamond. The ball's force left a long crack at the base of the windshield on the driver's side. We were sure that Dad would notice it when he drove to work the next morning. My brothers and I stood in the yard behind the house where Dad could not see us as he started the engine. We were relieved when he backed out of our driveway and turned south to drive through town. He did not come back. Apparently, he did not see the damage I had done. My brothers and I were relieved even more when he said nothing about it when we sat down to eat supper that night. I especially felt good with my reprieve. I did not want to experience another whipping from him. I knew if I did, both legs would have been cut off at the knee.

Roy Weber had bought baseball and softball equipment for his sons, so when Weber played in the park with us, he brought bats and softballs, three fielder's gloves, and a first-baseman's mitt; we brought our brother Tom's fielder's glove. Weber hit ground balls to us as we took infield positions. Richie played third, I was shortstop, Dave took second, Jerry played first, and Rollie did the catching. With Weber hitting the ball to us, we fielded grounders, threw to single bases, and turned double plays.

For all the kids in Mead, Highlandlake resident and freelance writer Louise Mowry and her husband, Johnny, organized a softball workup game once a week in the park. Johnny took time off from his job with the Highland Ditch Co. to play. He was difficult to "get out" because he always hit home runs. The ball usually left the park when he batted.

We entered a softball tournament in Longmont after we recruited Herb Newman, Billy Amen, and Vernon Widger to play with us. With those three and the five of us and with Weber pitching, Roy Weber agreed to be our coach. But this was a fast-pitch game, and my brothers and I had could not hit the ball. I was frightened by the speed of the pitch and the fear of getting hit. The rest of our recruits could not hit either. Their ground and fly balls turned into outs; only Weber got on base with a single and a double. We were beaten decisively and eliminated in the first round of tournament play.

We had become enamored with the game of pool, and whenever we could, we slipped into the pool hall to watch the men play, and if we had a spare dime and Dad's permission, we would play on the eight-ball table. While walking down the alley behind the Dempewolf house, I noticed they had placed a small pool table in a storage shed in their backyard. Unabashed, I knocked on their door to ask Mrs. Dempewolf if we could have it. She consented, and we placed it in our upstairs middle bedroom. While playing one summer evening, we were so engrossed in our "round-the-world" game, we did not want to take the time to descend the stairs to use the outhouse. Instead, we chose to pee out one of the opened east-bedroom windows. We did not realize that this would interrupt the conversation that our elder sisters and

Mom were having at the table right next to the open kitchen windows. Our urgent relieving stunt was abruptly brought to a halt when sister Kathleen opened the door to the stairwell and yelled up to us, "That's enough of you yay-hoos dropping that 'yellow rain' down here on us. Cut it out right now! For cryin' out loud, don't be so lazy!"

In the fall of the year, Dave, Richie, Rollie, and I finished our supper quickly so we could play tackle football on the soft grass in the United Brethren Church yard, across the street and west of our garden. We played with a football we crafted out of a twenty-five-pound cotton sugar sack stuffed with rags and molded into an oblong shape. I recall catching a "deep pass" from Rollie by grasping onto a torn shred of cloth hanging from the tattered bag-ball. Snagging the ragged shred with the fingers of one hand, I scored a touchdown as Rollie and I opposed Richie and Dave in an aggressive game of tackle. I wore a faded red sweatshirt that had been handed down to me by Gary Olson and upon the back of which I painted the block number 14, the same number on the jersey of Donnie Owens, the halfback on Mead High School's six-man '49 state champion football team.

When winter came, we grade-school-age brothers played one-on-one basketball in our small enclosed porch, attached to the southeast corner of the house. I had constructed a miniature backboard and a hoop rounded from a coat hanger, complete with a net made from string. I mounted the backboard over the porch door. The "ball," consisting of a rolled-up pair of socks tightly compacted by the stretch band of one, was imaginatively "dribbled" in a simulated up-and-down motion with the sock mass remaining clutched in the hand and never touching the floor. I had difficulty shooting my jump shot over Rollie because he had grown taller than Richie and me, and with Rollie's more aggressive physical style of play, I was defeated repeatedly and becoming deeply aware of the competitive nature of both my brothers and the game of basketball.

However, playing basketball outdoors on our backyard court was what we liked best. It was a priority after each snowstorm for one or more of us to remove the snow so we could begin playing as soon as possible. With our rubber basketball developing air leaks, we had difficulty keeping it inflated. We sought help from Mead Garage owner Duck Newman, who first pumped the flat ball with air, dipped it into a tank of water to detect the leak, and then deflated it. He burnt a rubber patch over the hole for which he charged us twenty-five cents. He always allowed us to use his compressed air source to keep the ball filled. A rubber ball, tightly compressed with air, and a hoop into which we could throw it was all we needed. It did not matter that there was no net to soften the throw of the sunken ball. Our biggest self-imposed obstacle was remembering where we placed the needle and finding it so we could keep the ball inflated.

L-R: Richie, Ronnie, and Rollie Newton, 1949. *Newton Family Album*

L-R: Dave and Jerry Newton, 1948. *Newton Family Album*

Ronald Weber and Loe Hernandez, 1950. *Mead Consolidated Schools Yearbook*

Chapter 5

The Gym

The Mead and Highlandlake school districts were consolidated to form District 117 in 1917 when a single new building was constructed, housing the combined elementary, junior high, and high schools. District 117 included twenty-one sections of agricultural land, an area where the families of sixty-five students lived. Students were transported in two buses from a radius of eight miles to a new Mead Consolidated School on the south side of town, built at a cost of $32,000. Besides the seven classrooms, an assembly hall, and home economics and manual training rooms, the two-and-a-half-story building with basement also included a gym. However, the gym was not built specifically for basketball, and the first high-school games, starting in the 1930s, were played in the Farmer's Union Town Hall.

In 1938, the old gym was converted to classrooms because a new gym was being constructed. A gray stucco-covered building that was a Works Progress Administration project was built as an attachment to the northwest side of the school. In the bitter cold of winter with freezing temperatures, the gym became a gathering place and refuge for students, athletes, Mead townspeople, and farm families. On Friday evenings, Mead High played basketball in the gym, competing against other rural high schools in Weld County.

In January '47, the sun had set over the mountains south of Mount Meeker and Longs Peak; darkness had closed in over the Front Range of Colorado. I walked hurriedly westward up the street with the town park on my left. The fallen snow two days earlier was packed hard from the many cars carrying kids to school, going to work, and traveling to the post office and the grocery store. The packed layer had been melted by the Chinook winds coming over the mountain a day earlier, but freezing temperatures that day had turned the road into ice. The snow was piled a foot and a half high in the park and in the vacant lot on each side of me. Since there were no sidewalks, I walked on the street wearing calf-high buckled rubber boots.

I wore a brown parka given to me last Christmas by my brother Raymond, who lived in New York City. Raymond had sent home five beautifully wrapped packages containing parkas for us five brothers, blue for Dave, a gray one for Jerry, and three brown ones for us triplets. All had the inside label of Saks Fifth Avenue. My sister Kathleen said, "Saks Fifth Avenue is a high-priced store, and your coats cost Ray a lot of money. They sell mostly to rich people." Its thick sheep skin lining efficiently captured my body heat.

I approached the north end of Main Street, where there was an overhanging street light suspended with a dual wire attached to two telephone poles. The light from the bright incandescent bulb beamed down from the white enameled lamp, and it glistened off the icy pathway where I walked. I concentrated on each step and paced carefully, trying to keep from slipping and falling as my smooth boot bottoms met the glassy roadway. The toes of my cold feet were starting to hurt, and I was looking forward to warming them beside the coal-burning stove in our house now just a block away.

I had just finished delivering the *Denver Post* to subscribers on the east side of town, following the instructions of elder sister Maureen, who had been asked to substitute for Sally Roberts. Sally had inherited the paper route from her brother Donald, who had received it from elder brother John. It was Friday, and Sally was away for the weekend. In her absence, the Newtons could always count on being asked to deliver the *Post* for 50¢ a day for two hours of work.

On this night, I was a concerned that I was unable to deliver a paper to the Dempseys, who lived next to the Mead Inn. They had a fat golden-brown husky-like dog, which snarled and growled as I entered their front yard. I was afraid to go any farther, and instead of dropping the paper off inside the screen door, I simply threw it into the yard while the furry monster nipped at my knees. The paper went flying with page after page lying in the snow. I knew I couldn't tell Maureen about this, but I also knew that Sally would hear from Mr. Dempsey about his paper, and the Newtons would hear from Sally. But for now, I closed my mind to this and thought about what was to happen that Friday evening.

As I approached the Main Street crossing, Sally's father, Mr. Roberts, coming home from the barbershop turned the corner in his '46 Ford. He proceeded west in front of me and pulled over to park in front of his house, next door to ours.

As Mr. Roberts stepped out of the car, I yelled out to him, "Hello, Mr. Roberts! Are you goin' to the game?"

Mr. Roberts, wearing a long overcoat and a gray fedora with his warm breath mist and cigarette smoke combined into a dense white cloud around his head, answered, "I'm afraid not, Ronnie. Mr. Palinkx is off tonight, and Frank Schell is expecting me to cut his hair as soon as I eat supper and get back to work. Who's Mead playin'?"

I stopped in the middle of the street and blurted out, "Platteville. They're at the top of the league and are even better than Windsor, who always beats us." Then remembering what my sisters had told me, I said, "Those schools are bigger than us, and we have a hard time beatin' 'em."

"I hope the boys win," Mr. Roberts said as he walked to his front door, his cigarette dangling from the side of his mouth. Mr. Roberts, also one of the finest horse trainers in Colorado, usually worked with a couple of quarter horses in a corral next to our backyard. That night, because of the cold weather, Mr. Roberts would not be working with his horses. That night, the horses would have the luxury of the warm shelter in a corrugated tin barn that Mr. Roberts and his boys had built.

I walked to the entrance of the alley that separated our properties. I passed their magenta-colored octagonal-sided granary and their outhouse. As I entered the back porch of our house and removed my boots, I was no longer thinking about how cold it was. I was euphoric about going to a basketball game. I thought about how fortunate I was to be able to go for the first time with my two triplet brothers. Furthermore, I couldn't imagine how anybody in the town would want to do anything else. At age ten, I deemed there was nothing more exciting than the prospect of watching basketball on a cold winter night in a warm gym.

At the Newton household, going to any event, athletic or otherwise, was a privilege and was based on seniority. Our brother Jerry, a year older, had already attended several home games. Going to the game was costly, and it was not easy for Mom and Dad to come up with ticket money. However, that night, the three of us were paying our own way. We had delivered advertising circulars for Mr. George Snider to all the houses in Mead, and he had paid us 75¢. Mom said we could spend part of our earnings for the game.

Earlier that afternoon, the whole school was filled with excitement. A pep rally had been held just before school was let out, and the cheers and yells echoed through the building. The sounds penetrated our second-grade classroom, disturbing Mrs. Abbot as she conducted our spelling lesson but exciting me with joyous anticipation.

That night, with our parkas and boots on and Mom giving each one of us a dime, we headed out, with brother Jerry leading the way. We heard Mom's admonishment as we stepped out the door, "Now you boys behave, ya hear?"

As usual, we chose the path of the snow-packed street, where the corner streetlights lit the way. We resembled four frozen "walking Frankensteins" as we hunched our shoulders and pulled our arms into our coat sleeves, trying to keep our hands warm. We had no gloves; they were a luxury item, way down on the priority list for clothing to be purchased. Furthermore, if gloves or mittens were bought for one child, they would soon be borrowed and quickly lost, never to be seen again.

We passed by the house of Mrs. Emily Newman, Mead's fifth-grade teacher and the mother of our friend Herbert. We walked by Coach Spencer's and Supt. Carl Carlson's houses. Edwin Spencer, the coach for both the B- and A-teams, was already at the gym, and so was Mr. Carlson, for it was his job to collect admissions. The B-team always played first at seven o'clock and was followed by the A-team at eight.

As we approached the school, we saw a big yellow bus with Platteville Consolidated Schools painted on the side. We could hear the sounds of bouncing balls and running footsteps on the gym floor as we stepped into the small foyer that led into the gym.

The foyer contained glass cases of trophies from past basketball and football victories and pictures of graduating classes hung high on three walls. The senior class sizes at Mead High had been small, perhaps five to eight in number. Starting in 1933 with the letter M, the school started the custom of placing individual student pictures within the perimeters of large block letters surrounded by silver-colored frames. As each succeeding class picture was hung, the words MEAD HIGH SCHOOL were spelled out. Senior pictures of our elder siblings— Orbin ('38), Raymond ('40), Eunice ('41), Roberta ('43), and Rosemary ('45)—were among those spread over the letters I, G, H, S, and O. Our cousin Bill Newton ('35) appeared on the letter A, along with Margaret Baker Olson, mother of our classmate Gary.

I saw brother Jack's name engraved on the consolation trophy he and his team had earned in 1946 in the Colorado State Basketball Tournament. The trophy had a wood base with a bronzed basketball player on top with arms extended and holding a ball with both palms.

We left our boots in a corner in the foyer and proceeded through the double doors into the gym. I sensed a "special energy" as I stepped into its large expanse. It was electric with excitement as the crowd roared and as players raced up and down the floor. The ongoing game produced sounds I had heard as a young player and had learned to love and appreciate—but never with this intensity. I immediately sensed that the Mead gym was a special place, a special place for special events. That special event was basketball, a game that now had become my sole obsession. The sharp contrast of the warmth in the gym with the coldness outside certified in my mind that watching basketball in the comfort of the gym was the best place to be that Friday night. I was lucky; in my mind, God had bestowed a tremendous privilege on me and my brothers.

Mr. Carlson was seated at the east end of the court behind a small wooden table with a metal money box, watching the game while he collected admissions. A bespectacled, pale-complexioned man in his late forties, Mr. Carlson parted his graying hair low on the left side and wrapped long thin strands over the top of his bald head. In the winter, when he walked the short distance from his house to the school, he covered his exposed head with a gray fedora, and he tucked his suit trousers into his unbuckled calf-high rubber boots. That night, he was wearing his customary double-breasted Penney suit of gray window-pane check. Mr. Carlson had obtained his master's degree in Colorado school policy at Colorado State College of Education in Greeley, qualifying him to be a superintendent. Gentle, kind, and forgiving, he devoted his whole being to the school and often substituted as a bus driver or teacher.

"Hello, boys," said Mr. Carlson with a smile. "The game has just started."

"Hello," responded Jerry, speaking as we placed our dimes on the table.

Each of us was on his own to find a seat among the thin crowd. Jerry found a spot with Marvin Blazon and George Ulibarri, who were sitting on the top row of the south-side, brown-stained, three-tiered bleachers that Marion Humphrey had built. Rollie and Richie were hoisted onto the stage by Herb Newman behind the east basket, where they found folding chair seats near Ronald Weber, Loe Hernandez, and Vernon Widger. I waited until the referee called time-out and quickly ran past the two teams as they huddled with their coaches. I found a seat where no one was sitting on the west side of the Mead team. I wanted to sit where I could listen to the conversation of the team with Coach Spencer and retrieve any errant balls that might come my way.

I shed my warm parka and leaned back against the cold plastered wall; its coolness felt good next to the hot skin on my back. I could feel the condensed moisture running down the wall but now was penetrating my shirt. The Mead gym was the largest room I had ever been in, and that night, it seemed more immense than ever.

Mom had told us, "Your dad helped build the gym about the time you triplets were born."

I said to myself, "I wonder what part of this gym was built by Dad." Did Dad help lay the large cement blocks and place mortar between them as the walls rose upward? Did he plaster the stacked rows of blocks just as he had done in our house? Perhaps he helped lay down the floor. I was certain he probably helped paint because that's what he did for a living.

Although the Mead gym was gigantic in my eyes, it was one of the smaller courts in the Poudre Valley League, surpassing only the renowned "cracker box" at Windsor. At Mead, the distance between the center circle and the outer curvature of the keyhole on each half-court was only a few feet, with the court width about two-thirds of regulation size. The west basket was permanently attached to a box structure with two openings above the backboard for showing movies on a screen on the stage at the opposite end of the court.

With a wide mop, Marion Humphrey had dusted the floor immaculately clean at 5:00 p.m., and he would dust it again between each game and at each halftime. That preceding summer, Mr. Humphrey had also given the granular surface of the plaster walls a new coat of gray paint, which he had applied about eight feet high from the gym floor, finishing the remainder of the walls up to the ceiling with a pale yellow color.

The scoreboard, a black rectangular box, hung in the northwest corner next to the ceiling. With a push of a button by the scorekeeper, the numbers rolled from behind into open rounded slots, providing the double digit score for each team. When our sister Helen told us about Mead getting an "electronic scoreboard" for the first time, she explained, "It's really not new. Mr. Carlson bought it secondhand from Greeley High School."

Across the court, I could see student spectators with their opened, unbuttoned colored blouses or shirts displaying the orange-and-black bulldog mascot logo on the front of their white T-shirts. B-team cheerleaders Marilyn Muhme, Mary Louise Peters, and our sister Pat, all dressed in black skirts, white blouses, black suspenders, and black-and-white saddle shoes, led the cheers.

To my left and to the end of the east court, I saw classmate Barbara Graham descending the cement stairs leading from the "refreshments room" (the home economics classroom and kitchen), carrying a bottled Coke in one hand and a Butterfinger candy bar in the other. I wished that I too could have some candy or pop, but I quickly banished the thought from my mind, once again remembering how lucky I was to have the admission money to see the game. Tonight candy bars and soda pop were secondary, and I took solace from the fact that I would probably have some if I was in closer proximity to where Barbara was sitting with her dad. We had known Barbara since the first grade, and I knew that she would always share candy with us, even without us having to ask. Besides, I did not want to change my seat for another. From my perspective, I had the best seat in the house.

I could see Mr. and Mrs. Major sitting very tall against the south wall. They, along with their three sons, farmed about four miles southeast of town and had come to watch their second-eldest son, Charles, play. To their right was Martin Graham, the father of Barbara, and the elder brother of Dean, Charles's teammate.

The players wore black: black tennis shoes, black leather kneepads, and black jerseys. Coach Spencer was wearing a single-breasted black suit. Substitute players, sitting on the bench to my left, wore warm-up jackets of bright orange satin, with orange and black strips of stretch-knit rounding each shoulder.

When the A-team came on the floor, our sister Helen, along with Beverly Jane Walter and Violet Sekich, all dressed in long-sleeved black sweaters with the orange-and-black block letter M on the front and white socks and saddle shoes on their feet, led the crowd in cheers. Throughout the game, they spun their long black skirts and synchronized their stepping movements, using outstretched arms and closed fists to guide spectators with their yells.

I watched intently as Dean Graham shot his jump shot with his legs bent upward and his shins parallel to and high above the floor. The elegant and magnificent image of Dean flying into the air and releasing the ball with legs sprawled wide was one that I tried to emulate. I later discussed my observation with Loe, who also had seen Dean's athletic demonstration, and soon, Loe was able to mimic his form while shooting baskets in our backyard. Dean had also perfected the "long shot," and Richie and I would try to simulate his technique. Our admiration for Dean and our desire to emulate him had a special motivation—he was sister Helen's steady boyfriend.

Charles Major, tall like his parents, was playing center. He had excellent moves with his back to the basket and was given the ball many times but was unable to score with any consistency. Early in the game, with his jersey shirttail hanging out of his pants and a strained look on his face, he soon began to look lethargic and tired. He had a back brace on under his jersey, and he continuously stooped over, grimacing with pain.

Mead lost to Platteville 33–30, but Dean Graham was the high-point man with thirteen. As pep club girls left the gym singing, "Whether we win or whether we lose, we're Bulldogs just the same," the four of us slipped our boots on and hurried home to tell Mom about the disappointing outcome.

The next morning, as we sat at the breakfast table, Rollie said, "Las' night, Charles Major did not play very good. His back must have been hurting him. He had a brace on."

"Yal," said Richie, "don'cha remember during Thanksgiving, he was thrown out the back of Louie Rademacher's truck, and he landed in our garden? Louie was speedin' 'round the corner toward the Newmans' house on a Sunday afternoon with Charles, John Lind, and a bunch of others standing up in the bed. They were knockin' out street lights by throwing rocks at 'em as they drove by. I remember seeing him lyin' there on the ground with a hurting look on his face. He was lyin' in our garden. Dad went over there to help him. He was hurt bad."

"Yes," said Helen. "They weren't sure he would even be able to play after that. I sure hope he gets better soon. He is our best player. The basketball coach over at Greeley is hopin' he'll go there to college when he graduates."

Carl Carlson, 1949. *Mead Consolidated Schools Yearbook*

A-String and B-String Teams: Front row, L-R: Orville Markham, Dean Graham, Charles Major, John Lind, Don Martinez; Back row, L-R: Junior Stotts, Wayne Dempewolf, Tom Spencer, John Stotts, Coach Edwin Spencer, 1947. *Mead Consolidated Schools Yearbook*

A-String Cheerleaders: L-R: Violet Sekich, Helen Newton, Barbara Walters, 1947. *Mead Consolidated Schools Yearbook*

Chapter 6

Touch of a Teacher

As each winter and basketball season rolled around, I was exhilarated by the high-school pep rallies before each game. Sitting in class, I could hear the cheering and clapping of more than a hundred students in the gym just down the hall.

Feeling the fervor, I thought, "Oh, only if I too can go to the game," for it was not always a certainty that my brothers and I could attend. On the afternoon of each home game day, and as soon as we arrived home after school, one of us would ask Mom for permission. Many times, she would just look at us and not answer. Her indecision was always based on finances, but it also depended on recent behavior and if we had completed assigned household tasks.

On a Friday afternoon in January '49, I sat in my fourth-grade classroom listening to Mrs. Jepperson read a story about a killer tiger menacing a small village in India. Her voice was becoming hoarse, and she stopped reading to get a drink of water from the fountain in the hall. I was having difficulty paying attention because my mind was on the game against Eaton that night. With the break from her recitation, I focused entirely on the game, and I said to myself, "I hope Mom will find the money and let us go."

As the bell rang for school to be dismissed, Mrs. Jepperson said out loud before she permitted the class to leave, "Ronald, would you stop to see me for just a moment after school?"

I could not imagine why she wanted to see me. I was not a disruptive student, and I had never disobeyed in her class. Mrs. Jepperson had been our first-grade teacher three years before, and she was one of my favorite teachers, comparing very favorably with the Abbott sisters who had taught us in the second and third grades.

In the school yearbook, Mrs. Jepperson was quoted, "Nearly all the boys of the fourth grade are sports-minded. They enjoyed playing football, basketball, volleyball, and baseball, especially the games with the fifth grade." She also knew we especially liked basketball, and she persuaded Mr. Carlson to buy a basketball just for our class. It was smaller than the ball used by the high-school team. It was for soccer, a game I did not know anything about anyhow. Its smaller size allowed us to hurl it more easily above the ten-foot-high rim and into the basket as we played at recess and noon. On a cold winter day, when everyone assembled in the gym for lunch or play, Mrs. Jepperson would assign a male member of the class the responsibility and privilege of caring for the ball and making sure it was brought back to the fourth-grade coatroom for safekeeping.

As my classmates hurried out to catch the bus or walk home, I, seated in the middle of the room between Jim Brunemeier and Larry Nuss, gave a slight nudge to Jim and pushed him gently forward until I approached Mrs. Jepperson's large wooden desk. She pulled open a bottom drawer and took out her pocketbook.

With her characteristic warm smile, she said to me, "I have a surprise for you and your brothers."

She removed a coin purse from her black pocketbook, unsnapped it, and took out three dimes she then placed in an envelope. She took scissors and cut off half the envelope, and began to fold the rest of it around the three dimes. She then took a rubber band and wrapped it around the small parcel and handed it to me.

She said, "Take this home to your mother, and tell her I hoped she would give you permission to go the ball game tonight."

I took the wrapped dimes from her hand, clutching them in my fist. Not even thinking to say thank you, I ran to the coatroom, put on my boots and parka, opened the two wide doors of the school with a burst of speed and a bang, and ran all the way home, the parcel of dimes in my pocket.

I burst through the back-porch door, yelling, "Mom! Mrs. Jepperson gave us money for us triplets to go to the game tonight! Can we go? Please?"

"What? Let me see," she commanded.

I gave the small package to Mom. She opened it, and the three dimes dropped into her apron lap. Then she said, "Well, I suppose so, but you better be sure you have your chores done."

That night, we triplets wore white sweatshirts that our brother Jack had given us for Christmas presents. Helen had stenciled a bulldog mascot image on the front, and we wanted to show everyone we were proud supporters of the Mead Bulldogs.

"Those look pretty neat," said Loe as he helped us climbed on the stage to watch the game with Weber and him. We got there in time to see our brother Tom play on the B-team, which won easily. Tom scored twelve points and, just a sophomore, was beginning to demonstrate his skills as a basketball player. He briefly saw action in the A-team game, which Mead also won. Our sister Pat, a senior and a cheerleader, cheered Mead on to the win.

* * *

After basketball season ended and snowstorms had passed, the spring rains began, and soon, it was May, with the school year about to end. Mrs. Jepperson was reading to our class, covering the final chapters of a *Hardy Boys* book that Gary Olson had brought. We had finished cleaning up our textbooks in preparation for use by next year's fourth grade, and a picnic and picture show outing on the last day of school the following week was planned by teachers and Mr. Carlson. Mrs. Jepperson had placed our final letter grades for each subject in our report cards, and they were ready to take home. Six weeks before, Dr.

John Bothell, working for the Weld County Department of Education, had administered achievement tests to all the grades, one through twelve, at Mead.

On Wednesday afternoon that final week, Mrs. Jepperson reminded the class, "Remember now, you and your parents and brothers and sisters are all invited to come to Awards Night here in the gym. The program begins at seven o'clock."

That evening, I sat in a middle row of dual-attached wooden folding chairs set side by side on the gym floor by Marion Humphrey's children, Alberta and Robert. Gary Olson, Larry Heil, Rollie, and Richie were sitting with me. With the wooden chairs arranged in two columns facing the stage at the east end of the gym, we were surrounded by parents and students, all talking with excited, hushed voices. The east backboard and basket had been raised parallel to the floor so that they would not obstruct the view of the audience of a hundred or more. As Mr. Carlson ascended the temporary stairs placed in front of the stage, standing behind the podium, he introduced each event printed on the mimeographed program.

"And now," said Mr. Carlson, "we'd like Bobby Anderson to come up here and give us a recitation of the humorous speech he wrote and presented in the speech competition at the district meet in Greeley. Bobby, as you may not know, won first place among students from twenty-one other schools. He has titled his speech 'The Shoop Scovel.'"

Bobby, a high-school junior, began to tell a story with broken sentences and with an accent resembling German about a scoop shovel. The audience erupted with laughter as he recited his story from memory while gesticulating with rapid arm motions and walking around the stage. The audience clapped loudly when he finished, and Mr. Carlson smiled proudly as he took the stage once again to announce that Sandra Alexander would follow with a piano solo.

Business teacher Mrs. Lillian Spencer gave out awards for typing and shorthand, and Coach Edwin Spencer awarded the block-letter M to football, track, and basketball athletes. Our sister Pat and several of her classmates received forty-words-per-minute typing pins, as well as eighty-words-per-minute awards for shorthand. Our brother Tom and seven others in his sophomore class were awarded letters in basketball.

Awards for scholastic achievement were saved until the end. Mrs. Baker and Mrs. Crews, representing the second and third grades, followed first-grade teacher Mrs. Goodwin in giving out handcrafted award certificates to meritorious children while smiling parents watched approvingly.

"And now for the fourth-grade awards," stated Mr. Carlson, "we'll have Mrs. Isabel Jepperson announce the names."

Mrs. Jepperson, sitting on the side bleachers with the other teachers, rose and walked up to the podium. She started out saying, "I enjoyed being with the fourth-grade children this year and to see how they progressed so much from the time I taught them three years ago as their first-grade teacher. I am especially pleased to recognize two students who have progressed significantly since last year with their achievement test scores."

She had two award certificates in her left hand that she had made, each with eight-and-a-half-by-eleven-inch purple construction paper, folded in half into a booklet, into which she inscribed the following words:

◊   *For Scholastic Achievement*
◊   *Fourth Grade*
◊   *Mead Consolidated Schools*
◊   *May 1949*
◊   *Mrs. Isabelle Jepperson, Teacher*

She called Gary Olson to the stage first. She described how exceptional Gary's performance was and that his scores were comparable to those of a tenth-grade high-school student. As Gary descended the stairs to take his seat, she said, "Would Ronald Newton please come forward?"

Not expecting this, I had to be coaxed by the other teachers to leave my seat and proceed to the stage. With head down and feeling out of place with all eyes staring at me, I stumbled up the stairs and stood with my back to the audience and facing Mrs. Jepperson.

She then said, "Ronald Newton has shown significant achievement this year over last year, and we want to reward his achievement by giving him this certificate."

She handed the award to me, and I quickly left the stage, again with head down, looking at no one as I hurried to my seat. That night, I gave the certificate to Mom for safekeeping. She carefully looked it over and then placed it in her dining room chest of drawers. She said nothing. Complimenting her children for their achievements was never her style. She did not want them thinking that they were "the only star that twinkled."

A-String and B-String Teams: Front row, L-R: Leo Brewer, Don Giebelhaus, Buddy
Amen, Don Owen, Tom Newton, George Vonalt, Raymond Fiechtner; Back row,
L-R: Bobby Anderson (Mgr.) Glenn Markham, Willard Yakel, Tom Major, Eddie
Rademacher, Richard Yakel, Tom Spencer, Wayne Dempewolf, Coach Edwin Spen-
cer, 1949. *Mead Consolidated Schools Yearbook*

L-R: Richie, Ronnie, and Rollie Newton, 1949. *Mead Consolidated Schools Yearbook*

A-String Cheerleaders. Back row, L-R: Patty Lang, Loretta Adler; Front row: Alma
Amen, Patricia Newton, 1949. *Mead Consolidated Schools Yearbook*

Isabel Jepperson, 1949. *Mead Consolidated Schools Yearbook*

Chapter 7

Difficulty in the Fifth

Basketball was our favorite winter activity, and when we weren't playing, we wanted to watch others performing. "Peewee" and junior high basketball games were played on Saturday mornings, and my brothers and I would create every opportunity we could to see the games in the Mead gym or travel to the opposing school.

Our next-door neighbor Mrs. Emily Newman took Kathleen, Jerry, Rollie, Richie, and me in her car to a junior-high game in Frederick. Her son Herbert was playing for Mead, along with Ronald Weber, Freddie Sekich, John Schell, and Billy Amen. The Frederick Warriors had been a rival of Mead in basketball throughout the decade of the '40s, and I soon became aware of the intense competitive spirit between the two schools. The tradition of playing the children of Italian immigrant coal miners who were tough mentally and physically was on the minds of all Mead school kids every time they faced the formidable Warriors of Frederick.

Mead was defeated that Saturday morning, and Mrs. Newman was not happy with the outcome. She thought that the Frederick coach Al Tesone, a classmate of hers at Colorado State College of Education, intimidated the referee and had given Frederick the advantage, calling many more fouls on Mead rather than the hometown opponent.

Mrs. Newman said, "I dated Coach Tesone in college, and I thought he was one of the most wonderful guys I had ever met. Today I'm not so sure."

Mrs. Newman lived in the next block south of us Newtons. We saw her often. She came to our house on Saturday mornings to visit Mom, and she willingly provided transportation for Mom to shop and buy groceries in Longmont. If Mom needed to borrow a cup of sugar or needed to make an urgent phone call (before we had a phone), she prevailed on Mrs. Newman. She was also the fifth-grade teacher of Jerry and us triplets. As fourth-graders, our basketball team had defeated her fifth-graders. The outcome was a real surprise to her. Talking to Mom in a conversation I overheard, Mrs. Newman said, "I certainly wouldn't have expected it. My fifth-graders were so much bigger than those fourth-graders."

In her early forties, Mrs. Newman parted her long auburn hair in the middle, braided it into several strands, and wrapped these up and around her head. She dressed in suits and flowered dresses and used no makeup. She had opinions on many subjects and showed no hesitation in expressing them to her students or anyone else. When she was standing, her hands were always placed on her hips, giving the impression that she was observing and calculating and forming her own ideas and interpretations on what she was seeing and hearing. A strict disciplinarian, she was quick to punish those who infringed on her rules. In the eyes of a fifth-grader, Mrs. Newman was a woman to be feared. To a kid like me, she was a foreboding figure, inducing states of dread, dismay, and anxiety. At times, she was most generous, giving rides for Mom, my brothers, and me to Longmont and to school on cold winter mornings. At other times, classmate Gary Olson said, "She was just outright mean."

One day in our fifth-grade class, I was subjected to Mrs. Newman's forceful response to one of my stupid classroom shenanigans. She had left our classroom to visit another teacher after she had assigned us to quiet self-study. I took her absence as license to stand before the class and throw erasers at classmates in the back of the room, Leonard Smith and Johnny Minch. Sitting studiously at my desk before she returned,

I became concerned when she opened the door with a furled brow and a frown, fuming. She came directly toward me as I sat at my desk. She slapped me on one side of the face with one hand and on the other side with the other. With her left hand on the back of my head, she pulled me toward her and downward and then slapped me several times on the back, shoulders, and upper arms as I tried to protect myself. As she walked away, I placed my head on my arms on the desk top and began to sob. I cried for several minutes, humiliated and ashamed for what had transpired in front of my classmates. I was ashamed that our neighbor had to resort to those measures to correct my misbehavior.

Mrs. Newman had boasted of her cleverness in her ability to monitor our class. She said, "Don't try something when my back's turned. I have eyes in the back of my head, and I know what you're doing."

That day, I was unaware that Mrs. Newman had been standing at the top of the stairs outside our classroom and was observing my "pitching prowess" through the glass transom above our door. As the school day ended, I became concerned that when Mom heard about this episode, she would add her own punishment. I do not know for sure how Mom became aware of my antics; I presumed that Mrs. Newman had called her.

That evening, Mom grabbed me by the shoulders and forced me to look directly at her as she said, "I hear you've been acting cute at school. I've heard all about it. You're grounded for the next two weeks. There'll be no basketball games for you. You'll be stayin' home. I'll show you, young man. Don'choo ever show off again like that. Shame on you."

There was an emotional tension between Mrs. Newman and me, the cause of which I did not totally understand. One day, right after the lunch hour, Mrs. Newman stood in front of the classroom with hands on her hips and said, "I don't know why so many people think the Newton triplets are so great." She shook her head as she walked toward her desk. "I don't get it. I know them, and I know better."

I never knew for sure what caused her to make that statement. What had I done wrong? Did I say something to somebody that I shouldn't have? Was it Richie or Rollie who did something she thought was wrong? Furthermore, why did she say this in front of the whole class? Did she think the three of us were "big-headed" and needed to be "brought down a notch"? I was always aware that because we were triplets, there was a lot of public interest in us and that our actions were known to many in the community. I knew they and Mom expected us to behave in an exemplary way and never to think "we were the only star that twinkled." I sensed that Mrs. Newman had observed an episode that told her, "The Newton triplets are not all that they're cracked up to be."

Our class often had spontaneous discussions on a variety of topics. As a member of Longmont's Swedish Lutheran Church, Mrs. Newman said to me as I told her that we triplets were to be confirmed as fifth-graders, "I don't know why you Catholics are confirmed at such a young age. You don't have any idea what's goin' on. In the Lutheran Church, you're confirmed as teenagers." Mrs. Newman addressed the whole class as we discussed religions. "We Lutherans don't pray to the Virgin Mary. We find it very strange that Catholics do so. We pray only to God and Jesus."

Mrs. Newman constantly minimized whatever I said by upstaging me. In a discussion about buildings in our Mead community, I proudly stated, "My mom told me that my dad helped build the Mead gym," to which she emphatically retorted, "That's nothing. Curly helped build the grain elevator here in Mead and many others all over Weld County." Curly, her husband, was the on-site construction supervisor for the Denver Elevators company.

One afternoon, while halfway through taking a geography fill-in-the-blank quiz, I went up to her desk to ask her about one of the questions I didn't understand. As I placed the quiz sheet in front of her, she assumed that I was giving up and was leaving many of the questions unanswered. She took her red pencil and started grading it as I stood beside her. I was startled and was too timid to inform her I wasn't finished. I miserably flunked.

We started the fifth-grade school year in a small classroom, and as the year progressed and as more students transferred to Mead, Mrs. Newman moved us to a larger room. Mike Eckel joined our class, having moved to the Mead school district from Johnstown. Along with Mary

Helen Olson, Gary Olson, Elaine Leinweber, and Joan LaFollette, Mike began learning to play a musical instrument. Buying an instrument was not an option for us, and on Friday afternoons, instead of music, we had art lessons with the remainder of the class.

Joan LaFollette transferred in from Longmont's Columbine School and was a good student. She never misspelled a word on our weekly examinations. Even after she told me that she took the list of words home with her and studied them, it never occurred to me that I should do likewise. Mrs. Newman had not made that assignment. Homework had never been assigned during our elementary grades. After all, learning was supposed to take place at school. Our schoolbooks were never taken home. They remained in our desks, were the property of the school, and were on loan to us only during the day.

At the end of our fifth-grade year, our fourth-grade teacher, Mrs. Jepperson, learned of my low achievement test scores and said to me, "I'm surprised, Ronald, that you haven't done better this last year." I shared in her disappointment. I wanted to perform well. I wanted to be more like Gary Olson. his scores were always "way up there." My disappointment in myself was even greater when I learned that my new classmate, LaVerne Magnuson, had scored higher than I did. It would not be long before Lyle Schaefer would move to Mead, and he too would displace me, moving me further down the academic performance chain.

Rather than basketball, our '49–'50 school year was dominated by football. Mead High School won the state six-man football championship, defeating Nucla 40–8. Halfbacks Vernon Nuss and Donnie Owen and fullback Eddie Rademacher did most of the scoring for the Bulldogs. Eddie Rademacher's six-foot-three height and his one hundred and eighty-six pounds made him a formidable competitor. His large frame also served him well as a basketball player, playing alongside our brother Tom.

Front Row, L-R: Delores Leonard, Betty Lee, Barbara Hetterle, Richie Newton, Ronnie Newton, Rollie Newton, Charlotte Widman, Barbara Graham, Shirley Smith. Middle Row, L-R: Jim Brunemeier, Josephine Rademacher, Claudia Williams, Mary Helen Olson, Janice Fredericksen, Beverly Steving, Elaine Leinweber, Irene Stotts, Joan LaFollette, Shirley Hepp, Jacqueline Thompson. Back Row, L-R: Eddie Smith, Jim Landolt, Mike Eckel, Denver Spencer, Gary Olson, Leonard Smith, LaVerne Magnuson, John Minch, Emily Newman, 1950. *Mead Consolidated Schools Yearbook.*

Chapter 8

Inspiration and Support

I hurried home from school the day after a deep snow blanketed Northeastern Colorado. It was early December 1950, and I wanted to remove the snow from our outside basketball court right away. To my surprise, my brother Dave was already there in his stocking cap and jacket, using a large scoop shovel; tall mounds of dirt-laden snow lay on all four sides of the half-court he had cleared. I helped him remove what was left, and by the next day, the exposed ground was dried by the sun with the help of the arid winds coming down the eastern slope of the Rockies.

Within forty-eight hours, we were standing on dry ground, shooting at the net-less hoop ten feet above. Our elder brothers, Jack and Tom, had mounted it on a backboard attached to a single pine four-by-four post. I tried to improve my jump shot and then began working on the release of a "long shot" from the far corner of the cleared area. I experimented with a high arching shot that I had seen high-schooler Buddy Amen use with great success. Taking heed of Weber's admonition that "good basketball players need to be able to use both hands," I worked on my left-hand dribbling and layup skills until darkness fell and I could see no more.

That winter, my four brothers and I attended every high-school home game. Our admission had been paid by our sister Helen. Helen and our sister Pat had graduated from high school, and the two of them had moved to Longmont to work. Helen was a receptionist for a general practitioner, Dr. Malcom Cook, and Pat assisted a dentist, Dr. Alfred Carr. For Christmas, Pat gave us a miniature pool table with balls of marble size, and Helen gave season tickets to each of us for the high-school games. She had mailed the money to Supt. Carlson. Our gift was a Christmas card she placed under the tree for each one of us. Inside the envelope, she had placed an index card upon which she had typed the date and the opponent of the six home games.

Our brother Tom, a high-school junior, was a starting forward on Mead's basketball team. The team featured new warmups, and for the first time, team members had long pants to wear. The warmup suit of jacket and pants, made of wool, was all black with a large blazing-orange M on the left side. Mr. Carlson had also purchased new jerseys for the team—orange with black letters for away games and white with orange for home games. Black shorts with fine orange trim finished out the uniform. As a fifth-grader, I relished the thought that someday my brothers and I would wear the uniforms that brother Tom and his teammates wore.

On a February Saturday morning, I delivered Postmaster Hap Howlett's copy of the *Rocky Mountain News* to the Mead Post Office. Hap, stuffing the locked boxes from behind with the just-arrived mail, heard the post-office door open as I entered; he approached the barred window set among the mailboxes to determine who it was. Seeing I was one of the Newton brothers, he asked, "Do you know what your brother Tom did last night against Eaton?" Before I could respond, Hap said, "He won the game for 'em. Bub and I drove over to Eaton last night to watch. It was one of Eddie Rademacher's best games. He must have scored more than twenty points. With about fifteen seconds left to go, Eddie tied it up with a free-throw, making the score 46-46." Hap chuckled and said, "Then the damnedest thing happened. It was unbelievable. Eaton took it out of bounds and threw it to one of their players, who then let it fly in a final desperation shot. The damn ball hit the ceiling, so then it was out of bounds, and Mead got the ball at half-court."

"How much time was left?" I asked.

"Three seconds," said Hap. "Loe Hernandez threw in the ball to Tom, and we all yelled, 'Shoot! Shoot!' Tom pivoted and let loose. When it was in midair, the buzzer sounded, and the ball split the net. Mead went two points ahead and won the game."

"So the final score was 48-46," I commented happily.

"That's right. It was a real upset," said Hap. "Eaton is second in the league, two games behind Windsor, who has lost only one. Mead is in sixth place, one game ahead of Platteville, who's last."

I hurried to deliver the rest of my papers and to get home so I could tell Mom what I heard. I knew Tom would still be sleeping and that I would be the first to tell her about his accomplishment. I was proud of how Tom won the game for Mead, dreaming of the day when perhaps I too, with a dramatic shot, could win a game for Mead. I fantasized about the shot I would take. At the right baseline with my back to the basket, I would turn left to jump and twist in midair to face the basket with the ball above my head, pushing it off my left hand with my right, and "pumping it in with nothing but net." I practiced this shot many times on our dirt court at home. I preferred the right baseline for the start of the shot. I was certain that with this imagined game-winning shot, "my star" would shine brightly. Everybody in town, including Hap Howlett, would be talking about it!

For Christmas in 1951, my four brothers and I were once again anticipating that sister Helen would give us season tickets to the Mead basketball games. Expecting a card from Helen with the six home games listed on an index card, we were concerned when we saw that under the tree, she had placed a small wrapped box for each one of us. Had the tradition that she had established been discontinued? Would we no longer have paid admission to all the games? On Christmas Eve, we opened her present to see that inside was a tree ornament she had made. She had painted a face on the silvered glass ball, glued on "hair and eyebrows" of cotton, and capped the ornament with a top hat. Of course, I was grateful for the handmade decoration but was perplexed and disappointed. I concluded that Helen had broken the tradition she had established, and I knew she had no other gift under the tree for me. I wanted my season tickets!

Helen waited until all five of us had opened her present, and after watching our collective bewilderment, she finally said, "Look inside the hat." Each of us removed the hat to see that the index card with all the games listed was rolled up in a cylinder.

I stuck the index card in my pocket and walked over to the Christmas tree and hung my ornament gift. Helen's annual Christmas gift was always the one I coveted.

"I thought you had forgotten all about buyin' 'em this year," I said. "I was scared we wouldn't be goin' to any games. Thanks a lot."

Tom, now a senior and six feet and two inches tall, played center for the first two games of the basketball season, but Mead's new coach, Tom Peterson, switched him to guard when he brought up six-foot-four Clarence Newman from the B-team to play center. Two days before Christmas, Mead played its first league game against the Ault Bearcats, with Tom playing guard. Not knowing that Mr. Carlson had already received the admissions money from Helen, Mr. Carlson let us in to the game with no questions asked by him or us. Mead blistered the Bearcats. It was a real rout! Tom scored twenty-five points, which marked the beginning of his being one of the top scorers in the Weld County A-League.

In January '51, my brothers and I watched Tom score twenty-one points as Mead downed Johnstown. That night, Coach Peterson put Tom back in the center position so his sharp defensive skills could ward off the inside offensive game of Johnstown. Tom had an uncanny ability to block an opponent's shot from a side angle, thus avoiding a called foul while preventing the opponent from scoring. Tom's outstanding defense, in addition to his great offensive showing, contributed to Johnstown's defeat.

As I walked home from the game with Richie on that cold winter night, Richie said, "I can hardly wait 'til we get in high school and we're playin. I wanna play like Tom. I bet he made at least twenty points. I hope I can make twenty points in one game like he did tonight."

"Yal, me too," I said. "If Rollie made twenty and Jerry made twenty, that'd be eighty points. We'd win for sure. The other team wouldn't have a chance."

Helen and Pat Newton, 1950. *Newton Family Album*

Tom Newton, 1951. *Mead Consolidated Schools Yearbook*

Chapter 9

Coach Clark

On a weekday winter morning in 1951, it was snowing heavily. All of us Newtons scurried from bedroom to closet to bathroom to kitchen to porch to get ready for school by eight-thirty. That winter morning was a lot easier for nine kids to maneuver; we finally had an *indoor* bathroom. That previous summer, Mom and Dad had a bathroom and a sewer system installed. The sink, toilet, and bathtub were placed where the pantry had been, and Dad dug a large hole for the septic tank in back of the house. The final touch was an eighty-gallon electric water heater installed in the cellar. Rollie and Richie had already delivered the *Rocky Mountain News* and were washing up in the new bathroom. Jerry and I were washing breakfast dishes, rinsing them off with hot water from a kitchen sink faucet and placing them in the cupboard after drying. Twin sisters Kathleen and Maureen made peanut butter sandwiches, wrapped them in waxed paper, and placed them in paper sacks with an oatmeal cookie.

I went to the porch to locate my rubber boots my sister Rosemary had given me for Christmas. I looked for the pair that had my name written on the inner lining; there were four other pairs lying there, all the same shape and same color. With our stocking caps and winter coats on and lunch bags in hand, we scurried along a tire track formed in the fallen snow on the street to the school. Jerry and Dave and Marc had departed ahead of us and so had the twins. Tom was still back at the house.

"The hall clock says twenty-seven minutes after," said Richie as the three of us entered our sixth-grade classroom and stepped up the tiny flight of stairs into the front coatroom to remove our boots and hang up our coats and caps. The room was warm from the heat that Mr. Humphrey had turned on at seven o'clock and smelled of wax that had vaporized from the pine floors.

Because of slow travel on the snow-covered country roads, three school buses were running late; one-third of our thirty-two classmates had not yet arrived. Those who were there were talking loudly to one another and laughing. The bell rang, and we slid into our assigned seats for the roll to be taken. Mr. C.H. Clark, our sixth-grade teacher, led the class in reciting the Pledge of Allegiance, and then the school day began with solving long-division problems in our math books.

After serving four years in the navy and finishing a teacher training program at Colorado A&M College, Mr. Clark followed in the footsteps of his mother, Mrs. Myrtle Clark, Mead's seventh-grade teacher, and he took a job at Mead as teacher of sixth grade.

Mr. Clark was tall and lanky and had a Dick Tracy–shaped nose. Having dated him once several years before, Rosemary commented, "Dressed in his sailor uniform, CH was a very handsome man." His hairline had receded, but a small tuft of hair remained in front, which he grew long and combed back over his head. The Western-style shirts and trousers he wore reflected his passion for horses and the outdoors. He always wore a tie and, occasionally, cowboy boots. He commanded our respect and, like his mother, was a taskmaster. Learning was always taking place in his classroom.

Because we got to color maps, my favorite subject in Mr. Clark's class was geography. Mr. Clark gave each student a mimeographed reproduction of a geographical region that he instructed us to color with crayons. When finished, the class would vote on which were the five best of thirty-two maps. These five were then hung above the blackboard in the *middle* of the room for direct visibility, attention, and esteem. All across the front wall of the room and on both sides of the chosen five were the remaining twenty-seven. My maps were always among the best, but I was devastated one time by my failure to maintain my status. I hoped no one would notice which one was mine, but Barbara Graham did.

She inquired, "What happened, Ronnie?"

I had no answer.

Mr. Clark understood the importance of sports at Mead and particularly with his class of thirty-two pupils. That previous fall, he had arranged for us sixth-grade boys to play flag football against a sixth-grade class from Longmont's Columbine Elementary School. I had quarterbacked the team, and Richie and Rollie played at the receiver positions. We triplets, convinced that Mr. Clark could coach us in basketball just as he did in football, wanted to play a Longmont school.

"Mr. Clark, can you schedule a game with Longmont Columbine or Central for us?" Rollie asked.

"Yes," agreed Allen Thompson. "We'd like to play them. I know we can beat 'em." Allen, very athletic, had moved to Mead from Oklahoma, and we quickly befriended him. We invited him to play basketball with us, and he easily mastered the fundamentals.

However, when Mr. Clark arranged for us to play Columbine on its court, we were both ecstatic *and* intimidated.

"Mr. Clark, their schools are much bigger than ours, and we know they are going to have a lot of good players," said Rollie.

"We'll see," said Mr. Clark. "I'm sure you're going to do all right. You might be surprised. I know they have 'fan backboards' in their gyms, and that might take some gettin' used to. They'll furnish one referee, and they want us to bring one. Ronnie, do you think you can get Ronald Weber to referee for us?" he asked.

"I'll ask him," I replied.

"Ask him too if he can drive his car and take some of our players to Longmont," directed Mr. Clark.

Mr. Clark borrowed jerseys from the peewee and junior high teams, but each of us had to furnish our own trunks, preferably black. Mom found three sets for us, handed down from Jack and Tom. Two were colored dark blue, and these were worn by Richie and me. The other one, black, went to Rollie. With her sewing machine, Mom altered them to fit our tiny waists.

When we arrived at Longmont's Columbine Elementary, we were greeted by Mr. Jim Harper, Columbine's physical education teacher. He led us through the gym into the locker room, and while we changed into tennis shoes and uniforms, Mr. Harper and Mr. Clark continued their conversation.

"We'll be suiting up fifteen sixth-graders," said Mr. Harper.

"I brought ten players with me," Mr. Clark responded. "Not all our team could come. Some of them have to do farm chores, so they couldn't make it."

As they talked, Weber, then about five feet and six inches tall, walked up to them, and Mr. Clark placed his hand on his shoulder in anticipation of introducing him to Mr. Harper. Before Mr. Clark could utter a word, Mr. Harper blurted out, "Sure he can play today. It's okay. He's not too big. Let him suit up."

"No, no," said Mr. Clark. "He's not going to play. He's our referee."

Our team doubled the score on Columbine that afternoon, and everyone got to play. I made one long shot that Richie commented about on the way home. "Seeing where the shot was coming from, I had placed myself under the basket in the spot where I thought I could rebound, thinking Ronnie would probably miss. But his shot was perfect, with the ball hitting only the net as it went through the rim."

Mr. Clark then noted, "Those backboards didn't give you kids much trouble today, did they?"

I replied, "I didn't use the backboard for any of my shots except for layups."

Rollie acknowledged, "I liked 'em. I could take side shots closer to the end line without hitting the side of the backboard."

Playing on the court at Longmont's Central Elementary School several weeks later, we sixth-graders were again victorious—and again by a wide margin. Mr. Clark then decided to enter our team in the peewee tournament sponsored by Mead Consolidated Schools. The tournament was for "small" seventh-, eighth-, and ninth-graders on teams from the Weld County A-League. With our sixth-grade entry and the regular peewee team, Mead was entering two teams in the tournament.

The next week in class, Mr. Clark called out to me. "Ronnie, would you please come up here for a minute?"

I walked to the front of the room and stood next to where Mr. Clark was sitting. He said to me in a whispered voice, "We need to decide which of the seventh-graders should be on our team. Mr. Carlson wanted us to have some of them play with us. Who do you think we should get to help us out?"

I whispered, "I think we should get my brother Jerry and Marvin Blazon."

As I spoke, Mr. Clark wrote their names down on a sheet of paper. "How 'bout Jerry Sitzman?" Mr. Clark asked. "Do you think he could help us? Have you seen him play?"

"He's pretty tall," I answered. "I think he and Jerry can help us with the rebounding. They both can play center for us."

"Those three are all we need," said Mr. Clark. "We have seven from our sixth-grade class, and the limit is ten players."

Mr. Carlson and Coach Tom Petersen drew up the brackets, and our team was scheduled to play Johnstown the next Saturday at 10:00 a.m. Mr. Clark held practice for our hybrid team on Saturday afternoon, a week before the tournament. Mr. Clark had high expectations, and he, as well as we Newton brothers, looked forward to the next Saturday with much anticipation. We had never played in a tournament, and the possibility of playing more than one game in one day was an opportunity we relished. Adding to our excitement was the announcement at the supper table one evening that Mom and our sister-in-law, Ferne, the wife of Orbin, were going to attend. The Korean War had started, and Ferne and daughter Kathy were staying with us until Orbin, still in the marines, completed his assignment in Korea.

Come Saturday, we entered the gym and saw the gilded gold trophy that Mr. Carlson had bought for the tournament winner. It was magnificent.

At ten o'clock, Mead High social-studies teacher and the appointed referee, Mr. Ernest Maurer, blew the whistle to start the game. Mr.

Clark started us triplets, Jerry (Newton), and Marvin Blazon. Not too far into the game, Rollie tipped a jump ball to Jerry, who was crouched in the keyhole at the bottom of the circle; Jerry immediately pivoted to his left and dropped in his hallmark hook shot. But after that brief triumph, the morning was endlessly frustrating for Mr. Clark and our team.

Referee Maurer, who was not familiar with the game of basketball, made some "unusual" calls that began to inhibit the play of our team. Furthermore, the experience of the Johnstown five began to show, and the game got away from the Mead "second-team" peewees. Mr. Clark's frustration heightened when I, receiving the ball from Johnnie Minch on a fast break and seeing the defender rapidly approaching me, hurried my shot and missed the layup as the ball caromed off the backboard without even hitting the rim.

Richie, sitting on the bench at the time, heard Mr. Clark say, "I didn't think Ronnie would miss such an easy shot so badly." He then added, "We certainly have not played well today."

That morning, we brothers experienced our first loss as members of a team. I cried as I walked off the floor. Richie, Rollie, and Jerry remained stoic with saddened faces as we descended the stairs into the locker room. I showered and changed into street clothes.

I had finally regained my composure as Jerry and I left the school and started our walk home. However, I teared up again as I began to speak. "W-we shouldn't've lost that game," I said. "Th-they were not that good. I-I missed two easy shots. If I had made 'em, we would have tied the game."

"Mr. Maurer sure called some dumb fouls," said Jerry.

"Y-Yeah, he called two fouls on me!" I said. "Ahn one of em, I-I didn't even touch the guy. I-I was just goin' after the ball! Ahn the other one, I j-just reached in with both hands and took the ball away from the guy. I couldn't believe Maurer called a foul on me."

"He doesn't look to me like he's ever played basketball," said Jerry. "He didn't know what he was doin'."

"I don't know why they had him doin' the reffin'," I said. "They should've gotten Weber to do it. He knows how to call a game."

Several weeks later, our sister Rosemary came home for the weekend. Rosemary had dated Ernest Maurer, and he had taken her to Mead's high-school prom the previous spring. So I seized the opportunity to tell her about my perception of Mr. Maurer's inept performance in calling our game and to inform her of my thoughts about her boyfriend.

"Maurer's a lousy referee," I said to her. "He's never played basketball. He doesn't know anything about it. He really made some stupid calls. He called me for walkin' when I wasn't."

"He may not have played, but I'm sure Ernie knows the rules," said Rosemary.

"He doesn't know anything about basketball," I said. "He doesn't know how to ref it, and he doesn't know how to play it. He helped us lose. It's not fair."

"Well, Ronnie boy," said Rosemary, "just lump it. Get over it. Not everything is fair in this world. I'm sure he was tryin' his best to do a good job."

Sixth Grade Basketball Team. Front row, L-R: Gary Olson (Mgr.), LaVerne
Magnuson, Richie Newton, Ronnie Newton, Rollie Newton, Jim Landolt, Johnny
Minch: Back row, L-R: Leonard Smith, Mike Eckel, Bob Straight, C. H. Clark
(Coach), Denver Spencer, Allen Thompson, 1951. *Mead Consolidated Schools
Yearbook*

Rosemary Newton, 1951.
Newton Family Album

Ronald Weber, 1952.
*Mead Consolidated
Schools Yearbook*

Chapter 10

New Hoop

As we transitioned into our middle-school years in 1951, basketball was the dominant sport in Colorado, and we indulged in it at home, on the playground, at school, and in our social life. Every year, the Amateur Athletic Union held a national basketball tournament in the Denver Auditorium. For three consecutive years, family friend Walter "Walt" Slee bought tickets for my four brothers and me to see the quarterfinals. Collegiate players from all over the nation were recruited to play on teams, such as the Phillips 66ers, the Denver Nuggets, and the Akron Goodyear Wingfoots. All-American Arnold Short from Oklahoma City University played with the 66ers, and Denver East High School star and collegiate all-American Ronnie Shavlick from North Carolina State University appeared with the Nuggets. Along with the 66ers, the Nuggets were one of the most powerful amateur basketball teams in the country, with past players namely Jumpin' Jack McCracken and Vince Boryla, formerly of the University of Denver.

With the advent of television, the National Industrial Basketball League games were televised, and we saw the Denver Central Bankers and the Denver Truckers play the Peoria Cats, the Wichita Vickers, and the unbeatable Bartlesville Phillips 66ers. Utah State University standout LaDell Anderson played for the Bankers, and Colorado University all-American Burdette Halderson had linked up with the 66ers. At CU,

Halderson and his teammate Bob Jeangerard led their team to the NCAA Final Four, where they were defeated by the University of San Francisco's Bill Russell and K. C. Jones, both drafted by the Boston Celtics. On Sunday evenings after the ten-o-clock television news, we watched sports highlights featuring college basketball teams, such as Seton Hall, Furman, and LaSalle, all playing in New York's famed Madison Square Garden.

Walt Slee took us to see the Harlem Globetrotters and the Washington Generals play an exhibition game in the Longmont Memorial Coliseum, and we saw the Globetrotter story acted out on the movie screen. I was overwhelmed by the magical dribbling prowess of Marques Haynes, whom I attempted to emulate. Women basketball players from the Texas Flying Queens came to Longmont to play the ladies on the Denver Viner Chevrolet team. The Viners were coached by Les Major, the brother of Mead's Tom and Charles Major; Les's five-foot-ten wife Dorothy played center. The Viner ladies also played our high-school team in an exhibition at the Mead gym against Loe Hernandez, the Newman brothers, Billie Amen, Ronald Weber, Ed Hetterle, and others.

Although my brothers and I participated in all types of sports, basketball was what we liked best. We had "basketball hoops" of different sizes scattered throughout our front yard and backyard. A Folger's coffee can was nailed to the large silver poplar in front of the house. We shot at it with a tennis ball as we played one-on-one. Unable to bounce the ball on the soft dirt, we simulated a dribble with an up-and-down motion with ball in hand. Making a long-distance jump shot with an opponent/brother holding a raised arm up to block it was the exciting part of the game.

While poking around through trash in the alley behind Bunton's Red & White Grocery, I found an iron hoop that I knew would work well as a basketball rim. About ten inches in radius, I attached it to the east side of Bossie's cow barn by inserting a flattened soup can inside the hoop and nailing the whole assembly to the wall at a height of about eight feet. I then made a net out of string and tied it to the hoop. At first, my brothers and I played with a softball, but later, we switched to a small inflated rubber basketball, a little larger in size. Our younger brothers—Marc, Dave and Frosty—had collectively received it as a Christmas gift from our brother Jack, and with this inflated rubber ball, dribbling became an additional part of the one-on-one game. With the reduced dimensions of hoop height and hoop and ball diameter, younger brothers Marc and Frosty were now playing their own version of basketball.

Next to the coal house in the backyard, brothers Jack and Tom had placed a tall pine "four-by-four" with an attached wood-planked backboard. Mead blacksmith Fred Petersen had built a "rim" for them. He used a thin iron strip that he bent and molded into a ring, slightly smaller in diameter than the eighteen-inch regulation size. Mr. Petersen welded four support strips to the rim and drilled holes in them so the hoop could be bolted to the backboard. When Mr. Humphrey replaced the nets in the Mead School gym with new ones, he gave a used one to Jerry. Jerry brought it home, and Jack, standing on a top rung of our stepladder, attached it to the rim with electrician's tape.

My brothers and I shot baskets and played "horse" and two-on-two games with a regulation-sized basketball on the dirt court. On Sundays, we played with Jack, Tom, and our brothers-in-law, Wilbur Thornton and Jack Curran. We chose sides, comprised of young and old, and played a half-court game. After several years, when the metal rim broke, I took it down and transported it to Johnny Carlson, now the town blacksmith, so he could weld it back together. There was a short delay in the continual play on the backyard court.

The rim broke once again, and the pine planks on the backboard became warped and loosened. Deciding we needed a new goal, we began to mobilize and gather materials for construction. A sturdy steel rim had been mounted on a backboard attached to a telephone pole in the vacant lot across the street from our house. The rim had been crafted by a blacksmith and was of regulation size. I did not know who put up the whole apparatus, but whoever did abandoned it. No one was using it.

Wanting to construct our own goal in our backyard, I deduced the rim would work perfectly and that it would be ours if I took it down.

There were four lag bolts holding it to the backboard. I ran down the alley to the Mead Garage to see if mechanic Joe Jones would lend me his Crescent wrench. As usual, Joe willingly consented.

But where would we get the materials for the backboard? What could we use? The next Sunday, my brothers and I were in Allenspark, Colorado, at Walt Slee's cabin. Walt asked me to retrieve some firewood from the storage area beneath the new room that he had constructed in the front of his cabin. I noticed some one-by-twelve pine planks had been removed from inside the cabin when the remodeling was done. I quickly assumed that Walt most likely didn't need them anymore and that they would serve well as a backboard for our basketball goal. There were also some two-by-fours there that we could use.

Walt consented for us to have the scrap wood, and that night, we unloaded it from his car and placed it in the coal shed for storage. When I told Mom what we were going to do with the materials we had collected, she said, "Why don't you birds wait till Jack gets here? Have him help you with it. He knows how to build those things."

Our middle-school years were marked by the Korean War. Our brother Jack, a career marine, was assigned to staff headquarters of the First Marine Air Wing at the Korean Pusan West Air Base. In 1952, Jack returned from Korea. It was on a December evening, just a few days before Christmas. I was sitting at the kitchen table, cutting out articles and pictures from the *Rocky Mountain News* as part of the "current events" homework our teacher had assigned, when Jack suddenly opened the kitchen door. He was dressed in his marine uniform, concealed by a heavy marine-green overcoat that was covered with snowflakes. He wore a foldable side cap, leather gloves, ear muffs, and laced black boots. As he entered the kitchen, he carried a large leather suitcase.

"Hello there, squirt," he said as he extended his hand for me to shake.

"How'd ja git here?" I asked.

"I walked from the Washington Highway," he said. "I hitchhiked from Denver after I got off the train from California. Didn't take me long. Gotta couple of rides as soon as I got on the highway."

Jack's "coming home" made the 1952 Christmas very special for the family. He had come to no harm in the war, and after an absence of two years, we were all happy to see him. Mom cooked supper for him, and while he was eating, I asked him, "Can you help us build our basketball goal? We just about have all the stuff we need to build it."

"Maybe," said Jack. "We'll see. I'll think about it."

"Oh, you birds!" said Mom. "At least give the man a chance to get through Christmas. When it's over, you can ask 'im again. Just wait a while. He's only been here for thirty minutes, and you're askin' him to work for ya'."

Two days after New Year, I came home from school to see that Jack had already built the backboard. It was different from what I had expected to see. Side by side, Jack had placed four five-foot-long one-by-twelves and attached them together with two four-foot-long two-by-fours. I could see that the wood surface he had created was certainly the backboard, but I couldn't figure out what the two-by-four frame behind the backboard was for. What was its purpose? What was even more perplexing was that Jack had already begun to dig, and there were two holes, not just one as I had expected.

"How's this gonna work?" I asked.

"You'll see," he said. "I should have it all ready to put up by tomorrow."

Jack didn't use nails to build the backboard and frame; he used bolts and screws. He had purchased a new hand drill from the lumber yard, along with a large screwdriver and a Crescent wrench.

When I came home from school the next day, I could see that Jack had attached the rim to the backboard and that the backboard frame was attached to two four-by-four posts, both eighteen feet long. It was now clear to me what Jack was doing. With the frame extending the backboard three feet outward from the two upright posts, we could maneuver directly under the basket and backboard without bumping into them. From the perspective of a seventh-grader, this was indeed a very clever design. Each of the two holes had been dug to a depth so that when the posts were placed into them, the top of the rim would be exactly ten feet from the ground below.

Jack said, "Trust me. I have calculated it many times in my head, and I have measured it many times. I know it's goin' to be right."

With all the brothers standing and watching as Jack placed the final bolts, he said to us, "Okay, all of you help me lift this backboard up, and let's see if we can slide these two posts into the holes. But first, we have to carry the whole thing into the alley and line the ends of the posts right over the holes. Okay, let's all lift the backboard up to see if we can get the posts to slide in."

With Jack in the middle and with brothers on each side of him, we lifted the framed backboard and then moved our hands down the two posts as the structure rose and as the posts slid into the holes. The posts simultaneously hit the hole bottoms with a resounding thud, and the tall apparatus shook slightly as it settled in to place. We all stepped back and looked upward at the basket as it hung above us.

"My god," I said. "This is really somethin'. Wait till Walt sees what we've done with the scrap wood he gave us. He'll really be impressed."

"The rim looks ten feet high to me," said Rollie.

"Well, it better be," interjected Jack. "I've measured it a hundred times."

"Gosh, Jack," said Dave. "Now we can play underneath the basket. Thanks for buildin' it that way. It's just like playin' in the gym."

"Well, let's get goin' and fill in the holes with dirt so we can start playin'," said Jack.

The goal that Jack built was a magnificent structure. It stood majestically in our yard for all the townspeople to see, and it became the envy of all the kids in the neighborhood. Everyone marveled at its unique construction.

My brothers and I played under Jack's basketball goal many times. We shot baskets the year round. In summer evenings, after working in the beet fields, I worked on my drive-in shot going underneath the goal and laying the ball gently against the backboard, practicing this shot using both my left and right hands. Jack's newly designed goal allowed me to improve this important shot, which became part of my repertoire. Soon, the goal would become the play site for brothers Marc and Frosty.

They too were the recipients of Jack's ingenuity and benevolence, and they too would clear snow from the backyard court.

For our Christmas present, Jack bought us triplets, Dave, and Jerry each a pair of PF Flyer tennis shoes and a pair of white sweat socks. PF Flyers, manufactured by B. F. Goodrich, were a black high-topped canvas sneaker with a patch at the ankle that read "PF Flyers." PF stood for posture foundation, a patented insole technology that set the standard in tennis shoe comfort at that time. My basketball idol Bob Cousy, the famed dribbler and ball-handler for the Boston Celtics, wore PF tennis shoes.

"The salesman at the sporting goods store said you can jump higher with these than you can with those you buy at Penney," said Jack. "But I don't know about that. He was really wantin' ta sell me somethin'. When I bought five pairs, he was grinnin' from ear to ear."

For Christmas the year before, Walt Slee gave each of us a set of kneepads. Kneepads were considered essential for any worthwhile basketball player. Every boy playing the game at Mead wore them. They were expensive, and the school did not furnish them, nor did we have the money to buy them. When Walt asked what I wanted for Christmas, I told him, "Kneepads," and then I qualified my answer by saying, "But you can't spend that kinda money on us. They cost too much." The five of us were delightfully surprised when we opened our box and saw Bike-brand kneepads inside.

Like us triplets, most of our teammates on our seventh-grade peewee team wore kneepads. Ed Hetterle, a Mead High School senior and a member of the varsity team, coached our peewee team, while physical education teacher and coach Tom Peterson coached junior high. Our classmate, Allen Thompson, nine months older than us triplets and much taller and heavier, was moved up to the junior-high level playing with our brother Jerry and other eighth- and ninth-graders. Allen had demonstrated his great physical skills as an athlete, and his superiority over the rest of us seventh-graders was clearly evident.

Our peewee team practiced during our afternoon physical education class. On Saturday mornings, we competed against teams in the Poudre Valley League, including Ault, Windsor, Eaton, Fort Lupton,

Johnstown, Kersey, and Platteville. Fort Lupton beat our peewee team, and so did Windsor and Eaton. It was difficult to earn a victory over our more experienced and older opponents. That season, our Hetterle-coached PW team won only three games: Platteville, Johnstown, and Kersey.

Illustration of Basketball Goal, 2015. *Ronald Newton*

Jack Newton, U.S. Marine Corps, 1953. *Newton Family Album*

Seventh Grade Pee-Wee Basketball. Front Row, L-R: Leonard Smith, Rollie New-
ton, Ronnie Newton, Richie Newton, Marvin Blazon; Back Row, L-R: Coach Ed
Hetterle, Arvid Fietchner, Larry Nuss, Johnnie Minch, LaVerne Magnuson, Jerry
Frank, 1952. *Mead Consolidated Schools Yearbook*

Chapter 11

Middle School

In the classroom, with our minds mostly on basketball, seventh-grade teacher Mrs. Myrtle Clark worked to keep us focused on academics. Mrs. Clark, the mother of our sixth-grade teacher, C. H. Clark, was nearly sixty years old. She wore thick bifocal glasses and, in winter, sat at her desk with her fur coat over her shoulders, trying to stay warm. When one of us said something stupid in response to her question and the rest of the class began to laugh, she would immediately interject loudly, "Uh-uh, uh-uh! You can laugh with them but not at them." Mrs. Clark had total control of the class. No one misbehaved.

Mrs. Clark said, "You have to do well in mathematics. It is something you will use every day. That's why we study mathematics the first thing in the morning—when your mind is clearest and you think the best."

She drilled us in fractions: adding, multiplying, and dividing them. We had fraction word problems to solve. Mrs. Clark would recite the problem out loud. "Billy and his sister went for a walk. They saw eight dogs along the way. Five of them were gray. What fraction of the cats was gray?" She then called on one of us who raised a hand, thinking we knew the answer.

Mrs. Clark gave us mimeographed mathematics work sheets to complete. She took them home with her to grade and passed them back the next day. Our writing lessons included composing a letter.

While giving instructions on the components and style of a letter, she told us about letters she read from a soldier in World War II that were written to his sister, the mother of Mead high-schoolers Ralph and David Borgman.

"They were beautifully written," said Mrs. Clark. "He told about his experiences in North Africa. They were the finest letters I think I have ever read." Then she looked at me and said, "You boys know who he is. His name is Walter Slee."

Our classmate Jim Brunemeier asked her. "What should we write about?

"Anything you want to," she said. "You can always talk about the weather."

I wrote a letter to my brother Jack. I asked him about what he was doing in the war in Korea. I was curious if he was shooting at Chinese and North Koreans. I told him that we were playing peewee basketball and that our sister Kathleen's boyfriend, Ed Hetterle, was our coach. I asked him if he still remembered the high-school basketball game when he scored thirty-seven points against Frederick, and I signed it, "Love, Ronald."

Coaching responsibilities for peewee basketball were turned over to high-schooler Ed Hetterle by Coach Tom Peterson, who coached the junior high team. Besides us triplets, Marvin Blazon and Leonard Smith were team starters. Playing six other teams in the Weld County A League, we had a mediocre season, losing half our games.

In the eighth grade, our teacher, Mrs. Eva Jane Nygren, emphasized reading and creative writing. The first time she assigned our whole class to write a story, she was very disappointed with the results.

"I did not think anyone in the class wrote very well," she said.

I had tried to write something humorous. Mrs. Nygren was not amused, nor was she impressed with my writing, much less my story. She had many corrections of grammar, punctuation, and sentence structure.

Mrs. Nygren was the wife of Bill Nygren, a farmer who had graduated from Colorado A&M College. Her father was Carl Peters, an educated farmer whose holdings a quarter mile south of Mead had been homesteaded by his father, Albert. Carl and his wife Mary each had several years of college, and they sent their three daughters—Eva Jane, Helen, and Mary Louise—to the University of Wyoming. Carl was also a member of the Mead Consolidated Schools school board, along with Gary Olson's grandfather, Emil, and Glen Markham's father, Donald.

Mrs. Nygren had been injured in an automobile accident. She had been sitting on the passenger side of their family Chevrolet when her head hit the dashboard, and the chrome Fleetline logo jammed into her face, leaving a scar just above her lip. However, this did not detract from her beauty or her cordial and pleasing smile. Her attire was usually a colored blouse and business suit with a straight skirt. She was informed, smart, pretty, dignified, kind, and courteous.

As a "know-it-all adolescent," I misjudged her gentle demeanor as a sign of weakness, and I openly disagreed with her thoughts and commands by "talking back" and expressing my own views, sometimes disrespectfully. Usually, she said nothing in response and simply tolerated my arrogance.

One afternoon, Mrs. Nygren divided our class into subgroups to study our spelling word list. Not liking the group I was assigned to and wanting to be with Gary Olson, I said, "Why can't I be with Gary?"

"Because I want you in the group I assigned you," answered Mrs. Nygren.

"Oh shoot!" I said as I slammed my spelling workbook down on the desk in vehement disagreement.

Thinking that she heard me use the four-letter word, Mrs. Nygren was furious. "What did you say, Mr. Newton?" as her upper lip quivered.

"I-I-I said 'shoot,'" I stammered.

"I hope that's what you said," Mrs. Nygren retorted as she glared at me, her face red and her mouth twisted with anger. She chastised me with words I did not want to hear. "You are the 'smartiest' boy in here. No one else talks the way you do."

While the rest of the class was dismissed for gym class, I sat at my desk, alone with Mrs. Nygren, while she worked at her desk. I read a library book on Alexander Hamilton that she told me to read and on which I was to write a report. I would have plenty of time to do it because she told me that she was keeping me out of gym for one week—thus, no practice with my junior high basketball team for those five days. I knew it would take me out of Coach Schmidt's starting lineup for Saturday's game, a severe punishment.

I was hurt by her words, and I was ashamed and remorseful. I was hurt too that I had confirmed her low opinion of me, and I wanted to change it. I was afraid she thought I was lying when I repeated the "shoot" word I used. The thought of telling her I was sorry never occurred to me; apologizing to another was something I had never done. I was feeling so bad about this episode and how my past behavior had been so hostile and disrespectful to Mrs. Nygren, I resolved that I would not talk that way to her or any other teacher ever again.

I especially wanted Mrs. Nygren's approval. I was unhappy that she did not have the same esteem for me as she did for others in my class. I surmised it was not only because of my "big mouth" but also to my "place" on the economic and social charts of the Mead community.

Mrs. Nygren played bridge with the mothers of classmates Mike Eckel and Gary Olson. Mike and Gary's parents and Mrs. Nygren and her husband Bill socialized. I sensed the economic difference in the social stratum between their families and mine, and I envied the lives that Gary and Mike led.

I remembered how shocked I was when Mrs. Nygren's father, Carl, reprimanded me for taking pea vines off his truck while he waited for it to be unloaded at the pea huller. He reported me to the huller foreman, and my brothers and I were banned from the premises. We were puzzled by his action; other farmers willingly let us help ourselves to all the pea vines we could drag off their trucks. Mr. Peters's attitude toward my brothers and me was even more perplexing when he asked for our help that fall to pick up ears lying on the ground of his cornfield that the picker had dropped while loading them onto a truck. Was his sudden cordiality and courtesy on display because he needed our services? Nevertheless, whatever opinions Mr. Peters had about us Newton brothers, good or bad, he was most satisfied with our performance, and he paid us handsomely for a day's work.

In Mrs. Nygren's conversations with Mike Eckel and Gary Olson, there was a familiarity that seemed to be absent when she talked to me.

Their conversational topics were personal and "inside" where mine were limited to instructional topics. I was envious of Gary's and Mike's easy access in talking with Mrs. Nygren. I was timid and reluctant to utter any pleasantries. With the mantra I had heard over and over through the twelve years of my life—"Children are to be seen and not heard"—it was difficult for me to initiate a conversation, especially with an adult.

Both Mike and Gary had been trained to converse with adults with utmost courtesy. Mike always used their surname and prefaced it with "Ms., Mrs., or Mr." He used phrases such as "Yes, ma'am" and "No, ma'am" and "Yes, sir" and "No, sir." Observing that Mike's courteous speech was clearly respected by others, I began to address my teachers and all adults with "ma'am" and "sir" in hopes I would be treated with the same kindness and respect by my teachers.

I was excited one day when Mrs. Nygren told us she was going to attend one of our games. She was the first of our teachers to do so, and I interpreted her attendance as a sign that she had a genuine, heartfelt regard for my brothers, my teammates, and me. "You boys did real well," she told us the next day. Then glancing over at me, she said, "Ronnie, that long shot you made was just spectacular." Mrs. Nygren had also given me the lead role in the Armistice Day play that our class presented to the whole school, and now with the school year about to end, I felt redeemed, having finally earned her respect.

In spite of my behavioral shortcomings in the classroom, I continued to thrive on the basketball court. We triplets, now in the eighth grade, were playing on the junior high team, along with our brother Jerry, a ninth-grader. In addition to us, Coach Schmidt assembled a team that included Allen Thompson, Jerry Sitzman, Marvin Blazon, Jerry Frank, and Mike Eckel.

About five feet and four inches in height and weighing a mere hundred pounds, we triplets were overpowered by taller and heavier opponents, and our offensive output was meager. Nevertheless, our ball handling kept us in the starting lineup. We won a few games in league play, and in the Poudre Valley League Junior High tournament, Allen and Rollie each got seven points in the first game as we were defeated by Windsor 26–20. Then in the consolation bracket, we were defeated by Johnstown 29–20. By that time, losing had become a common occurrence and was readily accepted by us. As eighth-graders, we knew we had one more year to compete at the junior high level, and we were confident that winning would be more within our grasp.

Mead's high-school basketball team was not making any headlines either. Our neighborhood friends—Herb Newman, Ronald Weber, and Vernon Widger—were playing on the A-string varsity, and our sister Kathleen was supporting them on the sidelines as a member of the cheering squad. After a lackluster season, the Bulldogs found themselves facing the top seed, Windsor Wizards, in the first round of the Class B District 2 tournament on the campus of Colorado A&M College. Led by Newman and Weber, the Bulldogs mustered only twenty-nine points to the Wizards' 55. In the consolation round, Mead defeated the Ault Bearcats 30–20 using a ball-control slowed-down game, with Newman leading the charge. Windsor, the perennial champion of the District 2 tourney, entered the Colorado State High School Basketball Tournament for the third time.

In the fall of 1953, with us triplets now ninth-graders, our English teacher, Doris Eck, introduced us to the concept of "diagramming," whereby we analyzed a sentence in a visual illustrated scheme. We learned to break a sentence down into component parts—subject, predicate, and object—and to identify modifying adjectives and adverbs. Our writing assignments included such topics as composing a condolence letter and describing what we observed on our way to school one morning. Ms. Eck shared her experience of writing a condolence letter to the parents of her fiancé, who was killed in World War II. "It was the hardest thing I ever had to do in my life," she said.

I wrote my simulated condolence letter to Loe Hernandez, expressing my sorrow that he had lost his brother Max. My "on-the-way-to-school experience" included two paragraphs, one describing my observation of Ms. Mary Johnson as she stepped out the front steps of her house to sweep snow away and the second a description of a snowball fight I had with Ronald Weber when I hit him with one just as he emerged from his house.

Ms. Eck encouraged us to give oral presentations to our class. "I want you to tell the class about a funny incident that has happened to you," she said. But standing in front of my classmates and talking to them about a personal event in my life was frightening and threatening. Nervous and anxious, standing with my hands in my front pockets and hardly glancing at my audience, I said, "I was eight years old when I was standing and talking to my sister Pat. I backed up and stumbled into a water-filled scrub pan on the floor. I sat right down in it. I sat in eight inches of dirty water. My sister Pat was not all that happy about it. She and my elder sisters were always havin' to *change our clothes* and wipe up after we triplets made a mess."

"Well, I hope not at that age!" Ms. Eck blurted out jovially.

Hearing Ms. Eck's remark, my classmates howled with laughter.

Realizing what I had said, I blurted out, "No, no, what I meant was that Pat wasn't crazy about havin' to help me wipe up the water."

Not only did Ms. Eck's comment add levity to my presentation, which did not have much humor to begin with, but I am certain her words enhanced my grade, and I am certain that my face was red with embarrassment. In contrast to my nervous presentation, the deliveries of Mike's and Gary's stories were poised and calm, free from anxiety, voiced with confidence, and spiced with humor.

Our ninth-grade class went on a field trip with our general science teacher, Edwin Warner. He drove the bus carrying us to several ecological sites around Mead. We stopped to view the cattail swamp on the Redmond farm where Mamie Akers lived. Of course, my brothers and I had been there many times ourselves. It was late in the fall, and the red-winged blackbirds had already gone south, but the red-headed woodpecker was there rat-a-tat-tatting in the giant cottonwood.

"Just look at that elegant bird," said Mr. Warner as we stood around him. "He looks like he dressed up for a wedding party. On his head, he wears a top hat of scarlet. On his chest, he wears a shirt of bright white, and over his shoulders, he wears a black tailed coat. Don't you think he's the most beautiful creature you've ever seen?" Then he picked up a cattail head and pulled a tuft from it and threw it into the air. "Those tiny parachutes," he said, "are carrying minute seeds and scattering them all over the swamp. They will grow into new cattails next year."

Back in the classroom, Mr. Warner, explaining the parts of a flower, said, "The male anthers provide the pollen that lands on the stigma and fertilizes the egg in the ovary. The fertilized egg then turns into a seed."

Allen Thompson, sitting next to me, pointed to the bifurcated anther sacs in the illustration in our textbook and whispered, "They look just like 'balls.'"

I could not keep myself from chuckling. The two of us hunched over, and our bodies shook with laughter.

Watching and listening to us, Mr. Warner suddenly stopped his lecture and said, "Sex is not a laughing matter. It's a wonderful thing. Mother Nature developed sex for the purpose of propagation. Sex is the way of perpetuating the species, both plants and animals. You boys need to take these things more seriously."

Sex and reproduction were never topics of discussion at the Newton household. It had never occurred to me that flowers had a special purpose in procreation. I had always appreciated their beauty but had no understanding of their essential function. With animal and crop production all around me, I had not yet understood how it all came to be. As a naïve middle-schooler, I had a lot to learn, learning that would take me beyond the game of basketball, a microcosm that was still my primary world.

L-R: Myrtle Clark, Eva Jane Nygren, Doris Eck, James Warner, 1952. *Mead Consolidated Schools Yearbook*

Junior High Team: Front row, L-R, Richie Newton, Mike Eckel, Ronnie Newton, Rollie Newton, Marvin Blazon; Back row, L-R: Ronnie Johnson (Mgr.), Allen Thompson, Jerry Sitzman, Jerry Newton, Jerry Frank, Coach Bryan Schmidt, 1953. *Mead Consolidated Schools Yearbook*

A-Team: L-R, Coach Bryan Schmidt, David Borgman (Mgr.), Leroy Blazon, Oscar Whitman, Ralph Biederman, Ronald Weber, Vernon Widger, John Schell, Dwayne Stroh, Robert Humphrey, Donald Nelson, Herbert Newman, Conrad Hopp, 1953. *Mead Consolidated Schools Yearbook*

A-Team Cheerleaders: L-R, Shirley Giebelhaus, Eleanor Nelson, Norma Burback, Kathleen Newton, 1953. *Mead Consolidated Schools Yearbook*

Chapter 12

Basketball Saturday

A prominent family, the Eckels, moved from Johnstown to Mead to live in their renovated farmhouse situated on about three hundred acres a mile and three quarters north of Mead. Eleven-year-old son Mike enrolled in our fifth-grade class, and he was our teammate and close friend for the next seven years. The Eckel farm became a location for class parties, playing basketball, and later a place of work for me. The Eckels shared meals with us and many of Mike's classmates, and the conversations around the table were about sports, religion, education, and life. These conversations significantly shaped my outlook and behavior and provided a kind of "beyond my own family" guidance as I moved into my teenage years.

On a Saturday morning in November 1952, the ground was covered with snow that had fallen two days earlier. Temperatures had dropped below freezing the night before, but the forecast was for the day temperature to be in the low forties. My brothers and I were still in bed when the phone rang downstairs.

"Hello," said Mom in a soft voice. She heard a young male voice on the other end.

"Mrs. Newton?" the caller asked.

"Yes, it is," answered Mom.

"Mrs. Newton, this is Mike Eckel calling, and I was wonderin' if the triplets, Dave, and Jerry could come to my house and play basketball this afternoon. Gary Olson and I put up two basketball goals in the hayloft of our barn last weekend, and we have cleaned and swept the floor so we can have a regular game up there. I want to invite Allen Thompson and Lyle Schaefer to see if they can come also. My sister Pat said she would play, so if everybody can come, we will have five on a team."

"Well, for heaven's sake," Mom said, laughing, "they're not out of bed yet, but I'm sure they'll want to. They have a few chores to do around here this morning, and they have to go to catechism class at church, but I'm sure they will be finished by afternoon."

"Excellent, Mrs. Newton," Mike responded. "Marg said she would fix supper for everybody when we finish playin'." Unlike most children, Mike and his sister Pat referred to their parents by their first names, Marg and Frank. "Could they stay for supper with us, Mrs. Newton?" Mike asked.

"I don't know why not," Mom said emphatically. "They'd like that."

"Excellent," said Mike, "Mrs. Newton, Marg said she could come to your house about one-thirty and pick them up. Would that be okay?" Mike asked.

"Sure," replied Mom. "They'll be ready."

"That's spectacular!" Mike exclaimed excitedly. "Thanks a lot, Mrs. Newton. We'll be there at one-thirty."

Mom hung up the phone and walked across the room to open the door to the upstairs.

"Hey, you birds!" she yelled. "I just got off the phone with Mike Eckel, and he wants you all to play basketball in their barn this afternoon. You've gotta lot of work around here to do before ya go to catechism this morning, so get up and get movin'!"

Excited to hear the news, I was the first one down the stairs. Even though it would be in a barn hayloft, this afternoon, we would be playing full court, just like in a "real" basketball contest. The five of us ate a quick breakfast of cold cereal and toast and began to go at our assigned work. Richie and Rollie delivered the *Rocky Mountain News*.

Dave and I washed and dried the breakfast dishes. Jerry fed the chickens and walked to the grocery store to pick up groceries that Mom needed for Sunday dinner. Richie and Rollie chopped planks of wood into kindling and brought in two buckets of coal, while I dusted and cleaned the spare bedroom on the northwest corner of the house.

"Be sure to make the bed up," commanded Mom. "I laid out clean sheets and pillow cases. Be sure you wash the windows too. I want that room cleaned well for Helen when she comes home next weekend."

At ten o'clock, we walked five blocks to Guardian Angel Church for our catechism lesson. Jerry, now in the ninth grade, was no longer required to attend. Younger brothers Marc, Frosty, and Dave were learning from the Baltimore Catechism manual with Sister Marjorie as their teacher, while my two triplet brothers and I had transitioned from the manual and were now studying stories of the Bible as taught by Sister Laurance. Father Martin had bought small "Bible books" for us older catechists, and the assignment we had been given for that week was to read the story of David and Goliath. Sister Laurance read phrases from Samuel 17:45–46.

You come against me with sword and spear and javelin, but I come against you in the name of the Lord Almighty, the God of the armies of Israel, whom you have defied. This day the Lord will hand you over to me, and I'll strike you down and cut off your head.

"What do you think this story is about?" Sister Laurance asked our class.

Richie raised his hand to answer. "It's about bein' brave, even if ya don't think ya can win," said Richie. "That giant was much bigger than him, but David stood up to 'im and killed 'im. He wasn't afraid of 'im."

"It's 'bout believin' in God," said Josephine Rademacher. "David asked God to help him."

"Do you think God was on the side of David and not the giant?" asked Sister Laurance.

"I think he was," I said.

"Why do you think that?" asked Sister Laurance.

"I think David believed in God, but the giant probably didn't," I answered. "So God is goin' to take care of those who believe in 'im."

"What if the giant also believed in God?" asked Sister Laurance. "Whose side would God be on then?" Then Sister Laurance added, "You boys play sports, don't you?"

We all nodded.

"Whose side is God on when you're playing? Your team or the other team?"

"Most of the players on the other team probably go to church. They probably are Christian. They believe in God also. So wouldn't God be rooting for them as well as you?" queried Sister Laurance. "I think so. So if you have a big competitive event coming up—a sports event, a debate tournament, a music competition, whatever it might be—should you pray to God to let you win? I don't think so. So what should you pray for?"

"I guess then . . ." said Rollie, hesitating. "I guess you just pray that God will help you play your best."

"I think that's right," said Sister Laurance. "And if you and your teammates do your very best. You may win, but you may not. Win or lose, it's God's will. David had a lot of confidence in himself because he had confidence in God. He believed God would enable him to accomplish his objective of killing the Philistine warrior. He believed God would enable him to do his best. This story of David and Goliath is about when David was a young man. David later in his life became a great leader of his people. Do any of you know what else David did and what he is also known for?"

We all shook our heads. We didn't have a clue.

"The biblical scholars say he wrote some of the Psalms," said Sister Laurence. "Have any of you read the Psalms?"

Again, we shook our heads. "No."

"You need to read some of these," said Sister Laurance. "They're part of the Old Testament. Maybe at our next lesson, we'll study some of them. They're really good prayers. The other sisters and I read them all the time. They're part of our daily prayer."

With catechism class over, we hurried home for lunch, washed and dried the dishes, and waited for Mrs. Eckel. At one-thirty sharp, Mrs. Eckel arrived in our driveway in their '52 Pontiac. Mrs. Eckel, in her early forties, came to Colorado to attend the University in Boulder and graduated with a degree in business administration. She was raised in Sioux Falls, South Dakota, where her father was an electrical contractor. About five-foot-eight, she was slightly taller than her husband Frank, whom she met in a boarding house in Boulder where she lived as a student. She had prominent cheekbones that became even more pronounced when she flashed her beautiful smile that always accompanied her greeting. Her hair was golden brown, which she wore tucked back. She had light brown skin, which became heightened with a summer tan. Besides being physically attractive, she had very gracious manners and always addressed those she met by mentioning their name.

Mrs. Eckel, with us five Newtons in the car, slowed down to enter the Eckel driveway. She brought the car to a stop while she waited for Mrs. Thompson's car to leave after dropping off Allen. Lyle Schaeffer was already there and was standing with Mike and Allen, who each had a basketball in his hands.

"C'mon, let's go!" yelled Mike. "Gary and Pat are already up in there in the barn waitin' for us."

We walked across the short wooden bridge arching over the ditch that, just a few months ago, was carrying water to the Eckel farm and farms further southeast but now was only a deep furrow. We walked another fifty yards to the barn, a tall two-storied structure painted a dark cherry red, trimmed in white, and covered with gray composition shingles. The four borders of the half-octagon roof enveloped the expansive hayloft of the barn, which Mike Eckel had transformed into a two-goal basketball court.

We entered the barn through a side door into a small room stacked with bales of straw. Just a month before, they had been placed in the hayloft from outside with a tractor loader. The bales had been used as impromptu benches during the Halloween party the Eckel and Olson families hosted for our eighth-grade class. Here at the beginning of the long winter, the straw was now in storage, later to be used as bedding for Pat Eckel's horse.

Rather than use the stairs, we excited basketball players ascended one after another to the hayloft floor using the vertical ladder of plank steps. As I emerged through the portal, I gasped with amazement at the expanse of the hayloft floor, now a basketball court. Almost as large as the one in the school gym, I thought to myself. The area was well illuminated with four spotlights, one on each end of the floor overlooking each basket, and one on each side of the court.

"My gosh, this is big," I said to Mike. "You're lucky to have this. Thanks for inviting us, Mike. This is going to be terrific!"

My brothers and I had always dreamed about having a full court to play on, particularly one that had a floor other than dirt. We had plans of someday putting up goals in the abandoned Mead hay mill, where we could play on the cement floor underneath the steel roof. Now here in the Eckel barn hayloft, at last, we had a full court, one with a basket on each end, one where we could play a "real" game.

We shed our coats but kept moving all the time, shooting and dribbling, jumping and running, trying to keep our bodies warm with the temperature hovering below forty degrees.

"Let's get started," said Mike. "Lyle and I will be captains and choose sides."

This choosing-up ritual had occurred many times with us. It did not matter what side we were on. We knew we would have plenty of opportunities to handle the ball. When we played basketball, everyone was included. All players got to participate to the fullest, no matter their skill level. For us, it was not always who could win with the best players. It was making sure that everyone had fun and had a chance to improve. Basketball was a team sport; no one player was permitted to "hog" the ball. If that was even tried, there was a chorus of admonishment, "C'mon, pass the ball!"

My brothers and I had participated in many playground activities in Mead with playmates of all ages and skill levels. When we played workup softball in the backyard, Mom monitored the activities from her kitchen. She could hear through an open window when the performance of a younger child was being critiqued and when he was being discouraged from participating. If it appeared to her that her younger children were not being allowed to participate in an equitable fashion, she would shout from the window, "You let them have their turn now, and quit that bickering out there! If you don't, I'm going to make you all come in and sit in a corner!"

As a six-year-old, I remember being included with the adults in a Sunday afternoon basketball game. I made myself useful playing defense, knocking the ball out of the hands of an unwary adult brother-in-law who had his back turned to another defender and did not see me. I quickly grabbed the loose ball and threw it to one of my adult teammates. In this cooperative support role, I was appreciated and included, even though I was not as physically capable as the adults. They laughed with approval when I passed them the ball. I was learning there were many ways to be a useful and contributing member of a team. Being good on defense was one of them.

In basketball, we learned to be resourceful and to think where and under what situation we could contribute. A player always had to keep moving, not standing still. In this way, we could eventually be in a position to receive the ball from a teammate or a ball caroming off the rim or bouncing from the backboard. We learned that sometimes a player would be the successful scorer but that, at other times, a player could gain just as much satisfaction in making a key pass to a teammate and assisting with a score. If one of us became the dominant scorer, it was not because he "hogged the ball." It was because he was in the right position and because it was appropriate to shoot. To us, being an all-around excellent basketball player was not trying to be the best one on the floor. It was being at the right place at the right time.

That Saturday afternoon on the hayloft court went by quickly, with all players demonstrating their favorite skills. Allen, with the ball in a dribble, drove to the goal and started his leap far from the basket, twisting and turning high into the air before touching the ball softly to the backboard. Jerry, playing post, shot his "patented" hook shot, while Lyle, just getting started and learning the game, was demonstrating success with rebounding. Richie pumped up jump shots from all over the floor, while Rollie, playing forward on the left corner of the court, shot his jump shot while turning in midair. Mike and I worked on our dribbling and ball handling. Dave and Pat, being two years younger than the rest, were learning the varied facets of the game. Gary shot set shots and kept score.

We moved rapidly from one end of the court to the other, stopping only when it was apparent to all that a foul had been committed. Mike had painted a foul line and keyholes on each end of the court so that free throws could be taken.

"When we get to 60, let's take a time-out!" Gary yelled out.

Reaching that score, we stopped to rest, and our thirsty crew climbed down the stairs and walked outside to drink from the well on the south side of the barn. Our overheated sweat-soaked bodies cooled rapidly as we waited our turn at the spigot.

"I wish we could do this every Saturday," I said exuberantly, realizing it would be almost two months before junior-high competitive basketball started in January.

"It would be good practice for us in getting ready to play," agreed Mike.

Soon, it was five-thirty, and Frank Eckel came up into the barn to say that Marg wanted us to come down to eat. Knowing we were reluctant to stop, not even to eat, he watched us play for a few minutes.

"Okay, you kids!" yelled Frank. "Let's wrap it up. Marg's got supper ready. Let's all head to the house and get washed up!"

All of us scrambled down the ladder. We paused to get a drink from the well and ran across the yard to the house. The Eckel house had white-painted tongue-and-groove wood siding, and the two-story structure stood about forty yards east of the north–south gravel road leading from Mead. Two large cottonwoods grew in the front yard, surrounded by a bed of bluegrass. A large picture window had been carved out of the west side of the house, where the Eckel family had a panoramic view of Mount Meeker and Longs Peak.

Mike, entering the house first, said to us, "You can clean up here in the washroom," pointing to a doorway on his right.

One by one, we entered the kitchen, where Marg had placed a spread of food on the kitchen countertop. A new stove and refrigerator of white enamel had been installed in the kitchen. The cupboards were of a rich reddish-yellow knotty pine, and the kitchen table and chairs were constructed of the same wood. Throughout the house, upstairs and downstairs, were richly stained pinewood floors, which, in my eyes, epitomized the elegant life of the Eckel family.

"Take one of those paper plates and help yourself to the chips, beans, and coleslaw," said Mrs. Eckel. "I've got the hamburgers over here on the stove. The pop is there in the cooler on the floor. While you eat, you can go in and watch TV in the living room, or if you wish, you can eat here at the kitchen table."

Getting to the food last, I decided to eat in the kitchen. I sat down next to Frank Eckel, who was drinking a Coors beer and biting into a thick hamburger. Lyle Schaefer and Gary Olson joined us, sitting across from Frank and me. Having made sure that everyone had food, Marg sat down on the other side of Frank with her filled plate.

Marg asked, "Well, did everybody have a good time today?"

"We sure did," I said. "Playin' full court with two baskets is a lot of fun. We stopped to rest only once. Runnin' up and down the floor, we got so hot that we didn't notice how cold it was up there in the loft."

"It was a lot cooler today up there than it was when we had the Halloween party up there," said Gary.

"Boy, that was a good party you had for us, Mrs. Eckel," I said. "You sure had a cool-lookin' witch's costume on. And that was the first time I ever had apple cider. I liked it a lot."

"Frank and Gilman had a heck of a time getting all those bales up in the loft," said Marg. "Then they had to turn around and get them out of there for you boys to play basketball. What's goin' on at school?"

"We're all workin' on our civics class project for Mr. Johnson," said Lyle. "We have to write a report and put a notebook together on Colorado."

"I'm 'bout half done with mine," said Gary. "Mom bought me a couple of magazines that have a lot of stuff in them for tourists. They have an article on the state capitol and the Museum of Natural History. I got a lot of information I can use. Mom and I went to the Longmont library. I got a couple of books too."

"I got two books from the Longmont library as well," I said. "My brother Tom dropped me off there when he took Mom to buy groceries.

It was the first time I had ever been in a library. There was a nice lady there who helped me. I got some information about the Indians who used to live in Colorado. The Ouray tribe used to be here. I found out when the Colorado flag was designed and made and what our state bird is. It's the lark bunting. I'd sure like to see one. I don't know what they look like. I'm goin' to draw a picture of one that's in the book. I already drew a picture of the state flower, the columbine. It looks pretty good."

"I've seen a lark bunting," said Frank. "Saw them when I was huntin' antelope on a ranch up near Grover. It's a beautiful bird. It's like a blackbird, only it has white stripes on its wings rather than red, lives in the low cover of sagebrush and bunch grass out there on the plains."

"Mike's working on his report also," said Marg. "His uncle Clayt had a couple'a books for him. He told me he also found some things in our Encyclopedia Britannica. When do you boys have to have this done?"

"Mr. Johnson is giving us time to get it done over Christmas vacation," I said.

"Well, you boys need to do a good job with your assignment," said Marg. "You know good grades are going to be very important, especially if you want to go on to college. If you want to do that, you better do well in high school. How about you, Ronnie? Are you going to college?"

"I don't know yet," I said. "My eldest brother Orbin went to CU for one year. He had to quit when World War II started. He was drafted and decided to join the marines. He majored in journalism. Mom says he now writes stuff for a marine paper."

"CU has a good journalism program," said Marg. "When I was there, there were students from all over the nation taking it. They said CU's journalism school was second only to the one in Missouri."

"What was your major at CU?" I asked.

"Business administration," said Marg. "My dad was a businessman. He thought it would be a good major for me. It's turned out that it is the case. I use that education all the time now. I took a lot of accounting, finance, and management classes, but I learned a lot from the other classes I took too."

"Her education comes in handy in keeping the books and payin' the bills for our farm," said Frank. "She's a hell of a good manager. She knows what she's doin'."

"All you boys should think about going on to college," said Marg. "Nowadays, you're goin' to need it. My brother Clayton is now going to Colorado A&M. He's majoring in animal husbandry. He wants to farm after he graduates. Gary, I know you'll be going. Do you know where you'd like to go?'

"Well, Mom went to CU. She got a scholarship. She was the valedictorian of her high-school class at Mead. I'll probably go there. Maybe I'll go to Colorado A&M, but I'm not sure that I want to study farmin'."

"How about you, Lyle?" asked Marg.

"I know I will," said Lyle. "Both my dad and my mom went to Peru College in Nebraska. They studied to be teachers. I don't know what I would major in, but I'm pretty sure I'm goin' to go. I know my mother wants me to. She says I should be a doctor. To do that, I'd have to go to CU. That's the only place in the state where they train doctors."

"I hope all of you can go somewhere to school when you graduate from high school," said Marg. "But to get in in most places, you have to have a good grade average in high school. You better have good grades. From here on out, you boys need to take your studies seriously—study hard and do your homework. If you know how to study in high school, you will be well prepared to know how in college. Many freshman flunk out of college in the first year because they just don't know how to study. You boys have to be good students as well as good athletes. You're in school to learn as well as play sports."

On the ride home, I didn't talk. I reflected on what Mrs. Eckel said about going to college. I kept repeating over and over in my mind her advice of studying and doing homework in high school. Up till now, I never had a lot of daily homework. Mr. Johnson's assignment was the biggest homework assignment I had yet. I had studied my catechism, but I really had not studied very much for school. I knew I liked learning, and I remembered how fascinated I was when Mr. Warner told his class about the structure of the flower in general science class and how bees aided in pollination. Maybe if I went to college, I said to myself, I could learn more about plants.

I recalled telling Mr. Johnson one day, "I like to draw. I think I'll be an architect."

"If you want to do that," said Mr. Johnson, "you'll have to go to CU. That's where the architecture school is. I hear it's a good one."

Maybe I should start thinking about college, I thought. Mrs. Eckel had been to college. She said I should go. She must know what she is talking about. Her son Mike was going to go. Lyle and Gary were going. Why shouldn't I go? I wondered if I was smart enough. Mrs. Eckel said a lot of college students flunk out because they didn't know how to study, not because they weren't smart enough. I knew of several Mead High graduates who dropped out of college. I wondered if the course work had been too hard for them. Would it be the same for me?

Next year, I would be a ninth-grader. I would have to begin being a good student. But I probably shouldn't wait 'til then. I'd better do a good job right now for Mr. Johnson. I better work to get an A on his report on the state of Colorado. I knew that my drawings would be good, but I also had to write a good report.

Mrs. Eckel pulled into our driveway. She said, "Good night, boys. We enjoyed having you with us today. I know Mike and Pat had a good time with all of you."

"Thanks, Mrs. Eckel," I said. "I sure liked playin' in your barn. It was like playin' in a real gym."

"You're welcome, Ronnie," said Mrs. Eckel. "Maybe we can do it again some time."

As we left the car thanking Mrs. Eckel, she acknowledged each one of us, saying, "You're welcome," followed by reference to each one of us by name. Mrs. Eckel exuded great respect from everyone she talked to.

That night, all the Newtons knew she respected each one of us and cared for each of us as individuals and friends of her children. The advice she had given me that night, I took to heart. In four years, I knew I was going on to college.

L-R: Richie Newton, Ronnie Newton, Rollie Newton, Dave Newton, and Jerry Newton, 1953. *Newton Family Album*

L-R: Allen Thompson, Mike Eckel, Pat Eckel, Gary Olson, Lyle Schaefer, 1953 – *Mead Consolidated Schools Yearbook*

Marg Eckel, 1957. *Patricia Eckel*

Frank Eckel, 1957. *Patricia Eckel*

Chapter 13

Devastating Defeat

With the ringing of the 8:30 a.m. bell, we took our seats in Ms. Eck's ninth-grade English class. Sitting next to me was our longtime classmate Barbara Graham, and she said, "We saw the picture of you triplets in the *Denver Post* last night."

"I saw it too," I said. "My sister Maureen saw it first, and she showed it to Mom. She knew Mom wouldn't like it. Mom doesn't like to see that kinda stuff in the paper."

The night before, Maureen had held the paper up so Mom could read it as she stood over the stove frying pork sausage for the evening meal.

"I wonder who had the gumption to send that in," Mom said sarcastically.

Mom always discouraged all publicity about her family, particularly us triplets. Previously, she had denied a Rocky Mountain News reporter's request to come to our house and take pictures and interview members of the family. Mom said, "He wanted to take pictures of us sitting around the table eating. The thought of him doin' that made me sick to my stomach." Mom asked Maureen, "Who in the world would have given the paper the triplets' school pictures?"

"It had to be someone from the school," she said.

Mom's concern about too much recognition being given to her triplet sons was eased when she read the last line. "Coach Beers could be starting a five-brother team a couple of years from now."

In this special submission to the *Post* titled "Triplets Give 3 Rs New Meaning at Mead," the writer stated, "Rather than the traditional three curricular Rs, the Poudre Valley Junior High League is talking about Rollie, Richie, and Ronnie." Our team had gone undefeated, beating Johnstown, Kersey, Platteville, Windsor, Fort Lupton, Ault, and Eaton. That night, the *Post* article was again discussed at the supper table.

"Don't let it go to your head," Mom said to the three of us. "Don't start thinkin' you're the only star that twinkles," she added.

Oh, how I had come to hate that phrase! I had heard Mom say it so many times. I was proud that "our star was shining" and that we had been recognized statewide in a large newspaper. I was equally proud of the fact that our team was unbeaten. I knew our teammates had contributed to that success, but they had not been mentioned in the article. I said to Richie, "I think Allen's, Mike's, and Leonard's pictures should have been there with ours. They've helped us win."

"Also Jim Landolt," said Richie. "He's played a lot."

The tournament at Windsor was just two weeks away, and we looked forward to playing several teams we had beaten. My expectations as well and those of Coach Beers were high. Having been a student teacher at Mead, this was Jim Beers's first year as the head coach of both the junior-high and high-school teams. His high-school team was in the cellar of the Poudre Valley League, tied at the bottom with Eaton. In contrast, our junior-high team had won all seven games, and we were at the top of the Poudre Valley Junior High League. With Allen Thompson, Leonard Smith, Mike Eckel, and us triplets, Coach Beers had an excellent core group as well as strong bench depth with Lyle Schaefer, Jim Landolt, Larry Nuss, Gary Olson, Bill Harding, and Lanny Davis. In his mind, Coach Beers would have a successful basketball season at Mead if his junior-high team won the Windsor tournament.

His hopes were buoyed by our winning the first game 45–15 over Platteville on Friday night. Earlier that afternoon, Johnstown had downed Kersey, and Ault edged Eaton. In the game preceding the Mead–Platteville encounter, Windsor defeated Fort Lupton, the winner of last year's tournament.

On Saturday morning, Mr. Carlson drove the bus carrying Coach Beers, thirteen players, and fifteen members of the cheering section to Windsor to face the Windsor Wizards, the host team, in the tournament semifinals. Cheerleaders Barbara Graham, Josephine Rademacher, Anita Jones, and Susan Schell led a dozen other student supporters in cheers and singing as we rode. Barbara had been our classmate for all nine years at Mead School. She was a loyal friend to all, and now she was a loyal supporter of our basketball team. She never missed a game. I heard her calling our names and shouting encouragement each time we stood at the free-throw line.

The Windsor district had just built a new gym of regulation size, a third larger than our Mead gym. The stands were already lined with pockets of Windsor fans when we arrived. We were greeted by Windsor's junior high school principal, Mr. James Dudley. He was a friendly man in his mid-thirties with salt-and-pepper graying hair. He was about five feet and eight inches tall and wore brown horn-rimmed glasses. I heard him tell Coach Beers that in addition to his administrative chores, he taught mathematics and science.

Representing the host team, Mr. Dudley welcomed the Mead team and showed us to the visitors' locker room. He wore a gray sweatshirt and a black shoestring with a silver whistle attached hung around his neck. His well-worn "dress pants" matched his black tennis shoes. He stayed to visit for a few minutes with Coach Beers and then left to work with other Windsor staff to get ready for the start of play. Mr. Dudley had been designated as the referee.

Coach Beers started the game with Rollie and Leonard as forwards, Allen as the center, and Richie and me as guards. Rollie had had a growth spurt in the last year and was now taller and heavier than Richie and me and was developing into an excellent rebounder. Allen was the tallest and the heaviest member of the team and was perfecting both a jump shot and a hook shot. Leonard was fast with his dribble and moved the ball down the court in dashing speed. Richie and I, as principal ball handlers, were skillful enough to protect the ball from defenders as we dribbled and passed effectively to teammates. Shot opportunities availed to us were usually layups; outside set shots were rarely taken.

The game was low scoring and progressed to where there was one minute and twenty-six seconds left. Neither team had played well, but we were ahead by two points, 20–18. Windsor had just scored, and I received the ball from Richie from the end bounds, and I began to dribble downcourt. As I switched from my left hand to my right hand and began to dribble around the Windsor defender, Referee Dudley blew his whistle. He motioned with his right hand by exposing his palm down, and then up, and then down and up. As he did this, he yelled, "Palming and carrying the ball!" He raised his hand and pointed it in the direction of Windsor's basket and said, "Windsor's ball."

From the side at half-court, Charles Hettinger immediately tossed the ball to his Wizard teammate Reed Warnick, who drove in for a layup to tie the score, 22-22. Deeply frustrated by the unusual lackluster effort of his team that afternoon, Coach Beers yelled to Richie, team captain, "Call time-out! Call time-out!"

Richie ran up to Referee Dudley and motioned with a two-handed T signal—fifty-two seconds left on the clock.

As Rollie, Richie, Allen, Leonard, and I assembled around Coach Beers to hear his last-minute instructions, he threw a towel to the floor in frustration. Glaring at the five of us with anger and his face flashing red, he stammered, "Wh-wh-what's wrong with you guys? I-I-I've n-never seen you play like this. W-what's g-goin' on here? We b-beat these guys by fifteen points the last time we played 'em."

I had no answer, nor did any teammates. I could not look at him. I hung my head and stared at the floor. No one said anything. All stood in silence.

Finally, Coach Beers blurted out, "O-okay n-now, g-get the ball into Allen. See if he can hit a shot close-in and win this thing."

Referee Dudley blew his whistle to start again, and he gave the ball to Richie to inbound. Receiving the ball, I dribbled downcourt, and as I crossed the midline, I threw the ball to Rollie on the right wing. Rollie bounce-passed to Allen, who turned and attempted a soft jump shot ten feet from the basket. The ball fell short, bouncing from the front of the rim, and was rebounded by the Wizards' Hettinger. Hettinger threw an outward pass to Larry Leffler, who dribbled twenty feet downcourt before passing to teammate Darrell McNabb, who had already crossed the midcourt line. McNabb, now at center court, drove toward the right side of the key, where Rollie met him and slowed his forward movement. The stocky McNabb moved to the right and set himself to shoot. He raised the ball above his head and poised toward the basket as he jumped.

Located to the left of the key, I had an excellent perspective of the play that was about to ensue. I watched Rollie jump and place his left hand directly on the ball still in McNabb's hands, forcing McNabb to return his feet to the floor with the ball still in his possession. I saw clearly that Rollie had prevented McNabb's shot cleanly with no body contact. Suddenly, I heard a whistle, and I saw Referee Dudley running toward Rollie and McNabb, descending on them like a banty rooster on a night crawler. Both were on the floor, each holding onto the ball, and struggling to gain possession. Unlike mine, Referee Dudley's view of the play was from fifteen yards back, and he ran up to the fighting duo and pointed to Rollie, calling a foul.

As Rollie raised his hand, signaling his presumed transgression to the scorekeeper, I was overcome with incredible astonishment. I was positive Rollie had not committed a foul. McNabb should have been called for "traveling." I wanted to immediately protest to Referee Dudley, even though I knew it would be futile. However, I refrained. In a previous heated protest I had given to a referee on the Fort Lupton court, I was assessed a technical foul. It would not be helpful to our team to give Windsor a third chance at the foul line.

A feeling of futility overwhelmed me as Referee Dudley announced, "That'll be two shots," and he held up two fingers for the scorekeeper to see.

With nineteen seconds left, the partisan Windsor fans were standing, yelling, and clapping, providing their confirmation of the referee's call. The crowd noise waned as McNabb attempted the first free-throw. The shot, not quite long enough, bounced off the front of the rim. McNabb had missed the first one. There was an instant loud groan from the Windsor fans and a yell of gleeful approval from Mead supporters. Coach Beers, my teammates, and I looked with disbelief as McNabb sank the second free-throw to nudge the Wizards past us 23–22.

The game ended that afternoon with our team experiencing our first and only defeat of the season. There was silence and saddened faces in our locker room as we showered and changed to our street clothes. I left the gym to go outside to use a phone booth. Inside the booth, I dropped two quarters into the slot. I dialed long distance—9-246-2802. On the other end of the line, I heard Mom's hello.

"This is Ron," I said. "We lost the game. We lost by one point. We won't be playing tonight. So you and Helen won't have to come."

"Oh, for heaven's sake," said Mom. "Helen just got here, and we were getting ready to drive over. Will you be coming right home, or are you staying for the final game?"

I said, "We're going to stay. We want to watch Ault and Windsor play for the championship. They have a concession stand here, and we are all going to eat here. Mr. Carlson says we'll be home about ten-thirty."

I hung up the phone and went back into the gym, where I saw Coach Beers sitting by himself, waiting for the Ault–Johnstown game to begin. I could see the disappointment in his eyes. My own sadness was magnified when I thought about how I had let him down. I saw that winning was just as important to him as it was to me. Losing was also disappointing to teammates, classmates, my brothers, and now my whole family. Like Coach Beers, I knew folks in Mead would be asking, "What happened to you guys?" I was certain there would be some town folks who would be saying, "The Newton triplets are 'too big for their breeches.' Their cocky attitude has caught up with 'em."

On the long sad bus ride back to Mead that night, my spirits were uplifted when I heard the loyal chants of our cheering supporters. "Whether we win, or whether we lose, we're Bulldogs just the same." I finally consoled myself with the thought That's the way God wanted it. Although saddened with how the junior high basketball season ended, I was looking forward to high school. I knew I had three years of basketball ahead of me. There would be plenty of other opportunities for my brothers and me to excel on the Mead High School basketball court.

On the following Saturday on my way home from biweekly confession at Guardian Angel Church, I stopped at the pool hall for a bottle of Nehi orange soda.

Grover Roberts, standing behind the bar, said, "I heard you kids lost the game to Windsor. What happened to ya'?"

"I don't know for sure," I said, "but when I talked to Ronald Weber about it, he said he thought Windsor threw a 'zone' at us. We've never played against a zone. We don't even know what it is. Weber said he could explain it to us someday in the gym. He said there's a special way to beat it. He learned how from Coach Peterson."

I wanted to tell Mr. Roberts about Referee Dudley's foul call on Rollie that I thought was wrong, but I decided not to. I knew if I did, he would think I was trying to make excuses for the poor showing of my brothers and me. I was beginning to realize what our friend Walt Slee meant when he said, "Referees are just like the players. They make mistakes. Mistakes are part of the game." I was beginning to learn that I should accept what has been done, roll with it, and move on. I was moving on and thinking about next year and playing basketball for Mead High School.

The 3 R's of the Future
This Is Rollie . . . Here's Ronnie . . . and Richie

Triplets Give 3 R's New Meaning at Mead

Denver Post, February 29, 1954

Junior High Team. L-R, Jim Landolt, Leonard Smith, Mike Eckel, Allen Thompson, Rollie Newton, Ronnie Newton, Richie Newton, Coach Jim Beers, 1954.
Mead Consolidated Schools Yearbook

Chapter 14

Sophomore Entrée

For athletic competition, Mead High was grouped with Ault, Eaton, Windsor, Johnstown, Platteville, Kersey, and Ft. Lupton. All were members of the Poudre Valley League (limited to high schools with enrollment between one hundred and two hundred students). Most often, athletic teams from these schools were coached by men who had learned their skills as athletes and students at nearby Colorado A&M College or Colorado State College of Education. James Beers had earned his student-teaching practicum credit at Mead by teaching social studies and coaching three sports, and at the end of the '53 academic year, when Mead's Coach Schmidt resigned, Jim Beers was offered the teaching and coaching position.

In late November 1954, Coach Beers was in his second year as coach at Mead. The football season had just finished, and the Bulldogs had won only one game. Mead had defeated Berthoud 33–0 in a nonconference game but lost eight others, one to Kersey, 67–0, and another to Fort Lupton, 51–7. Although it was the second year for brothers Rollie and Jerry to play football, it was the first year for me. Richie decided to be student manager. As a substitute lineman at 112 pounds, I saw very little action. I regretfully remember playing on our kickoff team when the second half began with Kersey. I was afraid to tackle the Kersey running back as he whizzed by me next to the sideline.

Jerry had made an attempt to trip him by catching his foot, but I made no effort. I stood there like a statue, petrified. I simply watched the runner ran past both Jerry and me for a touchdown—a real pantywaist.

Observing my lack of response, Arvid Fietchner barked, "Newton! What are you doin'? Why didn'cha hit 'im?"

Embarrassed by my lack of courage, I blurted back, "I didn't know what to do. I didn't know how to tackle him."

"Well, you had a good angle at 'im," said Arvid. "Ya should've put a cross-body block on 'im and knocked him into the stands."

Obviously, I had learned very little about playing football that year. I tended to avoid the harsh shock when two bodies collide full force. Instead of hitting my opponent with my shoulder, I preferred to step aside and finesse the tackle by wrapping my arms around the runner's waist and sliding them down to clasp his knees to bring him to the ground.

With only one coach at practice, there was little time for instruction in the intricacies of the game or for one-on-one teaching of techniques. However, math and science teacher Mr. Arthur Troutman agreed to help out with practice on several occasions, and he tutored the offensive linemen in the mechanics of blocking. Crouched down in the stance with me across from him on defense, Mr. Troutman demonstrated by pushing his right shoulder into my thighs, followed by a rapid swing of his torso into my legs. At first upright and trying to resist his advance, I was bowled over backward and lay flat on my back.

Proud of what he had just done and getting himself up from the ground, Mr. Troutman said, "Whatcha want to do here is swing your rump around quickly and strike your opponent across the knees and thighs as you pivot with your hand on the ground. But 'cha have to do it quickly, and you have to move with a lot of force to knock him down."

Later in the season, with Windsor ahead by three touchdowns, Coach Beers put me in the game to play offensive right tackle. In the huddle, quarterback Ralph Biederman called for a halfback running play over the right side. At the snap of the ball, I placed my body across Windsor's 185-pound defensive lineman, Ron Greenwald. Greenwald, holding his ground as I thrust into him, put his left hand through my crotch and his right hand under my chin, grasping my whole body. He proceeded to simply lift me up, all 112 pounds, and throw me aside like a sack of chicken feed. This was done just in time for him to meet Allen Thompson attempting to carry the ball through the line. Allen was met instantly with a big bear-hug tackle from Greenwald, who immediately threw him to the ground, stopping him for no gain.

Unlike me, Mead's starting tackle, Conrad Hopp, weighing 195 pounds and using Mr. Troutman's technique, took out two defenders at the same time as he swung his hips and legs into their bodies. Hopp was so effective that on one occasion, he unintentionally lacerated the face of the defender with his rubberized cleats.

From my perspective, the fall and football season were interminable, and I was glad to see winter approaching. With high-school basketball, winter was my favorite time of year. I was just completing a half year of typing with Mrs. Thelma Bachman as my teacher. The class was made up of sophomores. Rollie and Richie were also enrolled. She had taught brother Jerry and sisters Maureen and Kathleen.

One day, as class was over and we were waiting for the bell to ring, I asked Mrs. Bachman, "Are you going to come to some of our basketball games this year?"

"Well, I might be able to," she said. "I like basketball. I played it in high school back in Iowa. What team will you boys be playing on this year?"

"I know we'll be playin' on the B-team. I think Allen will be playin' A-string," I said. "At the end of last year, Coach Beers brought him up from junior high to play on the A-team tournament team. This year, he might even start."

"You boys all need to keep your grades up. So far this year, you've all been eligible to play football. After Christmas, most of you will be taking our advanced typing class, so you need to keep working hard," said Mrs. Bachman.

"I'm glad I'm taking typing," I said. "Mrs. Eckel told me that typing is one of the best things you can learn how to do. She said you will be using it all the rest of your life, no matter whatcha do."

I was also taking algebra from Mr. Troutman. Mike Eckel told me, "Marg [Mike's mother] said that if you're goin' to college, you need to understand mathematics. She said algebra and geometry would both be good preparation for college."

Algebra was very challenging for me, but it was not difficult to meet Mr. Troutman's very relaxed standards. There were no homework assignments, and often, the class period was taken up by his discussion of school events, athletics, and national politics. Quizzes were seldom given and haphazardly scheduled. Following this one-semester course, Mr. Troutman was scheduled to teach geometry starting in January.

I was ecstatic that football had finally come to an end, and anticipating the upcoming basketball season, I was as excited as a four-year-old at Christmas time. I had endured the football season and the humiliation of eight resounding defeats with my teammates by thinking of football as a necessary evil and keeping me in shape physically for the basketball season. Basketball was the game where I knew I could excel. I had demonstrated that to Coach Beers and to my teammates in junior high last year. My passing and dribbling skills compensated for my lack of physical strength and stature. Many of my football teammates would put their cleats aside and don gym shoes to join me on the hardwood.

I was certain my three brothers and I would start on the B-team, but I believed all of us were good enough to play on the A-team. Basketball was the Newtons' game. We could shoot, dribble, and pass. We understood the subtleties and nuances of basketball. We had played together many years on our backyard court and in the Mead gym. We had competed with older neighborhood friends—Loe Hernandez, Ronald Weber, Vernon Widger, and Herb Newman. We had competed against each other. We each had learned from the others. We understood that basketball was competitive. The goal was to be better than a brother, better than a friend, and now better than our high-school opponents.

Coach Beers scheduled the first basketball practice in late November, the week after Thanksgiving. Jim Beers, twenty-four years of age, came to work each morning dressed in a tweed suit and tie. He had a blue suit, a gray one, and one that was brown. He kept them meticulously clean; his white shirts were starched and pressed. He shed his suit coat when teaching, and for practices, he wore a white sweatshirt and light-blue denims with a whistle hanging from his neck on a black shoestring. He was of Irish origin, and he parted his short reddish-brown hair on the left side and combed it back on the right side, elevating it an inch above his head. Clear horn-rimmed glasses sat on the nose of his ruddy-complexioned, pock-marked face, which flushed red when he was frustrated or angry. Coach's short-fused temper was ignited easily, and his outcry of displeasure was preceded by a reddened face. The tip of his nose was red from the constant rubbing it got from his right thumb and index finger.

A shy man, not accustomed to group speaking, Coach Beers addressed his charges in a mumbled and stuttering monotone. "Bu-boys," he said, addressing twenty-three young men who showed up that Monday afternoon, "fu-football is over. It goes without saying that we did not do well. Bu-but I know we will do better in bu-basketball." Hesitating briefly to rub the bottom of his nose, he continued, "Our first game is a practice game with Timnath in less than two weeks, so, bu-boys, we have a lot of work to do. I want you to work hard. Let's forget about football and move on."

He instructed the seniors and juniors along with us triplets, Leonard Smith, and Allen Thompson to take one end of the court and the rest of his players to take the other end. With the blast of his whistle and a short verbal command, he guided both groups through layup, dribbling, and passing drills and then had us run laps around the gym perimeter. He finished the first day's session with all of us shooting free-throws. The '54–'55 basketball season for Mead High School had officially begun. Four Newton brothers would play for Mead, undoubtedly a first for the state of Colorado and most likely a first in our nation's high-school basketball history.

Like Mead High, the professional basketball season for the National Basketball Association (NBA) had also begun, and for the first time in their history, they began televising the games. The ball-handling skills of Bob Cousy of the Boston Celtics caught my attention. I wanted to be like him. My goal was to be the best passer and dribbler on Mead High School's team.

Thelma Bachman, James Beers, Arthur Troutman, 1954.
Mead Consolidated Schools Yearbook

L-R: Jerry Newton, Ronnie Newton, Rollie Newton,
and Richie Newton (Mgr.), 1954.
Mead Consolidated Schools Yearbook

L-R: Arvid Fietchner, Conrad Hopp, 1954.
Mead Consolidated Schools Yearbook

Chapter 15

Dual Playtime

Coach Beers had already concluded who would be the starting five for his Mead Bulldog A-team. He had coached us all, and he had plenty of time to assess our talents. He had a great respect for the skills of Johnny Schell, who would play forward. Johnny was six-foot-one, gangly, and strong. He had been a very physical football player and pursued this same approach in rebounding. He had a deadly jump shot from the left side. With his back to his opponent, Johnny jumped and twisted in midair, releasing the ball high above his head with the trajectory parallel to the backcourt line—an effective shot he exploited time after time and to which defenders had difficulty stopping. Johnny's vivacious girlfriend from Longmont, Irene Ghesquire, attended every game, even driving to the away games in her own or Johnny's car.

Junior Jerry Sitzman, six feet and four inches tall, played center. Although inexperienced, he was good inside at rebounding and shooting short jump shots. Tall and spindly and at 165 pounds, he had to work hard to outmuscle heavier defenders.

However, Connie Hopp made up for Sitzman's lack of girth. Connie, as tall as Sitzman at six- feet-four, weighed 195 pounds and was seldom challenged by anyone for the space he occupied near the basket. In the stance of an upright burly bear and his back to the defender, Connie, as the other starting forward, was an effective rebounder. Connie and Jerry Sitzman would carry the inside game for Mead with help from Johnny.

Ralph Biederman started as a guard along with Allen Thompson. Ralph's father had played basketball for Mead in the 1930s and was always in the stands supporting his son. Ralph, a senior, had come to Mead his freshman year. He played quarterback on the football team, and he would be the primary starting ball handler on the basketball court.

Allen Thompson, just a sophomore, had become an excellent athlete since arriving in Mead in the seventh grade. My brothers and I had befriended him immediately, and we included him in our backyard sports activities. Because he was the tallest of all our classmates, Coach Beers had him playing center on our junior high team. In that position, Allen perfected a good hook shot.

Allen was nine months older than us and most of our classmates, and he was physically more developed than the rest of us. And as young boys will often do, Allen would boast of the particulars of his advanced stages of growth and liked to poke fun at those whom he perceived as deficient. Allen added to his inherently powerful physique by lifting weights, and he was strong as steel.

"Look at these veins that are starting to pop out," boasted Allen as he gazed from side to side at each forearm.

He was proud of his well-proportioned body. It was as sculptured as Michelangelo's David, and it contributed immensely to his exceptional athleticism. My brothers and I respected Allen's physical superiority and were careful not to provoke him. When we did, he took no prisoners.

As a freshman, Allen played the receiver position on the football team, and this year, he had been a running back. As a basketball player, Allen was a leaper, leaving his feet early and many yards away from the basket as he drove for the layup—hanging in the air, winding his body and the ball through the outstretched arms of defenders, laying the ball gently on the backboard, and letting it arc gracefully into the net. Allen had also combined his vertical leaping skill with a one-handed shooting delivery over his head, giving him a jump shot that could be hurled over a defender with ease. He had a unique ability to roll the ball off his single right hand as he shot, and he developed great accuracy. At the height of his jump, Allen seemed to give himself a little more kick upward and more time to hang suspended by bending his legs at the knees and bringing his calves parallel to the floor.

I was envious of Allen's early successes as a freshman athlete. Hearing Mr. Troutman say one day in Algebra class, "That Thompson is one of the best athletes I have ever seen at the high-school level," my jealousy was heightened. How could this be? I asked myself. We've been playin' basketball longer than he has. Besides, we're the ones who taught him how to play. Now they say he's better than us.

However, I knew I could outperform Allen with my ball-handling and dribbling skills. I knew I was quicker with my hands; I could also be a better defender. I knew that I, like Allen, had a contribution to make to the team. I believed that a year from now, the contributions of my brothers and me would be needed and appreciated. Dave would be on the team then. We five Newtons would then complement Allen no matter what position he played. But for now, my brothers and I would have valuable playing time. We would be learning. We would be ready next year when skills would matter even more. Next year, any one of us five Newtons could be starting on the A-team—a goal to which we all aspired.

Besides Johnny, Connie, Jerry S., Ralph, and Allen, Coach Beers rounded out his A-team with juniors Jerry Newton, George Flores, Keith Stotts, and sophomores Leonard Smith, Mike Eckel, and us triplets. Rollie was the tallest and the strongest of us three. He and our brother Jerry were about the same height at six feet. Both Jerry and Rollie played forwards when Johnny or Connie got into foul trouble or needed a rest. Either one of them could be called upon. Jerry was not a big scorer, but he could work the boards tenaciously. Sometimes though, Coach Beers put him in as center. He maintained his position on the right side of the keyhole. When the Mead guards passed the ball into him, he would take one step to his left, pivot on his left foot, and hook the ball over his head, hurling it forward, allowing it to drop lightly over the front of the rim and into the net.

Because of their jump shots, Johnny and Rollie were most effective on the left side of the court. Their jump shots were similar—both twisting almost ninety degrees to directly face the basket while in upward flight, holding the ball with two hands just above the head, and thrusting it forward with both hands toward the basket but guiding it with the lone right hand.

Rollie could always outrebound taller defenders. With Rollie, rebounding was knowing where the ball was going to be once it was shot and then getting into position to block out the defender. With his precise timing, he always managed to get both hands on the ball at the height of his jump and pulling it inward to his body to protect it, all before landing back on the floor. Rollie was a physical player—"tougher than a shoe-sole steak," said Frank Eckel as he watched him play. He always had been in every sport. He was the "toughest" of the Newton brothers, and his physicality was demonstrated most while rebounding. His "space" near the basket could not be inhabited by anyone else; he guarded it with the ferocity and the stance of a prize fighter. As far as he was concerned, fisticuffs were appropriate if the defender became too aggressive and tried to move him out or take over the ball. Because of this constant backboard combat, Rollie had to wear a wire mask over the fragile eyeglasses that he wore. The mask gave Rollie a "tough guy" image and was a constant reminder to defenders that they should never start something that they couldn't finish.

Richie was the scorer. He was so accurate every time he shot that Mike Eckel called him "Dead-Eye Dick." Accuracy was Richie's hallmark. He was a sharpshooter. In every way and in everything he did, he was a gifted marksman. At twenty feet, he could knock a ten-inch wooden doll off the shelf at the church picnic concession. He could pitch a baseball over the plate at any location he wanted. With a rock propelled from his slingshot, Richie could hit a rabbit between the eyes, and he could hit a cantankerous rooster on the head with a rock at forty paces. On the basketball court, Richie could hit a jumper with precise accuracy at fifteen to twenty feet out. Farther from the basket, he had a deadly set shot, and at the foul line, he shot a remarkable 80 percent. The only way to stop Richie was to not let him set up for a shot or to keep him from getting the ball. Against zone defenses, he was a killer. His perimeter shots always found the net. Richie was a superb passer—behind his back or otherwise. His long "baseball throws" of the basketball were always on target to the open man downcourt and led to frequent fast-break scoring.

Although our brother Jerry, George Flores, Keith Stotts, Leonard Smith, Mike Eckel, and us triplets all played on the A-team, we would also play in the preliminary game as B-stringers at every competition. Eighteen players suited up for the B-team. Usually, Richie and I started as guards, with Rollie as a forward and Jerry at center. George Flores, Lawrence Jensen, or Lyle Schaefer started at the other forward spot. As the game progressed with Mead often far ahead, our other eleven teammates would finish out most of the game time that was left.

We Mead B-stringers won sixteen out of eighteen games, losing to Eaton 33–32 and to Johnstown 61–49. Our team overwhelmed the opposition by an average of nearly 10 points a game with an average score per game of 42.1 points with our opponents at 32.5. Defeating our opponents by wide margins was a trend the Mead team established at the B-string level in '54–'55 and would continue for the next two years. The Mead B-stringers were the genesis of a basketball powerhouse coming out of the farmlands of Northeastern Colorado. For the next two years, Mead would be the menacing opponent, consistent contenders for league, district, and state titles.

As members of both the B- and A-teams, my brothers and I got a lot of playing time. Often we played as many as six quarters, sometimes seven, allowing us to gain valuable game experience. This was when I learned to be a "floor general."

The role of the floor general was to bring the ball down from the defensive end-court to the offensive half-court and, if necessary, to break the opponent's full-court press with both dribbling and passing. On the offensive half-court, the floor general controlled the tempo of the game, giving his teammates time to set their positions and initiating the first pass to start offensive play. To effectively get the ball to his teammates, he must know how to pass with either hand. In essence, the floor general takes control of the game, not necessarily with his shooting but with his ball handling.

My role as floor general was not one to which I was formally assigned; it was a role that I assumed whenever I was on the floor. I took pride in my ball-handling skills. On our backyard court and for many hours and days, I had practiced dribbling with both hands. I continued this habit at every practice, emulating Marques Haynes of the Harlem Globetrotters. Like Haynes, I could spin the ball on the tip of my finger (but so could my brothers).

For the first tilt in early December, our A-team lost to Timnath. On our home court, Rollie, Jerry, and I saw action against Berthoud, Mead's second nonconference foe. Rollie, Johnny, Connie, and Jerry Sitzman all scored in double figures as Mead walloped Berthoud 85–53. A week later, we met an improved Berthoud team on their home court. All four Newtons played. I was playing in the third quarter when Berthoud came within four points. Coach Beers called time-out and collected his players into a huddle.

Coach said, "Connie, you've got to stop Vigil. He's scored three of their last four baskets. I know you've got four fouls, so try not to foul 'im, just keep 'im from gettin' the ball."

As Coach continued talking, Johnny stepped back from the huddle and tapped me on the shoulder. "Hey," he said. "Get me the ball. There's nobody guardin' me. I know I'll have an open shot."

Unlike in his earliest years of coaching, Coach Beers had learned to recognize a zone defense, and he said, "They're still in their zone, so keep the ball movin'. Ronnie, make sure you're at the point. Get it to the open man. Johnny, you rotate from side to side. Keep movin' so we can get the ball to ya."

When play resumed, Richie brought the ball across the centerline and passed it to me, and I took it to center court. I passed it back to Richie, who had positioned himself on the right wing. Richie, seeing that neither Jerry Sitzman nor Connie were open, bounce-passed it back to me, and I immediately threw an overhead pass to Johnny on the left wing. Johnny dribbled to the baseline and turned his upper torso toward the basket. He raised the ball above his head in synchrony with his jump, releasing the ball into a tall arc that rainbowed into the basket. Through the rest of the game, Johnny rotated from wing to wing along the backcourt, getting open before the defense could shift. As guards, Ralph, Richie, Allen, and I got the ball to Johnny, and each time, Johnny connected on his high-arced jump shot. Before the game ended, Johnny had hit seven of them and scored a total of twenty-one points; we beat Berthoud for the second time.

Right before Christmas, Rollie and I saw action in games against Kersey and Johnstown, with Mead winning both. Over the Christmas holiday, we took a break from school and basketball. The Christmas holiday with family, church, and basketball was an exhilarating time. My young life was at its best. With basketball foremost in my mind, I wanted those days to never end. My sophomore season of basketball was just beginning. There was much more for me to learn before I reached the excellence I expected to attain as a player.

B-Team. Front row, L-R: Ronald Vogel (Mgr.), Marvin Blazon, Bob Camenisch, Leonard Smith, Bill Harding, Richie Newton, Larry Nuss, Ronnie Newton, Lanny Davis, Jim Landolt (Mgr.); Back row, L-R: Coach Jim Beers, Rollie Newton, Mike Eckel, Keith Stotts, Gary Olson, Lyle Schaefer, Byron Jillson, Darrel Gettman, Jerry Newton, George Flores, and Lawrence Jensen, 1955.
Mead Consolidated Schools Yearbook

A-Team. Front Row, L-R: Coach Jim Beers, Ronnie Newton, Richie Newton, Mike Eckel, Rollie Newton, Ralph Biederman, Keith Stotts, Allen Thompson, Jerry Newton, Johnny Schell, Connie Hopp, and Jerry Sitzman, 1955.
Mead Consolidated Schools Yearbook

Chapter 16

Off Court

Playing basketball is like building a house; you can't do it well until you've learned the basic trade. A young man must first serve as an apprentice and learn from the more experienced practitioner before he embarks on the complex objective of constructing a dwelling. In our sophomore year at Mead High, my triplet brothers and I served our apprenticeships on the varsity (A-team) basketball team, learning from the older and more experienced players. We listened to their advice and followed their leadership. We learned from their mistakes as well as our own. We developed our skills and techniques, striving to be more proficient, preparing for when *we* would be the starters on Mead's varsity.

But my sophomore year was not only a learning season on the basketball court; it was a constant learning process for me off the court as well as I interacted with teachers and classmates in and out of the classroom. For me, my first year in high school posed many obstacles that challenged me, and I struggled to deal with them. I had much to learn.

In mid-December of '54, Mead High transitioned into the second half year of its class schedule. Several sophomore classmates and I had just finished a half year of woodshop. Now we would choose what we would take next.

Mike Eckel said, "Marg thinks I ought to take a foreign language. Spanish I is being taught by Mrs. Carlson. I talked to Mr. Johnson, and he thinks I should take it. What about you? What are you going to take?"

"Spanish is okay for me," I said. "My sister Kathleen took it, and she liked it. I think I will too. Let's both take it. We can study together just like we did for English and history."

With the twelve-fifty-five bell, the lunch hour ended, and Mike Eckel entered the Spanish I classroom through the side door. Seven or eight girls were sitting in the front, waiting for Mrs. Carlson to begin class. In unison, their heads turned abruptly, looking at Mike as he swaggered into the room. They all knew Mike and, each with an adoring smile, acknowledged the presence of this engaging, handsome young man who was about to become their classmate. Mike had received much of his good looks from his dad Frank, who looked like Humphrey Bogart. However, his mother Marg had also given him an almost ever-present smile that emanated from a slim elegant face that was so well proportioned, Mike looked more like Paul Newman. Marg and Frank also had instilled in Mike a very polished social manner, rich in politeness and courtesy. This, coupled with his matinee-idol looks, made him the center of attention for all the girls in Spanish I.

As Mike walked to the back of the room, he tugged at the back of his Wrangler jeans, pushing them down until his belt lay just at the top of his buttocks, producing a baggy bulge below his muscular butt. Laying his books down and still standing, he turned to the front and said, "Buenos días, Mrs. Carlson." Mike had worked with migrant workers on his dad's farm, and he was proud of the Spanish he had learned.

"Buenos días to you, Mr. Eckel," said Mrs. Carlson with a smile as she flipped through the pages in her roll book.

With the girls turned around and looking back at him, seeing their interested faces, Mike blurted out, "Buenos días, all you senoritas. Me no speaka español very well. I'm just a gringo ready to learn," he added.

Just then, I walked into the room. He pointed at me. "This hombre here is my friend Juan. But in English, we call him Ron," Mike said with a boisterous laugh, pleased with his display of wit. Seeing that Ronnie Johnson was the only other boy in the room, Mike said, "Boy, we have a lotta senoritas in the class."

As the one o'clock bell rang, Mrs. Carlson, still at her desk, started to call out the roll. "Senorita Janice," said Mrs. Carlson in a soft voice, "are you here? Please answer with si if you are present."

"Sí. Yes, I am," answered Janice Barnes, raising her hand.

As Mrs. Carlson proceeded through the list of names, Mike continued talking, his ingrained courtesy deserting him. "Hey, Elaine!" he yelled. "How do ya say 'You're beautiful' in español?"

Now Elaine Becker, a cheerleader knowing Mike was very interested in her, was beginning to appreciate his attention. She blushed and started to laugh.

"I know, I know," I said loudly. Then trying to mimic Mike's humorous phrases, I said, "She's el beautifico, el chichi."

The girls laughed gratuitously at my lame comment, and Mrs. Carlson waited until the laughing stopped before continuing her task. Her voice was soft and could only be heard when others were not talking. Frustrated that students were neither hearing nor responding, Mrs. Carlson said, "Please do not talk, and you boys back there, please hush."

The laughter ceased for a short time while Mrs. Carlson introduced the first lesson on "the Spanish you already know." Mrs. Carlson mentioned words such as tacos, tortillas, siesta, rancho, and San Francisco. Then she went over some Spanish words that were written similarly in both English and Spanish but did not have the same meaning.

When hearing the word constipado in Spanish, meaning "having a cold," Mike exploded with laughter and blurted out for all to hear, "It still means that your plumbing is stopped up. The only difference is that in Spanish, it's your nose. In English, it's your bowels."

The whole class convulsed with laughter.

Mrs. Carlson went on to introduce the Spanish alphabet and pronunciation. Each time she presented a phrase, symbol, or word, Mike and I somehow found them to be funny. Our laughter became uncontrollable and disruptive. Our random, unsolicited comments resonated with classmates, and the whole class was consumed with giggles, grins, and guffaws. Mrs. Carlson, unable to control the class, sighed and shook her head. Her soft-spoken words were disregarded or not heard.

When the one-fifty-five bell rang, Mrs. Carlson dismissed the first-day Spanish I class and said nothing about the havoc she had experienced. It was not an easy task for Mrs. Carlson to confront students directly. Instead, Mrs. Carlson would choose to deal with our misbehavior in another way.

The next morning, Betty Ann Bernhart, secretary of the school, knocked on the door and delivered two written notes to Mrs. Bachman, standing in front of our typing class. She read them and then handed one to Mike and one to me.

She said, "You two are supposed to meet with Coach Beers during the lunch hour at twelve five. He wants to meet you in Mr. Carlson's office."

Reading the note, I told Mike, "I wonder what this is for."

"You got me," said Mike. "I have no idea what he might want." Chuckling, Mike whispered with his hand over his mouth, "I guess he wants us to wipe his ass."

Sitting at Mr. Carlson's desk, Coach Beers looked at the two of us. We were very puzzled about what was taking place.

"Boys," said Coach Beers, "I'm told that you two have been cuttin' up in Mrs. Carlson's class. She says she doesn't want you in there anymore. So we're takin' you out of Spanish I, and we're puttin' you in my geography class. At one o'clock today, I want you to give your Spanish books back to Mrs. Carlson and report to my class. We'll be in the room next to the study hall."

Then he said, "You will not be playing this Friday. Neither one of you will be suiting up. You won't be playing in either game. Also, you won't be practicing with the teams for the rest of the week. During the last period, you will report to study hall instead of going to the gym for practice."

We were shocked and devastated. I felt ashamed of my behavior and how I had treated Mrs. Carlson with disrespect. I knew Spanish was an important subject for me to learn. Now I would not have that opportunity. I had blown it. I had wanted to experience a subject that I had never been exposed to before. And now I had deprived myself of participating in the sports activity I loved most. Worse still, I would have to face Mom; she would not be happy. I would have to explain my behavior. I knew Mom would find out about my misconduct in school. As usual, she meted out her own punishment. I was grounded for two weeks, and she gave me additional chores.

Mead had a week to prepare for the first league game against Kersey. On Tuesday, I went to the gym after study hall to watch my teammates practice. I did not want to go home early because I knew Mom would put me to work if I did. She had already told me that for the next two weeks, I could not leave the house on the weekend to be with friends. I noted that Allen Thompson was not there for practice. I had seen him yesterday, but that afternoon, Allen was absent. Allen also missed Wednesday's and Thursday's practice; he was not even in school. He was not in school on Friday, even though there was a game that evening. Allen was gone that week because he and his brother Delbert were working with their dad, a mule skinner, clearing trees and brush on the Lang farm near the South Platte River.

Allen arrived at the Mead gym on that Friday night, ready to play, and Coach Beers put him in his regular starting lineup. I had begged Mom for several days to let me go to the game that night, and she finally consented. Sitting with Mike in the bleachers and watching as Allen took the floor, I became furious. I thought that his being able to play was grossly unfair to the rest of the team.

I asked Mike, "Why is Allen startin'? He hasn't practiced all week."

Mike, not wanting to discuss the matter, said nothing and just stared forward to watch the opening tip-off.

"Why isn't Richie startin'? I asked in a loud voice. "He didn't miss practice all week. He should be in there." Looking over at Mike, I asked, "Don't you think so, Mike?"

Looking back at me, Mike said, "Yes, yes, I do." Mike's agreement with me renewed my confidence about my own judgment.

Mead beat Kersey that night, but Coach Beers's perceived favoritism toward Allen angered me, and it triggered my jealousy of Allen. Furthermore, I reasoned to myself, Allen should be disciplined. If he didn't practice, he shouldn't play. I rationalized further that as far as I was concerned, missing school to work and make money was not a good excuse for missing practice. In my mind, basketball and school work were more important than making money.

The next Monday, Mike and I were back practicing with the team. As we dressed in the locker room after a two-hour workout, I shouted over to Allen, who had showered and had just put on his jeans, "Hey, Allen! How come you've missed so much school last week?" Before Allen could answer, I lashed out at him, "You shoulda been here practicin' with the rest of the team. How come you were gone? Where were you?"

"F——k you, Ronnie," retorted Allen. "F——k you and the horse you rode up on. It's none of your goddamn business where I've been."

"Ya shoulda been here!" I shouted once again, this time much louder so all our teammates could hear.

Allen, now agitated and angry, walked over to me. The muscles on his bare chest were heaving, and the veins on his biceps were bulging. Allen cocked his arm and growled, "Look here, you scrawny sonuvab——." He raised his fist in front of my face. "I've got a knuckle sandwich right here for ya. You keep talkin', and I'll bust ya one in that big mouth of yours right now."

Frightened at what was about to happen, I realized I had made a tactical mistake. I put my head down, turned away, and reached into my locker for my shirt. Allen turned away from me to face the rest of our teammates as they all watched with fear in their eyes. Everyone in the room knew Allen could scatter my chattering teeth all over Weld County with one blow. Allen had made his point to them and to me. He was tough, he was independent, and he was a dominant physical player on our team. He lorded over us sophomore teammates. Never again would I confront Allen on anything. The consequences to me would be physical and psychological annihilation.

In the social world of male teenagers, it is most often the physically tough who rule. Those with muscles and high testosterone levels call the shots. They enforce adherence to their own wills by threatening and using physical force on others. If you were among their circle of friends, you did not confront them to change their behavior; you were the one who had to change, not them. They addressed conflict with physical force. A rational discussion or debate was out of the question. When physical conflict required collective resolution on the part of many, it was the toughest and the strongest who led the pack. The physical hierarchy in the social organization of teenagers in the '50s was not new. The ritual had not changed for eons.

As a high-school teenager, there were many times where I was dragged into the gang culture of attempting to settle disputes with fists. It was then when I appreciated the physical attributes of my peer friends. It was then when I wanted my "rival," Allen Thompson, to be on my side.

Eventually, I "mended fences" with Coach Beers and Mom, and I was permitted to rejoin the team. Mead won its next game with Johnstown, but Coach Beers, prolonging his disciplinary action for my classroom misbehavior, still did not allow me to play, nor did I play in the preliminary B-string game. Mike received the same treatment. We sat on the bench together and watched our teammates win both games.

L-R: Mary Carlson, Elaine Becker, 1955.
Mead Consolidated Schools Yearbook

Allen Thompson, 1955.
Mead Consolidated Schools Yearbook

L-R: Mike Eckel, Ronnie Newton, 1955.
Mead Consolidated Schools Yearbook

Chapter 17

Sophomore Seasoning

In mid-January '55, the sophomore basketball season resumed with a league game against Platteville. Early in the second half, Allen Thompson attempted to dribble and drive through Platteville's zone and was called for traveling. With our next possession, Ralph Biederman had the ball taken away as he attempted to dribble past a defender. Coach Beers, watching his two guards turn the ball over two times in a row, jumped from his seat in frustration and turned toward me. Red-faced with anger, he yelled, "R-Ronnie, git in there for R-Ralph!"

Thereafter, I remained in the game. Rollie, Richie, and Jerry also played. Mead went on to win 57–38.

We surprised Fort Lupton, beating them resoundingly, 48–30, on our home court. Ralph was away attending a funeral, and Coach Beers started me in his absence. Midway through the third period and possessing the ball near the right-side baseline, I attempted to dribble to my right and drive around six-foot-four Ron Cerreto. Cerreto, stepping and reaching to his left, hit me across the mouth with a swing of his forearm as I stumbled over his outstretched leg. The referee blew his whistle and signaled a charging foul on me. The hometown crowd yelled in protest.

Standing up on the stage and looking down on the referee, Ronald Weber yelled, "What? What da ya mean a charge? The guy clobbered 'im right 'n the chops!"

When Connie Hopp fouled out, he was replaced by Rollie, and Rollie finished the game with one of his finest performances, scoring three baskets and six free throws and holding Lupton's stalwart forward Gary Tway to just seven points. It was Tway's poorest offensive performance of the season.

Mead was tied with Windsor for the Poudre Valley League lead when we faced off with them, and although Johnny Schell had his best game of the season, with eight field goals and eight points at the foul line, we lost, and Windsor took sole possession of the league lead.

With Eaton, Coach Beers stuck with his starting lineup for most of the game, and I was the only substitute. Ahead at 41–29 with three minutes to play and wanting to slow the game down, Coach Beers changed to a zone defense. Then with less than a minute left, Eaton had made an offensive run of twelve points to tie the score at forty-one. Connie followed with a two-point jump shot, putting us ahead by two. Coach Beers then yelled to our team captain, "Johnny, Johnny, call time-out!"

With his team huddled around, Coach Beers barked loudly, "A-Allen, you throw the ball in bounds and git it to Ronnie! R-Ronnie, you hang on to it. K-keep dribblin'. Stall until the clock runs out. We only have twenty-eight seconds left. The rest of you guys, stand back and let Ronnie have it."

As soon as the referee handed the ball to Allen standing out of bounds, ready to start the final seconds of play, I screened off my defender, Bob Pappenheim, cutting closely next to Connie. I ran across the center line to the backcourt to receive the ball from Allen. I dribbled the ball across the half line, where I was met once again by Pappenheim. I immediately cut to my right, taking the ball with me and eluding him totally. With Pappenheim trailing, I continued to dribble around defenders. I maneuvered in and out, alternating from hand to hand with my dribble as I avoided the reaching-in hands of defenders. My teammates assembled closer to the baseline, keeping the defenders away from me as I zigzagged about the floor. None of the defenders could get close enough to me to foul. Time ran out. The final buzzer sounded, and we won 43–41.

The next morning, I descended the stairs from my bedroom to eat breakfast. Mom was sitting at the kitchen table reading the paper, drinking a cup of coffee, and eating her breakfast of toast and cereal.

"Well, did ya win last night?" she asked as I headed through the kitchen to the bathroom.

"We lost the B-string game by one point, but the A-string won 43-41," I answered as I closed the bathroom door.

I sat down at the kitchen table and poured milk over my Cheerios. I knew since Mom had not seen the game, she would be asking me about it. I knew too that she would ask the same question she always asked. She took it for granted that Jerry and we triplets would play together on the B-team in the preliminary game and that all four of us would most likely get adequate playing time. But she was always curious about Jerry's playing time in the A-game.

"Did Jerry get ta play in the second game?" she asked.

"No, he didn't," I said. "Neither did Rollie or Richie. Beers put me in in the last quarter. I don't know why he didn't play any of them. I was the only one who got in the game."

Mom just looked at me and said nothing. I knew Mom thought all her boys should play, no matter the circumstances. In her mind, basketball was about letting everyone participate. Participation was more important than winning, particularly when it came to her own children.

"What happened in the first game?" Mom asked.

"All four of us started. Jerry played a lot," I said.

"Why'd you lose? Mom asked.

"I dunno," I said. "We only scored thirty points, and they hit an easy shot right at the end to beat us. That's the first game we've lost this season. Coach substituted a lot. We probably would have beat 'em if he had kept all of us first-stringers in longer."

In the final game of the first round of league play, Allen Thompson scored fifteen points to lead Mead over the Ault Bearcats 51–40. Mead finished the first round in second place with a record of five and one. Windsor was the league leader at six and zero, and Ft Lupton was third at four and two. At midseason, Lupton's Gary Tway led the league in scoring, averaging seventeen points a game. Mead's Johnny Schell was third at fourteen, behind Kersey's Don Miller with sixteen.

Mead's second-round league game with Kersey was brutal. Three Kersey players and two Mead players fouled out before game's end. With Johnny and Connie each with five fouls, Coach Beers replaced them with Rollie and our brother Jerry. Rollie was the high scorer for Mead with thirteen points, with Allen getting eleven. Rollie and Connie held Kersey's high-scorer Don Miller to eight points—half his season average—and Mead earned its seventh win of the season, 67–46.

Mead had a return match nonleague game with Timnath and the opportunity to avenge the loss Timnath handed Mead last December. It was a high-scoring game with Connie, Johnny, and Jerry Sitzman all scoring in double digits. Mead trailed throughout the game but finally caught up with the Cubs with three minutes to go, tying the score at 62. With fifteen seconds left in the final quarter, Johnny potted his turnaround jump shot to tie the score again, 65 to 65.

Mead fans were ecstatic when the game went into overtime. Head cheerleader Barbara Graham assembled her three cheering mates— Elaine Becker, Colleen Wright, and Mary Helen Olson—onto the floor to lead them and the pep club with the traditional school yell. "M!" Clap-clap. "E!" Clap-clap. "A!" Clap-clap. "D!" Clap-clap. The foursome jumped in unison with their right fists thrust into the air, shouting, "Yay!" as the partisan crowd of two hundred loudly applauded.

With a time-out before the overtime started, Coach Beers decided he now wanted his key ball handlers in the game for those three overtime minutes. Pointing to me sitting on the bench, he said, "R-Ronnie, take R-Ralph's place." Then with his team bunched around him, he said, "Let's get back into our zone defense. Allen and Ronnie, get the ball in to Johnny. Screen for him if you can so he can get his jump shot off." Remembering that Connie had four fouls, Coach Beers barked, "Connie, be careful in there. Don't foul!"

With Jerry Sitzman controlling the ball at the center jump with a tap to me, I dribbled to our offensive half-court and passed to Johnny on the right wing. Johnny was fouled by Timnath's Jerry Schilling as he attempted a jump shot. Johnny made the first free throw but missed the second. With us ahead by one point, the Timnath guards moved the ball down and quickly passed it to Schilling, who had already scored twenty points. This time, Schilling's hook shot failed to go in, and Connie grabbed the rebound. Connie passed to Allen, who brought the ball across the centerline. With Timnath in a man-to-man defense, I screened past Johnny, and Allen got the ball to me as I cleared from my defender. I set for a twenty-foot shot and dropped it in to give us the lead, 68–65. The Mead fans were delirious.

However, the crowd's excitement subsided when a foul was called on me as I blocked the driving layup shot of Timnath's Chuck Byers. Byers made the first free throw and missed the second. Now his team was behind by only two. With a minute and a half to go, Timnath put on a full-court press. Allen and I, with three quick passes back and forth to each other, got the ball past the defense and to Johnny standing underneath our own basket. He laid it in for the score. We were up four points with a minute left. In a quick exchange, Timnath's Schilling attempted a twenty-foot jump shot. It took a long bounce off the rim into the hands of Connie. Connie passed to me, and I hit Allen with a bounce pass as he moved to center court. As I followed him and crossed the centerline, Allen threw the ball back to me, and I went into my control dribble.

With two Timnath defenders swarming around me, I leaped into the air with the ball above my head and passed it to Connie. Connie went into a dribble and was immediately fouled by Schilling; then going to the line, Connie sank one free throw. With twelve seconds to go, the score was Mead, 71; Timnath, 66. That's how it ended.

The victorious Mead spectators jumped to their feet, yelling and clapping. Mr. and Mrs. Hopp stood proudly and watched as supporters rushed onto the floor to congratulate the team and their son Connie. Irene Ghesquire grabbed Johnny by the arm and held his hand as she walked him to the shower room entrance. Martha Borgmann, smiling happily, stood next to Connie with her arm around his waist. Leaving her husband Delbert in the bleachers, Mrs. Jessie Thompson went down on the floor and kissed Allen on the cheek.

Barbara Graham walked among players to offer congratulations. "Good game, Ronnie. You did a good job tonight," she said.

"Thanks, Barbara," I said as I moved through the crowd toward the locker room.

Mom, who attended all our home games, remained in the bleachers with my brothers Marc and Frosty. She was standing next to Martin and Mary Graham, all of them with broad smiles on their faces.

That night, Laura Dreier Newton saw only one son playing in the most exciting basketball game she had seen in her lifetime. Her other sons did not play. That night, she would be very proud of her one son. Yes, Ronald had played an important part in the win, but Laura would not acknowledge that verbally. It was not her practice to tell her children she thought they had done well. She would not openly express pride in their success. Besides, she was disappointed her other three sons did not play, especially Jerry.

I never expected Mom to say anything about my performance. I did not seek her out or look to acknowledge her presence at game's end. Her presence was enough; that was all I needed.

The next morning at the breakfast table, I did not mention anything about the game for fear Mom would think I had an inflated ego. I only nodded when she benignly said, "Those overtime games are not good for my heart. I thought I was goin' to have a stroke right there in the stands."

It was cold outside that following Friday evening in mid-February as our team, one by one, climbed on a bus to travel to Johnstown. Coach Beers stood up to see if all his team members were accounted for. As Mr. Humphrey shifted into compound and as the bus slowly moved out of the school parking lot, Mike Eckel asked Coach Beers, who was sitting two seats in front from him, "Hey, Coach, who does Windsor play tonight?"

"Kersey," Coach Beers answered. "T-they could have a tough time with them. T-they're playin' at Kersey, and that Miller kid there is really hot. He and Lupton's Tway are the top scorers in the League. W-Windsor is still one game ahead of us. I sure hope somebody beats them in the second round of play. W-we won't be playin' them again until the first week of March. If we win tonight and Windsor loses, w-we'll be tied for first. W-we're goin' to have ta be sharp tonight. W-we barely beat Johnstown last time," Coach Beers added.

Johnstown played a tight man-to-man defense, and this put them in foul trouble. It was fouls that decided the game. Mead made twenty-five free shots, while Johnstown sank only five. With 40 percent of Mead's points scored on free throws, Mead won handily 61–49. Mead followed this win by whipping Platteville and remained in a first-place tie with Windsor, who had lost to Kersey.

But Mead's first-place position was short-lived. The Bulldogs were defeated by Fort Lupton. Lupton's six-foot-four forward, Ron Ceretto, dominated the defensive boards and held Johnny to his lowest scoring game of the season. Ceretto was effective in cutting off the passing lane from the Mead guards so Johnny could not get the ball.

Coach Beers concluded that Johnny was not hustling and voiced his displeasure at a time-out in the fourth quarter. "Johnny, you're just standin' around out there. You've got to keep movin' and move toward the ball."

Johnny, frustrated and angered by his lack of offensive output, became enraged and lashed back at Coach Beers. "Jesus Christ, Coach," he said. "What do you want me to do? Nobody's gettin' the ball to me!"

"C-cut out that c-cussin'," said Coach Beers angrily.

"Goddamn it, Coach, I can't help it. It ain't my fault!" Johnny yelled back defiantly.

"W-well, if you're goin' to talk like that, you can just s-sit down for a while and c-cool off a bit, Mr. Schell," Coach Beers said sternly. Looking at Rollie, he said, "Y-you get in there for Johnny."

Ft. Lupton beat us that night 49–43. Johnny got back in the game, but he ended up with only five points. Johnny showered and dressed. He said nothing. He left the locker room with his duffel bag strapped over his shoulder. He did not say goodbye to his teammates. He had not even bothered to pack his perspiration-soaked uniform. It was still lying on the floor.

Minutes later, Coach Beers walked into the locker room where his team was still dressing. He noticed Johnny's uniform wadded in a heap. Picking it up, he asked out loud, "What is this?" Seeing the number 44 on the jersey, he knew instantly that it was Johnny's. "Where's Johnny?" he asked.

"I dunno," I said. "He left a couple of minutes ago."

Coach Beers picked up the trunks and jersey and handed them to Larry Nuss, the team manager.

"Here," he said, "put these in your bag and take them back to school."

The bus returned to Mead without Johnny. Johnny had not waited for the bus; he had ridden home with his girlfriend Irene. She was driving his car.

On Monday, Johnny talked to Coach Beers. No one knew what was said; what went on during that lunch-hour discussion was between the two of them. However, it was apparent that they had settled their differences. Johnny was in the starting lineup on Tuesday night when we played Eaton, winning 36–34.

Thereafter, Mead went into a downslide and lost to both Ault and Windsor. Windsor won the league outright with a 13-and-1 record, and Mead tied with Ft. Lupton for second place at 10 and 4. The District 2 tournament was scheduled the following week. Nine teams were slated to play in the tourney, so the top two teams, Windsor and Mead, had a playoff first to determine which team would enter the winner's bracket and which would move into consolation play. The game, played on a neutral court in Loveland High School's gym, was a disaster for Mead, losing 60–34. Mead went into consolation play at the Colorado A&M College gym in Fort Collins, defeating Berthoud and then losing to Lafayette in the consolation final.

Although the '53–'54 basketball season had ended for Mead High, we took pride knowing that our second-place finish in the league with a 10-and-4 record had been one of the best for our school in the last decade. The pride of the community and of the school for Mead's basketball program remained steadfast. In his two years at Mead, Coach Beers had moved the basketball program forward, and now it was poised to move to the next level with an excellent crop of junior and senior players, all experienced and dedicated to play next year. The careers of Connie Hopp, Johnny Schell, and Ralph Biederman had ended, and now they were passing on their winning legacy to us.

The '53–'54 season had been one of learning for my sophomore and junior teammates, my three brothers, and me. My triplet brothers and I had been given a lot of valuable playing time, and so had brother Jerry. Each game night had been an opportunity to compete against opponents who were bigger, better, and stronger. Next year, Jerry and us triplets would be playing together as seasoned, experienced basketball players and still with Allen Thompson and Jerry Sitzman at our sides. Juniors Lawrence Jensen and George Flores would also be moving up to help out.

Throughout the season, seniors Connie Hopp, Johnny Schell, and Ralph Biederman had worked with us Newtons on our shortcomings, guiding us with their mentoring, badgering, and encouragement. Our collaborative play with these three seniors provided valuable experiences that would pay great dividends. With the nurturing leadership of Connie, Johnny, and Ralph, the '53–'54 competition had truly been a learning season for us.

In this same season of '53–'54, our eighth-grade brother, Dave, coached by James Beers, had led his junior high team to win the Poudre Valley League Junior High Tournament. Next year, Dave would be a freshman, and it was certain that he would be ready to play competitive varsity basketball with his triplet brothers and his brother Jerry. Next year, it was probable that Dave, we triplets, and Jerry would be playing on the A-team for Mead High School. Next year, believed to be for the first time in our nation's history, it was probable that there would be five brothers, perhaps as starters, playing on a high-school basketball team.

I finished the season with regret. I had remembered Coach Beers's bitter disappointment of last year when our junior high basketball team was defeated in the league tournament. I had hoped my brothers and I could help him and our varsity team win a tournament this year, but my hope was not realized.

A-Team. Front Row, L-R: Richie Newton, Mike Eckel, Rollie Newton, Ralph Biederman, Keith Stotts, Ronnie Newton; Back Row, L-R: Coach Jim Beers, Larry Nuss (Mgr.), Allen Thompson, Johnny Schell, Jerry Sitzman, Connie Hopp, Jerry Newton, Ronald Vogel (Mgr.), 1955.
Mead Consolidated Schools Yearbook

Back Row, L-R: Barbara Graham, Elaine Becker; Front Row, L-R: Colleen Wright, Mary Helen Olson, 1955.
Mead Consolidated Schools Yearbook

Chapter 18

Brothers

I read in a sports magazine that Ronald Weber gave me about two sets of three brothers playing college basketball. It especially piqued my interest because I dreamed that one day Richie, Rollie, and I would be a threesome playing basketball for a college somewhere, I hoped in Colorado. In the '54–'55 basketball season, the three of us had played on Mead High School's varsity, along with our brother Jerry. Although we were the first foursome of brothers to play at the same time, I learned that in the school's short history of thirty-four years, there were several pairs of brothers who played together at Mead.

I was a sophomore when Supt. Carl Carlson asked me to help custodian Marion Humphrey clean out the athletics storage area in the basement next to the boys' shower room at Mead High. Mr. Humphrey had been custodian for the school since it opened in 1918. Early on, he saw most of the basketball games played in the Farmer's Union Town Hall before the school gym was built in 1938.

"Back then," said Mr. Humphrey, "Mead was playing schools such as Gill, Gilcrest, Kersey, Milliken, and Galeton. Those schools were still purty small. Mead had forty or fifty high-school students, and there were probably 150 in grade school."

I saw some of the old score books on the equipment room shelves. It was a surprise to me to learn that many of the area farmers and townspeople had attended Mead and had played basketball. "Hap Howlett told me he played in the town hall," I said.

"He sure did," said Mr. Humphrey. "And I think his brother Bub also played. Back then, both the girls and the boys played. The girls stopped playin' each other sometime in the '40s. I don't know why. I guess they just liked cheerin' and yellin' on the sidelines better. I dunno."

"These books show that my brother Orbin played with my cousins, Jim and Merle Newton, sons of my uncle Spaulding," I said.

"I remember all of 'em," said Mr. Humphrey. "They called Merle Red. He was a real carrot-top."

"Carl Hansen, who plays with my brother Dave on their junior high team, said his uncle Herb played. Do ya remember 'im?" I asked.

"Yes, I do," said Mr. Humphrey. "He was a tall lanky kid, just like all the other Hansens who played."

"Ya know," I said, "these ol' score books show there were a lot of brothers on Mead's teams."

"That's right. Mead has a history of brothers playin' at one time or another," said Mr. Humphrey. "The Mudd brothers [Glenn and Clarence] played together, and so did the Adlers [Delmer and Art]." Your brother Ray didn't play basketball. He liked to sing, and he was more interested in 4-H stuff than he was sports. But I watched your brothers Jack and Tom play. Your brother Jack's team played in the state tournament."

"Well, next year, I hope there will be five Newton brothers playin' for Mead," I said. "Us triplets will be juniors, and Jerry will be a senior, and Dave will be a freshman. I think we'll all get to play on the A-string."

"Mead's never had five brothers playin' at the same time," said Mr. Humphrey. "The most has been two. Five playin' has probably never happened before anywhere."

We five were physically and mentally strong and well prepared to compete as basketball athletes. For the previous three years, we had spent our summers working in the sugar beet fields of Weld County with backbreaking hard toil that toned our muscles and conditioned our bodies for the physical challenges of basketball. Further, the mental and psychological demands that my brothers and I faced each day, working as a team in the farm fields in the heat of summer, had given us a toughness that would serve us well on the basketball court. Hoeing and thinning beets required teamwork to get the job done. Everyone had to contribute. Slackardness was not permitted. Each had to do his share. The five of us were never intimidated by challenges posed in the fields or on the basketball court. Working together was something we had done all our lives. A team of five brothers was especially conducive to basketball, and with many years of experience working and playing together, we brothers were developing into a formidable unit. Our presence ignited great interest throughout Northeastern Colorado and brought commanding notoriety to our school, our team, and our town.

As a high-school senior, Jerry was eighteen years of age and a year and a half older than us triplets. At six-foot-one and weighing 150 pounds, Jerry's facial features resembled our dad's, and he sported a crew cut. As a youngster, Jerry liked to build things, preferring that to sports, but very often he could be persuaded to play on a sports team. Of all the sports he tried, basketball was his favorite.

In our early teens, Jerry and I worked as a pair doing daily chores, while Richie and Rollie performed similar duties as a duo. As Jerry approached his midteens, he became more independent and began working outside the home. As a consequence, Dave became my work partner. As a junior, Jerry bought his first car. He began working evenings at the Longmont Drugstore, where he swept and scrubbed floors and washed windows.

Jerry had sustained a broken leg as a three-year-old when he fell down a stairs, and when he was eight years old, he broke it again. He had jumped onto the running board of our brother-in-law Wilbur's car as he was backing out of the driveway. Jerry slipped off and fell behind the front wheel, which ran over his ankle and broke the foot of the same leg he had broken years before. It was in a cast for a long while, and when the cast was removed, Jerry continued to walk and run with a slight limp, hampering his mobility as an athlete.

Dave, the youngest of us five, was fourteen years old and a freshman good enough to play on the A-team. Dave, with his crew-cut hair and good looks, was described as the "cutest of the lot" by the older girls in the school. Dave had an unassuming demeanor and did not take himself seriously. Although spending a lot of sports playtime with us triplets, Dave, in his younger years, preferred to play "cowboys and Indians" with younger brothers Marc and Frosty.

At an early age, Dave displayed an unusual capacity to endure long periods of physical stress. He was an exceptionally hard worker, and he loved the challenge associated with a physical task. He had no trouble competing physically with us, and he was a consummate teammate in any game of two on two, no matter the sport. As an athlete, Dave practiced a technique incessantly, often into the dark of night, never satisfied with his proficiency. Although a year and a half younger, Dave was stronger than me, and he could outrun me in the fifty-yard dash. His muscular calves enabled him to jump unusually high, higher than any of us four elder brothers. As a freshman, Dave was five-foot-eleven and weighed 145 pounds. Mom attributed Dave's rapid growth to his huge appetite; Dave ate everything Mom placed in front of him—in large amounts.

Fiercely competitive in all facets of our lives, we often resorted to physical fights to settle disagreements, which usually resulted in nothing more than wrestling matches where we tried to pin one another to the ground or floor. As a fourteen-year-old, I attacked Dave as a way to solve a serious argument that started at the town park during a workup softball game. Dave immediately pinned me. Thinking this must have been a fluke, I went at him again. To my surprise, he pinned me a second time. In my mind, Dave had humiliated me in front of my brothers and friends. I had been unexpectedly disgraced and embarrassed. Thereafter, I never tried to settle an argument with Dave by physical means. Dave had clearly demonstrated to me, my brothers, and my friends that he, a mere sixth-grader, was already my physical superior.

Although encounters with Dave were rather benign, fighting with Rollie was another story. Rollie came at me with clenched fists and slugs to the midsection. Rollie was tough, particularly in a defensive mode. He would not accept mistreatment from anyone and would fight back with more force than was inflicted on him. Rollie had weighed a little over five pounds at birth, the smallest of us triplets. In our elementary grades, his height and weight were slightly less than Richie's and mine. But this changed dramatically when he entered junior high. Maturing more rapidly than the two of us, Rollie became the biggest and the fastest runner. As a junior, he was six feet tall and weighed 145 pounds.

In contrast to Richie and me, Rollie's skin had a slightly darker pigmentation. As a consequence, he tanned easily and suffered no burned skin when exposed to the sun as did we light-complexioned brothers. Like our dad, his face was thin, and his eyes were set back and overshadowed by the ridge of his eyebrows. His darkened hair was parted and combed in pompadour style in front, which he twisted and turned with his left hand while sitting idly or reading a book.

If Rollie did not like something, he was brutally frank in expressing how he felt. He disliked milk and avoided drinking it if not forced by Mom. Rollie began reading adult novels at an early age. He borrowed books from classmate Gary Olson, and he checked them out from the Weld County bookmobile when it came to Mead. If you did not know his whereabouts, you could always find him in the upstairs bedroom staring into a book. An individualist, Rollie was the first to abandon our practice of "dressing alike." In junior high, it was discovered that Rollie had poor eyesight, so the Kiwanis Club of Longmont bought him a pair of glasses. We called him Four-Eyes, the name assigned to him by our friend Ronald Weber.

At birth, Richie's weight of a little over six pounds was intermediate between Rollie's and mine. He inherited his broad face and square jaw from Mom, making him the most handsome of us triplets. The end of his nose had a slight downturn, differentiating his looks further from his fraternal triplet brothers. In our elementary grades, Richie was heavier than Rollie and me and was somewhat chubby. Mom referred to him as Fatso-dolen.

Unlike Rollie, Richie was not combative, and I never got into fights or arguments with him. However, Richie was a mischievous practical joker, and I was often on the receiving end of his annoying pranks. His personality always seemed to connect with that of Mom and his teachers, and he could easily extract a smile from them no matter what the situation or what wrong he may have committed.

As a junior, he was five-foot-eleven and weighed 140 pounds. Like Rollie, Richie's hair was dark brown, parted, and curled in front. He walked with his toes pointing inward in pigeon-toed fashion, and his thin calves and muscular thighs were deprecatively perceived by him to be "bird legs." None of us were swift runners, and Richie was faster than me. In school, Richie's favorite subject was history, and in his personal life, he was a historian. He remembered the exact details and dates of most events, family or otherwise. Like all of us, Richie read the newspapers daily.

My facial features were a blend of my triplet brothers. I inherited a tinge of curliness in my light-brown hair from Dad, and my pompadour front had a long curl to it. Because I was the heaviest of us three when born, I always assumed that I had been born first, a "stated fact" that was never disputed by either Mom or Dad (and, to this day, still not totally resolved). As a junior and shorter and lighter than any of my four brothers, I was five-foot-ten and weighed 135 pounds. I was a serious student, intrigued most by the study of science, particularly biology. Because of my penchant for strict adherence to the teachings and practices of Catholicism, it was predictable for me to "stand on high moral ground" on issues of an ethical nature, which often placed me in direct conflict with friends and family. Like many young males influenced by the clergy and the rituals of Catholicism, I too had thoughts of becoming a priest.

Our brother Marc was twelve years old and in the sixth grade when he was tapped to be a student manager of our basketball team by Coach Adams. Marc was beginning to become a good player in his own right, having played in our backyard with his elder brothers, where he received no special treatment. Constantly competing with brothers much older than him, Marc was verbally combative. He took no abuse or nonsense from anyone, not even us, his elder brothers, or from our teammates or coaches. He was smart, independent, and defiant.

As the '55–'56 high-school basketball season began, there were five brothers on the team and another serving as student manager. Six

Newtons were poised to face opponents with fierce familial cooperation, loyalty, and competitiveness. Rather than Mead High, our opposing foes were jokingly referring to us as "Newtonville High"—an endearing phrase coined by townspeople and residents from all over Northeastern Colorado, not only in reference to our five-brother team but also to our large family of twenty siblings, who accounted for nearly 10 percent of the population of Mead. Newtonville High was a team with a long-established Newton family tradition dating back to two decades, when eldest brother Orbin and several of our cousins first stepped on the court to play for Mead.

L-R: Richie Newton, Rollie Newton, and Ronnie Newton, 1956
– Mead Consolidated Schools Yearbook

L-R: Dave Newton, Marc Newton, and Jerry Newton, 1956.
Mead Consolidated Schools Yearbook

Chapter 19

Brothers Court

By mid-November '55, our high-school football season had ended. Although Mead had not won a single game, we were not demoralized, thanks to the leadership and encouragement that Coach Jack Adams had given us each week. Our young team and our new coach learned from our failures. We all knew that come next fall, things would be different. For now, we had time to learn from the past and focus on the immediate future. Basketball would start soon, and we all looked forward to this with great anticipation and excitement. We knew basketball was where our skill and interest levels lay, and we were ready.

Nearly thirty of us assembled in the gym to hear what Coach Adams would tell us about the upcoming basketball season. There was a mixture of sophomores, juniors, and seniors with one freshman invited to attend—Dave Newton. Coach Adams had observed Dave's athletic skills as a football player, and he was certain Dave could play at the varsity level as a freshman. Dave had played second-string quarterback behind me and was first-string safety on defense. Traditionally, at Mead, freshmen played at the junior high level with eighth-graders, but Dave's precocious maturity and skills led Adams to believe he could contribute significantly to the varsity A-team's success.

Adams had replaced Jim Beers, who had realized his coaching interest was best satisfied by working with players of a younger age.

Beers resigned from Mead and moved to the mountain town of Craig to take a coaching job in the junior high school. This was Jack Adams's first coaching stint after graduation from Colorado State College of Education.

Coach Adams and student-teacher Coach Richard Alsup stood before us as we climbed on the bleachers to hear what they had to say.

"We'll have our first practice on Monday," said Coach Adams. "We'll have tryouts starting Tuesday, and by the end of the week, we'll know at what level we want you to play. Practices begin at three-thirty and will end at five-thirty. You'll be outta here by six."

Then Lawrence Jensen interjected, "I heard there was a town team here in Mead that wants to play us in a practice game. Our senior class was thinking about having that game as a fundraiser for our class project. We want to make enough money to buy a new scoreboard for the gym. Are we going to have that game?"

"I think we might," said Coach Adams. "Ronald Weber asked me about it. He said he, Loe Hernandez, Vernon Widger, and several others who graduated would like to play us. Mr. Carlson said we could do it and that most likely, we could have it on Tuesday of Thanksgiving week."

By the end of tryouts that first week, Coach Adams had selected a team of ten for his varsity A-string: Jerry Sitzman, Lawrence Jensen, George Flores, Mike Eckel, Allen Thompson, and the five Newtons. These ten conveniently provided two squads for scrimmage purposes, but often Walter Ayres, Lyle Schaefer, Jim Landolt, and Paul Hopp were brought up from the B-team to practice with us.

Coach Alsup and Mr. Schaefer had their B-stringers at one end of the court, and Coach Adams took the other end for the A-stringers. Earlier that fall, Adams had asked Mr. Humphrey to mount two backboards and goals on the balcony, facilitating more shooting and free-throw practice for Mead's nearly thirty players.

There was great enthusiasm with the team as the date of the "practice game" with the Mead locals approached. Adams had spent the previous two weeks concentrating on individual fundamentals: passing, dribbling, rebounding, and defending. We had had little opportunity for team play, so a team competition with a crowd on hand was a very exciting proposition.

Laura Dreier Newton was especially looking forward to this date. She had started attending basketball games the previous year, watching her triplet sons and son Jerry play B-string basketball and then suit up for the A-string as substitutes. This night, she would have five sons playing. Her next-to-the-youngest son Marc would be on the team bench as student manager and ball boy. Her youngest son Frosty would sit next to her, watching intently as he visualized that someday he too would play for Mead High along with his brother Marc. Her husband, James Elmer Newton, would remain at home. His interest in watching his sons play had not yet been kindled. That would occur later.

Laura sensed the cold night air as she emerged from her house to walk to the gym five blocks away with nine-year-old son Frosty beside her. "Hurry," she said as Frosty lagged behind. "We don't want to be late. The game starts in ten minutes." Laura's scarf, which had been wrapped around her head and tied under her chin, was draped around her neck and shoulders as she and Frosty entered the gym foyer.

"Hello, Mrs. Newton," said Mr. Carlson as he saw her approaching his table with a dollar bill in hand and Frosty at her side. "That'll be 75¢ for you and a quarter for the young man."

"Hello to you as well," Laura responded. "It's a cold night, isn't it?"

"It's supposed to get near freezing tonight," said Mr. Carlson. "I hope you enjoy the game. We have a pretty good crowd here tonight, with it being a practice game and all. It will make a good bit of money for the senior class."

"That's one of the reasons I'm here," said Laura. "Jerry wanted me to come. I guess his class wants to get a new scoreboard. He said they want to get a new one like Windsor and Eaton have, one where the numbers light up."

"Well, tonight's fundraiser will certainly get them started toward that goal," said Mr. Carlson.

As Laura walked across the east end of the gym toward the south-side bleachers, she spotted Barbara Graham's parents, Martin and Mary, sitting on the top row with their backs against the wall. Looking up at them, she asked, "Is there room up there for us?"

"We'll make room," said Martin. He motioned for Mr. and Mrs. Hopp to move over and then stepped down to the floor to help Laura to a seat beside them. The Hopps shuffled again to make more room for Frosty and Laura. Beads of perspiration sprung up on Laura's forehead as her body began to adjust to the warm temperature of the gym. She looked around her. Bub Howlett was sitting to her right next to the Hopps. Mr. and Mrs. Delbert Thompson were on her left several yards away. Thirty or more pep club girls dressed in white sweaters with block-letter Ms on their chests had assembled on her lower left. Down on the floor, she saw Marion Humphrey standing near the locker room door with a dust mop in his hand. Mr. Humphrey was talking to Mike Eckel's dad, Frank, who was drinking a bottled Coke.

The sparse crowd of 150 fans watched the cheerleaders go through their orchestrated motions as they, synchronized with the pep club girls, shouted words of encouraging support to the team of boys that was about to enter into competition with men who graduated from Mead several years before.

The lone and only referee, Greeley-ite Bill Elliott, had invited the captain of each team to the center of the gym to explain the rules peculiar to the gym. Jerry Newton and Vernon Widger listened intently as Elliott stated, "The ball is out of bounds if it hits the large 'movie box' behind the basket over there," as he pointed. "It's also out of bounds if it bounces off the balcony or off the side-mounted baskets. Same goes for the ceiling. It's out-of-bounds."

Finishing pregame warm-ups, the teams sat on each end of a single bench row along the north wall of the gym. Ronald Weber coached the graduate team. They were dressed in shorts of a variety of colors and wore orange jerseys with a scripted "Mead" across their chests and black numbers on their backs, previously worn by players such as Don Owen and Eddie Rademacher during the late '40s. Coach Adams had retrieved these faded garments from the depths of cardboard boxes storing sports uniforms in the basement closet adjacent to the east end of the gym.

Facing his team, Coach Adams said, "Let's start this with all Newtons. Jerry, you take center. Rollie and Dave, you guys play forward. Richie and Ronnie, you take the guard spots."

We five brothers shed our black warm-up pants and jackets emblazoned with large orange Ms on the left side, the same warm-ups our brother Tom and his teammates had worn six years before. Displaying white jerseys with orange numbers, our fivesome walked to the center of the floor for the opening tip-off. Smiles were flashed as each of us shook hands with our familiar opponent friends. We Newtons had played against all these guys many times before in our own backyard, and although they were all adults and had grown into manhood, their size and maturity did not intimidate us. We were confident we could outmaneuver them with quickness and skillful shooting.

Jerry and Herb Newman squared off for the opening tip-off. Loe Hernandez lined up to guard me, and Leroy Blazon guarded Richie. Vernon Widger defended against Dave, and Ronald Weber took Rollie. Referee Elliott blew the whistle and tossed the ball up. A loud roar from the crowd marked the beginning of the season as Loe Hernandez took possession of the ball with a tip from six-foot-four Herb Newman.

Laura Dreier Newton and the crowd watched, but they did not realize the significance of what had just happened. Five brothers had started on the Mead High School basketball team, a first for Mead High School and undoubtedly a first in the nation's high-school basketball history. Only Adams realized the significance of what he had just done. Laura attached no special meaning to what she was witnessing. Not understanding all the subtleties of the game, she attributed no importance to all her sons starting and all five of them playing together at the same time. This was not news to her. After all, they had been doing this all their lives.

Likewise, those in the crowd saw nothing unusual. They had been seeing bunches of Newtons playing basketball all these years. What else was new? Before anyone present that night could think long and intensely enough to appreciate the significance of the event, Adams started substituting, and the five Newton brothers playing on the same team at one time that night ended. Adams wanted to see how everyone on his team performed. Fourteen players played, including Paul Hopp, Carl Hansen, Jim Landolt, and Walter Ayres.

In the beginning, Herb Newman dominated the game, with Weber and Loe getting the ball inside to the tall lanky southpaw. However, by the fourth quarter, Coach Adams's high-schoolers put the game out of reach from the former students of Mead High, who were bending over, hands on their hips, and gasping for air. They could not keep up with the fast-breaking, rapid pace that their younger opponents inherently played. They were no match for Adams's well-conditioned thoroughbreds, who had just finished a brutal football season.

For the next two weeks, Coach Adams scrimmaged our team at every practice, mixing and choosing, trying to find the right combination in preparation for the first nonconference tilt with Windsor. Not wanting his team to tire before their opponents did, he initiated running drills of long duration, ensuring that the long-wind capacity of his team was beyond that of the competition.

At the end of drills each day, Rollie began to experience a dull ache in his chest. He had experienced this pain during football season, but it was periodic, and he had dismissed it as pain inflicted by physical contact. This time, the pain was there after every basketball practice, and he became concerned.

One night Rollie said to Richie and me as we undressed for bed, "This pain in my chest is starting to get worse, and I'm short of breath, and I have a little dizziness. I think I better go to the doctor. If Mom was here, she could get me in to see Dr. Cooke."

"She won't be back from New York for another week," I said. "Ray called Dad last night, said he changed her flight schedule and extended her stay another couple of days."

Overhearing the conversation, Jerry stepped into the room and asked, "What was it that Cooke said when he examined you for football?"

"He found a heart murmur," said Rollie. "But he said it was okay for me to play."

"We better get you in to see Dr. Cooke right away," said Jerry. "Let's go tomorrow morning. We'll see if he can fit you in. We'll take a chance."

Upon examination, Dr. Cooke attributed the ache Rollie was feeling to the heart murmur he had detected last fall.

"You probably had this when you were a child," Dr. Cooke reminded Rollie. "You probably had strep throat back then, didn't you?"

"I probably did," answered Rollie. "I know a lot of others in the family had it. I heard Mom talkin' about how sick they were."

"Well," said Dr. Cooke, "sometimes the strep bacteria reach the tissue lining of a heart valve and inflame it with infection. The body's immune system then attacks the tissue, and when it is injured, it is called rheumatic fever. The injured rheumatic tissue interferes with your heart valve. The flawed valve function is the murmur I detected with my stethoscope."

Although Dr. Cooke had consented for Rollie to play football last fall, this time, he said, "I think you need to cease playing basketball and sit out a year to see if this murmur eases up. I'll write you a prescription for digitalis. It's the standard medicine for this sort of thing. We'll keep you on this for a while and see how it goes. Get as much rest as you can, and lay off the physical activity."

Jerry and Rollie stopped at the Longmont Drugstore to pick up the medication. Rollie took the digitalis religiously for the next several months and took naps after school whenever he could. By spring, he appeared to have recovered, but he missed the whole basketball season, and as a consequence, the five Newton brothers never played together again on Mead's varsity A-team.

At the beginning of the season, the Greeley Tribune had picked Mead to win the North Central League. Mr. Carlson had pinned the article on the bulletin board outside his office. The Greeley Tribune said the following:

> Mead is loaded and ready. The Bulldogs have it this year
> with seven topflight lettermen back—good size, good
> defense, and good teamwork. Back are Jerry Sitzman,

Allen Thompson, George Flores, and four Newton brothers, Jerry, Richie, Ronnie, and Rollie. This year, freshman Dave Newton is now eligible to play.

Mead won the North Central League title that year but without Rollie's help. Rollie sat on the sidelines, sometimes keeping score and sometimes sitting in the stands with Mary LaVerne Graham, his girlfriend.

Rollie was happy when Dr. Cooke gave him the green light to play both football and basketball his senior year. This time, he would perform with his senior triplet brothers, Ronnie and Richie, and with sophomore brother Dave. But there was a bittersweetness to this. Jerry had graduated in the spring of '56. He would not be playing. The Newton five would never again play together at the same time on Mead High School's basketball team. A historical moment had vanished.

Four brothers—three of them regulars—are members of Mead High School's excellent basketball team. They are the Newtons. Left to right are Jerry, Dick, Dave and Ron. The team already has won eight of nine games and is averaging more than 72 points a game.
—*Rocky Mountain News Photos by Bob Talkin*

Frosty Newton, 1956.
Mead Consolidated Schools Yearbook

Laura Dreier Newton, 1956.
Newton Family Album

Chapter 20

Coach Adams

History is filled with notable instances in which a person has been at the right place at exactly the right time. Listening to a conversation between my dad and my career-marine brother Jack one evening, I heard Dad say, "FDR is the only one that could have helped us win the war. The same can be said about the Great Depression. If he hadn't brought us out of it, there would be no way in hell we could have beaten the Japs or the Germans, for that matter."

"Well, they say the same thing about Eisenhower," said Jack. "We were lucky to have him there to beat the Germans. They say no one else could have done it."

And from the perspective of my brothers and me and our teammates, we thought the same could be said for Jack Adams and our Mead High School basketball program. Our '55–'56 team was poised and ready to be led by a coach with wisdom and knowledge, one who could wrap his arms around our basketball talents and lead Mead High to a level of achievement greater than ever. We were ready for Coach Adams, and it turned out that he was ready for us.

On a Sunday morning in the summer of '56, as I was walking home from church, I saw Ronald Weber's Buick parked on Main Street in front of the Handy Corner. I hadn't seen Weber since basketball season ended, and I went in to visit him. Sander Adler and his wife, Esther, had purchased the Handy Corner from the Georges who had previously bought it from the Sniders. "Sandy" had quit farming and moved into town. In addition to running the soda fountain and ice cream shop, the Adlers were serving sandwiches and hamburgers and were still selling over-the-counter medications.

"Hello, Mrs. Adler," I said as I walked past the soda fountain, where she was preparing banana splits for Weber and Herb Newman, who were sitting in a booth in the back of the store. I hadn't seen Herb Newman for a couple of years. Herb left Mead before his senior year. Mrs. Emily Newman, still teaching the fifth grade at Mead, rented an apartment in Longmont to establish residency so Herb could go to Longmont High School.

"I wanted to play basketball and football at a larger school," Herb said before he left Mead. "And my mom thought I'd get a better education in Longmont. My brother Clarence didn't do well at the Colorado School of Mines, and my mom thought it was because he never learned what he needed at Mead."

Herb, a six-foot-four southpaw, was attending the University of Colorado and had tried out for the CU basketball team. Weber was learning carpentry and construction working with his dad and was playing softball and coaching baseball for Longmont teenagers.

I sat down next to Weber, ordered a Nehi orange soda, and began to listen to the conversation.

"I've thought a lot 'bout what makes a good coach and why some people are better at it than others," said Weber. "I coached all you Newtons before you became teenagers, and I do some coaching now. I think I know how to do it."

"When playing sports at Mead, I had three different coaches," said Herb. "In junior high, I had Edwin Spencer, and in high school, I was coached by Tom Petersen and Brian Schmidt."

"I had all of them too," said Weber. "Then Schmidt left, and Jim Beers came."

"Both Schmidt and Beers coached me too," I interjected. "Petersen was here when I was in junior high, but he left after two years. It seems that all our coaches stay just two years, and then they go somewhere else. I'm glad we've got Jack Adams now. He's a real good coach."

"I think he's the best coach Mead's ever had," said Weber.

"You know, Adams came to see me in Mead several times before he told Mr. Carlson he was going to take the job," said Weber. "He wanted to know all 'bout you guys. I told 'im all five of you were good athletes, 'specially in basketball. But I told him you could play any sport. I told 'im there were a lot of good athletes at Mead besides you Newtons. He said he wanted to coach track. That was the sport he did best at Greeley, where he went to college. He told me he also played football in high school and college."

Then Weber laughed and looked at me, giving me a slap on the shoulder as he boasted, "I told him you guys were so goddamn good because I was the one who coached you."

"Also," said Herb, "you were always playin' against us, guys much older than you. I think that's how you learned to play so well. I think a good coach is one who has played the game and has participated in a lot of other sports too."

"You're right on," said Weber. "I think I'm a good baseball coach because I've played a lot of softball, and I know how to hit. I learned good techniques of hittin' by playin' with you Newtons in your backyard. We used a tennis ball instead of a baseball. We took turns pitchin', and we learned how to put a lot of movement on it. We could throw curves and sinkers."

"Yal, Richie had a good curveball and could throw real hard," I said. "And I learned to throw a knuckleball that would drop suddenly, just like it was fallin' off a table."

"I remember very well, Ronnie," Weber said with a chuckle. "I used to wait and anticipate when you would throw it, and when my timin' was right, I'd come right underneath it, and I'd knock it 'out of the park' and over the fence into Grover Roberts's horse corral."

"I couldn't ever strike you out," I said. "You'd homer, battin' right- or left-handed. It didn't matter which way you went."

"I'm a real good hitter now," said Weber. "I think it helped me to watch the fast movement of a tennis ball. I don't have any trouble hittin' a curveball. Now I only bat left-handed. Playin' with you Newtons really helped me with my hittin'. now I'm the battin' coach for some of the high-schoolers in Longmont. I think I'm a good coach because I've played a lot myself."

"I think you're right," said Herb as he took a bite of his melted banana split. "My freshman basketball coach at CU played in college. He was a real good coach. He left CU when he was offered a head coaching job."

Coach Adams too had played the games he coached. He played in high school under Coach Jim Baggot. Baggot was a winning basketball coach from Greeley High School who had taken his team to the State playoffs in '55 and '57. In 1957, he won the Class AA boys' basketball state championship. Adams had learned from Baggot, and he sought Baggot's advice when there was need. Adams played football and ran track at Greeley High and at the Colorado State College of Education. His college classmate and our assistant coach, Bill Callahan, said to me, "Adams was faster than a galloping horse on a moving freight train."

One day, Coach told me, "I hold the record at CSCE for the hundred-yard dash at 9.8 seconds. I was clocked once at 9.6 seconds, but it didn't enter the record books because I had a tailwind."

Coaching at Mead was Adams's first professional position. He had signed on with Mr. Carlson for $2,900 a year with the responsibility of coaching three sports and teaching physical education and driver education. He and his wife, Arden, and young daughter lived in a rented house two blocks north of the school. Mrs. Adams, also a graduate of CSCE, taught physical education and was Mead's pep club sponsor.

Coach was six feet tall and muscular. He was accustomed to doing chin-ups regularly and had strong biceps and broad shoulders. He was fair skinned and sensitive to sunlight, and his gold-blond hair had thinned visibly. He wore horn-rimmed glasses, and when not in the gym or on the athletic field, he sported a bow tie.

Coach did not practice any formal religion, but in my eyes, his spiritual side was demonstrated in many ways. He was never profane but would discipline those who were with running extra laps or doing push-ups. He knew the significance of sport in high school and in the lives of young men. In a letter he sent to every member of our football team at the beginning of the season, he wrote,

> The sad thing about high-school athletics is that once spent, they can never be relived. Yours are here now, not last year or ten years from today but now. You are about to make athletics in high school a memory that will last your entire life. Make the most of what you have to offer.

> REMEMBER: There are no bargains or easy roads in the field of athletics. You get out of a sport exactly what you put in to it.

Coach studied each game he was coaching. He read books and posed questions to experts. He learned from his mistakes. In our Mead High football season in 1955, he started us out with an offensive formation that he called the "Short Punt," which he abandoned after the second game. He realized his offense was a failure; it was easily predictable to the defense, and it provided too few options. He replaced it with the "Split T." Weber told me he learned about this new "T" offense by reading a book written by Bud Wilkinson of the University of Oklahoma and from talking to Longmont coach Gil Everly, who was winning a lot of games with it.

Coach did not make great strides that first year with the "Split T"; our team scored only two touchdowns, and we never won a game. Our lateness in the season in instituting the new offense hurt us, and this, coupled with our small athletes and lack of experience, was too much to overcome. However, we improved the next year, and by November '56, our experienced Mead team was in contention for the North Central League title.

Weber and Coach saw each other frequently. They used to meet at the Handy Corner and talk about sports and coaching.

"Adams served in the air force on a base somewhere in Kansas," said Weber. "He said he developed skills of leadership and established a pattern of discipline, habits that are necessary for success in the military. He said he had to give orders and take orders. He said he learned what it takes to be a leader and what it takes to follow. He said you gotta know how to do both if you're goin' to be a good coach. I've watched 'im, and I've listened to 'im. He'll inspire the hell outta ya when he talks."

Coach had maturity and experience in life. He was more than eight years older than those he was coaching. This age difference proved valuable to him, and he could draw on his knowledge of life and athletic experiences. Although he was in his first year of coaching, he had strong opinions about athletics, basketball, and life in general.

One night at the end of practice, he assembled us on the bleachers before he sent us to the showers. He said, "You know, I don't think you guys need to wear those kneepads. I think they just slow you down. Why don't you try playin' without them? I think you'll find that you won't miss them at all, and you'll play even better. None of the college teams are wearin' 'em. Tomorrow I want you to leave 'em in your lockers and see how it feels. Also, Ronnie"—he looked toward me—"that chain that you're wearin' around your neck is dangerous. I'm afraid somebody is going to grab it, and you'll get cut pretty seriously. I think you need to take it off when you're playin'. I'm afraid you're goin' to get hurt, and I don't want that to happen."

I said nothing. Normally, when a person in authority told me that I had to stop a religious practice I had followed for years and with firm convictions, I would have rebelled and argued. But this time, I would do as Coach said. Both the team and I had developed a powerful sense of trust in him. I would continue to wear the medal, but I would take it off when playing basketball. From then on, I would adhere to whatever Coach said. I would jump off the Denver Elevators if he told me to. I had already sensed that he was a very special person, and I knew we were going to have a good year playing basketball; I knew we would win with skills, not with knee protectors and religious icons.

I saw Coach work out regularly. He was in excellent physical condition. He had Mr. Humphrey construct a chin-up bar adjacent to the football field. He used it himself, and he required all football athletes to use it. Coach could do more chin-ups at one time than all of us on the team put together.

Our basketball workouts included ball handling and passing drills with a lot of running up and down full court. Coach emphasized cardiovascular conditioning. He said, "I don't want to ever lose a basketball game because we got tired and couldn't keep up with our opponents. We have to be in better shape than they are."

A one-on-one drill with two players was often part of our daily workout, emphasizing specific facets of the game, including guarding, dribbling, shooting, blocking out for rebounds, and learning to anticipate where the ball would carom after a shot. Often Coach himself would participate, challenging each player with his superior strength and experience, forcing young players to learn from him and from their mistakes. He had an awkward unorthodox jump shot that originated at his forehead rather than above his head, but he had quick hands and was a good ball handler and an excellent defender.

One afternoon, when I was going one-on-one with Coach, I slapped down on the ball as I tried to take it away from him. Coach stopped to teach me a more effective way. He placed the ball in my hands and demonstrated as he spoke.

"Don't slap down on the ball," he said as he came downward, knocking the ball from my hands. "There will be greater tendency for you to foul, and even if you do get 'all ball' with your hand, the referee will often think it was a foul just because of the downward motion."

Then giving the ball back to me and asking me to hold it again, he showed that it was better for the defender to attempt to gain possession of the ball from an opponent's hands by slapping at it with an upward motion.

Coach posted a daily workout schedule on the west wall of the gym. These drills were all new to us. No coach at Mead ever required individual independent drills. He instituted "skipping rope," and he specified the number of skips he wanted us to take. He designed a drill simulating a "tip-in" when the ball rebounded from the backboard. Standing next to the concrete block wall at the west end of the gym, each of us had to tip the ball against it, with an arm extended above our head and timing the tip from the hand at the height of our jump. After fifty times with one hand, the drill was repeated with the other.

We used a "medicine ball" in passing drills, whereby a heavy large-diameter soft-leather ball stuffed with weights and padding strengthened the muscles of the arms and fingers as the thrower attempted to use the same techniques of throwing a standard regular-sized basketball. All passing, dribbling, and shooting drills were designed by Coach to require his players to be accomplished with either hand.

Coach always provided adequate time from each daily session to practice shooting free throws. He repeatedly said, "Games are won by making foul shots." Often I would shoot foul shots for thirty or more minutes, extending my practice time to 6:00 p.m. Coach said, "Your whole body should be directly facing the basket, and to do this, it is best to place the toes of both feet directly next to the foul line."

He noted that Rollie shot his free throws underhanded, while the other three of us used the typical "set shot" delivery, but he did not ask Rollie to change. "It doesn't matter which way you shoot it," Coach said. "Just keep both feet next to the line, and keep your shoulders square with the basket. Be consistent with your delivery. Use the same motion each time."

I took his advice and developed my free-throw shot by starting it with the ball directly in front of me and close to the middle of my chest. I bent my knees slightly and delivered the ball to the basket with the upward thrust of both my arms and my legs. I always held the ball in the same way, with the seams parallel to the floor and the tips of my fingers notched into them. Before each shot, I visualized how the ball should feel in my right hand as I released it with the appropriate trajectory to the basket. I knew as soon as it left my hand whether it would be another point on the scoreboard or just another missed shot. I repeated these sequences over and over. I used the same motions and the same touches of the ball, and soon, my free-throw percentage improved.

During free-throw practice, my brother Marc stood beneath the basket and tossed the ball back to me after each attempt. One night I was hot and on fire. I made fifty-five straight before I missed.

It did not take long for me to realize that Jack Adams's arrival in Mead and the matriculation of my brothers and me into high school were events whose timing appeared to be inspired by divine providence. These two "partners," a coach and a large cadre of brothers, were a combination that would lead us to great heights as a basketball team. We realized that Coach's arrival was a blessing to our town and our school. I knew my brothers and I were fortunate, and I began to believe in Coach Adams, in everything he said. We labored doggedly and constantly to meet his expectations. In my mind, we Newtons and Coach working together was a "match made in heaven." In refining the rough edges of our raw talent, Coach Adams was a lifesaver.

Coach liked to perform in front of a crowd, both as a coach and as a storyteller. At pep rallies in front of the student body, he would make up yarns about his players and tell jokes about them. He would single out a player and invite him to stand up in front while he good-naturedly poked fun at them, embarrassing them and enjoying it immensely. There, he would stand, hands in his pockets, knees slightly bent, weaving back and forth and spinning his tales.

One afternoon he parodied a situation with Rollie beside him. Coach said, "It was a real close game, and Rollie was on the bench, and I needed to get him back in, so I said to Rollie, 'Rollie! Rollie! Get back in there. We need your athletic support!'

"And then Rollie said, 'Coach, I can't. My mom washed it, and it's still hangin' on the clothesline.'"

The students loved it. They roared with laughter.

Coach led a disciplined life—working out regularly, not using alcohol or tobacco, and never swearing. He expected athletes under his tutelage to do the same. There would absolutely be no smoking or drinking of beer by any member of a team on his watch. Good physical conditioning was the hallmark of his approach to athletics. To win, you had to be in better shape than your opponents. In his mind, an athlete would not be in peak condition if he smoked or drank.

"I don't think you guys should even drink Coke," said Coach. "If you're goin' to drink pop, drink orange or 7Up. They're better for you."

In this vein of leading a disciplined life as an athlete, Coach was concerned about the exorbitant amount of time we Newtons and Allen Thompson spent at the Mead Pool Hall. From his perspective, a pool hall was an environment where the bad habits of drinking, smoking, and swearing could develop or be encouraged.

"You guys are spendin' too much time in the pool hall," he said one day in a pep talk. "That's not a place you should be. Among all those men, you're liable to pick up a lot of their bad habits."

One day when I was sitting in his barber chair, Grover Roberts said to me, "I hear Adams said he didn't want you kids hangin' out in the pool hall."

"Who told you that?" I asked.

"I'm not sayin' who told me," said Mr. Roberts. "All I know is that Adams doesn't know what the hell he's talkin' about. If any of his players are actin' badly, it ain't because they've been here in my pool hall."

I told Weber that Mr. Roberts was angry about what Coach said about the pool hall. Weber said he would mention it to Coach next time he saw him. Later, Weber told me that Coach said he was wrong for saying what he did and that he would apologize to Mr. Roberts. In my view, this was a most admirable gesture. Coach's impeccable integrity and honesty was evident. He admitted he had made a mistake, and he made amends.

Coach was convinced beyond doubt that smoking interfered with athletic performance. He stated this many times. However, smoking was ingrained in the culture of Mead society and, unfortunately, in the culture of the Newton family. All my elder brothers and sisters and my Dad had smoked. Even our junior high coach, Brian Schmidt, was seen standing outside the school building puffing on a cigarette. Smoking was socially acceptable. It was drinking by athletes that was highly disdained.

As a youngster, I had tried smoking many times. My brothers and I had constructed corncob pipes and rolled cigarettes using whatever materials we could find. I found metal tubing behind the Mead Garage that I used for a pipe stem. I stuffed corn silk and coffee grounds and Dad's Prince Albert tobacco into the hollowed-out corncob bowl and attempted to light it. I gave up in frustration when the material failed to ignite. We pulverized dried leaves, rolled them into newspaper, and tried to smoke them with limited success.

My brothers and I swiped cigarettes from anyone who left them around—from Dad, from elder brothers and sisters, and from brothers- and sisters-in-law. We smoked behind the barn, in the tree house, in the town park, and in any place beyond the watchful eye of Mom.

For me, smoking was just taking smoke into my mouth and blowing it out again. I never tried to inhale, and I had never experienced the sensation of the nicotine high that cigarettes provided. In my mind, cigarettes were expensive, and I had other plans for my hard-earned money. Furthermore, my circle of friends, Mike Eckel, Lyle Schaefer, and Gary Olson, did not smoke. Although Mike's mother Marg did, she instructed Mike and me to never start the practice.

"Smoking is a bad habit," she said. "Once you start, it's hard to quit. And if you do start, you'll regret it the rest of your life."

I had no trouble adhering to Coach's dictum on smoking, and drinking beer was never an issue for me. I had tasted beer, and I could not understand how anybody would want to drink the stuff; it was downright repulsive.

I also remembered what our friend Walt Slee told us. "One year, Coach Jim Baggot kicked the whole startin' five off his Greeley High basketball team. He found out that one night they had all gotten drunk on a case of beer." That wasn't a risk I ever wanted to take.

L-R: Jack Adams,
Lawrence Jensen, Russell
Schaefer, and Jerry
Sitzman, 1956.
*Mead Consolidated
Schools Yearbook*

Coach Jack Adams,
1957.
*Mead Consolidated
Schools Yearbook*

L-R: Herbert Newman
and Ronald Weber,
1951.
*Mead Consolidated
Schools Yearbook*

Rollie Newton and
Coach Jack Adams,
1957.
*Mead Consolidated
Schools Yearbook*

Chapter 21

Discipline

In December '55, Coach Adams had guided our basketball team to victory in two nonleague games with Windsor and Johnstown, and now it was the Saturday before Christmas, which fell on the following Wednesday. An unexpected event happened that afternoon, and it threatened the integrity and fabric of our team.

Allen Thompson was driving his '53 Chevrolet on Highway 66, heading west toward Longmont. Rollie was in the back seat with Mary Laverne Graham, while Mary Laverne's elder sister, Barbara, a Mead cheerleader and our classmate, was in front with Allen. It was 2:00 p.m., and they were headed to Longmont for their Christmas shopping. Despite it being rather chilly, Allen had his window halfway down so smoke from his cigar would not remain in the car.

As they talked, they approached an oncoming vehicle heading east on Highway 66. As they got closer, it was clear that this automobile was one that they all recognized—Coach's yellow '52 Chevrolet. He had been to Longmont and was on his way back to Mead.

"Hey, that's Coach Adams!" yelled Barbara. Barbara waved to him as he passed, and so did Allen, the cigar between his fingers.

Rollie, slumped down in the back seat, leaped toward Allen and asked, "Do you think he saw you smokin'?"

"Naw," Allen said confidently. "He probably only saw my hand. He couldn't tell I was holdin' anything."

Rollie slumped back in his seat with a dazed look. "Boy, I hope not. Ya know how he feels about smokin.' He'll kick ya off the team for good if he saw you. He won't put up with it."

Allen turned to Barbara and smiled. "I don't think he will," said Allen. "I don't think he saw anything."

Barbara, staring with eyes wide open, yelled, "I hope not! Our team really needs you." She had watched Allen play as a sophomore as our starting guard. She also knew Allen was top scorer in two games we had just played. Barbara, an ardent supporter of basketball at Mead, knew more than anyone that Allen's absence would seriously jeopardize the success of our season.

That night, Rollie described what happened that afternoon to Richie and me. "Allen always takes chances," said Rollie, "but nobody would've thought Coach would be drivin' down the road then."

The Christmas holiday week was over, and Coach had scheduled practice to resume the day after Christmas. Our whole A-team was there. Rollie, who had been advised by the doctor to sit out for the year, watched us go through our customary drills. With his team off for more than a week, Coach emphasized more running than usual, and it was a quarter after five when he blew his whistle for practice to end.

Dispensing with free-throw practice, he pointed to the bleachers and said, "Everybody, sit over here. I want to talk to you for just a minute or two." Standing before his team, he said. "Ya know we have a rule here that we don't want anyone smokin'. There's talk around town that some of you guys are. I wanna know if it's true. I want you to tell me if you know if anybody here on this team is weedin'."

He reached into his pocket and pulled out small squares of paper, and he handed one to each of us, including Rollie. Reaching into his other pocket, he pulled out pencils and handed them to us. Then with a stern voice, he said, "If you know of someone smokin,' write yes. If you don't know anyone, write no."

My mind began to spin, and I began to rationalize about what I knew about my brothers and teammates. I knew about Allen's cigar, but I rationalized, Smokin' a cigar is different than smokin' a cigarette. Allen was probably not inhalin'. It wasn't hurtin' him.

I had heard Rollie talking about Allen smoking cigarettes, but I had never seen him doing it. I had seen all four of my brothers smoking last summer. I had seen Dave and Richie on one knee next to our upstairs bedroom window, cigarettes in hand, and blowing smoke through the screen to the outside. However, I didn't see them doing it often, but maybe they were doing it more than what I saw. They usually finished practice before I did and were at home before I arrived; maybe I just didn't see them smoking. I didn't think they were inhaling much, and therefore, I didn't think it was all that wrong for them. I couldn't recall seeing Jerry recently smoking.

I also knew that Mike Eckel, Lyle Schaefer, Jerry Sitzman, and Lawrence Jensen didn't smoke. If George Flores did, I had never seen him. Furthermore, I speculated that none had seen any Newtons or Allen smoking. I had the most knowledge of smoking habits of my teammates.

I faced a moral quandary that, in my young mind, was of great proportions, perhaps the most significant of my sixteen years. Sure, I knew who was smoking, but I could not lie. If I did, I would be offending God, and on Saturday, I'd be confessing my sin to Fr. Martin Arno. I also needed to be truthful to my new coach. After all, I trusted in him, and he trusted me. I would lose that trust if he found out I was lying. But I did not want to betray my brothers. I had established a code not to tattle on my brothers about any indiscretions. If Coach was to find out about any misbehaviors, he would have to find out from someone else.

Facing with serious ethical consequences, I was in a substantive logjam, both rationally and emotionally. I kept my head down, not wanting anyone to see I was deeply upset by what Coach was asking us to do. I wrote no, folded the small paper, stepped down from the bleachers, and handed it and the pencil to Coach. I couldn't look at him. I knew I had lied, denying any knowledge of smoking by my brothers and my teammates.

I was the first to enter the shower room, and as I sat down to undress, I started to cry. I had been faithful to my brothers, but I had lied to Coach, and I had violated his code of honesty. I was angry with myself, with my brothers, and with Coach for putting me in the situation. I was questioning my personal worth, not even thinking about the outcome. I was feeling self-pity and was concerned what others might think if they found out I had not told the truth. I quickly showered, washing away all tears. Saying nothing, I picked up my books and notebook and walked home.

That night after supper, I lashed out at my brothers in the upstairs bedroom as we undressed for bed. Standing before Richie, Rollie, and Dave, I said, "I been tellin' you guys to stop smokin', and you won't hear of it. I had to lie and tell Coach I didn't know anything about what you guys were doin'." Unable to control my emotions and my anger, I began to cry again. In a hysterical voice, I bellowed, "When are you guys gonna learn? You know you ain't supposed to be doin' this stuff! When Adams finds out you guys have been smokin', he'll kick ya off for the whole year. There goes our team. We won't win another game!"

My brothers said nothing. They sat on the edge of the bed, not looking at me. This is what they did when they perceived me "on my soap box" and on a rampage directed toward them. In these circumstances, they thought I was portraying myself as a "martyr," and that night was no exception. In their minds, my brothers were again suffering a tongue-lashing from a "holier-than-thou" brother. I was once again trying to reshape their behavior. They had grown weary of listening to their "march-toward-sainthood" sibling. To them, I seemed to cry all the time. I was always more sensitive about things than they were.

As I sobbed, Richie barked out at me, "Quit cher cryin'! I'm tired of listenin' to ya." But Richie too was worried. He knew this was more serious than anything we brothers had ever encountered.

The next day, I was feeling as timid as a mouse in a room full of cats. I was not looking forward to basketball practice. I was concerned that Coach would ask us more about what was really happening. I was afraid I might be confronted by Coach to be more truthful. I was afraid one or more of my brothers or my teammates would be told they would not be playing, perhaps for the rest of the season.

But on that day, Coach said nothing about what he had learned the day before. As a matter a fact, he said nothing about it for the rest of the season, and he took our team to the state semifinals, and we finished the season with twenty wins and four losses. Allen Thompson and Richie had a stellar year. Both were named to the all-state team. I never said anything again to my brothers about smoking, nor did I ever again try to tell them how they should behave. They were their own people. They may be brothers, but each was different. Each had established a life path that was his own, and so had I.

The following summer, I asked Weber if he knew if Coach had seen any of the Mead athletes smoke.

"He told me he thought he saw Allen Thompson with a cigar in his hand as he drove by him in his car last winter, but he couldn't be sure," said Weber. "He said he never saw any of you Newtons smoke. He just heard that you did."

L-R: Allen Thompson, Mary Laverne Graham, and Barbara Graham, 1956.
Mead Consolidated Schools Yearbook

A-Team. Front row,
L-R: Russell Schaefer (Mgr.), Assistant Coach Richard Alsop, Coach Jack Adams; Middle row,
L-R: Dave Newton, Richie Newton, Allen Thompson, Ronnie Newton, Mike Eckel; Back row,
L-R: Lyle Schaefer, Lawrence Jensen, Jerry Sitzman, George Flores, and Jerry Newton, 1956.
Mead Consolidated Schools Yearbook

Chapter 22

A New Beginning

The infamous Indiana Hoosier basketball coach Bobby Knight once said, "Basketball is the toughest game in the world to play. There are no huddles, no time between pitches, no breaks. You have to be able to think on every possession. If you can't think, you can't play."

To lead a team of "thinking athletes," the coach has to be a thinker as well. Coach was just that, and he brought a list of ideas and innovative approaches that neither his players nor his adversaries had ever seen. He was fortunate that he inherited a large cadre of talented athletes who were serious and academically proficient. They were thinkers, and they were eager to learn. They welcomed Coach with open arms. His arrival and the start of the '55–'56 basketball season marked the beginning of a new era at Mead High. Jack Adams as the new coach, coupled with the abundance of talent emerging from Mead's four high-school classes, marked the beginning of a Class B basketball powerhouse never before seen in Northeastern Colorado, a generating factory that would be seen throughout Weld County for the next two years. For the first time in its forty-year history, Mead was picked by the Greeley Tribune as the team to win the North Central League championship.

> The Bulldogs are rated the team to beat for conference honors this year, with Gilcrest the most likely threat.

Mead and Gilcrest both have size, talent, and experience plus adequate reserves, with the Bulldogs' all-around talent giving them the edge in the preleague rankings. Mead is loaded and ready. The Bulldogs have it this year with seven top-flight lettermen back—good size, good defense, and good teamwork.

The season began in early December in a nonleague game with Windsor. Windsor had been a long-time rival of Mead but now was a Class A school. Windsor's student population had increased to more than two hundred, so it joined the Class A Platte Valley League, which included Brush, Lafayette, College High, Eaton, and Fort Lupton. In preparation for this first game, Coach initiated a practice never used at Mead. He had scouting reports for each team Mead played. I never knew where he got these detailed accounts, but Weber told me he thought Coach visited with other coaches who had played them.

With clipboard in hand, Coach reported in great detail about our opponent. "They defeated Fort Lupton last week 70-54. They are a good-scorin' team. We have our work cut out for us. Their high scorer was Reed Warnick with twenty-one points. Jack Winter scored sixteen, and Roland Margheim had eleven." Pausing for a moment, he said, "Reed Warnick is their big man, their leading scorer and leading rebounder. He gets a lot of easy shots inside from offensive rebounds. We're goin' to have to box him out. They say he has a good jump shot in close to the basket."

Addressing Jerry Sitzman, Coach said, "Jerry, we're goin' to start out with a man-to-man defense, and we're goin to put you on Warnick. Your height and his at six feet and three inches match pretty well, but you're goin' to have to be tough on the defensive boards. We can't let him get those easy shots. You'll have to maintain your space there between him and the basket. And Ronnie, I want you to take Margheim. He handles the ball well, can dribble with either hand. He likes to shoot a jump shot off the dribble, especially when he's goin' to his right. He's a good free-throw shooter, so you don't want to foul 'im. You'll have to play him close. Try to keep him from gettin' the ball. Without it, he won't be a scorin' threat. He's about your height at five-foot-nine. Richie, Darrel McNabb is the other guard. He's only five-foot-six. He didn't score much against Lupton. He dribbles only with his right hand, so he will be tryin' to drive on ya' goin' to your left. Play him that way. Make him go to his left. Take his drive away from him. He shoots his jump shot down low. I think at his height. you can block his shot. If you take his drive and his jump shot away, I don't think he will do much scorin'.'"

Coach flipped through several pages to read further on his clipboard and then looked over at Allen Thompson. "Allen, you'll be startin' there at the forward slot. You'll be guardin' Melvin Martin. He's a good rebounder but not a high scorer inside. However, he's accurate at the free-throw line, so you don't want to foul him. He's a little taller than you. Don't let him get between you and the basket. If he wants to shoot from the outside, let 'im do it. He's not a big scorer."

Now focusing his gaze on all of us, Coach added, "This team is a good reboundin' team. They're big. So we've got to be aggressive on both the offensive and defensive boards. Lawrence, we're countin' on you to help us out there with the reboundin'. You'll be guardin' Winter. He shoots jump shots from the base line. He is more of a scorin' threat than he is a rebounder. Play him tight. Keep that hand up there in his face. Don't let him get to the basket after he shoots. Block him out.

"I think these are goin' to be their starters Saturday night. But they have some good bench strength with Sam Reichert and Bill Seibert who play forward and guards Roy Betz and Alvin Andres. You guys who are not startin'—Jerry [Newton], Dave, Mike, George, and Leonard—I want you to be thinkin' about these guys you may be guardin'. I want you to watch them as they're playin'. When you get into the game, you'll know what to do. We're goin' to start out man-to-man, but we may change on and off to a zone. We may even use our 'rabbit defense' that we've been workin' on. We'll see."

Wanting to comment, I raised my hand, and Coach nodded. "Ya know, Coach, Warnick, Margheim, and McNabb were on the team that beat us in our junior high tournament when we were in ninth grade. They beat us by one point."

"Y'all, I remember that," said Richie. "It was at Windsor. The ref called a foul on Rollie. He said he fouled McNabb, but none of us thought he did. McNabb made a free throw to win the game. That was the only game we lost the whole season."

"This time, it's goin' to be different," Allen boasted. "We ain't goin' to let those guys beat us."

"Back then, we didn't know how to play against a zone," I said. "That's how they beat us. Now we know how to go against it. It'll be different this time."

The Windsor game was close until the third quarter. That's when Allen made 8 of his twenty-one points and gave Mead a twelve-point lead. I had a difficult time stopping Margheim; the Windsor guard ended up with nineteen for the night. However, Richie held McNabb scoreless, and Richie and I each accounted for four baskets, and we both made three foul shots. This kept Mead in the lead, and we won 49–40.

I'm sure Windsor was surprised by the outcome. Our loss to Windsor three years before was avenged, and it was on the same Windsor gym floor. We had defeated a respectable "Class A school" team from the Platte Valley League, a team that had defeated another good Class A team, Fort Lupton.

It became Coach's practice to assign me to guard the opponent's top-scoring guard. I knew that letting Windsor's Margheim score nineteen points was not my best effort. I knew I had to work on defense. I had to get better. I had foolishly fouled Margheim several times. However, the season was just beginning. I would feverishly work on it over the next month.

The next morning, a Saturday, I was out of bed by seven-thirty. Mom was already up, drinking coffee and reading the Rocky Mountain News at the kitchen table.

"That was good game last night, but I don't like it when they're close like that," she said. "I'm always afraid you're going to lose. I feel like I'm goin' to have a stroke."

She was expressing her sense of helplessness, unable to help except by hoping for the best. Always caught up in the intensity and competition of the game, I had learned to not let fear become entangled with my effectiveness. I thought Mom was just overreacting, and I minimized her feelings. I just grinned at her and smugly thought, That's just the way it is.

Taking another sip of coffee, Mom said, "I was glad all you birds got to play last night."

"Yal, Coach needed all of us, especially Jerry. Coach put him in when Lawrence got all those fouls called on 'im." I scooped several spoons of oatmeal into a bowl and sat down at the kitchen table across from her. "Where do you want me to start cleaning this morning?" I asked.

"We need to start on the back bedroom downstairs," Mom answered. "You need to dust the furniture and scrub the floor. The same goes for the living room and the dining room."

All our sisters had left home. They had done the cleaning and most of the cooking. Now Mom was at home alone with seven boys. Mom did the cooking, but we brothers helped with all other household chores. We would wash and dry dishes, clean the house, bring in kindling and coal, and sometimes hang out the wash and iron clothes.

I chose to clean downstairs so I could listen to the radio in the living room. I tuned it to the Englewood KGMC station. It was my favorite. It played the top fifty popular tunes, starting with number 50 at eight o'clock and finishing with number 1 by noon. Although Bill Haley & His Comets had initiated the rock-'n'-roll craze with their tune "Rock Around the Clock Tonight," "Unchained Melody," "Love is a Many-Splendored Thing," and "Sincerely" were still high on the chart. The onslaught of Elvis Presley's hip-shaking tunes had not yet arrived.

At noon, we lunched on chicken noodle soup that Mom had prepared with a chicken from the freezer and homemade noodles she made the day before. Coach told us to eat lightly before each game. Mom would serve the soup again that evening.

That afternoon, Marc and Frosty attended catechism lessons at Guardian Angel Church, and all seven of us went to confession.

Richie and I arrived at the church at one forty-five. We entered a pew up in front and away from the students being instructed by Sister Marjorie. There was already a line of folks along the right aisle waiting to confess to Father Martin and ask forgiveness. Richie and I, with our knees on the wood-plank kneelers, searched our minds to remember failings and remind ourselves of the codes we had violated. This was a ritual that my brothers and I performed every two weeks. With hands clasped in front of us and our heads bent downward, we closed our eyes and thought intently about our offenses.

Emulating Coach, I had eliminated swear words from my vocabulary. I no longer had to confess their use. I had missed saying my prayers a couple of times. My most serious sin was that I had sassed and "talked back" to Mom. I knew it wasn't right, but I couldn't help myself. I lashed out at her when I thought I had been maligned. I knew she was hurt and angered at my quick-tempered responses. To Mom, this was interpreted as a lack of respect, perhaps because I was becoming conceited and self-centered. She thought my successes on the basketball court had gone to my head.

Raising her voice, her anger heightening, she retorted, "Listen, you little overbearing brat, you're not goin' to talk back to me like that! Who do you think you are? You're gettin' mighty stuck on yourself, young man!" At other times, she'd bark back at me, "I'll bring you down from your high horse. You just watch. I'll ground you so fast, you won't be playin' basketball for a week."

I knew this was not an idle threat, and I had stepped over the line. I knew I had angered Mom and offended God. This would be the sin I would confess. Father Martin would give me absolution and bid me not to disrespect my superiors again. I wondered if he remembered it was me who was committing the same offense time and time again.

After confessing and expressing contrition in the tiny cubicle with Father Martin behind the curtain, he assigned me to say three Hail Marys, and I saw the shadow of his hand making the sign of the cross as he said, "I absolve you in the name of the Father and of the Son and of the Holy Ghost."

Leaving the confessional, I then knelt in the pew once again, quickly recited my penance, and left the church. I waited outside for Richie to finish. For me, confession created a remarkable feeling of goodness and put my life "back in order." I was convinced that a "clean soul" made me a better basketball player, and I could focus on that evening's game with peace of mind and an enhanced sense of purpose.

When home, I tried to rest, but I couldn't sleep. I got up, went downstairs, and sat down at the dining-room table to do my American history homework. Mrs. Irene Hausken had assigned our class to read ten or so pages on the Civil War by Monday. I would get an early start on the assignment and finish up on Sunday if I needed to.

Mom warmed up the noodle soup for us, and after supper, I went upstairs to change clothes. Coach insisted all his players wear dress pants; no jeans allowed. All of us Newtons wore white corduroys and sport shirts. If Mom had no time to iron them, she would assign this chore to one of us. My brothers and I wore "letter jackets" of black and orange with leather sleeves, but we never bothered to sew the letter on them.

Around six-thirty, not waiting for my brothers who were still getting dressed, I walked to the Mead gym. I wanted to watch the B-team game. Dave would be playing. Soon, Rollie, Jerry, and Richie entered the gym, and I joined them and the rest of our teammates as we descended to the locker room to suit up. We A-team members would warm up at halftime of the B-team game.

In our A-team game, Coach stayed with man-to-man, while Johnstown played a zone the whole game. On offense, Richie played at the front point, and Allen and the other forwards (our brother Jerry, Dave, and Lawrence) played on each wing. With Jerry Sitzman at center, I rotated under the basket from wing to wing, getting the ball from our forwards as I came in behind the Johnstown defenders. This created great opportunities for open jump shots, and I paced Mead's scoring with sixteen points, four from free throws in the last quarter. Midway in that final period, we went ahead by four points with Richie's basket and my two free throws.

Coach called for a time-out. He wanted four good ball handlers in the game. He was preparing to hold onto the ball and let the clock run out. Pointing at Dave, he said, "Dave, go in for Lawrence."

With Allen, Richie, Jerry Sitzman, Dave, and me huddled around him, he said, "Let's start stallin'." Pointing to Jerry Sitzman, Coach said,

"Jerry, you stay under the basket. Let the other four stay outside and handle the ball. If they can get it into you for an easy shot, go ahead and take it. Hold onto the ball as long you can with the dribble. Then pass it on to any of the other three when they double up on you. They may try to foul you. If they do, try to pass it off before they get to you."

In our stalling mode, Johnstown began to foul to get the ball back. We scored thirteen points that final quarter, nine on free throws, and we came away with another nonleague win, 40–34.

In the locker room at game's end, Coach said to us, "It was a low-scorin' game for us because of the zone they threw on us, and we weren't hittin' from the outside. We only shot 38 percent, but it's early in the season, and we'll get better as the season progresses, and we've had more practice. But I'm proud of you guys shutting them down with our man-to-man defense. We stuck with man-to-man because we want to get in as much practice with it as we can before league play starts. A good man-to-man defense is a must. We have to get better at it." Glancing at me, he said, "Compared to last night, you had a good night defensively, Ronnie. You kept that Elsberry kid down to only nine points."

"Thanks, Coach," I said, basking in his praise.

On the following Friday against Estes Park, Estes was without two of its starters, and Mead jumped to a 20–7 lead by the end of the first quarter. Coach then substituted. I ended up with nineteen points, and Allen had eighteen. Richie scored seventeen, while Jerry Sitzman connected with fifteen. With a final score of 87–47, we were certain our eighty-seven points was the highest ever recorded by a Mead Bulldog basketball team.

We defeated LaSalle 45–41 the next night. We were ahead by a wide margin most of the game, but LaSalle narrowed the lead in the final quarter with a fifteen-point rally.

With the next week being Christmas vacation, Coach conducted practice through the last school day and bid us goodbye until the twenty-sixth of December. The start of basketball season had gone very well for Mead and our new coach. We had won all four games.

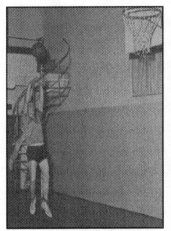

L-R: Jerry Newton, Richie Newton, and Jerry Sitzman, 1956.
Mead Consolidated Schools Yearbook

L-R: Allen Thompson and Ronnie Newton, 1956.
Mead Consolidated Schools Yearbook

Chapter 23

Marching Onward

The week after Christmas, my only obligation—a pleasant one—was to play basketball. Each day, Coach had us A-stringers in the gym, sharpening our skills in preparation for the remainder of the season. Since we had not played for more than a week, the afternoon practices were longer, and so were the drills. Figure 8 passing with three players at a time up and down the court continued for fifteen minutes until Coach was satisfied we were regaining our wind. There was no time for rest as he transitioned us into a full-court baseball-pass drill, followed by a fast-break exercise.

In rehearsing the fast break, one of the most exciting plays in basketball, we started at half-court with three rows of players and with the ball starting at the center. The ball handler dribbled to the top of the keyhole, and two players moved downcourt on the wings, one on each side. Either was a potential receiver of a pass to take it in for a layup as the ball handler approached the foul line. Coach had a fourth row at the baseline that also moved toward the foul line, attempting to take the ball away as the central ball handler moved in.

Intense one-on-one half-court pair-offs were next at each of the four baskets. Coach watched intently, shouting defensive instructions. "Crouch lower in your stance, and keep one hand in the ball handler's face!" Coach barked at us. Then Coach, getting into the fray, challenged each player with his own superb defense, laughing and chuckling when he swiped the ball. I looked forward to the exercise with Coach, where I learned to protect the ball with my back to him and then driving around him, dribbling with either hand for a layup, or putting up a hook shot with either hand. Coach smiled approvingly when he was beaten, and when I blocked his low-release jump shot, he laughed with satisfaction.

Coach paired up his charges in a rotating pass drill, tossing the "medicine ball" with two hands or one. He divided us into teams of five and scrimmaged us full court for thirty minutes. He then released us from team drill to begin our individual drills.

Looking at the individual practice schedule Coach had taped to the gym wall, I saw he had increased the number of practice tip-ins against the wall by twenty-five, and he had increased the skip-ropes from 100 to 150. Most importantly, he wanted us to shoot a hundred practice free throws instead of the customary seventy-five. The first of January was just around the corner, and Coach wanted our team to be more than ready to resume play. Once again, our team was continuing its quest for the North Central League crown.

As New Year of '56 began, we marched onward with much confidence, having won four games in December and suffering no defeats. However, that confidence was shaken when College High from Greeley handed us our first loss. Since College High was a nonleague team, we brushed it aside as unimportant. With our next contest, we defeated Johnstown, another nonleague opponent.

Two weeks previously, we had established a new Mead High School record by scoring 87 points against Estes Park, a record that was short-lived. Playing Evans at home, we scored a whopping 106 points, while Evans had only 40. Allen Thompson scored the highest of his career with 31, and I scored 25. Richie and Jerry Sitzman ended up with 16 apiece. Most of these resulted from a full-court press when the Evans guards could not protect the ball from our aggressive defensive play.

That night, our new electronic scoreboard, a gift from the senior class, was in use for the first time.

"Hey, Coach!" shouted Lyle Schaefer. "Let's see how many points we can score and break in our new scoreboard."

Coach, seeing the scoring frenzy building, acknowledged with a smile as the crowd roared with anticipation that Mead might score 100 points. We continued to press full court, and Walter Ayres swiped the ball from an unwary Evans guard and drove to the basket to drop in a layup for the hundredth point. Double zeroes lit up on the scoreboard for Mead. Yelling and screaming broke out from the crowd. A new scoreboard had been "broken in" with a three-digit score that was beyond its two-digit capabilities, and the largest point total ever recorded at Mead High was scored. The Greeley Tribune erroneously reported that this was the highest scoring game ever recorded in Colorado but three weeks later corrected itself by reporting that Cheyenne Wells had scored 112 against Arapaho in 1953 and that Glenwood Springs had scored 111 against Steamboat Springs in the 1916–1917 season.

Reflecting on this mammoth score several weeks later, Coach was sorry he had done it. Coach said, "Their coach was really mad at us for running up the score, so I called him up and apologized."

The scouting report on Gilcrest indicated they were the best team we had to face in league play. Gilcrest had a big frontline and a small and speedy backcourt. Addressing us on Monday before the next day's game, Coach said, "Their big man is Rudy Peralez. He's six-foot-four. He's their big scorer. He's averaging eleven points a game. They have two forwards at six-foot-two, Bruce McLeod and Norman Cogburn. With their height, we're going to be challenged on the boards. Their guards are fast and small, especially Richard Lopez. The other guard is Fred Keil. They both are five-feet-seven. They're good scorers, so Richie and Ronnie, you two are going to need to play good defense. Stay on 'em. Keep 'em from gettin' the ball. Ronnie, you'll take Lopez. He'll drive on ya, mostly goes to his right. Richie, Keil likes to shoot jump shots. He doesn't drive much, likes to pass the ball off. Also, they have a couple of substitutes—a guard, Gary Meek, who is five-nine, and a five-foot-eleven forward, Jerry Righthouse, who plays quite a bit. They have lost only to Grover and have beaten Keenesburg, Berthoud, and Estes Park."

Coach turned to the last page on his clipboard and said, "Oh yes, they have a brand new gym with fan backboards, so this will be an adjustment for you guys. We haven't played anywhere yet where they've had 'em. They may take some getting used to. When you warm up, try banking a few shots to see how it feels. That's where you might have the most trouble. Don't let the smallness of the backboard fool you. There's plenty of room for you to bank a shot."

At that juncture, we were tied with Gilcrest atop the North Central League. That night, Richie and I held Gilcrest's two guards to less than ten points each. Allen Thompson hit twenty-five, and we won easily, 55–35, giving us the league lead at four and zero.

The following Friday night against Berthoud, who had not yet won a game, Coach started our second string, and we won handily 74–36. On Tuesday, we faced Timnath on our home court, and Jerry Sitzman tallied twenty-four points, and Richie dumped in eighteen. Coach used eleven players as we scored seventy points, far ahead of Timnath's forty-one.

At school the next morning, Mrs. Hausken met with our American history class. Mrs. Hausken had assigned us to answer questions at the end of the chapter, and they were due that Wednesday. After taking roll, she asked us to turn in our homework. Briefly surveying to see how few had completed their work, Mrs. Hausken angrily lashed out, "Why haven't more of you completed your assignment? You can't use last night's ballgame as an excuse. There are players on the team who got theirs done. Furthermore, you've had a whole week to do this. I want these answers turned in by tomorrow!"

History was a subject Richie and I both liked, and we had done our homework. Before every test or quiz, the two of us studied diligently with Mike Eckel during the noon hour. History was the only class in which the three of us could compete with Gary Olson and Lyle Schaefer for the highest grades.

Our final first-round game in league play was at Erie, the school who had defeated us in football to win the league title and then the district playoffs. Now we faced those same players on the basketball court. Although Erie was not a tall team, they were strong physically, and their small gym, just like ours, was well suited for a huddled zone defense. We had a difficult time finding the basket and barely squeaked by with a win, 35–33.

In another nonleague game the next night, we faced the Frederick Warriors. Like Erie, they had defeated us in football. With six-foot-one Larry Petras at center, six-two Red D'Orazio at forward, and five-foot-eight Alex Hattel at guard, the Warriors were leading the Poudre Valley League.

Starting out against Frederick's zone defense, Coach had Allen Thompson rotating from wing to wing with Lawrence Jensen and Jerry Sitzman moving along the baseline. Richie and I found Allen open for his jump shots, and by the end of the first half, Allen had potted six baskets.

We played a glove-tight man-to-man, trying to stop Frederick's Petras, who was playing with his back to the basket with defender Jerry Sitzman right behind him and with further defensive help coming from Lawrence Jensen. Frederick's Hattel constantly got the ball inside to his teammate Petras, and Petras, driving around his defenders, found opportunities for easy layups, and by the end of the first quarter, he had hit five field goals. Finding Petras tough to defend, Jerry Sitzman fouled him three times and Lawrence twice. As a consequence, he connected on seven foul shots, and coupled with the five buckets, Petras scored a whopping seventeen points in the first half. Petras and D'Orazio dominated us both offensively and defensively, and at halftime, Frederick was well ahead, 33–24.

In the final quarter, Jerry Sitzman fouled out, and Coach substituted with George Flores and Jerry (Newton). Although Allen netted twenty-five points, it was to no avail; by game's end, Petras had thirty-six points with twelve field goals and twelve free shots. Coach Alex Tesone's Frederick Warriors handed a second loss of the season to the trampled Bulldogs of Mead 67–58.

As my teammates and I showered and tried to overcome our disappointment, Coach Tesone came in to the locker room to acknowledge our valiant but losing effort. He consoled me by shaking my hand and saying, "Nice game, Mr. Newton. I've been coaching against Mead for at least ten years, and this is one of the best Mead teams we've ever faced."

Coach Tesone went around to each Mead player to offer compliments of a "nice game." When he got to Jerry Sitzman, he said, "I know Petras was really hard to stop, but here's what you should do. Play in front of a guy like him. Don't let him get the ball. Cut off the passing lane. Once he gets the ball inside like that, you can't stop him. The secret is to not let him get the ball."

Coach listened carefully; he was always learning more about the game. He had been coached well by Greeley's Jim Baggot in high school, but now he had a chance to learn from another skilled high-school coach who was one of his toughest competitors. I'm certain that Coach also had thoughts that night that he and his team might meet again with the Frederick Warriors, perhaps in the district tournament or in the state tournament. Up to that point, Coach's team had won seven games, and this was only its second loss. In his mind, there was a lot of basketball to be played. Still, he knew he had been beaten by a good team and a good coach. Frederick's legacy as a formidable opponent was unarguable. Mead had only beaten Frederick once since 1946.

Rollie, sitting out the year because of a heart murmur, remained in the stands, unable to help his brothers and his former teammates. Rollie had badly wanted to play Frederick. Rollie wished he had had the chance to spar off with Petras and D'Orazio on the boards and to contribute offensively. Rollie said that night as we went to bed, "I know if I'd been playin', we'da beaten those b———ds. God, I hate gettin' beat by those sons-a-b———s!"

In the second round of league play, Mead walloped Estes Park, Evans, and Berthoud and easily beat LaSalle, Erie, and Timnath. Then the Gilcrest Spuddiggers came to Mead with league high-scorer Rudy Peralez, averaging more than twenty points a game. That night, Jerry Sitzman equaled Peralez in rebounding, but Jerry fell short on scoring, with Peralez getting fifteen points and Jerry making only three. Allen and I kept Mead in the game, scoring fifteen points each. Repeatedly fouled inside, Peralez got seven points on free shots. We had the lead until the end of the third quarter, when Gilcrest tied it up at thirty-four.

Midway in the fourth quarter, Gilcrest grabbed the lead at 41–40 and then got four quick baskets, while we made only three points. Gilcrest finalized the score at 49–44, and that put them in a tie with us for the league lead.

Although Gilcrest was touted as the team for Mead to beat at the beginning of the season, we had already beaten them easily in the first round, and the loss was unexpected and painfully disappointing. On Monday afternoon at practice, Coach talked to our downhearted team and provided his customary postgame analysis.

"Their backcourt three—McLeod, Peralez, and Cogburn—are all taller than our backcourt," said Coach. "They got nine more rebounds than we did. All three of them scored. They got some easy baskets, most of them from offensive rebounds. Peralez got half of his points on free throws. Gilcrest shot twenty-one free throws and made sixteen of 'em. We shot eighteen and missed ten. Now, guys, we've got to do better than that. Their free-throw percentage was 76 percent. Ours was a miserable 56 percent. I made a quick calculation here."

Coach looked at his clipboard. "If we had hit 76 percent of our free throws like they did, we'da beat 'em by one point. Work hard on your free throws this week, all of you. Fifty-six percent is the lowest it's ever been. I know we can do better. Concentrate on what you're doin'. Work on your technique. That Fred Keil of theirs had an exceptional game—at least, it was for him. He got a lot of clear jump shots on the screen. Ronnie and Richie, you two have got to switch men sooner. We can't let those front guards get those open shots like that. We're gonna work on switchin' this week."

Mead and Gilcrest shared the league lead but not for long. That Friday night, Gilcrest was upset by LaSalle, and a week later, they were beaten by Erie. So going into the final game of the season with Timnath, Mead was already the league winner, regardless of the outcome.

After beating Timnath 44–34, Coach stood in front of us in the bus. Mr. Humphrey had started the engine, but we were still in the Timnath gym parking lot. "Well, we've officially won the league championship. Tonight we can celebrate."

"Hey, Coach!" hollered Richie, "I'm goin' to ring the fire siren."

Coach looked at Mr. Humphrey, and they both broke into laughter.

"Well, this is certainly something the whole town needs to know about," said Coach. "Mr. Carlson [superintendent] says it has been ten years since Mead won the league title in basketball. Go ahead and celebrate tonight, but Monday, we'll have ta get ready for the district tournament, which will start week after next. I've scheduled a scrimmage with Windsor for Wednesday of next week."

The bus pulled in front of the Mead school about eleven-thirty. We unloaded our basketball gear in our lockers, and Richie, Lanny Davis, and I climbed into the Eckel Oldsmobile for a ride home with Mike.

"Mike," said Richie, "we've got to ring the siren before you take us home."

"Yal," I said, thinking I had a brilliant idea and the wisdom of Solomon, "let's stop in front of the firehouse with our lights off and let Richie set it off. You can then drive us to park in our yard. Nobody will see us. Nobody will know it was us."

Mike drove down Main Street with the car lights off and parked. Richie jumped out and pushed the white button on the small red box on the outside of the firehouse wall. The siren screeched into the night as Richie jumped back into the car, and Mike drove to the driveway in front of our house.

It was several minutes before our laughing, mischievous foursome heard the noise stop. Moments later, we anxiously watched the headlights of a car coming down Main Street and turning toward us at Grover Roberts's house. With the driver knowing exactly where he was going, the car turned north on the street leading to our house and pulled into our driveway. Wilbert Peppler, the town mayor, stepped out of the car with a flashlight in his hand. He peered into Mike's Olds, seeing the four of us slouched down, trying to hide and appear ignorant of what had just happened.

He came to my side of the car, and knowing we were going to have to converse with him, I reluctantly rolled down my window.

"Was that you boys who set the siren off?" asked the mayor.

"No, it wasn't us," I said, looking directly at him with a confident glance.

"That's right, Mr. Peppler," said Mike. "We've been sittin' here for an hour, just talkin'. We heard a car drive off when the siren went on, but we couldn't tell whose it was."

"I'll bet it was you boys," said the mayor. He then walked to the front of Mike's Olds, knelt down, and reached under the bumper to put his hand on the radiator. "It's just what I thought," he said. "The radiator's still hot. You boys were driving this car just a few minutes ago."

"It wasn't us," said Richie.

"I know it was," said the mayor. He grinned at us and repeated, "I know it was you boys." He turned off his flashlight and walked back to his car.

As the four of us watched him drive off, I said, "That Wilbert is a smart son of a gun. I'm glad he didn't do anything."

"Yal," said Richie, "knowin' him, it's a wonder he didn't put us in jail for the night."

Wilbert Peppler had married Bonnie Muhme, a junior-high teacher at Mead. He lived in Mead and was recently elected mayor. Wilbert knew all us Newtons. We had thinned beets for him a year before. His sleep had been interrupted, but he would soon learn why we rang the siren. Mead High had won the North Central League basketball championship. The trophy would be displayed on a table in front of Mr. Carlson's office for all the school to see.

With the league season over, Mead's record was thirteen and one, while second-place Gilcrest's was eleven and three. Our Mead team scored a season total of 867 points, averaging sixty-two points per game, twenty points more than our opposition.

L-R: Mike Eckel, Dave Newton, George Flores, Lyle Schaefer
and Lawrence Jensen, 1956.
Mead Consolidated Schools Yearbook

Mead Firehouse with siren mounted on roof, 1957.
Mead Consolidated Schools Yearbook

Chapter 24

Tournament Time

March was tournament time for high-school and college basketball teams all over the nation. In March '56, the NCAA Division I basketball tournament began with twenty-five schools and four regional tournaments. In the Far West Regional, John Wooden's UCLA Bruins were knocked out by the San Francisco Dons, headed by Bill Russell and K. C. Jones, two all-Americans. Defeated by Iowa, famed coach Adolph Rupp's Kentucky team did not make it out of the Midwest Regional. Iowa went on to the final four and then the final, only to be defeated by the Dons.

Also in March '56, the Colorado Class B District 4 tournament was in Fort Collins on the Colorado A&M campus. Top-seeded Mead was pitted against Evans, while second-seeded Gilcrest played Berthoud. Third-seed Erie was matched against LaPorte, and fourth-seed LaSalle went against Estes Park. The district tournament winner would go on to the state tournament.

We breezed by Evans 61–39, and Erie whipped LaPorte 57–39 to meet Mead in the semifinals. Gilcrest doubled the score on Berthoud 54–22, and LaSalle sneaked by Estes Park 63–60. Gilcrest and LaSalle would meet in the second semifinal game. In the semifinals, we overpowered Erie, winning 48–41, and Mead entered the finals against Gilcrest, who had crept by LaSalle 60–57.

It was low scoring in the championship game, and it was tied 18–18 at the half. But we took over in the third quarter, making thirteen points, and in the final period, we surged ahead, scoring nineteen. With the game well in hand, Coach substituted, and we trounced Gilcrest 50–33. As winners of the district tournament, we took home our second championship trophy that year, and Supt. Carlson placed the coveted prize alongside the previously won league trophy on the table placed in the hall outside his office.

We would be going to the state playoffs. It had been more than a decade since brother Jack and his Mead High School team went to state, Mead's first appearance. Our '56 entry was Mead's second in its thirty-eight-year history. We entered the first round against Ordway, the Eastern Arkansas Valley League champion. The game was played in the late afternoon in Englewood High School's fieldhouse. Ordway kept the score close for the first quarter, but then their wheels fell off. By the end of the third quarter, Mead was ahead by twenty points. All ten team members played, and we won 59–45.

That night, Coach took our team to Joe "Awful" Coffee's Ringside Lounge Restaurant for dinner before we checked into Denver's Wynne Hotel. Coffee had been a prizefighter, and his establishment was ornate with pictures and plaques depicting the pugilistic world and Coffee's accomplishments. We all ordered T-bone steaks and french fries, topped off with apple pie and vanilla ice cream. Curious about his young patrons and their clean look, Coffee struck up a conversation.

"Where you all from?" Coffee asked.

"We're from Mead High School, Mr. Coffee," Mike Eckel proudly answered. "We're playing in the state basketball tournament. The Class B playoffs are in the Englewood High School gymnasium, not far from here."

"Well, I know where Mead is," Coffee said. "I see the sign on the Washington Highway when I'm headin' north to Cheyenne to see relatives. How big is Mead?"

"About two hundred," I answered.

"How big is your high school?"

"About 125 students, and that puts us in Class B. Greeley, about thirty miles from us, has almost three hundred students, and they are Class AA."

"Yes," said Coffee, "Greeley's playin' here in Denver also. They made a reservation for their team to eat here tonight also. We expect them to be here about ten. Didja win today?"

"We sure did," said Coach. "We beat Ordway 59-46 about an hour ago. We had a good game tonight. Richie Newton here on my right and Allen Thompson over there at the other table combined for thirty-two of our fifty-nine points. Richie was hot from the outside and Allen from the inside. The whole team played real good defense, stealing the ball six or seven times. We're going to get a good meal here and then head to the Wynne Hotel. The boys will have plenty of time to sleep and rest. We don't have school tomorrow. We'll be back in Englewood tomorrow afternoon to play Sanford."

"I think I know where Sanford is," said Coffee. "Isn't it south near the New Mexico border?"

Coach nodded and said, "Yes, that's right. I would guess it is more than a hundred miles southwest of Pueblo."

"Well, thanks for comin' in tonight, and good luck tomorrow," said Coffee as he shook hands with Coach.

It was no coincidence that another strong team from Weld County, Frederick High School, was also in the state playoffs. Frederick, one of only three teams that beat Mead that year, was in the alternate tournament bracket and had defeated Stratton in the first round. Frederick would play Oak Creek immediately after our game.

That afternoon, four teams—Mead, Oak Creek, Frederick, and Sanford—were on the floor simultaneously, taking pregame warm-up shots on the eight basketball goals around Englewood High's gym. I stopped to talk to Frederick's Alex Hattel at midcourt.

"Good luck to you tonight," I said to him as I shook his hand.

"Same for you," said Alex.

"Was Stratton tough to beat last night?" I asked.

"It was real a close game. We caught up with them in the last quarter and tied it up. It went into overtime, and we won, 69-67," Alex said. "D'Orazio and Petras both scored twenty points."

"We got by Ordway pretty easily," I said. "But today with Sanford, we're facing a real good team. They won the state tournament several years back. Coach tells us they have a good shooter named Reynolds. I hope we can stop 'im."

"I hope you do too," said Alex. "Let's both win, and then we can battle it out tomorrow night in the final."

As our second state playoff game began, cheerleaders Elaine Becker, JoAnn Strausheim, Barbara Graham, and Elaine Leinweber led the small contingent of Mead supporters with the victory yell.

Victory, victory is our cry!
V-I-C-T-O-R-Y!
Are we in it? Well, I guess!
Mead High School!
Yes, yes, yes!

Barbara, our classmate for our eleven school years, had been a cheerleader the last six. She never missed a game. She was always calling out with her support for us, oftentimes encouraging my brothers and me individually. She was captain of the cheerleading squad. They were outfitted in orange corduroy skirts and orange sweaters with the familiar block Ms on the front. Rolled-up white anklets and saddle shoes adorned their feet. Four vertically striped orange-and-black megaphones rested on the floor next to them, to be used when Mead fans were invited to cheer at critical times.

After the first half, Sanford led Mead 30–27. In the final period, with less than four minutes left, Sanford went ahead, 48–46. For two minutes, we were unable to score.

On one occasion in those final minutes, we had a chance to make a bucket. I took the ball to midcourt on a fast break with Dave, moving fast toward the basket on my left wing. At the key, I bounce-passed to Dave, who went up with the shot, only to have the ball slip from his hands before he could bank an easy layup. The ball ended up out-of-bounds and in the third row of Sanford's yelling fans. The Sanford supporters screamed with delight, realizing that Mead had missed an easy opportunity to score.

With two minutes left and Sanford ahead by two points, Sanford went into a stall. Trying to gain possession of the ball, Mead incurred three quick fouls, and Sanford responded with three more points at the charity stripe. With the ball in my hands, the whistle blew with the referee alleging I had committed a charging foul. It was my fifth. I had fouled out.

When I got to the bench, Coach, very much disgruntled, said to me, "You got a little too aggressive on that one, didn'cha? Now ya got yourself and us in real trouble."

Right then, Coach knew that the season was over. His Bulldogs were defeated in the semifinal game 55–46.

After congratulating Sanford's Lloyd Reynolds, who scored a whopping twenty-six points, I left the gym through a side door to the hall and to the locker room entrance. There I saw Arden Adams, Coach's wife, talking to him. She was in tears. Her eyes were red, and he was consoling her with his arm around her shoulder. I realized how important this game was in their lives and to others as well as to my brothers and me and our teammates. This was Coach's first year, and this was the first loss of a key game he was to experience. I had not had a good tournament, and once again, I felt I had let my team and my coach down.

That night, Frederick defeated Oak Creek, and the next night in the Denver Coliseum, Frederick beat Sanford to become the 1956 state Class B champions. Frederick's Larry Petras and Red D'Orazio were named to the all-state team, along with Mead's Allen Thompson and Richie Newton.

A week later, Frank Eckel had another perspective on the negative outcome of our game with Sanford. It was a Saturday, and I had helped Frank's son Mike haul bales of hay and store them in their barn for their nearly a hundred milk cows. Marg Eckel, Mike's mother, invited me to stay for supper before they took me home. Mike's younger sister Pat also joined us. As we shared dinner, we discussed a variety of topics, including the upcoming track season, Catholicism, attending church, and milking cows. Mr. and Mrs. Eckel always invited their children to engage in meal conversations, and I was also encouraged to take part. Finally, our conversation turned to the basketball defeat the week before.

"What do ya think happened there?" Frank asked me.

With all their eyes on me, I stammered, "W-w-well, they had a good team. Their best player scored twenty-six points on us. W-we couldn't stop 'im. I-I fouled out. The ref called a charge on me. I didn't think it was. Coach was pretty mad at me. I didn't play a very good game."

"You know what I think?" said Frank. "I think you guys started celebrating your good fortune before you should've. You were out on the town eating steaks and good food and stayin' in a fancy hotel after winning the first game. You should've gone home right after the game that night and started thinkin' about the game the next day instead of celebrating your win. You kids started to celebrate too soon!"

Not knowing how to respond to a rationale for losing I had not thought about before, I acknowledged Frank Eckel's comments, saying, "You may be right."

Mike then said, "I think they won because they were a better team than we were. I wonder how we would have done if Rollie had played, not having him hurt us. We needed 'im."

As I undressed for bed, my mind went back to our loss. Maybe Frank Eckel was right. Maybe our premature reward activities had lulled us into complacency. I remembered what Sister Laurance told us in catechism class. "You should pray for God to help you play your very best, not to win. God does not control who wins a game." I reflected on our defeat. It was part of God's plan because we did not play our very best, no matter the reason. Losing must be accepted as a potential price to be paid when participating in an exciting high-stakes event such as a state basketball playoff, especially when one has not played well. As I knelt beside my bed, I asked God to help my brothers and me to play our very best throughout next year and lead us to the state tournament again. I vowed I would always be in my best behavior in the coming year so I could earn God's favor. With God's support, I knew I could help my team win.

The past year was one from which many lessons were learned by Coach, by me, and by my teammates. These would provide valuable experiences and would allow all of us to develop skills and attitudes that could lead to our eventual success as a winning basketball team, perhaps state champions. The next year, Coach would give some thought to what Frank Eckel and others were telling him and his players. Next year, we conjectured, could be a different ball game.

L-R: JoAnn Strausheim, Elaine Becker, Barbara Graham, and Elaine Leinweber, 1956. *Mead Consolidated Schools Yearbook*

Ron's Drive Stopped

Ron Newton's potential drive for Mead is curtailed by Phil Peterson of Sanford in the first half of action in the Mead-Sanford game in the semis Friday. Mead lost a close contest and was eliminated from the tourney.—Tribune Photo by Jerry Kessznich.

Chapter 25

Misstep

With basketball season over, our junior class focused on plans for the junior-senior prom. Following tradition, juniors had the responsibility of hosting the event for the seniors. This meant we had to raise funds for decorations and hire a band. That spring, Mr. Arthur Troutman, our biology teacher and our class sponsor, was presiding over reports about our favorite animal he had assigned to our biology class. Mike Eckel had given his report on sheep, and Gary Olson discussed deer populations of the Rocky Mountains. I was scheduled to talk about eagles. The only information I had garnered was from the *World Book Encyclopedia*, and it was sparse. I gave no consideration to using the Longmont Library to find additional resource material. Not finding enough on which to report, I expanded my topic to include ospreys and falcons.

Unknown to any of us in our biology class was the fact that three years before, in 1953, Watson and Crick had made a most important biological discovery of all time. They had characterized the DNA molecule, the building block of the gene. Even the inheritance characteristics of "the gene" were beyond mention in our biology class. Our outdated textbooks were scarcely opened. In that same year, Jonas Salk had developed a vaccine against polio, which we all knew about because it was being administered to students in the lower grades. In just a few years, this dreaded disease would be wiped out in America.

Our stricken friend, Frank Melchior, paralyzed in both legs nine years before, was still attending Mead as a junior and was climbing up and down stairs clinging to his crutches and the rail.

As we presented our animal report to the biology class, Mr. Troutman took notes and encouraged us to do likewise, and he later tested our knowledge of what we had learned. In between reports, Mr. Troutman sandwiched discussions of our upcoming prom project, and he assigned us to carry out a variety of tasks. I volunteered to help with the decorating.

"I've been looking at this catalogue," said Mr. Troutman. "They have rolls of royal blue paper with silver stars on it. We can make a false ceiling in the gym with this. It is pretty expensive, $15 a roll. I think we can get by with twenty-five rolls. That will cost us $375. Janice, how much money do we have in our treasury?"

Janice Frederickson, our class treasurer, answered, "I just checked with Mr. Carlson and the school secretary. They told me we have $326."

"But $150 of that is for the band we've hired," said Ronnie Vogel, class president. "We also have to buy food and drinks. We're going to need a lot more."

"We'll have to sell more tickets for our ham raffle and get some businesses to contribute," said Mr. Troutman.

"We haven't gone to Berthoud yet," said Ronnie Vogel. "They helped Mead out last year. We need to go see 'em. We still have to go to more businesses in Longmont too."

"You kids will have to do this after school or on Saturdays," said Mr. Troutman. "If you need it, I'll let you use my car after school."

With basketball over and not yet starting our track program, we juniors had free afternoons, so several of us could solicit support from businesses in Berthoud, fifteen miles from Mead. Mike Eckel drove Richie, Lanny Davis, and me to Berthoud in Mr. Troutman's '55 Nash. We made stops at the bank and several retail stores, asking for contributions. We sold tickets for the ham raffle, promising we would deliver if they won. Bank tellers and retailers went to their billfolds and cash registers and gave us dollar bills. As 5:30 p.m. approached, we had collected nearly $80, and we headed back to Mead, taking a shortcut on gravel roads.

"Why don'cha see how fast this tin can of Troutman's can go?" said Richie.

"Yal, crank this bucket of bolts way up there!" said Lanny.

When the speedometer needle reached 100 mph, Mike burst out with laughter and said, "I bet ol' Troutman has never had this contraption goin' this fast!"

With a heavy foot on the accelerator, Mike found himself going too fast as he made an abrupt southward turn five miles northwest of Mead. The car slid across the road into the ditch but stayed upright. The ditch bank incline was just enough that Mike could not power the car out. The car was at a standstill, with the rear wheels spinning in the soft soil at the bottom of the ditch. Richie, Lanny, and I got out and tried pushing the car as Mike gunned the engine. It did not help. The car languished in the ditch with the four of us looking on with guilt-ridden frustration.

"Looks like we'll need a tractor to pull us out," said Lanny, a farm boy who had experienced these such events many times before.

"I think you're right, Lanny," said Mike. "I'll run over to the farmhouse over there." He pointed to a building a quarter mile away.

Just then, we saw a pickup pull out of the yard and head toward us.

"Need some help?" asked the farmer as he drove up.

"Yes, sir, we sure do," said Mike. "I think we're going to have ta be pulled out."

The farmer got out of his pickup and walked around the car, assessing the situation. "I think you're right, young man. You're goin' to need pullin'. I'll go get my Oliver and a chain. I think we can getcha outta here. I'll be right back."

It was 6:45 p.m. when Mike drove Mr. Troutman's car into the school parking lot. A concerned Mr. Troutman was waiting outside on the school steps with a furled forehead and a frown of concern. He was most anxious because he still had an hour's drive to his home in Denver, and he had been concerned for our safety and his car.

Approaching as we all climbed out, Mr. Troutman barked out at us, "What's happened here? What's goin' on?" he asked.

"Sir, I ran into the ditch about ten miles from Berthoud. We had to be pulled out with a tractor," said Mike. "But your car hasn't been hurt. Nothing happened to it."

"We're real sorry we're gettin' back so late," I said. "It took a long time for the farmer to get us out."

"You boys could have called and let us know what was goin' on," said Mr. Troutman gruffly.

"We were out in the country," I interjected. "We were never close to a phone."

"Well, we can talk more about it tomorrow," said Mr. Troutman. "I've got to get home. My wife's waitin' supper for me, and I've got a long way to drive."

The Mead High School student council, with advice and input from our history teacher, Mrs. Irene Hausken, had initiated a hearing process where a newly formed student court would consider what disciplinary action should be taken in cases such as this. All four of us appeared before the court, comprised of the presidents and vice presidents of each class. After deliberation, Mrs. Hausken agreed to convey the ruling to us the next day.

"The court was very concerned that the car was going too fast and exceeded the speed that should have been followed while making the turn," said Mrs. Hausken. "Because you are all in my American history class, the court decided that each of you should be asked to give a report to our class on the life of an American patriot who contributed to the writing of the Declaration of Independence. I'll schedule you for a Thursday and a Friday, about three weeks from now."

I found a book on Ben Franklin in our school library and presented a fifteen-minute speech on his science experiments, enjoying the research but uncomfortable with the presentation. To begin with, I perceived I was imposing on my classmates, taking their valuable time to deliver a speech as a penalty for my wrongdoing. It was doubtful that any of them cared what I was saying, much less learning from it. Furthermore, brought up with Mom's dictum that "children should be seen and not heard" and not being encouraged to express myself, I was nervous and stuttering as I spoke. I sounded like a panicked six-year-old caught with his hand in the cookie jar. I was reminded again of the trauma I experienced as president of my eighth-grade class at a graduation dinner we had with the school board as our guests. I was terrified. In retrospect, it would have been better if I had rehearsed my Franklin speech. It also would have been better for me to have taken a speech class, but I never did. I never had the courage to do so. I was too much afraid of the fright, worry, and anxiety it would bring to me.

L-R: Irene Hausken, Arthur Troutman, 1956.
Mead Consolidated Schools Yearbook

L-R: Lanny Davis, Mike Eckel,
1956. *Mead Consolidated Schools
Yearbook*

L-R: Ronnie Newton, Richie
Newton, 1956. *Mead Consolidated
Schools Yearbook*

Chapter 26

Prom

I asked Ginger Palinkx to the prom, a first-time experience for both of us, although we had attended an Eddie Howard dance at Denver's Elitch Gardens the summer before. I had known Ginger for two years, meeting her one summer at Highlandlake, where she lived. The Highlandlake community was a mile and a half from Mead, and Ginger and her family lived in a house that my family lived in before I was born and before the Newtons settled in Mead. Although we had a fondness for each other, we did not demonstrate that outwardly at school or elsewhere, and our conversations were infrequent. I saw her at church on Sundays and on Wednesday evenings during Lent, and as a loyal member of our high-school pep club, I heard her yelling support for our basketball team.

I confided in Rollie that I was going to ask Ginger to the prom, and he told his girlfriend Joann Becker, Ginger's best friend. Therefore, Ginger knew weeks in advance of my asking and was patiently and eagerly waiting for me to say something. Finally, I posed the question to her as we passed each other in the cafeteria. I explained we would be going with my best friend Mike Eckel and Elaine Becker, Joann's elder sister. Elaine and Joann lived on a farm southeast of Mead, and Mike was to pick up Elaine first and then me and then Ginger.

On prom night, Mike had difficulty in finding Elaine's house, and he was more than an hour late picking me up.

Elaine said when they finally arrived, "Ginger called. She was very worried. She thought maybe you had changed your mind about goin'."

Arriving at Highlandlake after nine o'clock, corsage box in hand, I walked up the steps of the Palinkx house.

Ginger answered the door and escorted me in to the room where her dad was watching TV. Seeing me, he blurted out, "You're mighty late, Mr. Newton! The dance is almost over! Where have you been?"

Not expecting to be reproached by her father, I stuttered and stammered, saying, "W-w-well, well, M-M-Mike Eckel got lost. He couldn't find the Becker farmhouse. I-I had to wait for him."

By now, Ginger's milk-white complexion was flushed with embarrassment. Fumbling with the box, fingers trembling, I took out the corsage and nervously tried to pin it on Ginger. I had great difficulty, and finally, Mrs. Palinkx, observing from the kitchen, came to help me attach it to Ginger's narrow shoulder strap.

The four of us entered the darkened gym with the band playing loudly from the stage and couples two-stepping across the floor. Long strands of royal blue paper studded with silver stars hung high above the gym floor. Hanging from the ceiling right below the paper in the center of the gym was a rotating three-foot-diameter sphere constructed of chicken wire and papier mâché and coated with a blackened surface of plaster of Paris in which hundreds of broken mirror pieces were embedded. Beams from strategically placed lights all around the gym glanced off the tiny mirrors in all directions, landing and flickering on the paper sky, across the floor and walls.

Small tables and chairs, covered by large umbrellas, were along the west wall, with a large banner inscribed April in Paris, the theme for the prom evening and selected from the current movie title. Courtesy of the manager of Longmont's Trojan Theater, large pictures of Doris Day and Ray Bolger hung on the north wall. Our proud junior class was certain this was the most elegantly decorated prom ever in Mead's gymnasium.

Refraining from dancing, Mr. Troutman and his young wife stood off to the side with Supt. Carlson, Principal Wendell Johnson, and custodian Marion Humphrey. Dressed in their finest, they talked and smiled as they watched young couples and parent chaperones glide across the floor.

Once again, Ginger reviewed the two-step with me, and we slow-danced to "Unchained Melody," "Picnic," and "Canadian Sunset." Ginger and I worked on the jitterbug, dancing to "Chattanooga Choo Choo" and "In the Mood." We laughed heartily at Mike as he clumsily stumbled, weaving under Elaine Becker's arms and around her, holding his head up in stately fashion as if he was Fred Astaire.

Coach acknowledged us with a sly grin and a quick comment. "Ronnie, you really look like you know what you're doin'." He and his wife, Arden, moved briskly by us, knowing full well that I was struggling too.

Seeing Mike's parents, Marg and Frank, dancing, we stopped momentarily to talk and to introduce them to Ginger.

"Ronnie, your class did an excellent job in decorating. This is really beautiful," said Marg.

"Thank you, Mrs. Eckel. We've been decoratin' for two weeks, and we've been raisin' money all year. We made a lot on our ham raffle. Mr. Troutman has been a good sponsor. He has given us a lot of help."

We said hello to Richie and his date, Francie Palombo. Rollie and Joann Becker were there as well, and so was our brother Jerry and Rosemary Weingardt. Lyle Schaefer was paired with Helen Barnes and Gary Olson with Virginia Boll and Allen Thompson with Barbara Graham. Around the perimeter stood many classmates, girls clothed in floor-length dresses recently purchased from Longmont's finest shops, corsages on their left shoulders, holding hands with their dates dressed in sports coats or suits with collared boutonnieres. Richie, Rollie, and I wore sports coats made of different fabrics, which we bought in Longmont, along with knit ties, a green one for me and blue and maroon for Richie and Rollie, respectively. Jerry, already preparing for his pending graduation, was dressed in a suit.

Joann and Ginger excused themselves for a bathroom break, while Rollie and I stood watching the dancing couples and listening to the music. At intermission, dancers sat at tables or on bleachers, eating cake and cookies and drinking raspberry punch from Dixie cups. The gym echoed with boisterous conversation and laughter as couples sat and scurried from place to place, excitedly acknowledging one another.

Soon, the band was playing its last tune, and I knew that I had to get Ginger home by midnight. I did not want her to endure further chastening from her father about my behavior. It was a short ride to Highlandlake, and we arrived at Ginger's house a little after twelve. I walked Ginger to the front door.

She stood there for just a moment before she said, "I had a great time. Thanks for taking me. Your class really did a good job in decoratin' the gym."

"Thanks," I said. "We spent $300 for the silver-starred paper and $150 for the orchestra. It was well worth it, and we still have money left over for our class to spend next year. Thanks for goin' with me. I had a great time too."

There was a silence and a pause in our conversation.

Finally, I asked, "Can I kiss you?"

Ginger, afraid to answer affirmatively and not expecting to be asked, smiled shyly, saying, "No-o."

I understood her reluctance and was not surprised. She was only a freshman, and I wanted to be respectful of her vulnerability and considerate of her mixed feelings.

"Okay, I will see ya soon. Good night."

I was lying in bed when Rollie came up the stairs to bed after taking Joann home. Knowing that he was going to ask me, I blurted out up front, "She wouldn't let me kiss her."

"She didn't?" Rollie asked, surprised at my words. "I guess she was just afraid. Maybe she was scared her mother would find out. Sometimes Catholic parents can be pretty strict with their kids, especially when they're young like Ginger."

The next week, Joann told Rollie Ginger wished she hadn't said no. That respectful and guarded relationship and the affection Ginger and I had for each other continued into my senior year.

Ginger Palinkx, Elaine Becker, Joann Becker, Francie Polombo, 1956.
Mead Consolidated Schools Yearbook

L-R: Ronnie Newton, Rollie Newton,
and Richie Newton, 1957.
Newton Family Album

Jerry Newton, 1956.
*Mead Consolidated
Schools Yearbook*

Prom wall-mural, 1956. *Mead Consolidated Schools Yearbook*

Mike Eckel, 1957. *Patricia Eckel*

Chapter 27

Award

In 1956, Coach initiated track as the spring sport, replacing baseball, which had been started by Coach Beers. Having enjoyed running long distances all my life, I looked forward to competing, something my brothers and I had not done since grade school. Two years before, I had observed England's Roger Bannister and Australia's John Landy both breaking the four-minute mile barrier on television, with Bannister winning. Having finished the basketball season, I knew I was well conditioned as a runner, but I was not prepared for the rigorous workouts required to condition my body for track.

A sprinter at Colorado State College of Education, Coach was very knowledgeable about track-and-field events. Assessing the talents of his athletes, he began to assign each one to compete in one or more events. He had brother Jerry running the mile and me the half-mile, while Richie and Lyle Schaefer participated in the quarter mile and the mile relay. Jerry Sitzman, Allen Thompson, and Dave high-jumped, and Dave and Richie pole-vaulted. Mike Eckel and Al Frei sprinted in the hundred-yard dash and the 220. Allen, along with Ronnie Schneidmiller, high-jumped and broad-jumped, and Schneidmiller also ran the hurdles.

Running the mile for the first time, Jerry's time was slow at 5:48, but by season's end, he had whittled it down to 5:12, low enough to qualify for the state meet. Allen and Dave were high-jumping five feet and four inches, and Allen qualified for state with a height of five feet and six inches. In the pole vault, Dave, still a freshman, attained a height of ten feet and five inches. My best time for the half-mile was 2:20—far from the league record of 2:07 and definitely too slow to qualify for state.

With the track season finished and the '55–'56 school year winding down, warm weather prevailed, and my brothers and I began thinking about the activities of the summer. One Friday, as we were going to bed, Rollie confided with Richie and me that Allen Thompson and he had skipped school that afternoon.

"We were ridin' 'round town in Allen's car during the noon hour," said Rollie, "and we got a wild hair up our ass that we should go swimmin'. Allen wanted to go to Walker Lake. He had never swum there before, and neither had I. It was hotter 'n hell today, and it's Friday. We didn't want to go to Carlson's world history class. He'd just have us readin' anyhow, and I can do that at home. I wouldn't be missin' anything."

Allen, superb athlete that he was, was an excellent swimmer. With me not knowing the techniques of swimming, it appeared to me at first that it was Allen's strong arms and alternating regular immersion of his hands that propelled him so rapidly and so effortlessly. Trying to imitate him and learning to swim from his instruction, I came to realize it was the vertical up-and-down kicking of his muscular legs that contributed most to his speed. When Allen swam underwater, I could never judge when and where he would surface. He held his breath for long periods, forcing me to think he had surely drowned, only to see his head emerging thirty or forty yards away. Most of the time, my brothers and I were comfortable in the water when Allen was present, for we knew he would be able to take us to safety should the need arise.

"Allen was teaching me to swim, and we went out pretty far where the water was deep," said Rollie. "Out of nowhere, Allen decided he was going to swim to the other side of the lake."

I told him, "Don't leave me alone out here. You know I can't swim."

"He just looked at me and didn't pay any attention to what I said. He went anyhow," said Rollie. "Knowin' we were pretty far out, I got scared. I turned toward shore and started to dog-paddle as fast as I could. I got real tired and started swallowing water. I couldn't catch my breath, and I thought I was gonna drown. I was kickin' as fast as I could, and then finally, my foot felt the bottom. I stumbled with my head going down below the water as I tried to get my balance. Soon, I was able to stand on the bottom with both feet. I stood there and choked on water for a long time before I walked to shore."

"What'd you say to Allen?" I asked.

"I couldn't say anything," said Rollie. "I had already put my clothes on and was standin' there on the side, watching him as he came close. I gave 'im the finger! I was so goddamn mad! I wanted to jump back in the water and beat the sh——t out of 'im, but I knew I couldn't. I've never been so scared in my whole life!"

Richie and I broke into boisterous laughter as we listened to Rollie. He ignored us and continued his diatribe toward Allen.

"I didn't say anything until he came out of the water, and then I told him what a dumb s——t he was. He just laughed, lit up a cigarette, and put on his clothes. I didn't talk to him all the way home. I didn't tell him goodbye or nothin'. I slammed the car door and gave 'im the finger again and walked into the house."

"What are ya goin' to tell Carlson on Monday?" Richie asked, chuckling.

"I dunno," said Rollie. "It's a good thing it's the end of school. I'm hopin' he'll let me off since he's feelin' good about finishin' up the year. Otherwise, he'll probably flunk my ass and Thompson's too. If it were me, I'd give him an F and make that sonuvab——ch take it over next year."

Rollie was always one to express exactly how he felt about an issue, and he wasted no time showing his anger if he felt the situation warranted it. Rollie's anger at himself and at Allen was heightened when Mr. Carlson assigned them both to write a report on World War II heroes as their punishment for missing class. He assigned George Patton to Rollie and Dwight Eisenhower to Allen. They had one week to finish it. The school year was just about over. Allen never bothered to complete his.

During the last week of school, students, faculty, and parents gathered in the gym for the annual "awards night." As always, Supt. Carlson presided and introduced the teachers, who went to the podium to announce the names of the award recipients in their discipline. Coach was last on the program. First, he summarized the accomplishments his teams had made for the year in football, basketball, and track. He asked athletes to come forward and receive their block-letter Ms for participation on a varsity team, stating the sport in which they lettered as he shook their hands and handed them the award—a coveted orange-and-black cloth-bound M with a symbol for each sport in which they participated embroidered in gold.

Mom was there. She brought Marc and Frosty with her. The three of them observed as we five brothers approached the podium to receive our award letters. I'm sure Mom was not thinking about the fact that this was the last time her five sons would be competing on the same team. Instead, she was most likely thinking of her son Jerry. She was thinking that Jerry would graduate. He would be leaving home. He would be her twelfth child to leave. Each time each one walked out the door, it was difficult for her. But she had six more left. It would be several years before her brood was gone.

When finished with the letter awards, Coach said, "Tonight we want to start an award that has never been given at Mead High School. The award is for Mead's Most Outstanding Athlete for this past year. It is based on the athlete's attitude, training, scholarship, and ability, and he will receive this engraved plaque that I have here."

Reaching into his pocket, he pulled out a small jewelry box and opened it. He took a tiny object from the box and held it up for all to see.

"The outstanding athlete will also receive this gold-plated ball. The ball has seam lines etched into it, giving it the appearance of a basketball. A large block-letter M is attached on the front, and a tiny ring is on top. A chain can be slipped through the ring so it can be worn around the neck or arm."

Putting it back in the box, Coach continued talking. "We have chosen the basketball symbol for the award because the awardee's best performances were on the basketball court. However, the award recipient has lettered in three sports: football, basketball, and track. He quarterbacked our football team, guided team play on the basketball court, and ran the half-mile in track. He is a scholar in the classroom, and he has shown excellent leadership with our sports teams. Ladies and gentleman, I'm pleased to announce that Mead High School's Most Outstanding Athlete for this school year is Ronald Newton. Ronnie, would you please come forward?"

I was stunned and emotionally unprepared to respond. I could not believe what I had just heard. I rose from my seat and walked to the podium, looking down all the way, nervous and anxious as I listened to the applause.

Coach, smiling and proud, shook my hand and handed me the tiny box. "Congratulations, Ronnie," he said.

I said nothing to Coach. I could not speak, and I could not smile. As I walked back to my seat, I was so overwhelmed by the sudden joy, I began crying. Embarrassed by my display of emotion, I looked down and made no eye contact with anyone. At my seat, I still could not control my weeping. My only thought was an athlete should not be crying. I felt very vulnerable. I perceived myself to be a fragile weakling in front of all those people. But I was proud of my achievement. I knew this was a very significant event in my young life. I was proud I had been selected by my coach, a man whose opinions I greatly respected. I was proud that my selection was based not only on my performance as an athlete but also on my performance in the classroom. I was proud my coach recognized my leadership skills both on the football field and on the basketball court.

Mom never said a word to me about the award. It would have been uncharacteristic of her to shower one of her children with praise. I asked myself, Was she fearful that "my star" might start to twinkle too brightly and too often? I never knew what her thoughts were that night, but I bet Mom was deeply proud that the star of one of her children was glowing brightly for all the Mead community to see.

1956 Outstanding Athlete Award,
Mead High School, 2017. *Ronald Newton*

Illustration of 1956 Outstanding Athlete Award,
Mead High School. 2016. *Ronald Newton*

Chapter 28

Summer

For three summers in our early teens, my four brothers and I toiled in the sugar beet fields, thinning them from overplanting and removing competitive weeds. This was tiring and laborious work, and the pay was minimal. In the summer of '56, we were rescued from this boring, backbreaking endeavor when we were given other opportunities for summer work. I was offered a job helping the Eckels build a dairy barn.

While I worked on the barn construction, my best friend Mike Eckel worked for his dad cultivating corn, irrigating corn and barley, and mowing hay. Mike drove about the farm on a Vespa motor scooter Frank had bought for him. One Monday morning, he drove up to the well near the barn while I was taking a drink of water.

"You'll never guess what happened this weekend," said Mike. "I went with Marg and Frank to the Markhams' house yesterday. Glenn's gettin' married, so the Markhams had a reception for his fiancée. She's from Longmont. Her name's Pat Harvey."

"I know who she is," I said. "She used to go with Johnny Hartman, Longmont's quarterback. She lives on Collyer Street. Our friend Walt Slee drives by there a lot when we're in Longmont."

"Well, she has a sister who's in our grade at Longmont," Mike interjected. "Her name is Sue. Sue and I got ta talkin', and I asked her if she could line me up with some of the Longmont girls to go out with. She said she would." Mike then chuckled, "And you know what, Ronnie? I'll be darned if she didn't call me last night. She said she called a friend of hers, and they want me to go to Longmont this Friday and double-date with her and her boyfriend. His name is Jerry Green. The girl's name is Linda Miller. Sue says she's really good-lookin', a beautiful girl, about five-foot-three. She'll be a senior, so she's our age. Can you believe it, Ronnie?"

"You lucky dog!" I exclaimed. "Is Sue good-lookin'? Our friend Walt says her sister Pat is."

"You damn right she is," said Mike. "I'd ask her out, but she's already goin' with that other guy."

Mike was seeing Linda Miller regularly. Marg and Frank were letting him take the Oldsmobile to Longmont a couple of times a week. One day, as Mike and I were riding in their truck, I asked him, "Do you think Linda could line me up with one of her friends?"

"I don't know," said Mike. "I'll ask her and see what she says. She's got lots of friends. Longmont's a big school."

Several days later, Mike rode up on his Vespa as I was sitting in front of the barn, eating my lunch.

"I talked to Linda last night," said Mike. "She said one of her best friends just broke up with her boyfriend, and maybe she might be interested in goin' out with someone else. He's on the wrestling team. His name is Ronnie Schlagel. Linda didn't know what happened between them. They broke up about two weeks ago. Her name is Kathy Nottingham. She and Linda sat next to each other in typing class. I guess Linda sees her almost every day this summer. She drives her dad's car all over Longmont. Linda's goin' to ask her when she sees her. She'll let me know."

Hearing this, I was ecstatic. I hoped Kathy would give her consent.

I saw Mike riding his Vespa on the road over the next couple of days, but he did not stop to talk. I was worried that Kathy did not want to go out and that Mike was having a hard time breaking the news to me.

Finally, one morning Mike gave me the good news. "Linda told me Nottingham wants to go out with you. Shall we take 'em to a movie in Longmont Saturday night?" he asked.

"That's okay with me," I said casually, trying not to show my excitement.

That Saturday night in July was the beginning of the relationship that Kathy and I had, which lasted into our high-school senior year. At first, Mike and Linda accommodated us double-dating in the Eckel Oldsmobile. Then Mike said, "Ronnie, can you get your brother's car some night and go by yourself?"

"I'm sure I can," I said. "I think Jerry will let me use his. Sometimes Tom is home for the weekends, and he doesn't go anywhere. So I could ask him too."

One evening, while sitting in Tom's car outside Kathy's house, Kathy informed me, "We all came to Mead last year to see you Newtons play basketball. We sat up in the balcony of the gym to watch. Linda Moore wanted to see you play. She remembered meeting you when you played softball in Longmont. There were four of us, and there were all you brothers playin'. Linda wanted to cheer for you, so she told each of us to pick one of you to cheer for."

"We didn't have any idea that you were there," I said. "Was Linda Miller with you?"

"Yes, she was," said Kathy. "We were all proud that we yelled and helped you win. You were playin' Johnstown. We had a good time that night, yellin' for all you good-lookin' boys."

"Well," I said, "that's why we go to Longmont and drag Main. We want to see all you good-lookin' girls."

"That's what we do too," said Kathy. "We want to see you Newtons. We girls here in Longmont get pretty excited when we see you Newtons are in town."

"We like to go look at you girls at your football games," I said. "We play our games in the afternoons so we can go into Longmont on Friday nights to see all of you. It looks like Longmont's going to have another good team this year, doesn't it?"

"It sure does," said Kathy. "I think we'll win state again."

I noticed that Kathy's skin had been browned by the summer sun and that her auburn hair was sun bleached. I knew Kathy, like many of the girls in Longmont with parents of means, did not depend on summer jobs for discretionary spending and that summers for them were leisurely and fun-filled.

Knowing the answer before I spoke, I asked Kathy, "Whatcha girls been doin' all summer?"

"Not much of anything," answered Kathy. "We've been playin', goin' to Sunset to swim and sunbathe. We've also been hangin' out over at the Boulder Reservoir. There's some good sand for us to lie on and soak up the sun. That's where all the boys are too. Sometimes they take us water-skiin'."

"You look like you've been out in the sun," I commented.

"You too," said Kathy. "The hair on your arms is all bleached."

"I'm out in the sun a lot, but sometimes I'm workin' inside. Right now, I'm helpin' the Eckels build their milk barn. I been glazin' windows, layin' blocks, paintin' walls, mixin' cement, and doin' all kinds of stuff. I work with Mike once in a while too. We hauled hay and irrigated barley. We were up all night settin' up the water when it came in from Highlandlake. It was fun, but it was a tough job. We had to make sure the aluminum pipes from the ditch were carrying water down each row. They had to be checked 'round the clock every couple of hours."

"Sue Harvey's sister Pat lives on a farm now out here by Mead," said Kathy. "She's been a city girl all her life, says that livin' on a farm is really hard to get used to. She says her husband is up from daylight to dark doin' all the farm work. Her sister drives a truck for 'im during the grain harvest. That's why my dad quit farmin' and moved to Longmont. He couldn't do all that hard work anymore. We still have the farm out there near Genoa, but my dad rents it out. Boy, am I glad we don't live out there anymore and are here in Longmont. My elder sister helped my dad feed cattle and drove a tractor for him, but I never had to."

"I like workin' on a farm," I said. "I like irrigatin'. It's fun. Mike is teachin' me to drive a tractor. He says maybe I can cultivate their corn for 'em. What I've been doin' now on the Eckel farm has been all new for me. I've learned to do a lot of different things this summer. Matter'a fact, just about everything I've done these last several months has been a new experience, includin' meetin' you."

Ronnie Newton, 1957.
Newton Family Album

Mike Eckel, 1957.
Patricia Eckel

Eckel Farm Buildings, 1957. *Patricia Eckel*

Chapter 29

Gridiron Success

As the annual cycle of life revolves, humans hope for new successes. In the fall of '56, Mead High was no exception as the school year was about to begin. Our football team had every reason to expect the previous year's record of no wins could be surpassed, and now with our experience and talent, our expectation of a winning season was tucked in the corners of our minds. In both 1954 and 1955, our friend Walt Slee had taken my brothers and me to see the state Class AA football championship games with Longmont High winning both years using the split-T formation. Coach had schooled us with this same formation the year before. We were confident it would help us have a successful season.

Classes had not yet started when Coach assembled our football team for two-a-day practices. It was late afternoon when thirty very diverse-sized bodies, clad in all-white uniforms, congregated at the goal line on the north end of the football field. Small five-foot-tall ninth-graders with oversized pads falling off their shoulders contrasted sharply with senior teammates with well-fitted equipment. Helmets off and hands on our hips, we all breathed heavily while taking respite from the fifty-yard wind sprint we had just completed. We were all facing south, getting ready to run two more sprints downfield and then two more back. Coach lined players up at the goal line, ten at a time, and, with a blast of his whistle, sent us off to the fifty-yard line, where we met assistant coach Bill Callahan, who aligned them for the second fifty-yard dash to the other goal line. Coaches Adams and Callahan repeated these sprint drills three times and then sent us en masse to run around the track six times.

Now that football practice had started, I had to leave work on the Eckel farm at three-thirty rather than the usual five o'clock. Furthermore, I was no longer going to work at seven in the morning now that Coach had scheduled a second morning practice session at six-thirty. My normal nine-and-a-half-hour workday had now been cut to six. In spite of the reduced work time, Mrs. Eckel generously paid me the $7 a day for the two weeks before school started.

For most of the summer, I had helped contractor Frank Malevich install a milking operation in the Eckel barn, but now Mike and I were hauling hay, feeding cows, and building fences. I had built up my strength by carrying cinder blocks and two-by-fours, transporting wheelbarrows of cement, shoveling sand and soil, heaving hay bales, and slinging pitchforks of ensilage. Eating plate-loads of vegetables prepared by Mom from her garden, I tried to increase my weight. Last year, I had been listed in the football program as a 135-pound quarterback. This year, I aspired to be 145 pounds and a lot stronger.

However, I had not run long distances since the previous spring when I was a half-miler on the track team. But I was not alone. None of my twenty-nine other teammates had done any recent distance running. The six laps Coach asked us to run were challenging and, for some the laps, were overwhelming. I managed to complete all six without stopping, but many teammates slowed to a walk for twenty or thirty seconds before resuming a slow pace and finally finishing. But this stop-and-go pattern would change over the next weeks; Coach would have our team ready for the first game with nonleague opponent Denver Lutheran.

With all of us exhausted players sitting on the ground around him to rest, Coach said, "Tomorrow we'll start work on our offense. We'll still use the split-T. All you guys from last year know what it's like. Coach Callahan will be working with all you playin' on defense. We'll let you know tomorrow who that'll be. Most of you'll be playin' both ways."

Looking at Ronnie Vogel, who, at 185 pounds, played tackle last year, Coach said, "Ronnie, we want to try you at fullback. With your weight and speed, you'll be real hard to bring down. We may still keep you on the line some as a tackle, but I think you'll help us more by carryin' the ball." Then glancing toward Rollie, he said, "Rollie, we need some help in the middle on the offensive line this year, so I'm going to put you at center. You have good hands. We'll also play you on defense."

Missing from our team was Allen Thompson. Allen had not enrolled in school that fall. Instead, he was working for any farmer who could use his truck-driving service. Allen had to bring in money to pay for the new Dodge truck he had purchased that summer. Allen undoubtedly would have started at a halfback position, but Coach filled the void by inserting sophomore Al Frei into the lineup. Frei, running the hundred-yard dash in 10.6 seconds, gave Mead an outside scoring threat, and Mike Eckel, with an 11.2-second hundred-yard dash speed, provided Mead good power through the interior of the line.

I was playing the key position of quarterback. Coach did not want me to get injured and would not allow me to play defense. However, my three brothers played "both ways." Dave alternated with me at quarterback and also played defensive safety. Rollie was offensive center, and Richie was at the receiver position, and both played defense. Lyle Schaefer, a talented 170-pound tackle, was on the right side of the line both offensively and defensively, and Walter Ayres was on the left side in the tackle slot. Bill Schneidmiller and Clayton Knight were hard-hitting linebackers, while Larry Nuss played defensive halfback.

With my brother Dave and me quarterbacking, we scored in every quarter against our first opponent, Denver Lutheran, on a Friday afternoon game on our home field. Dave hit Al Frei with a twenty-five-yard pass for one touchdown, and I connected with two twenty-yard passes to Richie for two large gains. Mike Eckel, at halfback, galloped for a thirty-six-yard run for one touchdown. Our defense kept Denver Lutheran scoreless.

Our resounding win boosted our confidence and inflated our egos, but we were brought back to reality in our next game with Greeley's College High when we did not even score until the fourth quarter. A touchdown opportunity was set up when Bill Schneidmiller retrieved a quick kick and ran it back forty-eight yards to the College High thirty-four-yard line. Then I hit Mike Eckel on a short pass, and Mike carried it to the one-yard line. With the next play, I handed off to Ronnie Vogel, who scored over right tackle. On the ensuing kickoff, Vogel, now playing defense, recovered a fumble on the College High thirty-eight-yard line. On the next play, I faked the ball to halfback Al Frei with a dive play over right tackle and handed off to fullback Vogel, who carried the ball to College High's nineteen-yard line. Two plays later, I passed to Richie, who was alone in the end zone, for our second touchdown. We missed both extra-point attempts, and so did College High. The final score was a 12–12 tie.

In our first league game, Timnath scored in the second quarter when their Don Partridge burst through our offensive line and tipped my forward pass into the air. Partridge caught it and carried it into the end zone for a Timnath touchdown. They scored again on a safety in the final quarter when an errant hike went over my head and out of the end zone. We were impotent offensively throughout the game, and we lost 8–0.

However, we blitzed our next opponent, Estes Park, playing a night game beneath dim lights at an altitude of seven thousand feet, surrounded by tall mountains. The night air was comfortably cool, and there was dew on the freshly mown grass. On our first offensive play in our split-T formation with me at quarterback and receiving the snap from Rollie, I whirled to my left and circled back to hand off to right halfback Al Frei, who was moving left behind fullback Ronnie Vogel and left halfback Mike Eckel. All three, running parallel to the line, were gaining speed as they swept around Estes Park's defensive line. Out in front, Eckel placed his shoulder into the torso of their defensive end, knocking him to the ground, while Vogel placed a body block on their defensive halfback. Frei skirted the fallen opponents, gaining thirty-two yards before he was tackled on Estes's forty-four-yard line.

On the next down, I called the same play to the right, with Eckel carrying the ball and Frei and Vogel blocking. Eckel took it another thirty-five yards to their nine-yard line. The next play, I faked a handoff to Vogel over right guard and instead gave it to Frei, following through the same side over tackle. Frei found a big hole that Lyle Schaefer had made in their defensive line and carried the ball into the end zone for the touchdown.

Thereafter, we scored almost at will. Frei scored again over right guard, and in the second quarter, Vogel carried the ball into the end zone from five yards out. With Dave quarterbacking in the third quarter, Dave hit Frei on a thirty-one-yard pass, and Frei carried it another nine yards into the end zone. We stopped Estes Park from scoring on our own one-yard line, and with me quarterbacking, we marched downfield to the Estes twenty-eight-yard line in just five plays. With the next play, I handed off to Eckel, who flipped a twenty-five-yard pass to Richie, who carried it to the three-yard line. On the next play, Vogel scored the touchdown. With us far ahead, Coach substituted our second and third teams. Estes finally scored on a sixty-yard pass, and we went on to win 31–6.

A week later, we nudged Gilcrest 12–6. I completed two twenty-yard passes to Richie to set up two touchdown runs for Vogel. Both scores resulted from a fake dive play to halfback Frei over right tackle and then giving a reverse handoff to Vogel, running through the center of the line after Rollie, taking out Gilcrest's middle linebacker with upright blocks, opened the holes.

On the following Friday afternoon, we romped over Evans 35–6. However, our potent offensive machine sputtered the next week, and we barely eked out a win over LaSalle. Trailing 12–0 at halftime, we kept LaSalle from scoring in the second half and made two touchdowns and an extra point to win 13–12. The LaSalle victory was a significant one for Mead and kept us in the race for the league crown. In a tie for second place with Timnath with a record of four and one, we were only one game behind league-leading Erie, still undefeated at five and zero.

At our Monday practice, Coach stood before our team, all of us sitting on the grass ready to hear what he had to say about the important game at Erie on Friday. "This game is for the big enchilada," said Coach excitedly. "With a win this week, we'll be tied with Erie. They play the split-T just like we do. They've been beatin' people with high scores, beat Frederick, forty-four to nothin' and Evans, fifty-one to nothin'. But cha know, guys, we've been doin' purty well ourselves. I think we can match up with 'em."

We were playing at Mead, and folks were aware of the significance of the game, and more cars than ever were parked diagonally next to the field and in the school parking lot. The small set of aluminum bleachers was full of spectators, and many others were standing along the sidelines, while some viewed the game from the comfort of their cars. Town barber Grover Roberts stood by his '46 Ford parked outside the north end zone, while Tony Dempewolf, having the same north perspective, chose to sit in his Texaco truck to observe. Ronnie Vogel's dad perched on the hood of his car to watch, and so did farmer and cattle feeder Dean Seewald. It was rumored that Dean had a large bet on the game with a sizeable point spread and was pulling for the Bulldogs. With a small metal cash box in hand, Supt. Carlson walked among the cars and spectators, collecting admissions. Hoping to see Mead win, Ronald Weber took the afternoon off from his carpentry work, and Donnie Giebelhaus stopped digging sugar beets for a couple of hours on his nearby farm to support his alma mater.

Mead got the ball on the opening kickoff, and within four minutes of the start, Eckel scampered twenty-two yards on a dive play over left tackle for a touchdown, and Vogel went over right tackle for the extra point. Throughout the first half, our undersized tackles, Walter Ayres and Lyle Schaefer, took on Erie's big tackles with ferocity, and linebackers Clayton Knight and Billy Schneidmiller courageously held Erie's running backs to short gains. We held Erie scoreless for the first half and went into the locker room at halftime, leading 7–0.

In the third quarter, we again moved downfield on the ground and were soon in Erie territory. We were on Erie's thirty-five-yard line when a holding penalty was called on Rollie. On the way back to the huddle, Rollie said to me, "That wasn't me. Why'd they call it on me? Hell, I wasn't even close to that play. I didn't hold anybody."

Erie held us on downs and forced us to punt. At that point, the momentum of the game shifted in Erie's favor. Vogel broke a bone in his foot in the third quarter and did not play thereafter. Erie's Ron Miller and Jim Beshears each scored a touchdown in the third quarter, and Miller scored another in the fourth. The final score was Erie, 20, and Mead, 7.

We had lost our quest for the North Central League championship, and there was a somber mood in the locker room as we showered. I reflected for a few moments on the game. We had been beaten soundly, and our fullback had been injured. I recalled the great excitement I felt when Eckel surprisingly broke through their line to score the first touchdown. I recalled Coach's enthusiastic pep talk at halftime, encouraging our team to not let up. I took solace from the fact that Erie's Beshears fumbled on the Mead two-yard line with thirty seconds to go. The score could have been a lot worse. I knew Erie was the better team, but I also knew we had the best record of any Mead High School football team since Mead won the six-man championship in '49. I was proud that our school had not only earned success as a basketball powerhouse but had also shown that Mead High could also contend on the football field. If Mead could beat Berthoud the next week, Mead would have five wins and two losses for the season, a record of which we could be very proud.

I also knew it would be hard to concentrate on the Berthoud game now that we were no longer contending for the league title. And it would be especially difficult for me because I was more excited than ever about the upcoming basketball season. In two weeks, I would be playing basketball. My brothers and I would be on the court. For me, basketball season was the best time of the year. But what happened the next week caused me great concern about the Newtons' sports future at Mead High.

On Monday afternoon, while all of us were putting on our full dress of uniforms, Coach stuck his head into the locker room and said, "I want everybody to meet up in the gym before we go out to the field. I have something I want to talk to you about."

Coach stood in front of us, a football in his hand. He was dressed in his usual baseball cap, white sweatshirt, whistle hanging around his neck, and knee-length football pants with no thigh pads. He, like everybody else, was in his stocking feet. He was not looking at us and smiling as he usually was. Instead, he had his back to us and was looking down at the floor.

He turned to address us, and as he talked, he flipped the football from one hand to the other. He said, "We faced a good football team last week. They've won the league title outright, and it looks like they'll be going to the state playoffs. They're two games out in front of everybody else. They play Gilcrest this week. Even if they lose—which they probably won't—they'll win the league title."

Still tossing the football back and forth between his hands, he continued, "We were in the game last week until they called holdin' on us and stopped our drive. We were ready to score again. Then with Vogel breaking his foot, it was uphill the rest of the game. But you all did well, especially our defense. You held in there, at least for three quarters. This is the final game this week with Berthoud. It'll be the final game for you seniors, and it's our homecoming. We want to win this one. The season is not over yet."

Then looking at me, he said, "Ronnie, don't start thinking about basketball. It will come soon enough. We've got a whole week of football yet. I want you to focus on that. Don't be lookin' ahead." He gazed at our group. "That goes for all of you. We can't be thinkin' about basketball when we got Berthoud yet to play. They beat us up purty good last year. We don't want that to happen this year."

Then he looked sternly at us. He said nothing as he gathered his thoughts before he said, "Someone here this afternoon has been smokin'. He was seen last weekend. He must think the season is over, and so he's fallin' back into his old habits. It looks like he's given up on himself and his team." He paused for a moment. "Now that person knows who he is. He's sittin' right here with you. He knows he's broken the rule. He knows he shouldn't have lit one up."

Then looking directly at Rollie, who was nervously twisting at his hair with his left hand, he asked, "Isn't that right, Rollie? What about that? You know who it is. You've been smokin', haven'cha, Rollie?"

Rollie did not answer. He could not look at Coach. He looked down and continued twisting the front of his hair.

There was silence in the gym. I couldn't look at Coach either. I asked myself, How did Coach find out about this? Who would have told him? I was certain it wasn't anybody on the team. Did he himself see Rollie? I had not seen Rollie smoking. He wasn't smoking in our upstairs bedroom. Where did Coach see him? Did Coach see Rollie smoking in the car when Rollie was driving home after working at the Longmont Drug? Now what was Coach going to do? Will he kick Rollie off the football team? Would he kick him off the basketball team as well?

"Rollie," he said as Rollie held his head up to look at Coach and hear what was coming, "turn your suit in. You won't be playin' this week. You've played your last football game."

He placed the ball in his right hand and raised it above his head and behind him. He threw it swiftly at Rollie, sitting twenty yards away. Rollie, surprised to see it coming at him, reacted immediately and held out both hands to catch it.

Coach then said, "Rollie, get ready for basketball for next week, and for god's sake, cut out that dumb smokin'. I figured you to be smarter than that. Don't make that mistake in basketball. If you do, you're goin to be watchin' the game from the bleachers. Do you understand?"

Again, Rollie could not look at him, nor did Rollie answer. In his mind, he had been disgraced and embarrassed. I too was embarrassed. I was saddened that Rollie could not play the final game with us, but I was glad he would be able to play basketball. Our team would need him.

On Thursday, the first blizzard of the year came, and school was cancelled all over Weld County. All the North Central League Friday football games were cancelled and scheduled for the following Tuesday. And the Mead High School homecoming dance was postponed to the next Friday, following our rescheduled Tuesday game with Berthoud.

Our passing game was most successful against Berthoud. I hit Richie, our primary receiver, with six completions out of fifteen attempts. Most were short yardage where Richie cut in front of their outside linebacker, and I, after receiving the ball from center, placed it over my head with both hands and lobbed a soft basketball pass to Richie for a four- or five-yard gain. On longer passes to Richie, I had learned I had to throw the pass to him before he made his ninety-degree turn to maneuver past his defender. As Richie turned abruptly, my throw was timed so the ball was immediately there for him to grab and tuck before he was tackled.

Our first touchdown pass came in the fourth quarter, when I threw a fifteen-yard pass to Al Frei, who caught it on the thirty-five-yard line and carried it into the end zone for our first score. Dave, alternating at quarterback, hit Richie with two passes, giving Mead a total passing yardage for the game of 145 with ten completions. Billy Schneidmiller, playing fullback for the injured Ronnie Vogel, scored our second touchdown, and we won our final homecoming game 12–6.

I was ecstatic at game's end. We had fulfilled our expectations with a winning football season, and basketball season was to start on Monday, and I was going to the homecoming dance with Kathy Nottingham.

L-R: Dave Newton, Richie Newton, Rollie Newton, and Ronnie Newton,
1956. *Mead Consolidated Schools Yearbook*

Homecoming King and Queen.
Ronald Vogel and
Elaine Leinweber, 1956.
Mead Consolidated Schools Yearbook

Coach Jack Adams,
1956.
*Mead Consolidated
Schools Yearbook*

L-R: Dave Newton and Ronnie Newton, 1956.
Mead Consolidated Schools Yearbook

Chapter 30

First

Kathy Nottingham was from Longmont. I began dating her in midsummer, and with each date, we grew closer. I knew I liked her more than any other human being I had ever known. At five-foot-eight and model like, Kathy wore close-fitting straight skirts and sweaters that accentuated her curvaceous figure. Her hair, closely cropped at the back of her neck, framed her face, a face with beautiful skin and an infectious smile. Kathy's sparkling eyes, coupled with an ever-present smile whenever I saw her, conveyed to me that I was an important person in her life. Our conversations were vibrant and engaging. She had a great interest in my activities at Mead and I as well toward Longmont High. We talked a lot about religion and our life philosophies. She, from a family of three siblings and a Protestant, attended church each Sunday. Education was important to the Nottingham family. Her elder sister attended Colorado A&M College, and Kathy had aspirations attending an out-of-state university. Born into a family of moderate wealth, Kathy was a source of pride as a girlfriend who showed a sincere interest in me despite my lower economic and social status. Popular among her classmates, Kathy was elected vice president of her senior class.

Kathy lived on Longmont's Collyer Street in a house that was small and temporary. The Nottinghams had just moved to Longmont from a farm near Genoa. They would build a new house very soon. At the end of each double date, Mike Eckel and Linda Miller waited in the car, while I escorted Kathy to the door. There was a small alcove hanging over the three steps up to the front door from which a bright light hung and lit up the whole front yard. I wanted to kiss her, but I was afraid to. I knew Mike and Linda would be watching us, and furthermore, I was not certain Kathy wanted me to do so.

Each time, I would ask, "Can you go out next Saturday?"

She would always answer, "Yes, I can."

Then I would say, "I'll call ya next week."

One day, in physics class, Mike told me matter-of-factly, "Linda said Kathy was going to get you to kiss her if it killed her. She says she's goin' to get you to do it the next time you take her out. So, Ronnie, ya gotta get it done, son. Quit fartin' around!"

The next Saturday night, Kathy and I pulled up in front of her house in my brother Tom's '56 Ford. We walked up the sidewalk and up the stairs to the front door. Both of us understood what was about to happen.

I spoke first, asking, "Can I kiss you?"

"Yes, you may," said Kathy, knowing full well I had not phrased my question with the correct English and that she had responded correctly.

"You're goin' to have to show me how," I said. "I've never kissed anybody before."

"Well," she said, grabbing both my hands and placing them into hers as she stepped toward me, "you put your arms around me like this." She moved closer to me and wrapped both my arms around her. She reached upward and put her left hand gently on the back of my neck and placed her right arm gracefully around my waist. She, at nearly my height, brought her face toward mine and said, "Then you kiss me like this."

She pulled me to her and pressed her lips to mine. With Kathy in control of my whole body like a puppeteer with strings attached to a rag doll, I shifted my feet and placed my hands on her hips. With our lips still fastened, I moved closer to her and wrapped my arms around her once again. Our mouths then parted, and we remained silent as we clung to each other in a close embrace. I wrapped my hand around her waist. It seemed smaller than I had ever imagined. To me, Kathy's whole body seemed tiny, fragile, and delicate. My sudden sense of physical dominance over Kathy empowered me with overwhelming confidence.

Kathy softly voiced her approval. "I've wanted you to do this for a long time."

Driving home to Mead, I recalled the Broadway musical song "Some Enchanted Evening." I had heard Ezio Pinza sing that song many times on the radio. I had seen Mary Martin and Pinza on television singing this electrifying song that had a special resonance for me. It conjured up feelings of excitement and exhilaration whenever I considered the prospect of seeing "that stranger" for the first time. I imagined what it would be like, and I hoped that enchanted evening would come for me. It did when I first saw Kathy.

I remembered my feelings when I was introduced to her by Linda Miller and when Kathy opened the door to greet us at her house, and she invited us in to meet her parents. I could not stop looking at her. At that moment, I was feeling more than I ever imagined. At that moment, I knew that Kathy was a girl I wanted to see again and again. With that first kiss, I had come to know her like I had never known her before. I had thought hundreds of times how great it was going to be when I kissed a girl I really liked for the first time. With Kathy, my expectations of that magical moment in that enchanted evening had been fulfilled.

Shortly thereafter, the two of us decided that we should demonstrate our loyalty to each other more visibly.

"I don't have a class ring to give you," I said. "I didn't ever buy one. Mike Eckel's mother told us not to get one. She said you won't wear it after you graduate from high school. She sez they aren't worth it."

"You could let me wear that basketball you got last spring," said Kathy. "You know, the one you told me about, the one your coach gave you for bein' the outstanding athlete. I could wear it on a chain around my neck. I'll wear it every day to school."

During Christmas break, my mind was more on Kathy than on our traditional Newton festivities. As soon as our family finished unwrapping presents on Christmas Eve, I drove to Longmont to see Kathy and exchange gifts. She had just gotten home from a church service she and her family had attended. She was wearing a bright red sweater with a long gold chain and my tiny basketball hanging from her neck.

"Open mine first," I said, handing her a large flat box.

As she took off the Christmas wrapper, she unveiled the words Ann's Style Shop on the box.

"I bet you paid a lot for what's inside here," she said.

"You're worth it. I've been savin' the money I've made working for the Eckels. Mike bought one for Linda too. We went shoppin' together."

"This is beautiful," she said as she pulled a turquoise sweater from the box and held it in front of her. "Thank you. I really love it."

"Mike got Linda the same thing, only hers is blue."

Kathy then handed me a small box, the kind you get from a jewelry store. Inside was a silver medal attached to a sterling silver chain, sitting on a bed of cotton.

"Where did you find this?" I asked excitedly with total surprise.

"At Snyder's Jewelry," she said. "Can you see what's on it?" Before I could answer, she said, "It's an angel. The lady in the store told me it was St. Michael, the archangel. You told me you and your brothers were born on his feast day. I thought you might like to wear it."

"Oh, I do," I said. "The chain broke on the one I had. It had a picture of the Holy Family on it. I've wanted a new one. I'll wear this one all the time. I'd wear it playin' basketball, except Coach won't let me. Ya know, in the Catholic Church, they always show him as a soldier with a sword standin' on top of the devil. They say he's a warrior fightin' off evil."

Kathy took the chained medal from my hands and placed the chain around my neck. "When I think of you, I think of you as one who fights bad things. You're always tryin' to be good. You're so much better than me. You're the nicest boy I've ever known."

"I guess I am a fighter," I said, "'specially when I'm playin' basketball. I always think if I am a better person, I'll be a better player. Thanks! Thanks! This is the best Christmas present I've ever gotten."

As she kissed me on the cheek, I whispered, "I'm never goin' to take this off, only when I play basketball. Maybe what I should do is take it off and pin it inside my jersey so Coach won't see it."

Illustration of St. Michael the Archangel Medal, 2016. *Ronald Newton*

Chapter 31

Lesson Learned

As the '56–'57 basketball season began, sportswriter Bud Pitchford of the *Longmont Times Call* wrote the following on December 12, 1956:

Newtons Going Strong

The Newtons are going strong for the Mead Bulldogs, and that school should have another fine basketball season. In fact, if the Bulldogs had a tall experienced pivot man, we don't know who would stop them. As it is, all of Mead's opponents are going to know they have been in a basketball game before they get through with them.

If you want to see a cage team with loads of natural ability and average size but beautiful teamwork, drop out to Mead some night during the basketball season and watch the Bulldogs in action. Especially keep your eyes on those four Newton boys.

It still was not certain who the fifth man would be. We did not have a tall pivot man. Allen Thompson had not enrolled in school and so would not be starting the basketball season. Undoubtedly, Coach was looking forward to having Rollie back. Rollie had missed the previous year because of a detected heart murmur. Coach knew the starting five would include us four Newtons, with Dave and Rollie as forwards and Richie and me as guards. But Mead had lost all its big men; Jerry Sitzman, Lawrence Jensen, and George Flores had graduated.

In our scrimmages, Coach tried Lyle Schaefer at center. Lyle was six-foot-one and weighed 178 pounds. He was also smart, and under Coach's tutelage, Lyle caught on quickly and learned the subtle nuances on how to play the position. Lyle had played tackle on Mead's football team, and he had learned to "hold his own space." He would not be pushed around on the basketball floor. Coach liked what he saw with Lyle in the starting lineup; the team had gelled with four Newtons and a Schaefer.

Our basketball team had practiced diligently during the week after Thanksgiving. In early December on a Tuesday night on our home court, Mead took on Johnstown from the Platte Valley League in a nonleague contest. The place was jammed with spectators who were anticipating the basketball season just as much as my brothers and me. Walt Slee came along with Bud Pitchford. Mom took her seat beside Martin and Mary Graham and Bub Howlett. Conrad Hopp Sr. came to see his son Paul play. The president of our senior class, Ronnie Vogel, brought cheerleader Elaine Leinweber to the game. Ronald Weber and Herb Newman came, and so did Johnnie Schell and his new bride, Irene. Bobby Seewald, home from the army, brought cheerleader Elaine Becker. Absent from the stands were the Thompsons. Their son Allen was not attending school. A noticeable void had been created at Mead High both in the stands and on the court.

This was to be Lyle Schaefer's first start at center, the fifth member of a team of four Newtons. Together, we triplets made fourteen free throws, but Dave, Richie, and I also each missed three. We brothers made forty-eight of Mead's points, and Mead eased by Johnstown, 50–46. Coach, remembering the missed opportunities at the foul line, had us practicing free shots the rest of the week.

The following Saturday evening against Greeley's College High, a Class A team from the Tri-Valley League, Rollie pulled down seventeen rebounds compared to College High's team total of eighteen. Besides dominating the boards, our defense held College High to just two points in the third quarter. We earned seventeen points at the free-throw line while still missing eight and won easily 51–40.

On Tuesday the following week, we traveled to Windsor to play our former archrival, now a member of the newly constituted Class A Tri-Valley League. Windsor played us real tight inside with their sagging zone, leaving the outside free and allowing Richie and me to each score sixteen points from the perimeter, mostly with long set shots. The game was heavily contested until the end of the third quarter when we pulled away to a five-point lead and then went on to win 50–46.

Our North Central League season began the second week of December against Timnath. We took control of the game, leading by twelve at the half and by sixteen at the end of the third quarter. Throughout the contest, Rollie ferociously fought off Timnath's Larry Collier for rebounds. In the fourth quarter, Collier tried to wrestle the ball away from Rollie's clutched hands, only to be dragged over Rollie and onto his back as Rollie gained sole possession. This resulted in a foul called on the defender, Collier, but also caused Rollie to become "hoppin' mad" at Collier for committing such a flagrant physical foul. Rollie's anger was so intense, he had to be separated from Collier before a fight ensued.

Running up to Rollie and getting between him and Collier, I said to him, "Come on, Rollie. Don't let 'im get to you."

"Whataya mean 'get to me'?" Rollie burst out. "He was on top of me like I was a goddamn buckin' horse!"

As I walked with Rollie toward the foul line, Rollie said, "That dirty b——d. He does that again, and I'll cold-cock him. The dumb son of a b——ch shouldn't be playin' like that. This is not football."

Rollie, coming off seventeen rebounds the week before, had established himself as the best and toughest rebounder in the league, always holding his ground. If opponents weren't in position, they simply weren't going to get the ball.

With Mead leading by sixteen, Coach took his starters out of the game, and Lanny Davis, Carl Hansen, Paul Hopp, Mike Eckel, and

George Rademacher played the last five minutes. I scored twenty points, Lyle Schaefer had eight, Rollie got ten, and Richie dumped in nine. We won handily 61–47. We shot seventeen free-throws and made thirteen of them—a respectable 80 percent.

Now because of the upcoming Christmas holiday, the league had scheduled several back-to-back games on Friday and Saturday nights. On Saturday, Erie was scheduled to play Mead in the Erie gym. This would be the first time Mead would play three league games in one week, two of them on consecutive nights. We were thrilled. The basketball season was beginning with a bang, and we were enthusiastic about playing as often as we could.

During that same week, Mike Eckel had asked me, "Can you and Dave work on the farm this Saturday? Frank wants us to haul hay bales from the field and put them next to the cow pens. The cows are gettin' short of feed, and Frank wants to get it done before Christmas and before a blizzard sets in. We'll pay you two bucks an hour. Frank thinks we can get it done in a half day."

Realizing this would provide Dave and me spending money right before Christmas, I consented for both of us. I also knew Frank Eckel depended on Dave and me. He had hired us previously to work on Saturdays as well as on weekdays before we went to school. In recent years, Frank Eckel had been very good to me, hiring me and paying me well in the summer to help build a new cow barn. I felt I had an obligation to him. Furthermore, since this was to be just a half day's work, we would start early and be home with plenty of time to clean up and get ready to board the bus for the Erie game that night.

On Saturday, Dave and I arose at seven o'clock, ate breakfast, and drove our brother Tom's Chevrolet convertible to the Eckel farm. We parked next to the gas tank where Mike was filling a truck. Mike drove the three of us out to the baled haystack on the southeast corner of the farm. We rode down the lane leading to the lake, where we drove over the dike and then south to the haystack. The lane was covered with snow, and Mike had to track it with just his memory of the terrain. Six inches of snow were sitting on top of the stack. Mike stopped the truck about fifty yards away.

He said, "Let's put down the sideboards so we can get more bales on the bed." He reached into the glove compartment. "I got gloves for us all. We're goin' to need them with all this cold weather and us grabbin' onto the bale wires."

Then Mike drove the truck up next to the stack so Dave and I could stand on the cab and reach the top. We brushed the snow off and began to throw the bales down to Mike, who methodically placed them on the truck bed. With forty or more bales loaded, we hauled them to the barnyard and placed them into another stack next to the holding pens. By one o'clock and after four trips to the stack, we were finished.

After a bath, I lay down on my bed to take a nap but could not sleep. With still a couple of hours that afternoon left, I worked on an English essay and then dressed for the bus trip to Erie, scheduled to leave at five-fifteen. With our players boarded, Marion Humphrey eased the big "yellow dog" out of the school yard and headed east toward the Washington Highway.

Sitting a couple of seats back from Coach, I asked him in a raised voice, "Hey, Coach, who did Erie play last night?"

"Gilcrest," he said. "When I called the Greeley Tribune last night to give them our score and the stats after the game, they told me Gilcrest won. I guess Beshears was Erie's high-scorer. Rollie will be guarding him tonight. He's got a good jump shot, so we'll have to keep the ball away from him."

"What about Padia?" I asked. "You told me that I'd be guardin' him. How'd he do?"

Turning around to face me, Coach said, "I think he did pretty well also. They scored about forty points. But I don't think Lontine had a very good game." Seeing Mike across the aisle from me, he asked, "By the way, Mike, how's the milkin' business goin' out there on your farm now that you've got the barn built?"

"Marg says it's doin' real well. She keeps the books on it," said Mike. "I help out once in a while. I milk and feed the cows. We've got about seventy-five Holsteins. They're penned up now. Can't keep them out in the pasture with all the snow on the ground. Frank had me bring in four truckloads of baled hay today and stack them by the pens. Dave and Ronnie helped me. We finished up about one o'clock this afternoon."

Coach, not believing what he had just heard about the three of us working on the day of a game, said nothing more and turned to face the front of the bus. Unbeknownst to us, a tremendous rage was building inside him.

Richie and I started as guards, with Rollie and Dave in the forward positions and Lyle Schaefer at center. As usual, we started out with a man-to-man defense, but Erie predictably began with a zone.

Coach was disappointed with our first two quarters of play. He perceived us to be lethargic and lackluster. We did not have the "fire in our bellies" we had the night before. We were slow in reacting to the ball, and Erie's Beshears and Lontine had outrebounded us. By the end of the first quarter, I had not yet scored while missing two free-throw attempts and garnering three fouls, and Dave had scored only three points. Richie, with his outside shooting, kept Mead in the game. In the second quarter, I kept feeding the ball to Richie and on several occasions screened for him while he shot. At halftime, Richie had scored seven buckets and two free shots, while I had only four points. The halftime score was 21–18, with Erie holding a slim lead.

Richie, realizing he was getting all the shot opportunities and sensing that he might be perceived as "hoggin' the ball," said to me as we wound our way to the locker room, "Ronnie, you need to shoot more. Don't just let me do it."

I said back to him, "Don't worry about it. I'll take some if I can. Right now, they're lettin' you shoot, not me."

In the locker room at halftime, Coach was angry. We players sensed it, sitting in silence, waiting for him to speak.

He said, "You guys are pathetic. I don't know how we're still in this game. We certainly don't deserve to be. What's wrong with ya? What are ya thinkin' 'bout out there? Goin' to Longmont with your girlfriend after the game? C'mon now, getcher head in the game. We have a whole 'nother half to play. Your stupid mistakes are costin' us."

Then looking directly at me, he said, "Ronnie, what's this you leavin' your feet and not knowing what you're goin' to do with the ball when you're up in the air? That travelin' turnover cost us. C'mon, Ronnie, start thinkin' 'bout whatcher doin'. Also, lay off those fouls. Ya got three this first half. One more, and we'll have to set ya on the bench."

Turning to Dave, he said, "Dave, follow your shot when you shoot. Don't just stand there and wait for the ball to come back to ya. You know better than that. You'd think you had never played the game before."

Holding his finger up and pointing to Rollie, he said, "Rollie, stop gettin' mad and gettin' those dumb fouls. We don't want you foulin' out and Beshears bein' their high-scorin' man. Calm down a bit. I know it's rough there under the boards, but hold your temper."

Looking at Richie, he said, "Richie, you're the only one keepin' us in the game. Keep shootin'. Don't be dribblin' or passin' the ball off. Keep takin' the shot when you're open."

Coach spared no one. "Lyle, Lontine is eatin' your lunch on the boards. Ya gotta do better in boxin' him out. Ya can't namby-pamby in there. Ya gotta be tougher. Right now, you're just dancin' with him. Ya gotta move him out, get meaner."

Finally, Coach's frustration came to a crescendo when he shouted out furiously, "Dave! Ronnie! Mike! What's this I hear about you guys workin' today? You know you shouldn't do that on the day of a game!" Barking loudly as he gazed directly at Dave and me, he said, "Dave and Ronnie, the two of you look so tired out on the floor, you'd think you hadn't slept for a week. You're each movin' like you had a piano on your back. When you're too tired to play, you're lettin' the whole team down. I don't care how much money you made. It's not important. Workin' like that, you put yourself first and the team second. Listen, you two, the team is more important than you are. Don't you ever forget it! Don't you ever pull this stunt again. And Mike, don't ever ask them to do it again."

Dave and I had not expected this. We simply had not realized we had made a mistake. Now that we were being singled out and upbraided by Coach, we could not look at our teammates, and we just stared at the floor. None of us had ever seen Coach so angry.

Coach's voice softened a bit as he started talking about the second half. "Ronnie,' he said, "I don't wancha foulin' out, so I want Richie to guard Padia, and you take Heil." Then to the team, he said, "We're goin' to stick with our man-to-man. I'm sure they'll stay with the zone. Ya gotta move the ball around on offense. Ya been holdin' onto it too long. Get rid of it quick. You'll find the open man. Dave, you know what to do. Keep movin' back and forth on the baseline. When you get the ball, take the shot if you have it. Ronnie, get the ball inside to Lyle or Rollie. If none of you have an open shot inside, toss it back out and work it in again. And Richie, keep shootin'. I want ta see ya more fired up out there. Play this game like you mean it. I don't want ya standin' around like it's a cakewalk. I don't care if you are tired. Don't think about it, and play with some energy and enthusiasm."

Our team responded in the second half beyond Coach's expectation. The final score was 56–32 with us on top. Our defense was relentless and smothering. Richie ignited our team by sinking four outside jump shots and scoring twenty-two points for the night. Rollie had twelve points, and Lyle scored six. Dave and I ended up with eight points each.

There was no doubt that Dave and I had played poorly. Playing three games that week and working five hours heaving hay bales had taken its toll, but Dave and I and presumably the whole team had learned a useful lesson.

L-R: Lyle Schaefer, Mike Eckel, 1957. *Mead Consolidated Schools Yearbook*

Dave Newton, 1957. *Mead Consolidated Schools Yearbook*

Chapter 32

Midseason Woes

With the long Christmas break over, our team resumed the '56–'57 season with a renewed sense of purpose. Our goal was to remain undefeated in our quest for the league championship. We knew that both LaSalle and Erie would be tough opponents to face, but overcoming Gilcrest was paramount. They had defeated us once the previous year. Also, our team had "tasted" what it was like to participate in the state tournament, and we were determined to make it to Denver again. But getting there required us first to win the league crown and then the district tournament. We had many games to play and win before we could realize our dream of a state championship. Coach would have to keep us focused on one game at a time. Winning state was on our minds, but it was something we never talked about. Coach always made sure we concentrated on the game of the moment.

Immediately after Christmas, we took on Eaton, our third nonleague Class A opponent of the Tri-Valley League. We quickly went out in front 12–0, and by intermission, we doubled the score at 34–15, hitting with 47 percent efficiency. At the end of the third period, with the score still doubled at 47–23, Coach put in our reserves. I got eighteen points, with nine on free throws, but still shot only 69 percent at the charity stripe. Dave had fourteen, while Rollie had nine, and Dick had six. Lyle Schaefer contributed eleven points, and we won easily 59–41.

We resumed league play the first week of January and pounded the Berthoud Spartans. For the first three quarters, we four Newtons scored fifty-four of the fifty-five total points. Coach played reserves the entire final quarter, and we shellacked Berthoud 72–48.

With our lopsided Berthoud win, we continued winning with gusto, and we were doing it without the play of the previous year's star, Allen Thompson. Having missed the whole fall semester of school, Allen Thompson returned in January and joined Mead's basketball team again. In the previous season, Mr. and Mrs. Thompson had been to every game Allen played as Mead's starting guard. The Thompsons came that night to watch their son pick up where he left off. However, they were sadly disappointed when Allen only played in the final few minutes and didn't score.

On Friday the following week, we met Gilcrest for the first time on its court. Gilcrest, the only league team that beat us last year (surprisingly on Mead's home court), had already lost two nonleague games and was four and zero in league play, while we were undefeated at seven and zero. Gilcrest had the same three backcourt starters from last year: Rudy Peralez at six-foot-four, Bruce McLeod at six-foot-three, and Norman Cogburn at six-foot-two. At this first meeting, Peralez was leading the league in scoring with an average of 20.3 points per game, but Richie was close behind at 18.5. It was a tight game all the way. We were behind throughout the first half and all the way to the end of the third quarter with the score at 34-33.

Two minutes into the fourth quarter, Dave set himself for a shot and potted it to put us ahead. Then Gilcrest got three quick buckets, and Richie followed with a hit from the outside. With just under two minutes left, it was Gilcrest, 46, and Mead, 43. Richie tossed the ball inbounds to me, and I dribbled it downcourt and hit Rollie (who was underneath the Mead basket) with a pass. Rollie laid it in to give Mead forty-five points, with Gilcrest still ahead by one. Gilcrest's Peralez was fouled by Schaefer as he attempted a short jumper. Peralez missed the first free throw and made the second. With forty seconds left, Richie dribbled and moved into our end of the court. He passed to me, now twenty feet out from Mead's goal. I planted both feet to shoot a long set shot with twenty seconds left. The swish tied the score at 47.

With time running out, Gilcrest's Keil tossed an inbounds pass to teammate Torres, who dribbled downcourt and crossed the center line. Torres then passed to teammate McLeod, who was standing with his back to the goal right at Gilcrest's free-throw line. McLeod wheeled to his left and turned to face the basket, and with Rollie's hand in his face, he made the "shot of his life" to win the game for Gilcrest, 49–47.

Although Gilcrest was now the undisputed league leader, Coach was not terribly disappointed with our team's overall performance, but on Monday, he said to us, "Gentleman, if we had done better at the foul line, we could have won the game. We shot only 50 percent. We can do better than that. Every night this week, I want every one of you to shoot twenty-five extra free throws."

Then looking forward to the next game, Coach continued, "Shake off what happened with Gilcrest. Forget about them. We have a good team to worry about tomorrow night. LaSalle is tied with us for second place. Gilcrest beat them last week but only by two points. They have Frankie Vannest back this year. Remember him? Right now, he is the top scorer in the league. He got twenty-one against Gilcrest, mostly on drive-in layups. Tomorrow we're goin' with our 'rabbit zone.' We'll make Vannest shoot from the outside."

That Tuesday night in LaSalle, with Mead starting out with the "rabbit" defense and me as the "rabbit," a new referee, Vince Cyphers, was calling the game along with James Daubenmire. I had an excellent opinion of Daubenmire's ability to call a "good" game, but now I would experience a referee I had not encountered before.

I liked playing the role of the "rabbit." I was always going to the ball. I knew that Coach thought I was the best defender on the team and was depending on me to stop LaSalle's top scorer. I was pumped up, and I hustled to wherever the ball was, where my fellow defender teammate and I would surround the opponent, trying to make the steal.

With the ball in LaSalle's possession on their offensive half-court, LaSalle's Grossaint tossed a pass from the court perimeter inside to teammate Gary Cade, standing next to the keyhole. I aggressively pounced on Cade and grabbed the ball away from him. Referee Cyphers called a foul. Of course, in my mind, it was a clean takeaway.

For me, playing defense was just as much fun as shooting, passing, and dribbling. The challenge of stopping the opponent excited me. I moved my feet smoothly and quickly, keeping my position in front of the ball handler. I went for loose balls with abandon, diving to the floor to gain possession. If a ball in the clutches of an opponent was not protected, I would reach in with both hands to grab it and "tie him up" for a "jump ball."

As LaSalle passed the ball around the perimeter of our rabbit-zone defense, trying to find an opportunity for a shot or a pass inside, they finally found Vannest open—just for a moment. Vannest raised the ball up above his head to take a jump shot as I arrived in front of him. I placed my left hand on the ball, blocking the shot as Vannest was suspended in midair. Vannest fell awkwardly to the floor, and I was whistled for my second foul by Referee Cyphers. I was surprised, convinced I had touched only the ball. I was certain I had made no bodily contact with Vannest. I muttered to myself, "Couldn't this ref see this? This guy doesn't know what the heck he's doin'."

Still in the first quarter, with Mead behind by two points and with possession of the ball, I drove in for a layup, only to be called for a charging foul by Cyphers. It was my third.

I exploded with rage at Cyphers, who was approaching me to get the ball for the pending foul shot. "Come on, ref!" I shouted. "He ran into me. There's no way I fouled him!"

Not liking what he heard, Cyphers blew his whistle, signaled his hands with a T, and called a technical foul—my fourth, all committed in the first quarter. After Vannest sank both free throws, Cyphers blew the whistle and motioned for a substitution. Coach replaced me with Allen Thompson, and Allen played at the guard spot the next two quarters. I left the game, having only scored four points, and I did not return until the fourth quarter. I watched helplessly as Mead struggled with LaSalle, the lead exchanging many times. I was not happy that Allen was back and replacing me. I was not happy that I had heatedly voiced my objection to the referee. I was embarrassed about the technical foul, and I was worried about what Coach would say. However, I was certain that an inexperienced referee had done me in. I had been treated unfairly. This referee did not understand what aggressive defensive play was like, I concluded. All I could do was hope our team would prevail.

Deciding to abandon the rabbit-zone defense, Coach switched to man-to-man in the second quarter. I got back in the game in the fourth quarter but fouled out. This time, Daubenmire called the foul as I again attempted to stop Vannest. With one minute left, we were ahead by one point and went into a stall. With the score 52–51, desperate to get the ball, LaSalle fouled. However, three successive fouls resulted in Mead scoring a total of six points. LaSalle's Vannest got one more bucket, and the game ended, 58-53. We shot with 88 percent efficiency from the foul line in the second half, fourteen of our sixteen attempts.

Mead had successfully resisted LaSalle's late challenge and had performed well in spite of my anemic showing. That night marked my poorest performance since junior high school. I had played less than one quarter, scoring only five points, and I was accountable for one of the two free throws missed in the second half.

Our next game with Estes Park was scheduled in Longmont's St. Vrain Memorial Building. Two other teams in the region, Berthoud and Erie, were also scheduled to play in Longmont. The Longmont facility allowed for the larger expected attendance generated by the greater interest in area high-school basketball. Sportswriter Pitchford, touting Mead's game in the Longmont Times Call, wrote the following:

> The Bulldogs, with a good record to date, should even be tougher to beat from here on out with the return of Allen Thompson to the lineup. The fans, naturally, will be interested in seeing the Newton triplets (Richie, Ronnie, and Rollie) in action, as well as brother Dave

and center Lyle Schaefer, the two who round out the quintet that has been starting all this year's games.

However, fans coming to see the Newtons play may have been disappointed. At the end of the first quarter, Mead was ahead, 22-5, and Coach took his starters out of the game and played them only in the first four minutes of the last quarter. At halftime, Mead was ahead, 44–9, and went on to win, 71–26.

At midseason, Mead was ten and one, with Richie (averaging 13.9) and me (averaging 13.8) third and fourth in league scoring, behind LaSalle's Frankie Vannest (averaging 18.9) in first place and Gilcrest's Rudy Peralez (averaging 17.1) in second. Gilcrest, having not yet lost a league game, was still out in front with an eight-and-zero record, ahead of Mead at seven and one.

Our return match with Timnath resulted in another victory for us, and on the following Friday night, we breezed by Erie with no difficulty. Going against Erie's zone, we had trouble hitting from the outside in the first half but opened up in the third quarter with twenty points, while Erie had only seven. Midway in the fourth quarter, we were ahead by eighteen points, and Coach substituted our second and third teams. The final outcome was Mead, 72, and Erie, 58.

For the second time in the season, Mead had overwhelmed the Erie Tigers, the school that had been the league football champs. That same night on the ten-o-clock television news, Mead was chosen the Team of the Week by Denver sportscaster John Henry on his sports call show. A week later, a commemorative plaque arrived by mail at the school, and Superintendent Carlson displayed it on the table in the hall outside his office.

We continued winning by whipping the Berthoud Spartans for the second time. Rollie was fouled incessantly as he dominated the boards, and he sank a game-record high of thirteen from the free-throw line while missing only one. Dave hit ten field goals and two free shots. Our twenty-eight field goals, with Berthoud scoring only eleven, put us out in front 81–46.

Despite a loss to a key rival and lapses in offensive output in several other games, by midseason, Mead's offensive machine was operating at full throttle; thereafter, it would never again sputter. The Newton boys and a Schaefer were marching toward winning the league title two years in a row, and along the way, the Mead bench was seeing plenty of playing time.

MEAD CHOSEN "TEAM OF THE WEEK" ON JOHN HENRY SPORTS CALL; DEFEATS ERIE, 72-58

Last night was a big one for the Mead basketball team, the Bulldogs winning from Erie's Tigers, 72-58, at Mead to keep close on the heels of the Gilcrest Spuddiggers in the race for the North-Central League title and a little later in the evening was honored on the John Henry Sports Call show as the "Team of the Week." As a result of receiving the "Team of the Week" designation on the TV sports show, Coach Jack Adams' team will be awarded a trophy or plaque.

The Newton brothers followed the same pattern last night as they did in the first-round encounter with the Tigers, racking up 54 points in each game.

Rollie scored 18, Ronnie 16, Dave 12, and Dick 8. The rest of the Mead scoring was distributed like this: Lyle Schaefer 13, Allen Thompson 2, and Mike Eckels 3.

The Bulldogs held a narrow

1957. Longmont Times Call

Drive, Defense Face to Face

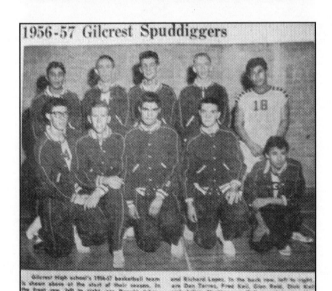

The old problem of the irresistible force meeting the immovable object is well illustrated in this shot from the Gilcrest-Mead thriller at Gilcrest Friday night. Dave Newton, (47) at right, one of sparkplugs of Mead's driving offense finds his drive cancelled out by Gilcrest's two stalwart guards, Fred Keil (4), at left and Dan Torres (6), center, who did a good job in hemming in the plunging Mead Bulldogs as Gilcrest went on to win in the last four seconds, 49-47.—Tribune photo by Jim Moore.

1956-57 Gilcrest Spuddiggers

Gilcrest High school's 1956-57 basketball team is shown above at the start of their season. In the front row, left to right, are Ronald Johns, Bruce McLeod, Rudy Perales, Norman Cochran, and Richard Lopez. In the back row, left to right, are Dan Torres, Fred Keil, Glen Reid, Dick Keil and Julian Martinez. — Tribune photo by Jim Moore.

Chapter 33

Conference Champions

The second game of the season with Gilcrest was one of the most important games in Mead's thirty-nine-year history. Gilcrest remained undefeated in league play. Beating Gilcrest would put us in a tie for the league lead and would avenge our previous loss to the Spuddiggers. This was the game that folks from all around Northeastern Colorado wanted to see. It would be played on Mead's home court.

That night, a Gilcrest bus loaded with student fans and streaming blue and white crepe paper drove into Mead's parking lot. It was followed by cars carrying Gilcrest supporters. Mead students, alumni, and fans arrived early to get good seats. Mom took her usual place in the upper bleacher next to Martin and Mary Graham. The Blazon brothers, Marvin and Leroy, both graduates of Mead, were there. Kenny and Connie Hopp sat next to their parents in the side bleachers; Connie brought his fiancée, Martha Borgman. Our brother Jerry drove up from Denver. He found a seat next to the Blazons. Ronald Weber and Herb Newman took their usual seats on the front row of folding chairs on the stage. Loe Hernandez and Vernon Widger joined them. Bub Howlett sat in front of the Grahams. Marion Humphrey and his son Robert brought in extra folding chairs and set more up on the stage and on the west end of the gym. Mr. and Mrs. Thompson, hoping to see Allen play, sat next to the Grahams. Because so many latecomers could not find seats, they resorted to standing in the gym entrance or near the locker room door. Frank Eckel and Dean Seewald found folding chair seats below the west basket. At game time, the Mead gym (normal capacity: 250 fans) was overflowing with more than 350 spectators.

For the first time ever, members of the Mead band played. As the teams warmed up with layups and jump shots, Ronnie Vogel, Janice Owen, and Barbara Vogel played their horns as they and other band members burst forth with the "Mead Fight Song," and the Mead Pep Club sang the following:

> Oh, the orange and black over all
> May they rise to the skies, ne'er to fall
> May the world look to them in flight
> For they are the colors for which we fight
> Oh, students of M-H-S
> The school that is always the best
> They've stood every trial, every test
> So with our might

Then accompanied by a loud horn blast from the music group, the club members yelled into a crescendo with "The orange and black shall reign forever!"

Five minutes before tip-off, Coach walked across the floor and beckoned us to follow him to the basement locker room.

"We'll start the same five we always do, and we'll play man-to-man," said Coach. "Lyle, you'll be on Peralez. Rollie, you're on McLeod, and, Dave, you take Cogburn. You two guys help Lyle out with Peralez. Double-team Peralez when you can. All three of you need to keep him from gettin' the ball. I know you three can outrebound them, so stand your ground, 'specially when they have the ball. Ronnie, I want you to stay on Torres like he was your girlfriend, and you, Richie, take Keil. I don't think he's goin' to do much scorin', so help Ronnie and double-team Torres when he gets the ball. Last time we played these guys, they threw a lot of zone at us. They'll probably do that again. But we can beat it. Just keep movin' the ball fast, and get it to the open man. If you're open and have a good shot, take it."

Then looking at me, Coach said, "Ronnie, you be the captain tonight, and for heaven's sake, don't pop off to the referee. We can't afford that mistake again."

Glancing at us starters, he said, "Listen up now. We're goin' to start out with the press, right off the bat. They won't be expectin' it. We didn't use it last time." Then he addressed me again as he handed out sticks of Doublemint. "Ronnie, you get on the man takin' the ball out-of-bounds, just like you always do. Get on him right away." Turning to Lyle, he said, "Lyle, you get back on defense as soon as you can. We don't want them to get any long passes for easy buckets."

Marc then came into the locker room and announced. "Coach, they want y'all upstairs. It's time to start."

"Okay," said Coach as he halted his remarks. "Here's the score. We let these guys stomp on us the last game. They outhustled us. Maybe they wanted to win more than we did, but tonight it's goin' to be different. We're goin' to turn the tables on 'em. Go out there and show 'em that we're a different team."

Now James Elmer Newton, our dad, with all the excitement the game generated, decided to attend. Our sixty-eight-year-old father had never seen a game of basketball. He had never seen any of his eleven sons play. Dad arrived right before tip-off and, unable to find a seat, was relieved when Marc, sitting at the end of the Mead players' bench, stood and gave him his seat. Marc sat on the floor between Dad's knees.

Gilcrest had the first possession but did not score. Dave got the rebound and hit Richie at side court with a long pass. Richie saw Lyle Schaefer alone and hurled a baseball pass to him. Lyle laid it in. We took the lead, 2–0.

I hurried to the end line where Gilcrest's Torres was taking the ball out-of-bounds. I waved my arms in front of Torres, trying to obstruct his view and force him to make a bad pass. Torres found his open teammate Keil, who received the inbounds pass, but Richie and I pounced on him like two buzzards on a dead rabbit. I knocked the ball cleanly out of

Keil's grasp, which bounced right into Richie's hands. Richie took three dribbles and drove in for the layup. We were now up 4–zip.

Then Richie, Dave, and I each sank buckets, while Gilcrest's Peralez dumped in one to bring the score to 10–6. Mead then got three more baskets and at the end of the first quarter was ahead, 16–6. Coach kept the full-court press on all through the first half. Each time the ball was stolen, it was passed to Richie, who got two quick easy layups. The fast pace of the game unnerved the Spuddiggers, and they hurried their shots, shooting only 18 percent the first half, while Mead hit 33 percent of their attempts. At intermission, Mead was well ahead, 24–13.

Coach stopped pressing in the second half, but he continued our man-to-man defense through the game. This strategy held Gilcrest to shooting just 24 percent. Schaefer held Gilcrest's Peralez to just eleven points, seven below his average. Despite our smaller size, we outrebounded Gilcrest, with Rollie getting fifteen and Dave nabbing twenty-two. Our sixteen-point lead was cut to ten in the third quarter, but we came back in the fourth, rampaging for twenty-three points to Gilcrest's thirteen. With Richie getting sixteen points and Rollie, Dave, and Schaefer all scoring in double figures, we blitzed Gilcrest by twenty-two points. The final score was 57–35. Defending Torres aggressively, I kept him to only ten points, and Richie kept Keil to just six.

This was the best game the '57 Bulldogs ever played on their home court. The Spuddiggers had been whipped soundly both defensively and offensively and were sent home with their shovels needing sharpening. Coach had mentored one of his best games, and Mead was tied with Gilcrest for the league lead.

As I went out on the gym floor to acknowledge the "good game" of our Gilcrest opponents, my eyes met those of Mr. and Mrs. Thompson, who were walking across the gym. Their faces were sad with disappointment; Allen had played very little. I could not say anything other than hello as I walked by them. They said nothing but simply nodded and quickly left without talking to anyone.

As the season progressed, Allen never managed to displace Rollie or Dave in the forward position or Richie or me as a guard. Dave's rebounding skills excelled those of Allen's, and Richie could score equally or better than Allen. Likewise, Allen's limited ball handling and leadership skills did not allow him to replace me as the floor general. Therefore, Allen had been relegated to the role of substitute when we got into foul trouble or when Mead was well ahead and when the outcome had been decided. Nevertheless, Allen was undoubtedly the best physical athlete spawned by Mead High School in its thirty-nine-year history.

The next night, Mead faced Grover, a top-flight Class C team from the Prospect Valley League in a nonconference contest. Again, I was assigned to defend their top scorer, Paul Timms. Timms, who averaged twenty points per game, scored only nine points for his team that night. We triplets each scored in double figures, and Mead won, 62–50.

In the second game of the season with Evans, Coach was confident that his team could easily win, and instead of starting his normal five, he started Rollie, George Rademacher, Mike Eckel, Allen Thompson, and Lyle Schaefer. Dave substituted for Rollie in the second quarter. Mead led, 35–13, at the half, overpowering the Rams' zone defense and shooting 42 percent from the field. Mead pulled down fifty-seven rebounds to Evans's twenty-two and won easily, 60–42.

The next day, a Saturday, a nonleague foe, Eaton, came to Mead for a return contest. We four Newtons, all scoring in double figures, canned sixty-two points to win 67–53. We were ahead by eighteen in the middle of the last quarter, and Coach played the reserves.

The following Sunday afternoon, Mom got a long-distance call from our third eldest brother, Jack. A career marine, Jack was serving in Korea. He had been there for almost three years, and Mom had not talked to him during that time. I listened to their conversation.

"Hey, Mom," Jack said. "I haven't written for a long time, so I thought I'd call you. What's goin' on there? Are the kids still playin' basketball? Is league play still goin' on?"

"Oh, they're still playin'. They have two games left with LaSalle and Estes Park," Mom said excitedly. "They're tied for first place with Gilcrest. Mead and Gilcrest each lost one game to each other. The boys said the other night that the district tournament would probably take place in another three weeks."

"Good," said Jack. "I'm takin' leave and want to be home when the tournament starts. I've got thirty days, so if they go to state, I'll still be there for that."

"Well, for heaven's sake!" exclaimed Mom. "That's good news."

"I'll call you when I get to the States," said Jack. "I should get there in a couple of weeks. Didja get the allotment check this month?"

"Why, sure," said Mom. "I got it two days ago. It came in at the right time. We had to buy some coal. It has been real cold here. We've been burnin' it up real fast."

"It should still be $325 through March," said Jack. "Come April 1, all the military are gettin' a raise, so I'm increasin' your check to $375."

"It sure does come in handy," said Mom. "With your check and the check I get from the school workin' in the cafeteria, we're squeezing by. But don't increase it if you need the money. We can get by with what you're sendin' now."

"I can handle it," said Jack. "It won't affect me . . . Well, I gotta go now. I'll have to win another poker game to pay for this call. It's costin' a bunch. Take care, and I'll see ya in a couple of weeks."

Mom hung up the phone and turned to those of us who were near. "That was Jack. He's comin' home to see you birds play in the tournament. Sez he got a thirty-day leave."

I could not believe what I was hearing. "Ya mean Jack is comin' home just to see us play?" I swelled with pride. My elder brother was coming home from Korea. He'd be here to watch Dave, Richie, Rollie, and me. It was a joyous moment.

Basketball had always been a part of Jack's life. He had helped Mead High win a state consolation trophy in '46, and Jack always found time to play a game of "horse" with us when he came home after work at the IGA Grocery Store. Jack gave white sweatshirts (on which sister Helen stenciled Mead's bulldog mascot) to us triplets at Christmas in '48 and bought sweat socks and tennis shoes for us five brothers for Christmas in '50. Over the '52 Christmas holiday, Jack built a magnificent basketball goal in our backyard for his seven brothers. And now in '57, Jack's compassion and benevolence to his family had not stopped. He was supporting his parents and his younger brothers with a monthly allotment from his military paycheck, a practice he had begun several years before.

Jack's homecoming on the Christmas holiday and his presence to see Mead basketball was an exciting time in the Newton household. The thirty days Jack spent back in Mead would be some of the most memorable days of my life.

But before Jack came home, Mead still had key basketball games to play. LaSalle, holding down third place in the league, came to Mead with the league's leading scorer, Frankie Vannest. A defeat by LaSalle would knock Mead out of first place.

Coach said, "We'll start out with the man-to-man, and Ronnie, you take Vannest. You've got to stop him tonight."

Following Coach's instruction, I stayed on Vannest like a cat with a captured mouse. When he did not have the ball, I stayed close to him, cutting off the passing lane so he could not receive the ball. My smothering presence restricted Vannest's movement. He moved aimlessly around the court, trying to get to the ball. Without Vannest, LaSalle's offense stalled, and we were out in front, 20–3, at the end of the first quarter. At the half, we had tripled the score 47–15, and Vannest was scoreless. Vannest and LaSalle never recovered. Mead held LaSalle to just thirty-seven points, while we tallied seventy-five. We Newton brothers had poured in forty-six points, and Schaefer had fourteen. Reserves played most of the second half, with Mike Eckel contributing eleven of the twenty-eight points scored. The league's leading scorer, Frankie Vannest, had been held to his all-time low of two points. LaSalle, Mead's only threat to their first-place league lead with Gilcrest, had been blistered.

In the final league game of the season, we dumped Estes Park 82–37. That same night, Gilcrest defeated Berthoud and remained tied with us with a thirteen-and-one record. LaSalle's Vannest and Gilcrest's Peralez remained the league's leading scorers, averaging seventeen points per game, while we triplets each had twelve points a contest, with Dave and Lyle Schaefer finishing with nine. Most likely, we Newtons' individual scoring totals would have been much higher had we not been replaced by reserve teammates when we were well ahead of our opponents, which frequently had been the case. Our regular season ended with one defeat and twenty wins. The '57 basketball team had established a winning tradition at Mead, unequaled since the school's inception in 1918. And now there was an opportunity for the Bulldogs to extend that legacy, setting their sights on winning the upcoming district tournament. The goal was to repeat Mead's district championship victory of the previous year.

We had two weeks to prepare for district. This time, Mead High would be playing close to home—in Longmont's St. Vrain Memorial Building. And just like the previous year, Mead was the top-seeded team in the tournament.

North Side Mead Elementary School Gymnasium (Formerly the Mead
High School Gymnasium), 2011. *Sheila Koenig*

Mead Consolidated Schools Gymnasium with total student body, 1951.
Mead Consolidated Schools Yearbook

Mead Elementary School
Gymnasium (Formerly Mead High
School Gymnasium), 2012.
Sheila Koenig

Entrance to Storage Room of Mead
Elementary School Gymnasium
(Former entrance to locker room
and shower room of former Mead
High School Gymnasium), 2012 –
Sheila Koenig

Basket attached to balcony of Mead
Elementary School Gymnasium
(Formerly the Mead High School
Gymnasium), 2012 – *Sheila Koenig*

Chapter 34

District Drama

In human competition, teams or individuals, there are winners and losers. Humans tend to remember and revere the winners, but the losers are often looked upon as those who just weren't "good enough." The memory of losers is often short. In athletics, winning is almost always foremost in the minds of seventeen-year-olds, and the stakes of gaining and maintaining the respect of friends and the community are high. For the '57 Mead basketball team, it had a tall mountain to climb. Mead had to redeem itself from the loss it had sustained in the state semifinal the previous year, and Mead had to prove to itself and to the community that the school *could* win a state championship and that they had to begin by winning the district tournament.

In March '57, Mead had just finished the North Central League play and shared the title with Gilcrest. The next step was the District 4 tournament, two weeks away. Rather than having us keep practicing hard for the two weeks, Coach wondered if it might be a good idea to lay off a few days and give his team some rest. He called one of his Colorado State College of Education instructors, basketball coach John Bunn, and sought his counsel. Bunn had coached at Stanford University and Springfield College and had a lot of experience on such matters.

Bunn said, "Give 'em a week off."

During the break, Coach had scheduled a scrimmage with the Longmont Trojans on Saturday, five days before the start of the tournament. Longmont, a Class AA high school of more than three hundred students, was a formidable opponent, an ideal one that allowed Mead to sharpen its skills in preparation for the three-day competition we would face the next week. Furthermore, we would play in the St. Vrain Memorial Building, where the Class B District 4 tournament was to be held. The scrimmage, lasting more than an hour with few time-outs, was handily won by us. Defeating the Trojans, a team with more height, boosted our confidence; we knew our Class B team was unusually superior and was ready to play. Our knowledge of our present skill level was bolstered by the fact that we had previously beaten Loveland High in a similar scrimmage during Christmas break, another Class AA high school. We had been tested many times in playing larger schools. Throughout the season, we had defeated Class A teams in nonconference games, including Windsor, Eaton, and College High.

When Mead resumed practice, we had six days to prepare. Managing and directing the tournament and representing the North Central League was our uncle, Earl G. Achenbach, superintendent of the Berthoud school district.

Gilcrest, Mead's archrival, was placed in the District 3 tournament in Greeley along with Johnstown, Evans, Wiggins, LaSalle, Kersey, Ault, and Platteville. LaPorte and Frederick from the Platte Valley League were selected to participate with four other North Central League teams in the District 4 tournament, including Mead, the top seed. For the opening round, LaPorte was paired with Mead, followed by Estes Park versus Frederick and Erie versus Timnath. Berthoud drew the long straw and received a bye into the second round.

Top-seeded Mead had no difficulty defeating bottom-seed LaPorte. We put a hustling man-to-man defense on LaPorte, which resulted in several steals coupled with fast breaks, with Mead going ahead 20–5 by the end of the first quarter. Coach kept his second stringers in for three quarters of the game, and we won easily, 67–27.

After Mead eliminated LaPorte, the Frederick Warriors, the previous year's state champion, whipped Estes Park by forty-two points and was bracketed to play Mead; Erie squeezed by Timnath and would meet Berthoud.

The next night, prior to our contest with Frederick, Coach had our team suit up early before the start of the Erie–Berthoud tilt so we could scout the presumed winner, Erie, and take a few warm-up drills during intermission. Early on, Erie struggled with the underdog Spartans, but finally, Erie's Sabino Lontine got hot and scored fifteen of Erie's eighteen points in the second quarter. Still only ahead 42–40 with one minute to go in the third quarter, pivot-man Lontine dumped in another eleven points in the final quarter to bring his team to a win 61–52.

However, just before the game ended, Erie's Lontine was roughed up by Berthoud's Alan King as the two of them vied for a rebound. Lontine swung at King with his fist, hitting him on the side of the head and knocking him to the floor. With whistles blowing and the crowd aw-ing at what they had just seen, Lontine was ejected with just a few minutes left.

Coach sat us five starters down on the players' bench, giving us last-minute instructions before the start of our game with Frederick. As Coach talked, Erie's Lontine, now in street clothes, emerged from the locker room on the north end of the gym and proceeded to walk to the other end to leave the building. As he walked past the Mead bench, his duffel bag in hand and his uniform on a hanger draped over his shoulder, hundreds of fans in the crowd of 1,500 booed, continuing as Lontine walked in front of them. Still hearing the crowd's disapproval as he approached the south end of the court, Lontine dropped his bag and turned to the crowd with his right hand held up with only his middle finger pointing upward. The booing crowd, flabbergasted by what they had seen, booed him even more as he departed.

Although only five-foot-eleven, Lontine was 185 pounds of muscle. He had made the all-state football team as a tackle, and with his wide body, he was an effective pivot man on Erie's basketball team, holding off defenders as he received the ball close to the basket and wheeling to his left with a right-hand hook shot. Besides his girth, his personal appearance also made him an imposing opponent. Lontine's left eye had been injured in his early life, obscuring his pupil until only the white showed, giving him a villainous and intimidating appearance. In the eyes of judgmental spectators, Erie's Lontine was the actor in this basketball drama whom they wanted to see punished. Many thought he should not be allowed to participate further in the tournament.

When the booing died down, Mead's tilt with Frederick started. The previous year, Frederick had defeated Mead in a nonleague game and had gone on to win the state championship by defeating Sanford, the team that beat Mead in the state semifinals. Having lost three starters from last year, Frederick faced Mead with a much smaller but still experienced team. Senior Alex Hattel was back with five classmates, and his brother Mike was on the team as a junior. Mead wasted no time in taking the game under control. With Richie hitting jump shots from twenty or more feet out, Mead had a 16-6 lead by the end of the first quarter. We shot 45 percent from the field, with Richie nailing ten field goals and me getting six. In the final quarter, Mead tallied twenty-two points to Frederick's five. Frederick's Alex Hattel, playing with an injured knee, scored only five points.

With two minutes left in the game, Mike Hattel and I both went after a loose ball near the sideline. Hattel, realizing he had no chance of getting to the ball, unwisely decided to shove his body into me, forcing me up into the stands. Referee Bobby Winkles called a technical foul on Hattel and ejected him from the game. Mead won easily, 62–37. The proud Warriors of Frederick had suffered the most devastating defeat ever by a Mead High School team. Mead would now face Erie in the finals the next evening.

The humiliation the Frederick Warriors experienced that Friday night was not forgotten by the Hattel brothers. The following morning, they wanted to avenge their loss in a place other than the basketball court. On Saturday morning, Rollie was confronted by the Hattels in Longmont.

Rollie, up at seven o'clock, drove our recently purchased '49 Ford to Longmont to begin work at the Longmont Drug, something he did every Saturday. Our brother Jerry had this job before Rollie, but now that Jerry had graduated and gone to Denver, Rollie took over. Rollie worked not only on Saturdays but also four nights a week from nine to eleven. On weekdays, Rollie swept and mopped the floor, but on Saturdays, he washed the store windows.

Outside the store, Rollie climbed a stepladder with a cloth over his shoulder, a squeegee in one hand, and a pail of water in the other. Glancing to his left, he saw two familiar faces moving toward him. It was the Hattel brothers, Mike and Alex. The Hattels came to Longmont quite often. Like us Newtons, they came to shop and to drag Main Street. That morning, they rode to town with their dad, who worked at Snyder's Jewelry. The Hattels stopped about ten feet in front of Rollie.

Mike Hattel scowled and said, "Newton, you chickensh——t son of a b——ch, youse Newtons think you're hot sh——t. Come on down. I'll show ya that you ain't nothin' but a cold turd."

"Come on, Mike," said Rollie. "I ain't got nothin' against you. What're ya tryin' to prove?"

"I'm goin' to prove that I can beat the holy crap outta ya," snorted Mike. "Youse Newtons ain't nobody. You're all pieces of sh——t. Y'all think you're good basketball players. I got news for ya. When I git done with ya, you won't be playin' any more basketball."

Alex, wanting to see what Rollie would do, never said a word. He was still suffering from his knee injury, and he was in no shape to fight. He stood beside his brother, grinning slightly and snickering, brimming with confidence, thinking his brother Mike was a superior fighter.

Meanwhile, Rollie, seeing that the back door of the drugstore was wide open, threw the squeegee and pail to the sidewalk, spilling the water in front of the Hattels. He quickly jumped down and lifted the ladder up, holding it between him and his adversaries, and he ducked through the open door into the drugstore's back room. Mike Hattel, enraged by splashed water on his shoes and now wanting to strike the first blow, ran after Rollie and followed him into the store.

Seeing his boss and storeowner Fritz Haverly watching Mike Hattel in angry pursuit, Rollie yelled out to Haverly, "Get this son of a b——ch outta here! He has no business bein' in here!"

Startled by the sudden appearance of two young boys who looked like they could kill each other right there in front of him, Haverly quizzically shouted, "What the hell's goin' on here?"

"This dumbass wants to pick a fight with me!" exclaimed Rollie. "I haven't done a thing to him. I'm out there washin' windows, and he's walkin' by and wants to start a fight."

"Young man," said Haverly to Mike Hattel, "you better run on down the street, and I don't want to see you in this store ever again."

Seeing there was now another "dog in the fight" and an adult as well, Mike Hattel turned to leave but not before saying, "I'll getcha later, Newton. I'll find ya when ya don't have somebody around to take care of ya, ya goddamn mama's boy!"

Rollie was certain the Hattels would be waiting for him when he got off work at one o'clock. Rollie gathered his coat and his weekly paycheck and ran lickety-split to his parked car. He jumped in and locked the doors. On the way home, he stayed off Longmont's Main Street, and he avoided Highway 66. Instead, he took the Weld County Road toward Mead and drove into our front yard without seeing the Hattels again that afternoon.

However, Rollie was still concerned that the brothers would start something that night at the memorial building preceding Mead's finals game with Erie. Frederick was scheduled to play Berthoud for third place. But the Frederick team left the building as soon as its game was over, not bothering to watch the Mead Bulldogs play, and the Hattel brothers were no longer in sight and were not seen again.

The finals game for the District 4 championship with the Mead–Erie faceoff was scheduled late that night at nine-thirty. Nearly nine hundred fans showed up, with large contingents from Longmont, Erie, and Mead. Brother Tom drove up from Denver to stay with our family for the weekend, and he took Mom and brothers Jack and Frosty to the memorial building. My girlfriend Kathy Nottingham was there to watch me play for the first time. She was accompanied by Linda Miller, Mike Eckel's girlfriend. Walt Slee closed his Lewis Furniture Store at nine and hurried to catch the nine-thirty tip-off. Walt sat with Bud Pitchford, who was covering the game for the Times Call. C. H. Clark, who had been we triplets' sixth-grade teacher and coach, came to see how his boys had developed in the last six years. Mead High School alums Dean Graham, Ronald Weber, Herb Newman, and Vernon Widger all came. Stalwart supporters—the Hopps, the Grahams, and Bub Howlett—were there. Mead farmer Dean Seewald came with Mike Eckel's dad, Frank. Dean had a $200 bet on the game for Mead to win by more than ten points. Dean had made a phone call to Coach that afternoon, encouraging Coach to run up the score. Coach benignly acknowledged his call and reported it to Supt. Carlson.

Although there was some doubt whether Sabino Lontine would be allowed to suit up for the Erie Tigers, the tournament director, our uncle Earl Achenbach, gave him the green light, and Lontine played one of his finest games. Our teams traded baskets in the first quarter with a tie at 10–10. In the second quarter, Mead's tight zone limited Erie's success by limiting them to shooting from the outside. Richie hit a jump shot to put Mead in the lead at 14–12, a lead Mead never relinquished. Lyle Schaefer hit two free throws, and Rollie put in a ten-foot jump shot for Mead to move ahead, 18–14. I found the range with three push shots and one jump shot, and my eight-point burst in the second quarter gave Mead a ten-point advantage at the half, 28–18.

Erie reduced Mead's lead to six points in the third quarter, with Lontine hitting highly arched, sweeping hook shots, but we four Newtons hit from the field to keep Mead twelve points ahead at the end of the quarter. With four minutes left, I was called on a charging foul, and Erie's Padia, defending me, went to the free-throw line to score, narrowing Mead's lead to five points. Lontine had been on fire the second half, scoring twelve of his eighteen total points. Erie was consistently able to get the ball inside to Lontine, playing next to the keyhole. In taking his patented hook shot, the burly Erie center was repeatedly fouled, and he connected on six straight free throws, all in the last quarter.

With a little over three minutes left, Mead went into a stall. Controlling the ball with my dribble, I broke loose from my defender and drove in for a layup. With Erie in possession, Richie stole the ball and quickly hit me with a pass as we fast-broke to the Mead basket, resulting in another two points.

Frank Eckel, sitting in the stands with Dean Seewald, watched his longtime friend suffer with anxiety through the game as Erie kept the scoring margin to less than ten points. Dean, with furled forehead, was understandably worried; his $200 was in jeopardy. With just forty seconds left, Richie sank two free throws and put Mead ahead by ten, 50–40. Frank and Dean Seewald jumped to their feet, raised their fists, and yelled triumphantly.

With Mead still stalling, I hit Mike Eckel under the basket with a pass. Mike laid it in for two more points. With Mead's next possession, Lyle Schaefer was fouled, and he dumped in two free throws to put us ahead by fourteen and the win, 54–40.

Dean Seewald won $200, and Mead won the District 4 championship, sending our team to the state tournament for the second year in a row.

While the partisan Mead crowd watched, our uncle Earl (Achenbach) presented the trophy to Coach. Along with the other nine hundred fans, Mom and my brothers Jack, Tom, Jerry, and Frosty stood and applauded. Dad, now taking a keen interest in basketball as he accompanied our brother Jack to watch us play, stood motionless with pride as he watched his boys walk off the floor. James Elmer Newton's four sons had dominated play in the District 4 tournament.

It was ironic that Larry Heil, our classmate and teammate in the second and third grades, was now attending school in Erie. Larry had contributed to Erie's success in winning the league championship in football, and now he was a guard on the basketball team. I have often wondered how good it would have been to have had Larry playing for Mead. It would have been a joyous occasion for both of us as Coach accepted the District 4 championship trophy for Mead.

Block That Shot

Laporte's Tom Davis (24) is shown above trying to block a shot by Mead's Lyle Schaefer (55) in the opening round game between Mead and Laporte in the District 4 class B tournament Thursday night at Longmont. Schaefer scored on this shot as he drove in from the side to help Mead to a 26-5 first quarter lead and eventual victory over Laporte. In the foreground scrambling for position are Mead's George Kademacher and, behind him, Laporte's Paul Corbett.—Tribune photo by Jim Moore.

Up for Grabs

The ball—and the tournament championship—is up for grabs in this picture from the first quarter of the Mead-Frederick game Friday night at the District 4 tourney at Longmont. At the left is Mead's Rollie Newton (34) in the center is Frederick's Dave Paul (55). The Warrior's center and rebounding mainstay. At the right is Mead's Lyle Schaefer (center, screened). A key factor in the game can be seen in the far right just behind Schaefer's left leg. It is the bar dy handicap left knee of Alex Nattel, an anchor the whole Frederick team had to pick up with it on offense. Mead won handily. 55-37.—Tribune photo by Jim Moore.

Ron Tries Jump Shot

Ron Newton in center jumps up for a try in shot during the Mead-Erie tilt at Longmont Saturday. Shown left to right are Mead's Lyle Schaefer (55), Rollie Newton (34), Erie's Bob Green (13), Sablon Lautlee (55) and Joe Padia (31). Mead won the championship tilt, 54-40.—Tribune photo by Ray Hedges.

Mead Cops 4-B Title

Mead's Bulldogs, co-champions of the North Central league and District 4, Class B titlists, are one of the favored teams in the state playoffs. Members of the team are: front row (L-R), Ron Newton, Dave Newton, Lyle Schaefer, Dick New- ton and Rollie Newton; back row (L-R), Paul Hopp, Mike Eckel, George Radamacher, Carl Hansen, Allen Thompson, Lanny Davis and Jim Landolt.—Tribune photo by Jim Moore.

St. Vrain Memorial Building, Longmont CO, 2014. *Ronald Newton*

Chapter 35

State Tournament

As we entered the state tournament for the second consecutive year, our team's sentiments could probably be best summarized in the dictum voiced by Iowa's renowned high-school wrestling coach, Robert Siddens. "Win with humility, and lose with dignity, but don't lose." We had won many games that year but never with arrogance or conceit. We had been defeated the year before in the semifinals, a devastating loss suffered without shame, malice, or bitterness. Inspired under the leadership of Coach Adams, we were determined that this year, our team would not lose. Our overwhelming successes in the season had provided us great confidence. We knew we were ready and able to take home the championship trophy.

On Thursday, following our capture of the District 4 title, we entered the Englewood High School gym, where the Class B state tournament first-round games were played. Mead, in the upper bracket with a record of 22 and 1, was paired with Bayfield (18 and 4), and Hotchkiss (19 and 1) was to play Granby (16 and 3). In the lower bracket, Sanford (12 and 8), the team that beat Mead in last year's semifinals, was to square off with Stratton (20 and 3), and Wiggins (18 and 4) was to face Fowler (15 and 6).

Coach would not take our team to Denver the night before to stay in a hotel. He wanted us to sleep in our own beds, so we drove to Denver the day of the game. Frank Eckel and Gilman Olson drove their cars, and Coach drove the driver's education car, the three of them carrying ten players and two managers to Englewood.

Playing before a sparse crowd, Mead squared off with the Bayfield Wolverines, a school from the southwest corner of the state. Mead exploded for twenty points in the first quarter, and we held Bayfield to only seven points in the second. Ahead, 20–16, at the end of the first period, Mead rolled to a 39–23 halftime lead. At game's end, we Newton brothers' combined fifty-two-point total was larger than Bayfield's final score of forty-nine points. All five Mead starters scored in double digits, and Mead closed with a 72–49 victory, with reserves playing most of the second half.

Coach hustled team members into our respective cars, and we all headed back to Mead, stopping briefly at a restaurant to eat. My brothers and I were home and in bed by nine o'clock. An "early night" was important; the next morning, we would travel back to Denver for the semifinals.

Unlike the year before, the '57 semifinals were held at the Denver Coliseum, built just a few years before in the shape of a Quonset. With a seating capacity of ten thousand, the coliseum was the site of the Denver Stock Show and Rodeo every year in January. But for basketball, the earth-floor arena was covered with an elevated gym floor, assembled in large square block sections.

Mead's semifinal opponent was Hotchkiss, a Western Slope high school that had defeated Granby. It was a coincidental "dogfight" between the Bulldogs of Mead and the Bulldogs of Hotchkiss. In the first quarter, Richie scored eight of Mead's sixteen points with three set shots and two free throws. By halftime, Richie had scored four more points, and Mead was ahead, 23–15. Richie scored another ten points in the third quarter, putting Mead ahead, 50–29. With two and a half minutes left, Mead gained a twenty-point lead, mostly with the help of Dave, who tallied fifteen for the game. Coach then played reserves. The final score was Mead, 59, and Hotchkiss, 49.

Unlike the previous year, Mead made it through the semifinals. The next day, Mead would face the Wiggins Tigers in the state finals.

Wiggins, playing in the Poudre Valley League, had placed second behind Johnstown, a team Mead had beaten twice in nonleague play and that had defeated Wiggins twice before. However, in the District 3 Class B tournament, Wiggins met Johnstown for the third time and finally triumphed by five points. Wiggins then squeaked by Gilcrest, giving it the berth in the state tournament.

In addition to winning games under the tutelage of experienced coach Elmer Cromer, who had played basketball for Fort Collins High School twenty years prior, Wiggins was winning games with superior height. Cromer installed a two-post offense with the Von Loh brothers, Willis and Allen, both six-foot-four. Gordon Ledford, at six-foot-one, played the small forward, and Danny Howell and Roland Rohn at five-nine and five-ten, respectively, played guard. In beating Stratton to get to the finals, Wiggins's Ledford scored eighteen points, and teammates Roland Rohn and Allen von Loh also scored in double figures.

Because of its size and Ledford's sharpshooting, Wiggins was picked to win the Class B title by the Greeley Tribune. Sports fans from all over Northeastern Colorado portrayed the upcoming game as a proverbial David-versus-Goliath contest. Longmont's Times Call cautioned that the quickness of the smaller Newton brothers should not be overlooked. Sportswriter Budd Pitchford said, "It should be a hard-fought contest all the way, probably no more than four or five points difference in the final score."

The Mead entourage arrived in the coliseum parking lot about 4:00 p.m., with the tip-off scheduled at six forty-five. Carrying our uniforms on hangers and our jock straps, socks, and tennis shoes wrapped in a towel, Mike Eckel and I walked toward the coliseum door.

A woman came up and asked, "Are you boys from Mead?"

"Yes, ma'am," said Mike. "We sure are."

"Well, I want to see those Newton brothers play," she said.

"Do you want to see a Newton?" Mike asked. Then he pointed to his chest. "I'm a Newton. My name is Mike Newton. You watch for me tonight. I'll be playin'."

I walked ahead, laughing.

"I'll be watchin' for ya," said the woman.

Inside and out of the woman's sight, Mike and I doubled over with laughter.

After our pregame warm-ups, Coach assembled our team in the locker room for his customary pep talk. He appeared confident. He had read the news reports of the Wiggins–Stratton game the day before and had concluded that Mead had to stop Gordon Ledford. Ledford was the leading scorer for Wiggins. He had a good jump shot and was a competitive rebounder.

"We'll start out man-to-man," said Coach. "Lyle, you take Allen von Loh. He's the bigger of those two brothers. Rollie, you take the other Von Loh. They both play post, so sometimes you'll have to play in front of them to keep them from gettin' the ball." Then he pointed at me. "You take Ledford. I know he plays forward a lot, but I want you on him. They're goin' to let him have the ball since he's their best scorer. Dave, you take Rohn, and, Richie, you'll have Howell."

Coach was as he always was before a game. He appeared calm and confident in front of his players. But I'm sure that inside, his gut was doing flip-flops. He knew this was the most important game he had coached at Mead. His team had been ousted in the semifinals last year. Now Mead was being challenged by a team that physically outmatched his. Yet his current team had lost only one game that year. Wiggins, with its bigger players, had lost four. They could be beaten, he said to himself.

"Play like you always do tonight," Coach said to his team. "Freelance on offense. Keep the ball moving. They usually play man-to-man, so you need to keep moving as well. Lyle, you're the captain tonight."

Hearing about the Wiggins players' height, I had not set my sight on winning. In my mind, beating Wiggins was a "long shot" proposition. All I wanted to do was hang in there. I hoped and prayed our team would play well. If we played a good game, I would be satisfied. However, I knew playing well would not be good enough for Coach. He expected his team to go for the win, playing its very best.

All the Mead supporters were sitting behind the Mead bench, a small group in comparison to the total five or six thousand fans that had assembled in the coliseum for this early game. James Elmer

Newton was there. By then, Dad had gotten "tournament fever." He had attended every game in both the district and state tournaments. Dad was accompanied by Mom, Walt Slee, and brothers Jack, Tom, Jerry, and Frosty. Herb Newman and Ronald Weber came; so did the Hopps, Martin and Dean Graham, the Thompsons, Frank and Marg Eckel, Dean and Bobby Seewald, and our cousin Spaulding "Tex" Newton. Sportswriter Bud Pitchford of the Longmont Times Call was at the courtside tables along with other reporters from the Tribune, the Denver Post and the Rocky Mountain News.

Barbara Graham came to watch. After seven years of cheering for Mead, Barbara had chosen not to be cheerleader her senior year. She had earned enough credits for graduation and had moved on with her life, earning money for college. JoAnn Becker, Elaine Leinweber, Elaine Becker, Helen Barnes, and Francie Palombo led Mead supporters in cheers. Mead pep club members had packed one bus to the brim to make the journey to Denver with driver Marion Humphrey and Supt. Carl Carlson. Team managers Marc Newton and Lyle's father, Russell Schaefer, were down on the court floor with the Mead team.

Greeley referee Bill Elliot threw up the ball for the opening tip-off. The Wiggins Tigers controlled the tip and made the first basket. With the Tigers' second possession, Gordon Ledford received the ball at his customary forward spot on the right side of Wiggins's half-court, with me defending him. Expecting Ledford to take a jump shot, I jumped in front of him, staying close as I put my hand in front of his face. Ledford put the ball to the floor to drive around me. As Ledford swept by me on my left side, I heard a loud exhaling whoosh coming from his mouth. It sounded like a freight train had just gone by. I stood there flatfooted as I watched Ledford go in for an easy layup. He put Wiggins ahead, 4–0.

Right then, I knew that Ledford's Wiggins team was ready to play and that I (three inches shorter than Ledford) had the biggest challenge I had ever faced on the basketball court. We four Newtons and Lyle Schaefer each scored field goals, and Dave hit one free throw. At the end of the first quarter, Wiggins was ahead, 13–11.

In the second quarter, Mead tied the score three times but could never take the lead. Halfway through the quarter, Rollie got his third foul. Coach yanked Rollie and sent Allen Thompson in to substitute. With his first possession with the ball, Allen Thompson pumped in his patented jump shot. Then Wiggins's Rohn came alive and sank five baskets, all in the second quarter. Ledford scored an additional five points to take Wiggins ahead by eight. However, Richie narrowed the margin to four by hitting two jumpers, and at half's end, Wiggins was leading, 28–24.

In that first half, I had accounted for only three of Mead's total twenty-four points. As I descended the stairs from the coliseum floor to the ground level, I glanced up at the scoreboard. We hung in there, I said to myself. They haven't blown us out of the water.

Although I felt winded, I was not especially tired. I'd never felt like that before. I knew I was in the best shape of anyone on the floor. Perhaps it was because I had to "go all out" throughout the first half more than I ever had to do before. It had been full throttle for me all sixteen minutes of the first half. I knew I had been challenged physically to stay up with Wiggins's Ledford. I knew that Ledford had scored ten of their points, but I was relieved that Mead had prevailed in keeping the score close. Mead still had a chance to win, and I could restore my wind during halftime.

My confidence was also restored when Coach spoke to us in the locker room.

"Men, we've got 'em where we want 'em," he said. "We're only down four, and we've got the whole second half to catch up. Rollie, I want you to go back in. I know you've got three fouls, but I know you can keep from foulin'. We need you in there to help with the reboundin'."

Hesitating for a moment, a thoughtful gleam now in his eyes, he continued, "Men, here's the score. We're goin' to switch to a zone. We'll foul less, and we'll be in better position for reboundin'. I'm hopin' also that with the zone, we can stop Ledford and Rohn better. Those two got most of their points drivin' to the basket. We'll keep Ledford shootin' from the outside. We'll make him beat us there, not inside as he is now.

Also, Richie and Ronnie, sag in on those two Von Lohs. Don't let them get a pass into 'em. Keep those inside guys from gettin' the ball."

Mr. Schaefer burst into the locker room and said, "Coach, ya got three minutes."

"Okay," said Coach, "let's go out there and take it to 'em."

Denver Coliseum, Denver CO. 2014. *Ronald Newton*

He's Got Him Covered

Mead's Rolly Newton ties up Byrfield's Sam Blomson (2) in Thursday's Class B State Tournament game at Englewood. Mead won the first round contest, 72-49.

—Rocky Mountain News Photo by Dick Davis

Mick Picks Off Rebound

Mick Springer of Hotchkiss goes high in the air to pick off a rebound as Mead's Rae Newton and Zore Hollenbeck of Hotchkiss watch. Mead defeated Hotchkiss, 59-48, in the Class B semifinals Friday.

—Rocky Mountain News Photo by Dick Davis

Newton (Dave, That Is) Hits

Dave Newton (22) of Mead goes high into the air to score a field goal as three Hotchkiss players—Mick Springer (44), Larry Lindersmith (41) and Larry Todd (32)—wait in vain for the rebound. Mead won the state B finals berth by beating Hotchkiss, 59-49, at Denver Coliseum Friday. Hotchkiss is coached by Bob Lord, December CSCE graduate.—Tribune photo by Paul Moloney.

Mead High School Cheerleaders.
L-R: Elaine Becker, JoAnn Becker, Francie Palombo, Helen Barnes, and Elaine Leinweber, 1957.
Mead Consolidated Schools Yearbook

Chapter 36

Championship

The second half of the final for the Class B basketball championship with the underdog Bulldogs facing the towering Tigers of Wiggins was ignited with renewed energy, and we immediately tied the score at 28—all with buckets by Dave and Richie. Thereafter, the lead changed four times and was tied five times. Wiggins was once ahead by four, but Mead could never get ahead by more than one basket.

Wiggins stayed with a man-to-man defense, and driving lanes opened up for me in the third quarter. I saw that I could vary the pace of my dribble and, with stops and starts, move around my Wiggins defender and go for the basket lickety-split for a driving layup. Midway in the third quarter, I got two more layup baskets, and I connected on a free throw when I was fouled by Dan Howell. Ledford connected on two jump shots and tipped in another. He then penetrated the Mead zone with his dribble and was fouled when shooting, making four of his five free throws. With just a few seconds left in the third, I hit a jump shot to put us ahead 40–38.

Our zone defense did not stop Gordon Ledford. By the end of the third quarter, he had scored another ten points, bringing his total to twenty.

Richie hit a jump shot from fifteen feet out in the first minute of the fourth quarter, and thereafter, all the scoring opportunities came to me. Going to my left on the dribble, I meandered through the Wiggins's towering backcourt Von Loh twosome and laid it in with my left hand to score. On the next possession, Richie found me open for a ten-foot jump shot, and I nailed it. With less than four minutes to go, I attempted a jump shot and was fouled again by Howell. I sank both free throws. Ledford then connected on a long jump shot and tied it up, forty-eight all. Richie brought the ball down and dribbled toward me to give me the ball and to screen out Howell. Richie's defender, Roland Rohn, switched to guard me, and as I drove toward the basket, Rohn fouled me as I attempted the layup. With two minutes and ten seconds left, I sank both free throws to put Mead ahead, 50–48.

Wiggins failed to score on its next possession, and we went into our proverbial stall. I maintained possession on the dribble, going with stops and spurts, changing hands, avoiding each Wiggins defender as they approached to take the ball away. With the clock running out, Wiggins got desperate, and Howell fouled me, hoping I would miss the free throws with Wiggins to get the ball back. I sank both of them to put Mead ahead, 54–50.

In a hurry to score, Wiggins's Allen von Loh put one up that missed the rim completely. Rollie, underneath the basket and seeing where the errant shot was going, leaped high for the rebound and maintained possession with a slow dribble. Rollie then threw the ball over the heads of the Wiggins defenders to me; I was standing near the perimeter of the court. Again, I went into the dribbling stall, and I was fouled by Ledford. I hit one of my two free throws, and I put Mead ahead, 55–50 with a little over a minute left. Wiggins moved the ball downcourt and got it to Ledford. Dave fouled Ledford as he attempted his jump shot, and Ledford sank both foul shot attempts. With fifty seconds left, we passed the ball around to one another, dribbling only when needed to get the pass away, and we maintained possession the rest of the game. The final score was Mead, 55; Wiggins, 52.

The partisan crowd, demonstrably behind the underdog Mead Bulldogs, let out a giant roar as the clock wound down. Mead had won the state championship. In a spectacular showdown between two powerful Northeastern Colorado teams, the taller Wiggins Goliaths were defeated by the smaller Mead Davids. Biblical history had been repeated. I scored nineteen of my twenty-two points in the second half, making seven of eight free-throw attempts and nailing six field goals. It was the finest performance of my life, and now, fifty-nine years later, it is an awesome memory.

My brothers and I did what we always did at the conclusion of the game. We shook hands with our opponents and went straight to the locker room. We showed little outward emotion of celebration. No extreme demonstrative signs of our success were displayed. We simply shook hands with one another and our teammates. Mead had previously won twenty-five ball games that season and now had won its twenty-sixth. We had become accustomed to winning. Although it was in the back of my mind, I never discussed the prospect of losing with my brothers or anyone else. It is only now, fifty-eight years later, when I contemplate the possibility of losing that final game. With a loss, things today would be much different for my brothers and me on how we perceive ourselves.

Our teammates were ecstatic about the win. Lyle Schaefer put a bear hug on Richie and then on me.

Mike Eckel, twirling his jock strap in the air around his finger, yelled loudly, "We beat those tall b———ds! Yippee!"

Lanny, smiling happily, shook hands with everyone. The usually stoic Carl Hansen yelled, "We got a state championship for the Bulldogs! Let's hear it for Mead!"

Coach did not participate in the celebration. He was trying to talk to reporters in the din of euphoria in the Mead dressing room. The next day in the Rocky Mountain News, Coach was quoted.

> We planned to win the state from the first night of practice this season. We lost out to Sanford in the semifinals last year, and these kids just decided this would be their year. They just wanted to win. That was the big difference tonight.

When our team emerged from the locker room, we sat in seats reserved for us to watch the remaining Class A and Class AA title games and finally to participate in the award ceremonies. When the announcer asked for Mead to send a representative forward to receive the trophy, Coach said, "Mike, you go."

As Mike Eckel extended his hands to grab the mammoth prize, the whole coliseum audience applauded. The clapping and yelling did not stop. Mead High had been the sentimental favorite, and the partisan crowd was clearly delighted with our victory. Budd Pitchford of the Longmont Times Call wrote the following:

> Mead was immensely popular with the crowd. Seemed as if everybody had heard and read about the Newton brothers, and they were pulling for their club to take state.

James Elmer and Laura Dreier Newton listened to the applause for the Mead High School basketball team. Many in the crowd had come to see the Newtons play, and they were not disappointed. For years, the Newton children had been cautiously admonished with Laura's favorite phrase, "Remember, you are not the only star that twinkles." However, that night, the stars of Laura's children more than twinkled. James Elmer and Laura Dreier Newton's children were the stars of the night. The light of Laura's children collectively lit up the Denver Coliseum like a celestial constellation. That night, the light of Laura's children illuminated the minds and hearts of nearly ten thousand coliseum fans, and the next day, the Newton children's achievements would radiate from local and Denver newspapers to readers all over Colorado. That night, James Elmer and Laura Dreier Newton (uncharacteristically) reflected with pride on the stellar performances of their children.

However, we brothers clearly understood we were not the "only stars that twinkled" on Mead's championship team. There was Lyle Schaefer, our fifth man. There was Allen Thompson, who filled in for Rollie when Rollie got into foul trouble. There was Lanny Davis, Mike Eckel, George Rademacher, and Carl Hansen. They contributed to our success. They showed up for practice every day and provided opposition in scrimmages, essential training components in Mead's preparation for the championship. But it was not just the Newtons and a Schaefer who had a starlit night; the stars of Mead's five second-stringers also had an opportunity to shine. Mead had dominated play in both the quarter- and semifinals in such an overwhelming way that Mead's bench bunch saw plenty of action.

With applause still thundering, Mike Eckel walked back to his team with trophy in hand. We swarmed around him as he held it high for all to see. When the applause ended, Mike noted that they had given him the Class A trophy by mistake. He turned and walked back to the directors to get the correct Class B one and returned to his team, holding it high above his head once again.

It was apparent that us four Newton brothers in the lineup were confusing to our opponents as well as others. Broadcaster Fred Leo, who called the game on KLZ radio, said, "If you don't think it's tough calling a game with four Newtons in it. It was a mess."

LaVerne Magnuson was a substitute guard for the defeated Tigers. LaVerne had attended Mead in grades 5 through 7 and had demonstrated his talents as a gifted student. LaVerne also learned how to play basketball by playing with us triplets on our fifth and sixth grade and peewee teams. Our brother Marc recalled a conversation he had with LaVerne after that championship game. "We should have won!" exclaimed LaVerne. "We had a much better team than you guys."

LaVerne may have been right, and that is what many others thought, including several sportswriters. But that night, we played our very best, and Jack Adams coached his very best. Perhaps Wiggins did not have a good night. That night, my prayers had been answered. God had supported us, who had done our very best, and in my mind, we were the better team.

The driver's education car with Coach driving and me in it was the first one to return to the school parking lot late that night at nearly two in the morning. I placed my playing togs in my locker, said goodbye to Coach, and walked home alone. Approaching our driveway, I saw that all the downstairs lights were still on. Walking past the dining room window, I saw Mom sitting in a rocking chair and sewing, while brothers Jack and Tom were sitting at the table. Only Dad had gone to bed. I walked into the room and was greeted by smiles from all three.

"Congratulations there, bub," said Jack. "You played a hell of a ball game."

"Y-you sure d-did," said Tom, slurring his words. "You guys showed those Wiggins farmers how to p-play b-basket-b-ball."

There was a bottle of Old Crow whiskey on the table. Both Tom and Jack had glasses in front of them.

"G-god-d-d-damn, those g-guys were b-big," said Tom deliberately and slowly. "I-I d-didn't think you k-kids h-had a chance."

"I was so nervous, I thought I was goin' to have a heart attack," said Mom, looking up from her sewing.

"Well, we had a good second half when Coach switched us to the zone," I said. "I'm sure glad Rollie didn't foul out. He kept us in the game with his reboundin'."

"You all played a good game," said Jack emphatically. "I know you'll make the all-state team for sure, and I'm hopin' the others do also. I want to see what the Rocky Mountain News does, also the Denver Post. In just a little bit, we're goin' to Longmont and pick up the papers and see what they say."

"Th-that lanky s-son-of-a-bitchin' Ledford w-will m-make it for sure," said Tom. "H-he musta made a hundred free throws t-tonight. R-Ronnie, you got that many t-too. Y-you couldn't miss."

Since it was so late when the tournament ended, we had not taken time to get anything to eat. I went to the kitchen to get a bowl of Cheerios and milk and went back into the dining room to converse.

"Don't forget," said Mom to me as I opened the door to the upstairs, "we have church in the morning. It's Sunday, ya know."

"Okay, get me up."

I went up the stairs and sat down on the bed to take off my shoes. From the silence of my bedroom, I could hear the talk below.

"Shame on you, Tom," I heard Mom saying. "These kids come home thinking they've done something real good, and seeing you like that with too much to drink—you oughta to be ashamed of yourself."

I heard Tom laughing, not caring about what she said. I knew Tom was happy about what had happened that night and that he was simply celebrating. That expression of his happiness made me feel even more proud of my accomplishments. I knew too that Jack was happy. I knew he had had the most exciting military leave of his life.

I knelt down to say my prayers. I thanked God for inspiring my brothers and me to play our very best. We were fortunate it was enough for us to win. Now, fifty-nine years later, I thank God for providing me one of the most memorable experiences of my life—playing basketball for Mead High School.

The next morning, I came downstairs from my bedroom. I noticed the Sunday morning editions of both the *Denver Post* and the *Rocky Mountain News* lying on the dining room table. I quickly perused them. My three brothers and I had all been selected on the all-state Class B basketball team. In the *News,* Coach praised his team, and he had singled me out. "I don't know any better player in the state." That accolade, like the victory itself and my whole life in that spring of '57, was sweet.

Newton Boys Have Solid Brother Act

Mead moved into the finals of the Class B State Tournament Friday afternoon and once again it was the Newton brother act that turned the trick. The boys are, left to right, Dick, Ron, Roland and Dave, Dick, Rollie and Ron are 17 year-old seniors and triplets, of course, and Dave a 16-year-old junior. Dick tossed in 22 point Friday, Dave 17, Rollie six and Ron five.

—Rocky Mountain News Photo by Dick Davis.

Mead's Class B State Champions

Front row, left to right: Roland Newton, Lyle Schaefer, Dave Newton, Carl Hamers, George Rademacher, Back row: Lanny Davis, Mike Ecke Ron Newton, Dick Newton, Allen Thompson.

—Rocky Mountain News Photos by Dick Davis

Bully Newton of Mead (right) looks like a diving champion as he tries to spear a rebound against Wiggins. Mead rolled to win Class B title, 52-32, over Wiggins.

Dave Newton (47) climbs high to grab off a rebound against Wiggins and looks to pass off to brother Bully Newton (54) as Mead starts its move downcourt. Closing in is Wiggins' Roland Rohn (24).

Gordon Ledford (14) of Wiggins looks like he has a "head for basketball" as he swoops in to take rebound against Mead Saturday in final game of Class B division. Mead's Dick Newton crosses his arm, and Rolly Newton (34) of Mead and Danny Howell of Wiggins moves in.

Wiggins, The Challenger

The Wiggins basketball squad, seated in the Poudre Valley conference, is shown above. In the front row, left to right, are John Brethauer, Roland Rohn, Marvin Sellers, Harry Rossman and Jim Thompson. In the back row, left to right, are Dan Howell, LaVern Magnuson, Allen Van Loh, Willis Van Loh and Gordon Ledford.—Tribune photo by Jim Moore.

1957 Colorado Class B State Championship Basketball Trophy. L-R: Mike Eckel,
Richie Newton, Ronnie Newton, Lanny
Davis, Coach Jack Adams, Rollie Newton,
1957. *Denver Post.*

1957 Colorado Class B State
Championship Basketball
Trophy, 2007. *Lyle Schaefer.*

L-R: Carl Hansen, Lanny Davis, and George Rademacher, 1957.
Mead Consolidated Schools Yearbook

Allen Thompson, 1957. *Mead Consolidated Schools Yearbook*

Chapter 37

Rejection

In the spring of '57, with the basketball season over, my senior year and my time at Mead High School were drawing to a close. With graduation looming for Richie, Rollie, and me and our classmates, we were all pondering the proverbial question bombarding us from almost everyone in the Mead community: "What are you going to do when you finish school?" And in that same spring, there was another complication for me. I learned that my girlfriend, Kathy Nottingham, was interested in another suitor.

"Linda tells me that Kathy is ridin' to school each day with this guy from Longmont," said Mike Eckel to me one day in English class. "Linda sez that she has seen them in his car together several times during the week."

"What's his name?"

"Jim Brown," Mike answered. "He's only a junior, and he's shorter than she is. He's kinda small. I guess he's a good-lookin' dude with his ducktail haircut and all. Linda sez that Kathy seems to like him a lot. Ronnie, you need to ask her what's goin' on and have her explain what she's doin behind your back."

I decided to confront Kathy. Although the cycle of spring had begun, that night, we had a cold snap, and at the end of the evening, Kathy, as she was accustomed to do, invited me into the Nottingham house so we could spend a few more minutes together in the comfort of their living room. We were sitting across from each other, she on the sofa and me in an overstuffed chair.

I started, "I hear you've been seeing someone else and that when you are with him, you ain't even wearin' your basketball chain."

Caught unaware and surprised at the direction of this conversation, Kathy said, "I guess Mike told you that, didn't he?"

"Y-yes, he did," I answered nervously. "Sez his name is Jim Brown."

"Well, he's just a good friend," she said. "We've been seeing each other when I'm with my friends Linda, Sue, and Marilyn. They all have boyfriends with them too. It's not all that serious. It doesn't really mean anything."

"Linda told Mike that you meet him in the halls at school and that you drive up and down Main Street sittin' next to him," I said. "They said it's been goin' on for a month, now." Then I blurted out, "I-I want my basketball back."

Kathy continued to defend her actions, saying there was nothing wrong with what she had been doing.

I persisted and said once again, "You need to give my basketball back to me."

Kathy unhooked the chain from around her neck and withdrew the basketball ornament from it. "Here, you can have it!" she said as she hurled the ornament across the room. I was taken by surprise when it glanced off my chest and landed on the floor.

I picked it up and held it in my hand as I put on my coat. Then I walked past her as I moved toward the door. She was sitting there, staring down at the floor. I said nothing, nor did she.

As I closed the door behind me, I began to weep. For the first time in my life, I had experienced serious rejection. I had lost the affection of a first love, and in my own mind, I had been defeated. I wondered if Kathy had concluded I was a hick-town loser and if she preferred a more sophisticated urbanite over me. I suspected my poverty-stricken past in a small town had not prepared me for meeting the challenges posed by a big-town upper-stratum culture. I felt inferior and full of self-doubt.

Perhaps Kathy's new boyfriend could offer her one thing that I could not: constant attention. Marg Eckel said to me one evening as we were eating supper at the Eckel house and discussing Kathy's departure from my life, "You know, Ronnie, young girls like to be attended to by their beaus. They want to feel important. They want to be smothered with kindness all the time, every minute, every day."

Jim Brown could visit Kathy every day, but I could not. Afraid that family members would listen to my conversations, I didn't call Kathy on the phone each night. I called her only once a week from the pay phone downtown. Our conversations were short. In my mind, I only needed to confirm our date for Saturday night and the time. We could talk then.

If Kathy needed daily companionship, I simply was not able to provide it. Afternoons were taken up with sports activities, and weekday evenings were spent at home doing homework and studying. I couldn't sacrifice those obligations, so Saturday evening had always been the special night when I could see her. In my mind, one night a week was what was needed. Anything more than that would divert me from achieving the important goals of going to college and playing basketball there. The girlfriend-boyfriend relationship had to be secondary.

But after that breakup, I missed sharing that one night a week with Kathy. I desperately wanted to see her again. One night, Richie, Rollie, Lanny Davis, and I dragged Longmont's Main Street with Allen Thompson driving his '53 Chevrolet. I was hoping I would see Kathy. If I did, I hoped that she wouldn't be with Jim Brown. I hoped she and her friends would be dragging Main in her dad's car.

Allen reached Johnson's Corner on the south end of Main Street and made a U-turn to head back north. As Allen picked up his speed, we passed another car with several passengers. I recognized right away that the one in the middle in the back seat was Jim Brown. He had been pointed out to me before by our Longmont friend, Vern Palinkx.

"Hey, that's Nottingham's boyfriend there in the back seat!" I announced.

"You mean, oh, what's his name?" said Richie. I had confided my hurt feelings to Richie, hoping it would ease the emotional pain I was experiencing.

Yal that's Jim Brown," I answered. Then with my bitter memories taking over, I said boastfully, "I'd like to take him on and beat the sh——t out of 'im."

"Well, let's just call him out!" shouted Allen. "We'll see if he wants to fight. I think you should take him on. He looks like a little fart. I think you can whip 'im."

Allen pulled up alongside their car at the stoplight. He rolled his window down and asked, "Is Brown in there?"

Brown, sitting in the back seat with his head down, slouched down further and did not look up or speak.

Not receiving any answer, Allen said, "Ron Newton's calling him out and wants to fight 'im."

Just then, the back door of the car opened, and a big, obese dude stepped out on the street and said, "He's not comin' out, but bring Newton out here. I'll take him on."

"Who are you?" asked Allen.

"I'm Fat Charlie. Do you want to make something of it?"

Fat Charlie was more than six feet tall, and he looked like he weighed more than 250 pounds. He wore jeans, and an untucked denim shirt hung over his protruding stomach. He must have been in his early twenties. He had most likely experienced many confrontations before, and he looked like he probably had been successful in all of them. I sensed that after a fight with this guy, they would have nothing more to do than to utterly haul my pulverized body across town to the Howe Mortuary.

"Come on out, you son of a b——tch," said Fat Charlie. "We'll take care of this right now."

In my mind, I was fighting for honor, and I could not back down in front of my brothers and friends. Furthermore, I wanted Kathy to know that I was picking this fight with her boyfriend, the one I perceived to be a winner. I had lost. I could settle the score if I overpowered him with my physical superiority. I was certain that I could whip Jim Brown, but Fat Charlie was another matter. Nevertheless, I felt I had to accept Fat Charlie's challenge.

I had opened the door and was ready to emerge when Rollie, a voice of reason, said, "Wait a minute here, Charlie. This is not your fight. This is with Brown. If he doesn't want to fight, we're leavin'. We're not goin' to fight you."

I closed my door, and the stoplight changed to green. Allen drove off, leaving Fat Charlie standing in the street.

Rollie had come to the rescue. He had saved me from stupidity, a dumbass confrontation that could have been physically debilitating, perhaps permanently. Rollie had shown a level of maturity and wisdom, neither of which I had.

Allen Thompson, 1957.
*Mead Consolidated
Schools Yearbook*

Lanny Davis, 1957.
*Mead Consolidated
Schools Yearbook*

Richie Newton, 1957.
*Mead Consolidated
Schools Yearbook*

Rollie Newton, 1957.
*Mead Consolidated
Schools Yearbook*

Ronnie Newton, 1957. *Mead Consolidated Schools Yearbook*

Chapter 38

School's End

Mead High School's capturing of the state championship in basketball had gotten the attention of many individuals and groups who wanted to honor our team. Our neighbor, Vernon "Bub" Howlett, a member of the Longmont Elks Club, wanted Mead to be honored by the Elks. For the past several years, Bub had attended most of Mead's games, both home and away, and he was proud of what the Newton kids next door had accomplished.

Bub told Mom, "I watched your kids play for years in your backyard. I knew they were goin' to do well. They've done a lot for our town. They are a real good bunch of boys."

Bub knew that not only were my brothers and I good basketball players, but we were also good workers when he hired us to shovel grain into augers in the tall silos of his Denver Elevator Co. Bub also knew he had not always been kind to us, but that was now behind both us and him. At the Elks dinner, Bub was happy for the Newton boys, and he smiled with great pride and clapped loudly as Coach Adams introduced each member of our team. Bub knew Mom's boys had done something of significance.

Greeley was the seat of Weld County, and the Greeley chamber of commerce also feted three county teams that played in the tournament (Greeley High, Wiggins High, and Mead High). After finishing dinner and being entertained with hula dancing by Hawaiian students from the college, I had the opportunity to talk to Gordon Ledford, Wiggins's outstanding forward whom I had tried desperately to defend against just a few weeks before.

"You really had a good game, Gordy," I said. "You made half of your team's points. You got twenty-six that night."

"Yal," said Gordy, smiling, "but we didn't win."

"Are you goin' to play in college?" I asked.

"I don't know yet," said Gordy. "I'm thinkin' about it. I may go here in Greeley. It's close to home."

"That's where I wanna go too," I said. "Our coach is helpin' my brothers and me get a scholarship."

Mead farmer Frank Barnes also treated our team to a chicken dinner at the Williams Wayside Inn in Berthoud. Frank's daughter Helen was one of our cheerleaders. Frank brought a tape recorder along.

He said, "You all need to say something tonight. We want to record it so that many years from now, you'll be reminded what it was like to be a member of this basketball team."

Mike Eckel, in his usual eloquent way, said, "It's been a privilege for me to have played with these Newton boys—Richie, Rollie, Ronnie, and Dave. I'm very proud that I've been an athlete at Mead High School. I want to thank Mr. Adams and Mr. Carlson for helpin' me and helpin' this team to the championship."

Our cousin Spaulding "Tex" Newton had also a special event planned for Coach Adams and our team. Tex was the regional representative for U.S. Rubber, the maker of Keds tennis shoes, and he had provided tennis shoes for our team for two years—that is, for everybody except Rollie. Rollie wore Converse shoes, the ones given to him by brother Tom.

"Why don't you wear Keds?" Tex asked Rollie prior to one game in the state playoffs.

"I don't like 'em," said Rollie emphatically. "They don't fit me right. They don't fit like these Converse shoes do."

Tex was disappointed, but he knew there was no chance he could convince Rollie to change his mind, especially if different shoes made Rollie less effective as a player.

Promoting his company's products, Tex planned a workshop for Colorado high-school coaches at the Park Lane Hotel in Denver. "Mr. Basketball," George Mikan, the former center of the Minneapolis Lakers and a spokesman for U.S. Rubber, was the principal speaker. Mikan demonstrated and described basketball techniques in the gym of Denver University, using players from DU and Mead's starting five to help with his teaching. We were dressed in our uniforms, and Rollie reluctantly but obediently wore U.S. Keds. At six-foot-ten, Mikan weighed at least 280 pounds, and his Keds shoe size was enormous. He towered over Mead's team members assembled around the keyhole as he demonstrated shooting underhand free throws.

On the way home in Coach Adam's car, I commented to Coach how big Mikan's hand felt when he shook hands with me. "Boy, he had big hands," I said. "Did you see 'im holding two basketballs, one in each hand?"

"Yes, I did," Coach Adams answered. "Your cousin Tex told me that every time he shakes hands with him, it hurts so much, he has to grimace in pain."

* * *

Coach Adams had initiated a track program as the spring sport in 1956, and I ran the half-mile. This year, I wanted to run the mile. Coach Adams had instructed me on the techniques of running long distances.

"Your arms are just as important as your legs," he said. "If they get tired, you can lose the race. Keep your thumbs tucked into your palms. Keep your fingers relaxed. Don't clench your fists. Always move your arms forward, never across your chest. All your body, including your feet, should be going forward, never sideways. Don't tighten up. Stay relaxed. If you tighten up, your muscles will get tired sooner."

Each day, Coach Adams created a workout program for me. Chin-ups and push-ups for arm strength were always part of it. Sit-ups and leg stretching were included. On some days, he would schedule wind sprints; on other days, he prescribed long-distance runs with targeted time goals. I worked out alone. With hooded sweatshirt and sweatpants, I did not miss a workout session, no matter what the erratic Colorado spring weather brought.

Running had always been a part of my life. As a youngster, I had Mom "time me" as I ran downtown to Bunton's Red & White to buy a grocery item. I could not run faster than my teammates, but I could run longer. Next to basketball, running the mile was my favorite sport activity but only after the event had taken place. Preparing for and running the mile were the most grueling experiences, mentally and physically, I had ever had as an athlete.

At the state meet, I stood upright with twenty other milers at the starting line. Having eaten only Cheerios and toast for breakfast five hours before, the growling feeling in my hollowed stomach marked the beginning of the intense physical agony I knew I had to endure. I was both anxious and nauseated. I tried not to think about how exhausted I would feel during that last quarter-mile lap, the time when milers are supposed to show that "kick," the time when the body, depleted of oxygen, desperately reaches for energy reserves and is carried to the finish line only by sheer will. I hated that suffocating feeling I experienced in the last stretch. It was what I dreaded most when running the mile.

I qualified for the state meet mile run at 4:54, a record for the North Central League. I had bested Mead miler Ralph Borgman's record of 5:05 and brother Jerry's record of 5:12, but I couldn't help but humbly compare it with English runner Roger Bannister's less-than-four-minute mile back in 1953.

As the gun sounded, I saw the sprint of my competitors as we all moved toward the center of the track. I had never experienced such a rapid pace in the first stage of a race. I did not try to keep up, and I fell back in the first lap.

As I turned into the second lap, I heard Coach Adams standing in the center infield, yelling at me, "Pick it up, Ronnie!" With each lap, Coach Adams ran from side to side of the track, yelling, "C'mon, Ronnie!"

With a half lap to go, I saw two runners in front of me. In spite of Coach Adams's yells of encouragement as he ran alongside me, I could not overcome them. Far out in front was a runner from the high-mountain Western Slope. He finished with a time of 4:27. He already had me beaten when he rapidly set the pace in the first lap. I was certain I had improved my previous best of 4:54, but I never found out what it was. Placing third was an accomplishment I had not expected.

However, Dave tied for first in both the pole vault at eleven feet and four inches and the high jump at five feet and eleven inches, both personal bests. Allen Thompson tied for fifth place in the high jump at five feet and eight inches. With the meet over, Dave, Coach Adams, and I said goodbye to Allen, who was driving back to Mead in his own car, and Dave and I helped Coach Adams tie Dave's vaulting pole to the door handles of Coach's '51 Chevrolet.

With three state medals in our possession, we drove down Highway 85 southward toward Loveland. Coach Adams commented, "We did real well as a team with only three athletes. We came in fifth outta twenty-two teams, scored eleven points. Limon won the state championship with twenty-nine points. They did it without winning first in any events. They had a heck of a lot of athletes that qualified. They won it with their sheer numbers. You guys must be hungry. Let's stop off to get something to eat." He pulled into the parking lot of a supermarket. "How about some fruit? It's good for ya."

I went in, and Coach Adams bought two bananas for me. I devoured both of them before I got back to the car. The hollow feeling in my stomach still had not dissipated, and there was a hollow feeling in my soul, a void that bananas could not fill. This was the last sporting event I would share with Coach Adams. My athletic days at Mead High were over.

Thompson Tries Broad Jump

Newton Eyes Height

Mead's Dave Newton gets ready to vault in the North Central
league track meet at Fort Collins Tuesday. He scored 10-6½ to
win the event.—Tribune photo by Jerry Kennerich.

Allen Thompson, 1957. *Tribune (Greeley)*

Ron Newton Wins Mile Run

Ron Newton, Mead, lunges across the finish
line just ahead of Darrell Emry, Ault, in a record-
breaking mile run. Larry Heinze of Galeton set
the pace in the first three laps but faded in the
final to finish third. Newton ran the mile in 4:54.6.
Tribune photo by Paul Maloney.

Chapter 39

Dedicated Learner

Since the school's construction in 1918, hundreds of students had come through Mead Consolidated School's doors, learning what they could before moving on with their lives. Graduating classes at Mead were small, some with only two students. The '44 class had fifteen seniors, and the class of '47 had nine graduates. The class of Vernon Weber (Ronald's brother) graduated twenty-five in '52; Ronald's graduating class of '53 had twenty.

At Mead Consolidated, young and old knew one another. We were friends and like family. We respected one another, and we were concerned about the welfare and future of our classmates. After graduation, many Mead graduates married and settled on farms right around the town, but some found work in neighboring Longmont and Denver. Others extended their education. The valedictorian of Weber's class, David Warner, went to Colorado A&M College, and classmate Charlyne Alexander attended Colorado State College of Education. Charlyne's sister Sondra, class of '49, went to CSCE, and so did her classmate Mary Lou Lee. Helen Peters of the class of '48 attended the University of Wyoming, and her sister Mary Louise of the '49 class followed in her footsteps. Donnie Owen, Mead valedictorian in 1950, went to Colorado A&M College. Two of Grover Roberts's children, Donald and John, attended A&M.

But some Mead folks chose not to remain at Mead High, seeking other alternatives for schooling. Several transferred to Longmont High School thinking they would have better opportunities in sports as well as the classroom. Emily Newman's son Herb left Mead his senior year and went to Longmont High. He had been a starter on Longmont's basketball team and went on to Colorado University to play freshman basketball. Four classmates of my brother Tom (Tommy Major, Jim Lind, Glenn Markham, and Donnie Geibelhaus) all left Mead for Longmont High.

"I played basketball with Tom when I was a sophomore," said Weber. "I know how well he played. He was one of the top scorers in the league. Would his team have won the league championship that year if all four of those guys had not transferred to Longmont? Would they have gone to state?"

"I dunno," I said. "I think they would've had a pretty solid team."

"I know of two Mead athletes who went on to play at the college level," said Weber. "Charles Major played freshman basketball at CSCE, but he dropped out of school to join the navy. Herb Newman tried out as a freshman at CU, but he didn't make the team."

"I hope my brothers and I can make it," I said. "Maybe we can be the first."

"Well, there are some players whom I competed against from the other high schools who did play for colleges," said Weber. "Ron McClary from Fort Lupton played football at Colorado A&M, and so did Kersey's Bill Mondt. Ault's fast halfback, Gerry Meek, played for CSCE, and Frederick's Mike Pappas played four years of basketball for CSCE."

"Gary Tway from Fort Lupton plays for the Aggies now," I said. "We triplets played against him in junior high and high school. He was a grade ahead of us. His team won the state Class A championship last year."

"I think you Newtons have a chance to play college basketball," said Weber. "But what you have goin' against you is your height. None of ya are very tall."

* * *

Throughout my high-school years, I pondered a lot about whether I was equipped to go on to college, and I took great interest in learning about the intentions and attributes of others older than me who chose to further their education.

One morning, in the summer of '52, next-door neighbor and fifth-grade teacher Mrs. Newman came over to talk to Mom. Several of us were eating breakfast when Mrs. Newman knocked on our back-porch door. She entered the kitchen and stood in the door, leaning against the door jamb.

Mrs. Newman said, "We went to Golden yesterday to enroll Clarence in the Colorado School of Mines."

"What does he want to take there?" Mom asked.

"He's goin' to be a meturgilist [metallurgist]," said Mrs. Newman.

"What's that?" I asked.

"They learn about takin' metals out of the ground and refinin' 'em," answered Mrs. Newman. "Metals like gold and lead are combined with a lot of other stuff too, so they learn how to separate the metal from the bad stuff."

Weber had told me that Clarence, like his brother Herb, was smart. But later one evening, I heard Mom and Kathleen talking about Clarence.

"Mrs. Newman said Clarence scored high on his achievement tests," said Kathleen. "I can't believe that he didn't make it and dropped out. Mines is a tough school. Maybe he wasn't ready."

Hearing Mom and Kathleen talking about Clarence no longer being in school, I curiously asked, "What happened, Mom?"

"Well," said Mom, "I really don't know, but sometimes kids don't work hard. They don't know how to study. Just because you're smart, it doesn't mean you can make it in college. Ya gotta work. Ya gotta really study."

"Ya know, Ronnie," said Kathleen, "some of the smart ones don't even go to college. Jack Landolt was valedictorian of his senior class. He didn't go. Junior Lesser was also a Mead valedictorian, and he didn't go. I don't know why they didn't. I guess maybe they didn't have the money. It takes a lot of money to go college."

"Mom, who paid for Orbin when he went to CU?" I asked.

"Why, he did, of course," said Mom. "I know he was workin', but I've forgotten where. But he only went one year. He had to drop out when he was drafted."

"If I go, I'll have to work my way through too," I said. "But maybe I'll get a scholarship playin' basketball."

"You can still go even if ya don't play basketball," said Kathleen. "Donnie Owens and Donnie Roberts played football in high school, but they aren't playing for A&M."

"I know," I said. "Donnie was a good football player. I wonder why he didn't go out for the A&M team."

"He and Donnie Roberts are studyin' to be veterinarians," said Kathleen. "Maybe they decided they couldn't do both. It's hard to be a good student and a good athlete at the same time."

"If I went to CU, I'd be an architect," I said. "CU has the only architecture school in the state. I wrote a report in English class on Frank Lloyd Wright. He was an architect. If I did that, I'd have to take more math. Ya gotta be good at math if you're goin' to be an architect."

I knew I wanted to go to college. Mike Eckel's mother Marg said, "The best way today to ensure success with your life is to have a college education." Besides, I enjoyed learning, and I knew that I would learn a lot in college. In English class, Mr. Johnson explained how students enroll for credit hours in college, and he described his experiences with night classes he was taking at the University of Denver. He and "commercial teacher" Mrs. Bachman emphasized that learning was the most the important aspect of high school; sports were secondary. Coach Adams, also proud of the academic achievements of his players, was quoted in the Rocky Mountain News—"And I have five straight-A students on the first ten."

Next to basketball, going to class, almost any class, was my favorite activity. I had been fascinated to discover the role of flowers in reproductive biology in Mr. Warner's ninth-grade science class. I had not realized that flowers on our lilac bush had other functions besides adding beauty to our yard. Mrs. Eck taught my freshman English class how to diagram sentences. I welcomed the challenge of breaking them down into component parts. As a sophomore, I experienced great excitement when arriving at complex problem solutions in Mr. Troutman's geometry class. That same year, I looked forward each day to maintaining simulated business account ledgers in Mrs. Bachman's bookkeeping class. I was proud that I finally was able to type fifty words a minute in Mrs. Bachman's typing II class, and I was awed by Gary Olson's ninety-words-a-minute achievement. Although having little understanding, I was still intrigued by the discussion of "simple machines" in Mr. Schaefer's physics class. Knowing I had not done well in algebra, I still declined an invitation from Gary Olson and Lyle Schaefer to participate in a correspondence refresher course that they were taking. I convinced myself that I would take it later in college. Furthermore, I had enough on my plate already; taking on another activity would put me on overload.

In the eleventh grade, I, my brothers, and our classmates connected very well with our new teacher, Mrs. Irene Hausken. Mrs. Hausken taught American history and English at Mead for one year, while her husband worked on his master's degree at the Colorado State College of Education. In English literature, we studied the classic Silas Marner, a story that resonated with me. I empathized with Silas, whose fiancée abandoned him, then familiar with the relationships of many of my schoolmates that had ended in heartache. I knew too that I would most likely be subjected to the same fate someday. I also related to Silas's strong moral and ethical attributes and his faith in God despite his terrible misfortunes.

"Silas was betrayed by his best friend, who then married his fiancée," said Mrs. Hausken. "As a consequence, he lost the love of two important people in his life."

I read that Silas Marner tried to overcome his despair by immersing himself in his work and saving the gold pieces he earned, but that was to no avail. His gold was stolen. What grabbed my greatest attention was Silas's devotion to the welfare of the orphaned child who had wandered into his home in the cold of winter.

"Finding and raising Eppie as his own daughter is what gave Silas renewed hope and new purpose in his life. The gold he lost was no longer important. What do you think was the most important thing in Silas's life?" Mrs. Hausken asked our class.

"It was another human being. It was the little girl Eppie," answered Gary Olson wisely.

"That's right," said Mrs. Hausken. "Silas had found his life's fulfillment in loving another person. Eppie was now his family. He would spend his life serving her."

I vowed that, if needed, like Silas, I would devote myself to serving family. Like Silas, I had already served my family, at times with great personal sacrifice, and I was determined to continue to do so whenever my help was needed. It was what my elder brothers and sisters had done, and I knew that was what I would do. I would follow in their footsteps.

In our young years, my brothers and I had learned to pool our meager financial resources so we as a group could prosper. As a high-school junior, I had bought winter coats for Richie and Rollie as well as myself. Each Saturday morning, I had cleaned the whole west-end downstairs of our house for Mom. Serving family also made me want to serve others as well. This led me to think that maybe I should become a priest. On the other hand, I could serve others as a teacher. Maybe I could teach science.

But then I wanted to coach. I wanted to learn how to be a coach and to play basketball. I wanted the chance to play college basketball. That opportunity was presented to me in April, several weeks after basketball season ended.

Coach Adams said to me one afternoon, "John Bunn, the CSCE basketball coach, is coming to Mead tomorrow. He wants to talk to you triplets about goin' there. He'll be here at 10:00 a.m. I'll talk to Mr. Carlson to get you all excused from class."

Coach Adams told me that Bunn joined CSCE in '56. As a student at the University of Kansas, John Bunn had earned ten varsity letters in football, basketball, and baseball. While at Kansas, Bunn worked with James Naismith, the creator of basketball, and was an assistant to Phog Allen at Kansas. Later, Bunn coached basketball at Stanford University and Springfield College before going to CSCE.

"He knows the rules of basketball better than anybody," said Coach Adams. "He sits on the rules committee for the Olympics, and he has been active in getting rules changed. One of the rules he got them to change was jumping the ball at center court after every basket. Just think how unfair that rule was and how it slowed down the game."

The next day, Coach Adams came to Mrs. Hausken's English class to get us and take us to the gym, where John Bunn was waiting. Mr. Bunn was sitting on the single row of benches on the north side, his fedora beside him. It was still winter, and he had on a long overcoat and was wearing unbuckled rubber boots.

"Hello, boys," he said as he shook each of our hands. "Please sit down. I want to see if you boys want to play basketball for CSCE this fall." He stood in front of us. "I'd like all three of you to play for me, but I have only one scholarship. The scholarship pays for tuition—no room and board. But we can give one of you a job in the dining hall or in the campus student union to help you pay for room and meals. Today I'm offering this package to Ronnie."

"I'm not sure I want to go to Greeley," says Rollie. "I'm thinkin' about goin' to A&M."

"I'm pretty sure I'm goin' to CSCE," said Richie. "I'll find a job somewhere."

"Who else are you recruitin'?" I asked.

"Theo Holland is getting out of the army, and he's enrolling in school this summer to get a head start. You remember he was an all-state player from Greeley a couple of years ago. We got two players from the Greeley High team, Ted Wright and Ken Miller. They both are comin.' Bein' from Greeley, they'll live at home, so they won't have a lot of expenses."

"Have you talked to Gordon Ledford from Wiggins?" I asked.

"Yes, I have. Gordy's not certain he's goin' on to college. He's goin' to think about it over the summer."

Several weeks later, we triplets received scholarship offers from coaches at Western State College and Adams State College.

"I know I'll get a better education at CSCE," I told Coach Adams. "That's where I want to go."

As the '56–'57 academic year drew to a close, Coach Adams assembled his players of football, basketball, and track in the gym. He wanted us to decide who would be the Outstanding Athlete for the year. The previous year, he alone had made the decision. He passed out small squares of paper with pencils and asked us to write the name of a teammate we thought most deserving. I voted for my brother Dave. Although he was just a sophomore, I knew he was a better athlete than me.

Finally, at the Mead High School awards night, Coach Adams announced that my fellow athletes had voted me as Outstanding Athlete. I received a gold-plated plaque.

"This is the second year in a row for Ronnie to be selected," said Coach Adams. "The criteria I asked the athletes to consider in their voting were scholarship, training, cooperation, and ability."

I was also designated to receive further recognition at Mead High School's graduation ceremony. Mead principal Wendell Johnson asked Lyle Schaefer, Gary Olson, and me to meet with him. Sitting in his office with the three of us, he said, "I've computed your grade point averages, and Gary and Lyle are tied with the highest, and Ronnie, you are second. Gary and Lyle, that makes you the valedictorians of the class, and Ronnie, you are salutatorian. We want all three of you to give a speech at graduation. So you need to get started writing them right away."

I was pleased that I was graduating third in my class, but I was terrified at the prospect of speaking. All my life, I had been influenced by Mom's dictum—"Children should be seen and not heard." I preferred to not say anything when with a group of two or more.

"You boys work on your speeches and get back with me on what you're goin' to say," said Mr. Johnson.

I went over my short remarks with him. On graduation night, Mr. Carlson introduced me. "As salutatorian, Ronald Newton has received an academic scholarship from the State of Colorado," said Mr. Carlson. "This allows him to attend any state-supported school he chooses."

Mr. Carlson then invited me to speak. As I approached the podium, I sensed a fright that I knew the audience would soon sense as well. I had never addressed a large audience. Furthermore, I had not rehearsed my speech, and I had not discussed it with anyone other than Mr. Johnson.

Being on the stage in the Mead gym and trying to say something "important" was intimidating. I never felt nervous before a crowd at the free-throw line in the same gym, but now I was standing at the podium without a ball in my hand. My body was trembling. I was not delivering a ball to the basket; I was delivering a speech. The audience would not be judging my athletic skill. They would be evaluating me as a person. They would ask themselves, Is this kid ready to face the real world?

At the podium, I unzipped the front of my academic gown partway and reached into my dress shirt pocket to pull out an index card. I had written on both sides of it. Reading from it, I told the audience that I was going to Colorado State College of Education and that I was going to major in physical education and be a coach. I went on to say how grateful I was for my four years at Mead High School. Being a student and an athlete at Mead High School had been the best four years of my life. I thanked Mom and Dad, all my teachers, and especially Principal Johnson and Superintendent Carlson. Upon reflection of the content of that speech, I should have thanked my brothers, but I did not. My brothers were the ones who contributed most to my happiness and success at Mead High.

I concluded by saying, "I especially want to thank Mr. Adams for being my coach and teaching me how to play basketball." Nothing inspirational, no flights of language—just a simple and heartfelt reflection of my four years at Mead High.

As we lined up to receive our diplomas, I noticed Frank Melchior, our classmate who had contracted polio in second grade eleven years before. He was walking with metal braces on his legs and a pair of crutches. Stricken by disease as a grade-schooler, Frank had never been able to experience the physical activity and the joy that high-school sports bring to those who had the opportunity to participate. Unlike us, his fellow classmates, Frank had already met the stark reality of the world head-on, and since then, he had not been deterred. In my mind, he had truly demonstrated a great success with his life, while that of us, his classmates, was to be determined. From my perspective, Frank was the one who should have been especially honored. He was the one who graduated with distinction.

L-R: Lyle Schaefer, Gary Olson, and Ronnie Newton, 1957.
Mead Consolidated Schools Yearbook

L-R: Frank Melchior, Richie Newton, Rollie Newton, Ronnie Newton.
1957. *Mead Consolidated Schools Yearbook*

L-R: Gary Olson, Lyle Schaefer,
1957. *Mead Consolidated Schools
Yearbook*

John W. Bunn, Basketball
Coach, Colorado State
College of Education, 1958.
Cache la Poudre Yearbook

Player of Year

For the second straight year, Ron Newton has been named Mead high school's outstanding athlete of the year. Newton, one of a set of triplets, lettered during the past year in football, basketball and track. His selection was based on scholarship, training, cooperation and ability. In football, Newton played quarterback. He was a guard on Mead's state championship basketball team. In track he specialized in the mile run, winning the conference and district championships. He placed third in the state. Ron's brothers are Rollie and Dick, both regulars on the class B state basketball champions. The player award was begun in 1956 by Coach Jack Adams. A permanent plaque has been given to the high school. Newton will receive a small trophy.

Chapter 40

Last Days

Early every summer, most high-school graduates make plans and embark on new futures, many of them quite different from their childhoods. Some go to work, while others continue their educations. But continuing formal education was not always easy. In the 1950s, most Northeastern Colorado graduates from rural areas had to leave comfortably familiar environments to pursue higher education beyond high school. In 1957, my triplet brothers and I were such students. All three of us had found summer jobs on farms around our hometown of Mead, and we were saving up for college. But we were also savoring time with family and friends, knowing our lives would change dramatically in a few months.

With the '57 school year ended and the start of summer, my triplet brothers and I and our friends continued one of our favorite pastimes, dragging north and south on neighboring Longmont's Main Street. Lanny Davis, Richie, and I went with Mike Eckel in his parents' Oldsmobile. After driving back on Main Street, several times, Mike said, "Let's go over to the St. Vrain Memorial Building. Frank [Mike used his dad's first name] said there's a farm exposition going on there. He sez it's a good one. Let's go see it."

The four of us entered the building lobby and began looking at several posters displayed on easels. Peering intently and reading the narratives, we did not notice Sabino Lontine come through the door with his girlfriend, Rosabel Cardenas, a freshman at Mead High School. Just like our Mead foursome, who had just graduated, Sabino had graduated from Erie High School, one of Mead's strongest rivals. Although Erie had defeated Mead twice in football the previous two years, Mead had beaten Erie four times in basketball.

Lontine weighed 185–190 pounds and was a very physical player on the football field and the basketball court. He was not pushed around by others, no matter their size. Of Mexican descent, his opponents called him Hombre el Mean-yo. That previous March, Lontine had "flipped the bird" to a booing crowd in that same building after he assaulted a Berthoud player in the District 4 basketball tournament. His physical features exuded toughness. He had the face of a bulldog and only one effective eye, his left one. His right eye had been injured so badly that he could not see out of it. The injury was such that only the white of the eye showed; the pupil was not visible.

Our teammate Carl Hansen one day in practice said, "Didja ever notice about Lontine? He stands to the right side when he shoots a free throw. That way, he can see the basket better with his one eye."

Walking up to our foursome cluster, Lontine said, "Well, if it ain't the mighty turdheads from Mead. Let's all go outside. We'll see if you can fight as well as you think you can play basketball."

"Why do ya wanna fight?" said Mike softly, looking into Sabino's one eye. "We ain't got nothin' to settle. We don't have anything to fight about."

"Come on outside, all four of ya," growled Sabino. "I'll take ya all on."

I knew if I was ever in a group brawl, I wanted Mike on my side. Mike was just as physical as Sabino. I myself had never had fisticuffs with anyone, and I was sure that Richie and Lanny had not either. With Mike there, I knew we had a chance.

I looked over at Rosabel Cardenas, a beautiful young girl with long wavy hair, looking uneasy, standing next to the wall, frightened and embarrassed about what was happening. Richie, Lanny, and I looked at Mike. We waited for him to speak. Mike said nothing. With a sly grin, Mike just stared at Sabino and appeared to be biding for time.

That night, Sabino looked tougher than he ever had. He exuded the strength and confidence of a prizefighter. The situation likened itself to a pack of stray dogs suddenly confronted by a mountain lion.

"Let's go, all four of ya," said Sabino. "I'll cool your donut."

I knew that I didn't want to fight Sabino, but I waited for Mike to say something first.

"No, Sab, I don't think so," Mike uttered. "Not tonight."

"C'mon, I'll cool your donut," said Sabino once again.

Turning to walk away, Mike said, "No, Sab, I don't think we're interested."

Mike headed for the entrance to the gym, and Richie, Lanny, and I followed. Sabino was left standing with Rosabel.

"You're all chickensh——ts!" yelled Sabino as we entered the gym.

We did not respond. The four of us walked from the lobby into the gymnasium area to see the other exhibits. We remained there for a long time. We did not want to emerge too soon, and we left the building by a side door, running to Mike's car. I never saw Sabino again.

What I learned that night and what I had previously learned from Rollie in a similar confrontation was that self-control and walking away are the real markers of wisdom and courage.

* * *

On a Sunday afternoon in June '57, I was at home reading the *Denver Post* when my brother Marc came into the living room and said, "There's a carload of girls out on the street, and they said they want to talk to you."

I got up and looked out the front window to see who they were. The car was a '55 Oldsmobile, but I could not see who was inside.

These aren't girls from Mead, I said to myself. They have to be from Longmont.

I walked through the kitchen and then onto the back porch and emerged from the back door of our house. As I walked down the driveway to the street where the car was parked, I still could not see who was in it. Getting closer, I recognized Kathy Nottingham in the back seat.

She poked her head out and said, "Hi, Ronnie."

"Well, hello. What brings you girls to Meadville?" I asked as I stooped down to look at them with hands on my knees.

"We came to see the Newtons," said the girl in the front passenger seat, whom I recognized as Sue Harvey. Sue, sister of Glenn Markham's wife Pat, had introduced Mike Eckel to his girlfriend Linda Miller, who had set up the introductory blind date with Kathy and me. Sue then questioned, "Isn't that why everybody comes to Mead? To see the Newtons?"

I smiled and chuckled and said, "Well, some people think we're the only ones who live here. There's so many of us. That's why they call it Newtonville."

"Where're all your brothers?" Linda Moore asked from the back seat with Kathy.

"I dunno," I said. "They all left with Lanny Davis in his dad's new Ford just a little while ago. They're probably in Longmont lookin' for all you girls."

"How come you're not with 'em?" asked Kathy.

"I'm workin' for Dean Seewald this summer, irrigatin' barley. I have to go to work this afternoon. I'm tryin' to make as much money as I can before I go off ta college."

"Where ya goin'?" asked Sue.

"I'm goin' to Greeley," I said. "I got a scholarship to play basketball."

"That's where I'm goin' too," said Roberta Jones, driver of the car. "They've got a good theater department. That's why I'm goin' there. I like actin'."

Trying to turn the conversation toward Kathy, I asked, "What're you girls doin' this summer?"

"Just goofin' around," said Kathy. "We're just havin' a good time. We just had our graduation two weeks ago. My mom said I should get a job, but I don't want to."

"Hey, you girls!" interjected Roberta. "We gotta get back to Longmont. My dad told me to get the car back by three. He an' my mom are goin' somewhere."

"Okay," I said, stepping backward as Roberta started up the car. "Maybe we'll see you on Main Street sometime."

Kathy looked at me just as she always had, rekindling feelings that I had thought were long dead. As Roberta drove ahead, slowly preparing the car for a sharp U-turn, Kathy said, "Goodbye, Ronnie."

"Tell Mike I said hello! We see Linda all the time," called Sue.

I waved as I watched the car drive away. I saw Kathy's waving hand as they passed by and watched until the car was out of sight. Somehow the human geography of Longmont and Mead had shifted tectonically toward me, raising the age-old question "How does one process and reprocess affairs of the heart?"

My life seemed to be a series of "visions and revisions." What had seemed sure and secure was overturned by a five-minute conversation. I never expected to see or talk to Kathy again. I was surprised by her sudden reappearance in my life, but I wasn't sure of her intent. Because she had been seeing someone else, I broke off our relationship three months before, a painful, emotional wrench for me. I wanted to be her only soul mate, but that was not what she wanted. I had heard from Mike Eckel that she was dating several guys, including Kenny Winters, halfback for the Longmont High football team and a high-ranking college prospect, perhaps for Colorado A&M College. I felt inferior to Winters, wallowing in self-deprecation.

I asked myself, What is Kathy thinking? If she's got Kenny Winters, why's she comin' back for me?

Complex and sometimes contradictory feelings washed over me. I surmised Kathy was most likely the one who had instigated the drive out to Mead to see me. I rationalized that if Roberta and Sue had been interested in seeing the Newtons as those two had asserted, they could have come by themselves. They didn't have to bring Kathy with them. Kathy wouldn't have come if she wished not to see me, and I wondered if Kathy was interested in resuming our relationship. After all, I had been the one to break it off, not Kathy. Maybe she had some regrets about what happened. Maybe she was ready to pick up where we had left off. My self-pity diminished. I was feeling better about myself and the world, bolstering my fragile ego and my self-confidence.

Two days later, I called Kathy.

Not wanting anyone in my family to hear me, as usual, I went down to the pay phone next to the Handy Corner. At the end of several rings, I heard the familiar voice of Kathy saying, "Hello."

"Hello," I said. "Is Kathy there?"

I was never sure of which female voice I would hear from the phone in the Nottingham household. It could be her mother or her little sister or perhaps her big sister who had come home from college.

I always inquired first, "Is Kathy there?"

Each time, without fail, it was always Kathy, and she would answer, "This is she."

At first, this response of she seemed unusual to me and not correct. I was used to hearing a female identify herself when asked with "This is her." I confirmed with my English teacher, Mr. Johnson, that Kathy's usage was the proper one. I was impressed with her precise, correct language. To me, it reflected a sophisticated, social status far and above my own.

Just as with earlier phone calls, the conversation with Kathy was short. The purpose of the call was simply to establish if she was able to go out on a particular night and what time I should pick her up, nothing more. A pay phone call interval was short, just a minute or two for a quarter; there was not a lot time for conversation. Besides, I didn't really like talking on the phone. I rationalized that any phone chatter beyond the necessary was wasting time and money. There would be plenty of time for talking when we saw each other.

Kathy never knew what car I would show up in. I often borrowed my brother Tom's '56 Ford, but I sometimes drove my brother Jerry's Plymouth or the '49 Ford we triplets had purchased together. This time, I would have a surprise for Kathy. I would be driving a brand new '57 "special model" Plymouth Fury that belonged to Dean Seewald, the farmer I was working for that summer.

The next day, when I returned the car to Dean, he asked me, "Did ya get any last night?" Before I could answer, he commented, "With a car like this, you shouldn't've missed."

I blushed, smiled, and did not answer. I knew that "scoring" was the expectation of many of my friends and many of the adult males I knew.

I suspected Kathy was more experienced than me and was perplexed by my guarded approach to our relationship. Although I knew I had the same desires as she did, I held back. My future was too uncertain. I remembered what Sister Laurance had said to our catechism class. "When the Lord calls you to serve, you will know it. You will be prepared to sacrifice the will of the flesh."

With Kathy, I understood, more than ever, what some of the sacrifices would be if I were to become a priest, but I also finally knew that at this point in my life, I had not yet been beckoned by that call.

I had never wanted to talk to Kathy about my thoughts and aspirations of the priesthood. I just wanted to be with her. The priesthood decision would have to wait until a later time. In my mind, I was still waiting, and I was certain I would know it if God's call came.

I saw Kathy all that summer. I knew that she was going on to college, but I had not known where until she told me, "I'm goin' to Stephens College in Columbia, Missouri. I found out two weeks ago that I passed all the interviews, and they have accepted me."

"Why Stephens?" I asked. "Why not Colorado A&M where your sister went?"

"Because I want to learn be a lady," said Kathy. "They teach you all the culture stuff and the social graces that women are supposed to know. A girl from our church went there, and she recommended it. There's a lady here in town who graduated from there, and she's the one who interviewed me."

"I bet it costs a lot to go there," I said.

"It sure does," said Kathy. "When Daddy heard what it was, he almost fell over dead."

I was impressed by the fact that Kathy came from a family of means in contrast to my own. When we talked about a future together, I conjectured about how I wanted it to appear to all interested observers.

In marrying Kathy Nottingham, Ronald Newton had moved up the social ladder! I was thrilled at the thought of Kathy's picture in the Longmont Times Call announcing our engagement to the glittering Longmont social scene.

Kathy said to me one night, "Ya know, Daddy asked me the other day, 'What about this guy from Mead? What do ya think about him?'

"I said to him, 'I'm goin' to marry him!'"

"I feel really lucky having you, Kathy," I said. "Other than you, I don't have much."

My personal scorecard was the confidence that I would perhaps someday be marrying into a family with financial security, security that had not been the norm in my own life.

A lot more than ten miles separated the homes of Longmont's Kathy Nottingham and Mead's Ronald Newton. Kathy's father had moved his family to Longmont from the family farm he owned near Genoa, Colorado. On the farm, he had earned good money and decided to go into business in Longmont, where he and his wife hoped to provide Kathy and her younger sister a better opportunity for schooling. They had lived temporarily in a small house on Collyer Street, but now Walter Nottingham had built a new house, and he had just moved his family into it at the end of the summer.

Even though Kathy would be living there only for a short time before she left for college, she was ecstatic that her parents and her younger sister were now living in the dream house that she and her family always wanted. The spacious brick rancher, its picture window looking out over the St. Vrain River Valley onto Mount Meeker and Longs Peak, was sited in a new upscale development on the west side of town on a picturesque cul-de-sac, and there was a detached garage for two cars.

The '57 summer was over, and the temperature was unusually cold that September midnight when Kathy and I pulled into the driveway of their new house in my '49 Ford. Although it had not snowed as it sometimes did in September, the wind swept between the house and the unattached garage with ferocity and a biting, unbearable coldness. An "alpha male," thinking I could withstand the cold, I had not brought even a light jacket. Kathy, wiser than me, had brought her long overcoat. She slipped it on as I walked her to the door for our goodbye. This would be the last time I would see her for nearly four months. She would be heading to Missouri, and I was moving to Greeley.

Kathy and I found ourselves under the overhang of the front portico roof, the wind pounding us as we held each other, wanting the moment to last as long as possible.

"I know what we'll do," said Kathy. "Let's go into the garage and stand next to the water heater. It'll be warm there, and we'll be out of the wind."

Entering, Kathy opened her overcoat and wrapped it around us as we kissed and kissed goodbye. Finally, we walked from the warm garage out into the cold and toward the front door.

"I'm goin' to write to ya."

Kathy said, "I'll write too. Good night, and I'll see you at Christmas."

* * *

One August evening, after working in the fields on the Eckel farm, I walked downtown to buy "fixin's" for my lunches that I would be preparing that week. As I left Bunton's Red & White Grocery, Ronald Weber drove by in his convertible, and he stopped to say hello. We decided to carry our conversation further and drink a soda pop in the Mead Pool Hall.

"When ya leavin' for college?" Weber asked as we sat down at the bar.

"Richie and I are leavin' for Greeley in a couple of weeks. Rollie's goin' to A&M. He doesn't have to be there for another three weeks. Richie and I are goin' to room together in a dormitory on the CSCE campus. I've got a job promised to me by Coach Bunn working in a student dining hall."

Bartender Emil Palinkx took our order, a root beer for Weber and an orange for me.

"I wonder if Adams's hundred-yard dash record still stands over there. It was well under ten seconds if I remember right," said Weber.

"It was 9.8 seconds," I said emphatically. "Ran it in 9.6 with a tailwind."

"I saw him in the post office last week," said Weber. "Said he was leavin' and takin' a job somewhere in Denver—Englewood, I believe."

"Ya know, coaches don't stay long in Mead," I said. "Ever since Spencer left after being here for a long time, we haven't been able to keep 'em. Peterson, Schmidt, Beers, and now Adams—they stay a couple of years, and then they leave. I wonder why they don't stay. Adams could have a good team next year with all those good players coming back."

"Well," said Weber, "sometimes when you have a good team, you get recruited away by another school. They give you more money, thinking you'll repeat your success at their school. That's what happened when Longmont recruited the Fort Lupton coach who won the Class A state championship to replace Montgomery when he retired. Ya know, Tway was on that Lupton team, and he now plays for A&M."

Weber took a giant swallow of root beer and continued, "But I don't think that is why Adams is leavin'. Ya know, nobody stays in this town. The coaches don't. The teachers don't. The preachers don't. The kids don't. There's nothin' in this town that makes people want to stay. They go somewhere else."

"But why do ya think Adams came here in the first place?" I asked. "A good coach like him could have gone anywhere he wanted."

"He was new, just outta school. He had no track record, so to speak—no pun intended," Weber answered. "I think he could've gone somewhere else, but I think he chose Mead because of you Newtons. Remember I told you he talked to me several times about you guys before he came here?"

"Yes, I remember. I'm sure glad he came," I said. "We sure couldn't have gone to the state tournament two years in a row without 'im."

Weber took another giant swig of root beer. He set his bottle down and let out a loud belch. He smiled triumphantly as if he had just hit a home run. I chuckled and took my final swallow of orange soda. We were silent for several seconds. I didn't feel like talking anymore. I was saddened with Coach leaving.

But Weber, now in deep thought, finally asked, "Do you remember seein' the movie Shane?"

"Yes, I do," I answered. "Walt Slee took us to see it. Alan Ladd was in it, and a kid named Brandon de Wilde was in it too. Ladd was Shane."

"Do you remember Shane was a gunslinger who came to that mountain settlement and wiped out all the bad guys in that bar scene?" Weber asked.

"Y'all, I remember! Shane's gunshots blew those guys back like they'd been hit by a tornado! After that, Shane didn't stick around. I remember the scene with him ridin' off with the Grand Tetons out in front of 'im. The film was shot in Wyoming."

"Well, Adams is like that gunslinger," said Weber. "He came into town and did what he had to do. He developed a winner outta you guys. But after he does it, he knows he can't stay. He has to leave."

"And I feel like that little kid runnin' after Shane and yellin' his name as he rides away on his horse. I want Coach to stay. I wish both of us could."

L-R: Richie Newton, Mike Eckel, Lanny Davis and Ronnie Newton, 1957
— *Mead Consolidated Schools Yearbook*

Epilogue

The dream of my two triplet brothers and me playing college basketball was not fulfilled. Rollie did not try out at Colorado A&M, and Richie and I dropped out of basketball after our freshman season at Colorado State College of Education. As freshmen, we had seen very little playing time and were convinced that would still be the case if we moved up to the varsity. Also, my athletic scholarship covered only tuition, $35 a quarter, and I, like Richie, needed additional dollars for room and board. This was accomplished by us working in the dining hall as waiters and as janitors scrubbing and polishing floors, a commitment of five hours each day. Participating in daily varsity basketball practice and traveling to away games would have negatively impacted our work schedule, significantly reducing our earnings. With this compelling economic rationale, Richie and I abandoned our goal of playing college basketball.

Our brother Dave, perhaps the best athlete of us all, went on to play for Mesa Junior College in Grand Junction for two years, and the Newton basketball heritage was carried on in our hometown of Mead by our youngest brothers Marc and Frosty. Mead High School was closed in 1961, and they transferred to the high school in Longmont. Today, Frosty maintains that he, not Dave, was the best athlete in the family.

Today, fifty-nine years later, I look back with nostalgia and pride on that historic night in '56 when we Newtons were the starting five on Mead High School's basketball team. Interestingly, only our coach, not any of us Newtons, realized the significance of those several minutes when we five brothers played together. But not even our coach could have realized that would be the only time, just those several minutes, when five brothers would be on the floor at the same time competing for Mead. One brother was abruptly withdrawn from participation when a heart condition was detected. So for the next two years, there would be only four Newtons simultaneously representing Mead on the basketball court. Four brothers would lead their team into the state tournament in those two years, and four brothers would be on the floor when Mead won the Class B state basketball championship in 1957. For us triplets, the journey to 1957 basketball "stardom" in Northeastern Colorado began with our birth in 1939 in a converted gymnasium in the abandoned town hall in Mead.

That '57 state championship game in the Denver Coliseum was witnessed by a vivacious cheerleader from Littleton High School. Mary Weingarth of Littleton recalled, "Our high-school coach told us to be sure and watch this game with all those brothers from this small high school. He said history was in the making, and we'd see a game played by a team with a very special chemistry that we would have never seen before. I remember the announcer was having a hard time telling all the Newtons apart, and in frustration, he blurted out, 'Oh, to hell with it, Newton passes to Newton, and Newton shoots!'" That beautiful cheerleader watching my brothers and me play that night later became my wife, Mary Weingarth Newton. Mary and I met as juniors at Colorado State College (CSCE had become CSC) and married in 1961. To this day, Mary has been my soul mate and friend and the lasting love of my life.

Fifteen years after Mead's historic game, my brother Marc, a journalist, wrote the following in a column for the Tribune (Greeley) as he reminisced about our championship game.

> I saw those big guys from Wiggins. I saw no way that Mead could do it. But looking back, I realize that Wiggins never had a chance. Sure, the game was close. But Mead was supposed to win it all. The coliseum crowd did its part by roaring every time Mead scored.

They all seemed to take a liking to this small town bunch that included four brothers. There was no way they were going to lose.

And thirty years later, after Mead's historic win, Lyle Schaefer wrote for the Mead High School reunion.

> In achieving our goal, we established bonds that are still with us today. Our high-school basketball team owes its success to a dedicated family support group and to Mr. Carlson (superintendent) who hired a dedicated faculty and staff at Mead High School and who created the environment that allowed this to happen.

My days as a basketball player with my brothers at Mead are laser-etched in my memory. I remember with great affection my other teammates. There was our fifth man, Lyle Schaefer, and there was Mike Eckel Lanny Davis, Carl Hansen, George Rademacher, and Allen Thompson. I love my basketball brothers as I do my blood brothers; Mike, Lanny, Carl, George, and Allen made unheralded contributions that were the underpinning of Mead's basketball success. Allen was the most gifted athlete with whom my brothers and I played. I'm grateful to Paul Hopp and Jim Landolt. They were occasionally moved up from the junior-varsity B-team to help us win.

Those glory days of almost sixty years ago are over, and since then, all my former teammates have married and have gone on with their lives.

Mead High School Basketball Team — 1957

Jack Adams, Coach	*Track and tennis coach*	*Junction City, OR*
Lanny Davis	*Print-operations technician*	*Rolla, MO*
*Mike Eckel**	*Real estate salesman*	*Naples, FL*
Carl Hansen	*Professor*	*Austin, TX*
*David Newton**	*Corporate executive*	*Washington DC*
Richard Newton	*Business owner*	*Aurora, CO*
Roland Newton	*Bank officer*	*Whitefish, MT*
Ronald Newton	*Professor*	*Coppell, TX*
George Rademacher	*Corporate officer*	*Bellevue, WA*
*Lyle Schaefer**	*Navy officer and pilot*	*Marietta, GA*
*Allen Thompson**	*Construction supervisor*	*Ganado, TX*

*Deceased

Dave graduated from Mead High in 1959. Unfortunately, his team, girded with the talents of Carl Hansen, George Rademacher, Paul Hopp, and freshman Marc Newton, was upset in the finals of the '59 district tournament, and Mead never again participated in the state tournament. Brothers Marc and Frosty played together for Mead High School before it was closed in '61; thereafter, they played for Longmont High School. For nearly fifty years, Mead High basketball ceased until the doors of a new school were opened in 2010. However, the "Bulldog" mascot was relegated to the Mead Middle School, and Mead High School now plays as the Mead Mavericks.

In 2011, the still-living Mead High School basketball team of '57 was reunited when we attended the induction of our championship team into the Colorado High School Activities Association Hall of Fame in Denver. At that same time, the '57 team was invited to attend a ceremony at the new Mead High School, where a banner celebrating our achievement was hung in the school's gym. The Hall of Fame trophy was placed alongside the '57 state championship trophy, and now both are prominently displayed in the case in the Mead High School gym foyer.

As I looked into that trophy case on that Saturday of 2011, I saw other trophies that Mead High School had earned over the years. On one, I saw the name of Jack Newton. Tom Newton's name was on another. The Newton brothers have left their mark on Mead High School basketball. I saw the graduation pictures of my seven sisters with those of their classmates displayed in large frames on hall walls. Three of them had pursued cheerleading roles, the only entre they had into the arena of competitive athletics and basketball.

But it was more than just the Newtons who contributed to the infamous history of basketball in the small rural community of Mead, a town spread over just a few acres and lying on the plains of Colorado at the base of the Rocky Mountains. It was the townspeople and the surrounding farm population that supported the team and sent their children to Mead High to play with and cheer for the Newton brothers.

Today Mead is ten times the size in land area as it was in 1957, and its population has exploded from a mere two hundred to nearly 3,500. The rich history of Mead, which has evolved over the last hundred years, will forever be highlighted and remembered by its rise to high-school basketball prominence in the decade of the fifties.

Back Row—Dave Newton, Carl Hanson, George Rademacher, Paul Hopp. Middle Row—Marc Newton, Larry Lee, Irvin Adler. Front Row—Danny Martinez, Robert Chinn, Coach—Lindy Everett.

Back, L-R: Coach Graydon Lord, Lowell Schaefer, Marc Newton, Bobby Frederick-son, Roger Olson, Keith Olson. Front, L-R: Frosty Newton, Willie Biddle, Danny Martinez, Jim Adler, and Art Stotts, 1959. *Mead Consolidated Schools Yearbook*

Coach Jack Adams, 2011. *Colorado High School Activities Association*

Mary Weingarth, 1957. *Mary Weingarth Newton*

L-R: Dave Newton, Richie Newton, Rollie Newton, Lyle Schaefer, Ronnie Newton, 2002. *Ronald Newton*

L-R: Rollie Newton, Ronnie Newton, Leonard Smith, Coach Jack Adams, Richie Newton, Mike Eckel, Lyle Schaefer, Lannie Davis, Carl Hansen, 2011. *Colorado High School Activities Association*

Bibliography

Denver Post. 101 W. Colfax Avenue. Denver, Colorado 80202-5315.

Feinstein, J. 1986. *A Season on the Brink.* Macmillan Publishing Co. 866 Third Ave. New York, New York 10022. ISBN 0-02-537230-0. p. 311.

French, P. A. N. 2013. *Childhood Memories.* 1235 Baker Street, Longmont, Colorado 80501. p. 6.

Gammill, Homer L. 1978. *A Little History of the Early Days of Mead.* Historic Highlandlake: Preserving the Rich History of the Highlandlake/Mead Area. Copyright 2009. Historic Highlandlake, Inc. http://historichighlak.org/mead/mead

Greeley Tribune. 501 Eighth Avenue. Greeley, Colorado 80631.

Hall of Fame. Colorado High School Activities Association. 14855 E. Second Avenue, Aurora, Colorado 80011. http://chsaa.org

Huff, D., and Chapman, M. 2010. *Siddens! Win with Humility, Lose with Dignity, But Don't Lose.* DWH Enterprises, 344 Rosehill Terrace, Waterloo, Iowa 50701. p. 217.

Johnson, G. L. 2010. *The Making of Hoosiers.* ISBN-13: 9781452891224, ISBN-10: 1452891222. p. 233.

Kluger, Jeffrey. 2011. *The Sibling Effect: Brothers, Sisters, and the Bonds That Define Us.* Riverhead Books (Penguin Group, USA, Inc.). New York, New York. p. 307. ISBN 978-1-59448-831-3.

Longmont Times Call. 350 Terry Street. Longmont, Colorado 80501.

Newton, M. E. 2015. *Meadean Standard Time.* 5213 W. Eleventh St. Road. Greeley, Colorado 80634.

Newton, R. J. 2015. *Light of Her Children.* Xlibris. 1663 Liberty Drive, Suite 200, Bloomington, Indiana 47403. p. 425. http://www. xlibris.com

Rocky Mountain News. 101 W. Colfax Avenue. Denver, Colorado 80202-5315.

Smith, Pauli Driver. 2009. *History of Mead, Colorado.* Historic Highlandlake: Preserving the Rich History of the Highlandlake/ Mead Area. Copyright 2009. Historic Highlandlake, Inc. http:// historichighlak.org/mead/mead

Students of Mead High School. *Mead Bulldog.* 1946–1958. Publishers: Students of Mead High School. Mead Consolidated Schools. Mead, Colorado.

Wooden, J. R., with Jamison, S. 1997. *Wooden: A Lifetime of Observations and Reflections On and Off the Court.* The McGraw Hill Co. New York, New York. p. 201. ISBN 0-8092-3041-0.

Index

A

Abbott, Gene, 15
Abbott, Hazel, 19–20, 24
Abbott, Shirley, 13, 17, 19
Achenbach, Earl, 272, 277–78
Adams, Arden, 163
Adams, Jack "Coach", vii, x, 151-52, 154-56, 160, 162-85, 187-94, 198-99, 201, 203, 213, 216, 219-20, 227-29, 231-235, 237, 241, 244-45, 247-50, 254, 256-57, 262-65, 267, 271-73, 277-78, 281-82, 284, 286, 292-93, 296, 300, 319-322, 333-35, 343, 345
Adams State College, 320
Adler, Art, 144
Adler, Delmer, 144
Adler, Esther, 160
Adler, Jim, 342
Adler, Sander "Sandy," 160–61
air force, 164
Akers, Mamie, 87
Akron Goodyear Wingfoots, 72
Alexander, Charlyne, 314
Alexander, Sondra, 49, 314
algebra, 113–14, 318
Allen, Phog, 319
Allenspark, Colorado, 75

allotment, 266–67
all-state, 273, 295–96
Alsup, Richard, 77, 152
Amateur Athletic Union, 72
Amen, Billy, 28, 32, 53
Amen, Robert, 18
American Dependent Child Act, 3
Anderson, LaDell, 72
Anderson, Robert "Bobby," 49, 52
Andres, Alvin, 180
animal husbandry, 100
Arno, Martin "Father", 92, 174, 183
Astaire, Fred, 213
A-string, 45, 52, 86, 113, 135, 152
A-team, 40, 43, 89, 114, 117, 119, 121, 124–25, 141–42, 157, 173, 184
awards night, 219
Ayres, Walter, 152, 156, 189, 229, 232

B

Bachman, Thelma (Mrs.), 113, 116, 318
backboard, 33, 42, 49
Baggot, Jim, 163, 170, 192
Baltimore Catechism, 92
Barnes, Frank, 309
Barnes, Helen, 5, 309
Barnes, Janice, 127
Becker, Elaine, 127, 132, 136, 142, 204, 211, 213, 215, 285, 289

Becker, Joann, 211, 213–15, 285, 289
beer, 15, 170
Beers, Jim "Coach", 104-06, 108, 110–16, 119, 122, 124, 128–31, 134–36, 138–41
Berthoud, Colorado, 3, 206, 309
Beshears, Jim, 233, 248
Betz, Roy, 180
B. F. Goodrich, 78
Biddle, Willie, 342
Biederman, Ralph, 89, 112, 118, 124, 133, 136, 141
Bike, 78
Blazon, Leroy, 155, 261
Blazon, Marvin, 22, 41, 68–69, 80, 82, 85, 89, 124, 261
blizzard, 235, 246
bookkeeping, 318
Borgman, Dave, 82
Borgman, Ralph, 82, 311
Borgman, Martha, 137, 261
Boryla, Vince, 72
Bossie, 29
Boston Celtics, 73, 78
Bothell, John, 49, 78
Brown, Jim, 302–4
Brunemeier, Jim, 17, 21, 47, 58
B-string, 45, 52, 121, 131, 135, 153
B-team, 40, 42, 48, 113–14, 121, 124, 135, 184, 339
Buick, 11, 160
Bulldogs (Mead), 48, 57, 85–86, 111, 139, 178, 191, 256, 282, 290–91, 340
Bunton, Bill, 28
Burris (reverend), 28
Byers, Chuck, 137

C

Cade, Gary, 254
Callahan, Bill, 163, 228
"Canadian Sunset," 213

Carbondale, 11
Cardenas, Rosabel, 326
Carlson, Carl "Mr." (Supt.), 22, 39–41, 45, 47–50, 60, 62, 68, 105, 128, 143, 152–53, 157, 194, 198, 206, 212, 217–19, 232, 257, 309, 321
Carlson, Johnny, 74
Carlson, Mary, 82
Carr, Alfred, 60
Catholic Church, 241
Catholics, 56
Central Elementary School, 67
Cerreto, Ron, 133
chamber of commerce, 308
championship, 57, 290, 338
"Chattanooga Choo Choo," 213
Cheerios, 135, 295, 311
Chevrolet, 172, 246, 304
Cheyenne, WY, 198
Chinook, 37
Christmas, 37, 60–61, 240–41
cigarettes, 169–70, 174
Clark, C. H. "Coach" (Mr.), 65–71, 276
Clark, Myrtle, 65, 81, 89
Class A, 244, 272, 294
Class AA, 199, 227, 272
Class B, 86, 178, 201
Class C, 11, 265
Cogburn, Norman, 189
Collier, Larry, 245
Collyer Street, 238, 332
Colorado A&M College, 65, 82, 86, 100, 111, 238, 314, 320, 329
Colorado High School Activities Association, 340
Colorado School of Mines, 161, 316
Colorado State College of Education (CSCE), 53, 152, 163, 216, 271, 314–15, 319–320, 322
Colorado University (CU), 72, 99, 315
Columbia, Missouri, 331
columbine, 66, 99

Columbine Elementary School, 57, 66
consolation, 86, 140, 266
Converse, 309
Cooke, Malcom (Dr.), 60, 156–158
Cousy, Bob, 78, 115
Craig, Colorado, 152
Crews, Elizabeth, 20
Cromer, Elmer, 283
Curran, Jack, 74
Cyphers, Vince, 254–55

D

Daubenmire, James, 254-56
David and Goliath, 92–93
Davis, Lanny, vii, 104, 124, 194, 206–07, 210, 245, 293, 297, 300–01, 304
Declaration of Independence, 194, 208
Dempsey, Charles, 38
Denver Auditorium, 72
Denver Central Bankers, 72
Denver Coliseum, 201, 282, 288, 293, 338
Denver Elevator Co., 308
Denver Live Stock Show and Rodeo, 282
Denver Lutheran, 228
Denver Nuggets, 72
Denver Post, 10, 103, 285, 295–96
Denver Truckers, 72
Denver University, 310
Denver Viner Chevrolet, 73
Dick and Jane, 10–12
digitalis, 157
District 3, 272
District 4, 272, 276, 278
Dodge, 229
Dons, 197
D'Orazio, Joe "Red," 191
drinking, 147, 169, 214
ducktail, 302
Dudley, James, 105–07

E

Eastern Arkansas Valley League, 198
Eck, Doris (Ms.), 86–87, 89, 317
Eckel, Frank, 97–99, 102, 120, 201–3, 246, 262, 278, 282
Eckel, Margaret "Marg," (Mrs.), 91, 93–94, 98, 100–102, 126, 201, 213
Eckel, Mike, vii, 56, 84–85, 89, 94, 104, 113, 119–21, 126, 138, 152, 170, 190, 196, 205, 216, 229, 239, 245–46, 265, 278, 292–94, 309, 325, 329, 339
Eckel, Patricia "Pat," 94, 96, 102, 201
Eisenhower, Dwight, 218
Elks Club, 308
Elliot, Bill, 154, 285
Elson-Gray Readers, 9
English, 86, 103, 126
Eppie, 318–19

F

Farmer's Union Town Hall, 1, 6
Fat Charlie, 305
fieldhouse, 198
Fietchner, Arvid, 112, 116
fight song, 262
Final Four, 30, 73, 197
First United Methodist Church, 14
Flores, George, 119, 121, 141, 152, 158, 174, 191, 244
Ford, 232, 330, 332, 335
Fort Collins, Colorado, 140, 197
Franklin, Benjamin, 208
Frederickson, Bobby, 342
Frei, Alfred, 216, 230–231, 236
full-court press, 121, 137, 188, 264
Furman University, 73

G

Gallegos, Sylvia, 30, 73, 197
Gallegos, Virginia, 30
Geibelhaus, Donald, 315
Genoa, Colorado, 225, 238, 332
geometry, 114, 318
Ghesquire, Irene, 117, 137
Golden, Colorado, 316
Graham, Barbara, 17, 43, 58, 66, 105, 138, 142, 172–73, 177, 200, 204, 213, 285
Graham, Dean, 43–45, 277, 285
Graham, Martin, 43, 138, 153, 244, 277, 285
Graham, Mary, 138, 153, 244, 277
Graham, Mary LaVerne, 158, 172, 177
Grand Tetons, 335
Great Depression, 1, 3, 10
Great Western Railway, 2
Greeley Tribune, 4, 157, 189, 283
Green, Jerry, 223
Greenwald, Ron, 112
Grossaint, Jim, 254
Guardian Angel Church, 92, 182
Gymnasium, 3, 270, 327, 338

H

Halderson, Burdette, 72
Hall of Fame, 340
Handy Corner, 160–61, 330
Hansen, Carl, vii, 144, 156, 245, 280, 293, 297, 301, 326, 339–40
Harlem Globetrotters, 73, 122
Harper, Jim, 67
Hartman, Johnny, 222
Harvey, Patricia "Pat," 222, 225
Harvey, Sue, 222, 328
Hattel, Alex, 191, 199–200, 274–75
Hattel, Mike, 274-76
Hausken, Irene, 184, 210, 318–319
Haverly, Fritz, 275–76

Haynes, Marques, 73, 122
heart murmur, 157, 192
Heil, Larry, 23, 50, 278
Henry, John, 257
Hernandez, Loe, 26–27, 35, 41, 73, 86, 114, 152, 155, 261
Hernandez, Max, 86
Hetterle, Edmund "Ed," 73, 78, 80, 82
Hettinger, Charles, 106
high jump, 25, 216, 312
Highland Lake, 211
High School
    Arapaho, 189
    Ault, 11, 104, 272
    Bayfield, 281–82
    Brush, 179
    Cheyenne, 198
    College, 179, 188, 230, 244–45, 272
    Denver Lutheran, 229
    East, 72
    Eaton, 78–79, 104, 134
    Englewood, 198
    Erie, 190, 231–32
    Estes Park, 192, 230
    Evans, 192, 232, 265
    Fowler, 281
    Frederick, 53, 82
    Ft. Lupton, 79, 104–5, 181
    Galeton, 143
    Gilcrest, 143, 178–79
    Gill, 143
    Glenwood Springs, 189
    Granby, 281–82
    Greeley, 42, 44, 163, 170
    Grover, 265
    Hotchkiss, 281–82
    Johnstown, 11, 62, 283
    Keenesburg, 13–15, 189
    Kersey, 104, 130, 139
    Lafayette, 140, 179
    LaPorte, 197, 272

Littleton, 338

Loveland, 140, 272

Mead, x, 7, 10, 11, 18, 36, 40, 57, 68, 78, 111, 115, 125, 140–41 143, 155–56, 158–59, 178, 188, 195, 198, 208, 220, 233, 235, 269, 274, 289, 293, 321–22, 337, 339, 340–41, 348

Milliken, 143

Oak Creek, 199

Platteville, 133, 139, 272

Sanford, 199–201

Steamboat, 189

Stratton, 199, 281, 283

Timnath, 115, 122, 136

Windsor, 140, 156

Highway 66, 172, 276

Highway 85, 312

Holland, Theo, 320

Holsteins, 247

homecoming dance, 235–36

Hopp, Conrad Jr. "Connie," 89, 113, 116–19, 122, 124, 134, 136–38, 141–42

Hopp, Conrad Sr., 137, 244

Hopp, Paul, 152, 156, 245, 339–40

Howell, Danny, 283

Howlett, Theodore "Hap," 60–61

Howlett, Vernon "Bub," 60, 244, 308

Humphrey, Alberta, 49

Humphrey, Marion (Mr.), 7, 41–42, 49, 65, 143, 154, 194, 213, 247, 261

Humphrey, Robert, 49, 89

hundred-yard dash, 163, 216, 229

I

Indiana Hoosier, 178

"In the Mood," 213

Iowa University, 113, 197

J

Jeangerard, Bob, 73

Jensen, Lawrence, 121, 141, 152, 174, 191, 244

Jepperson, Isabel (Mrs.), 7–10, 17, 46–48, 50–51

Joe "Awful" Coffee's Ringside Lounge Restaurant, 198–99

Johnson, Mary, 28, 86

Johnson, Wendell (Mr.), 98, 100-101, 212, 321

Johnson's Corner, 304

Jones, Anita, 105

Jones, Glen (Dr.), 3

Jones, Howard, 18

Jones, K. C., 73, 197

Jones, Roberta, 328–29

K

Kansas University, 319

Keds, 309–10

Keenesburg, 13

Keil, Fred, 189, 193

Kentucky, University of, 197

KGMC Radio, 182

King, Alan, 273

Kiwanis Club, 147

KLZ radio, 294

knee pads, 43, 78, 165

Knight, Clayton, 229, 232

Knight, Robert "Bobby," 178

Koenig, Sheila, xi

Korean War, 68, 75

L

Ladd, Alan, 335

LaFollette, Joan, 57

Lamberson, Wilse, 29

Landolt, Jack, 99, 316

Landolt, Jim, 104, 110, 124, 339

lark bunting, 99

LaSalle University, 73, 254, 267

Laurence (catechism teacher), 92–93

Ledford, Gordon, 283–85, 290, 309

Lee, Mary Lou, 314

Leffler, Larry, 107

Leinweber, Elaine, 57–58, 200, 204, 244, 285

Leo, Fred, 294

Leroy, Colorado, 3

Lesser, John "Junior," 316

Lewis Furniture Store, 276

Lind, Jim, 315

literature, 318

Longmont, Colorado, 2, 27

Longmont Drug Store, 145, 274

Longmont Times Call, 243, 256, 285

Longs Peak, 2, 37, 97, 332

Lontine, Sabino, 247, 273–274, 277, 325–27

Lopez, Richard, 189

Lord, Graydon, 342

M

Madison Square Garden, 73

Magnuson, LaVerne, 57–58, 71, 80, 294

Main Street, 37, 275, 304

Major, Charles, 44–45, 315

Major, Dorothy, 73

Major, Les, 73

Major, Tommy, 52, 315

Malevich, Frank, 228

man-to-man defense, 248, 264, 272, 290

Margheim, Roland, 179

marine, 68, 75, 265

Marjorie (catechism teacher) (Sister), 92, 182

Markham, Donald, 83

Markham, Glenn, 52, 83, 222, 315

Markham, Jim, 18

Martin, Mary, 240

Martinez, Danny, 342

Maurer, Ernest, 68, 70

Mavericks, 340

mayor, 194–95

McClary, Ron, 315

McCracken, Jack, 72

McLeod, Bruce, 189, 253

McNabb, Darrell, 107, 180

Mead, Colorado, ix, xiii, 1, 348

Mead Consolidated Schools, xiii, 1, 67

Mead Garage, 34, 75, 169

Mead Inn, 38

Mead Pool Hall, 20, 169, 333

Meadville, 328

medicine ball, 167, 188

Meek, Gary, 189

Melchior, Frank, 13, 206, 322

Mesa Junior College, 337

metallurgist, 316

Meyer, Linda, 328

Michael the Archangel, 241–242

Mikan, George, 310

Miller, Don, 136

Miller, Ken, 320

Miller, Linda, 223, 239–40, 276

Miller, Ron, 233

Minch, Johnnie, 17, 21–22, 54, 69

Mondt, Bill, 315

Montgomery, Al, 334

Moore, Linda, 224

Mount Meeker, 2, 97, 332

Mr. Basketball, 310

Muhme, Bonnie, 195

Muhme, Marilyn, 43

N

Naismith, James, 319

Nash (automobile), 206

National Industrial Basketball League, 72

navy, 65, 315

NCAA (National Collegiate Athletic Association), 73, 197

Nehi, 109, 161

Newman, Bernard "Duck," 34

Newman, Clarence, 62, 316

Newman, Emily (Mrs.), 23, 30, 39, 53–58, 161, 315

Newman, Herb, 28, 41, 86, 114, 155–56, 161, 171, 244, 261, 277, 285, 315

Newton, Bill, 40

Newton, David "Dave," vii, 5, 23–24, 26, 28, 33, 35, 37, 59, 74, 77–78, 91–92, 96, 102, 141, 145–46, 150–51, 155, 158–59, 175, 177, 180, 184, 196, 200, 217, 229, 231, 236–237, 244, 246–53, 257, 260, 262, 264–67, 280, 282, 284–85, 289, 297–98, 309, 312, 313, 337, 340, 342, 345

Newton, Eunice, 3, 5, 7, 40

Newton, Forrest "Frosty," xi, 5, 74, 77, 92, 138, 146, 153, 285, 337, 340, 342

Newton, Gerald "Jerry," vii, 4, 6, 22, 25, 28, 32, 35, 54, 64, 68–69, 78, 85, 89, 96, 102, 112, 116, 119, 124, 135, 141–42, 145, 150, 153–59, 174, 177, 180, 186, 192, 213, 215, 285, 311, 330

Newton, Helen, 5, 11–12, 42–45, 59, 61, 63

Newton, Jack, 5, 10–11, 18, 26, 40, 59, 66, 75–78, 82, 265–67, 276, 278, 285, 295–96

Newton, James Elmer, 1–3, 153, 263, 293

Newton, Jim, 144

Newton, Kathleen, 3, 12, 28, 37, 53, 64, 82, 89

Newton, Kathleen, 3, 28, 64, 113

Newton, Laura Dreier, 1–4, 31, 138, 153, 155, 159, 293

Newton, Marc, 92, 285, 340, 342

Newton, Maureen, 3, 28, 37–38, 64, 103

Newton, Merle, 141

Newton, Patricia "Pat," 5, 43, 48–49, 52, 59, 60, 63, 87

Newton, Raymond, 3, 5, 7, 37, 40

Newton, Richard "Richie," vii, xi, 4, 6, 8–9, 12, 15, 17, 20–22, 24–25, 28, 30, 32–33, 35, 41, 44, 49, 52–53, 55, 58, 62, 64–66, 69, 71, 80, 89, 92, 102, 104–106, 110, 113, 116, 120, 122, 124, 135, 142–43, 145–48, 150, 155, 158, 162, 176–77, 180, 182, 184, 186, 188–91, 193–95, 199, 201, 207, 210, 213, 215, 218, 230–31, 236–37, 244, 248-49, 252–53, 256–57, 262–64, 266, 274, 277–78, 280, 282, 284, 286, 291–92, 297–300, 304, 307, 309, 319–20, 323, 325–26, 336–37, 340, 345

Newton, Robert, 3

Newton, Roberta "Betty," 3, 5, 7

Newton, Roland "Rollie," vii, xi, 4, 6, 8–9, 12, 17, 20–22, 24–26, 28, 30, 32–33, 35, 41, 44, 49, 52–53, 55, 58, 62, 64, 66–67, 69, 71, 77, 80, 85, 89, 92–93, 102, 104–107, 110, 113, 116, 119–120, 123–24, 135–36, 139, 142–43, 145–48, 150, 155–58, 168, 171–74, 177, 181, 184, 192, 201, 211, 213–15, 217–18, 220, 231–32, 235, 237, 244–45, 247–48, 290–91, 295, 297–99, 300, 304, 306–307, 309–10, 319–20, 323, 337, 340, 345

Newton, Ronald "Ronnie," x, 4, 6, 8–9, 17, 24, 35, 47, 50–52, 57–58, 66, 68–71, 80, 99, 101–02, 104, 108, 110, 116, 124, 126, 130, 132–34, 136, 142, 150, 155, 158–59, 162,

165, 177, 179, 185–86, 204, 210,
213, 215, 220–21, 223–24, 226,
234, 237, 248–50, 263, 279–80,
287–88, 295, 297, 299–300, 302,
305, 307, 311, 313, 320–21, 323–
24, 328–29, 336, 340, 345
Newton, Rosemary, 3, 5, 7, 40, 64–65,
70–71
Newton, Spaulding "Tex," 285, 309
Newton, Thomas "Tom," 7–8, 25, 48,
50, 52, 57, 60-63, 66, 74, 224,
276, 285, 295-96, 315
Newton, Urban, "Orbin," 3, 7, 40,
68, 144
Newtonville, 328
North Carolina State University, 72
North Central League, 157–58, 164, 190
Nottingham, Kathy, 223–235, 236,
238–41, 276
Nottingham, Walter, 332
Nuss, Larry, 17, 47, 104, 140, 229
Nygren, Eva Jane Peters (Mrs.), 82–85

O

Oklahoma City University, 72
Old Crow, 295
Oldsmobile, 223, 325, 327
Olson, Emil, 83
Olson, Gary, 11–12, 17, 21, 33, 48–50,
54, 57–58, 83–84, 91, 98, 104,
147, 170, 190, 205, 213, 318–
19, 321
Olson, Gilman, 11
Olson, Margaret, 12, 40, 56-58, 99
Olson, Mary Helen, 17, 136, 142
Olson, Roger, 342
Ordway, Colorado, 198
Outstanding Athlete, 240, 321
Owen, Donnie, 57, 314
Owen, Janice, 262

P

Palinkx (Ginger's mother) (Mrs.), 212
Palinkx, Emil, 333
Palinkx, Ginger, 211–215
Palinkx, Vernon, 304
Palombo, Francie, 213, 285
Pappas, Mike, 315
Pappenheim, Bob, 134
Park Lane Hotel, 310
Partridge, Don, 230
Pee-Wee (PW), 78, 80
Peoria Cats, 72
Pep Club, 44, 136, 154, 163, 211,
262, 285
Peppler, Wilbert, 194–95
pep rally, 39
Peralez, Rudy, 253, 257
Peru College, 100, 330, 332, 335
Peters, Carl, 82
Peters, Helen, 314
Peters, Mary Louise, 43
Petersen, Fred, 74
Petersen, Tom, 62, 68, 161
Petras, Larry, 191, 201
PF Flyers, 78
Philistine, 93
Phillips 66ers, 72
physical education, x, 78, 322
physics, 239
"Picnic," 213
Pinza, Ezio, 240
Pitchford, Bud, 243, 276
Plymouth Fury, 330
pole vault, 217, 312
poliomyelitis "polio," 12, 205, 322
posture foundation, 78
Poudre Valley League, 78, 104
prom, 205, 211
Pueblo, Colorado, 199

R

rabbit zone defense, 180, 254
Rademacher, Eddie, 57, 60
Rademacher, Josephine, 17, 58, 105
Rademacher, Louis, 18
Red & White Grocery, 28, 73, 333
Reynolds, Lloyd, 201
Roberts, Donald, 314
Roberts, Grover, 20
Roberts, John, 18, 314
Rohn, Roland, 283, 291
Roman, Hulda, 3
Rosenoff, Eddie, 18
Russell, Bill, 73, 197

S

Saks Fifth Avenue, 37
salutatorian, 321
Schaefer, Lowell, 342
Schaefer, Lyle, 57, 98, 104, 121, 152, 170, 190, 213, 216, 229, 248, 257, 263, 267, 277, 285, 292–93, 318, 321
Schaefer, Russell (Mr.), 152, 171, 177, 285, 287, 318
Schell, Frank, 38
Schell, John "Johnny," 53, 117, 119-20, 122, 124, 134, 136-37, 139-42
Schell, Susan, 105
Schilling, Jerry, 137
Schlagel, Ronnie, 223
Schmidt, Bryan, 89, 161, 169
Schneidmiller, Bill, 229–30
scholarship, 320, 337
school board, 83, 209
Seewald, Dean, 232, 262, 277–78, 328, 330
Seewald, Robert "Bobby," 244, 285
Sekich, Freddie, 53
Sekich, Violet, 43
Seton University Hall, 73
set shot, 20, 106, 120, 167, 282

Shane (gunslinger), 335
Shavlick, Ronnie, 72
Short, Arnold, 72
short punt, 164
Siddens, Robert, 281
Silas Marner, 318
silver poplar, 25, 27, 73
Sioux Falls, 94
siren, 194–95
Sitzman, Jerry, 85, 89, 117, 122, 136, 141, 152, 157, 174, 179, 184–85, 188, 190–92, 216, 244
Slee, Walt, 73, 78, 222, 227, 285
Smith, Leonard, 54, 82, 119
smoking, 169–70
Snider, George, 28, 39
Snyder's Jewelry, 275
softball, 20, 25, 27
"Some Enchanted Evening," 240
Spanish, 126–27
Spencer, Denver, 21–22
Spencer, Edwin, 11, 18, 22, 39, 45, 52, 161
Spencer, Lillian, 21, 49
split-T, 227, 230
sports call show, 257
Springfield College, 271, 319
Spuddiggers, 192, 261, 264
Stanford University, 271, 319
Stephens College, 331
Stotts, Art, 342
Stotts, Iva, 25
Stotts, Keith, 119, 121
Stotts, Nadine, 23–24
strep throat, 157
student council, 208
student court, 208
St. Vrain Memorial Building, 268, 272
St. Vrain River Valley, 332
sugar beets, 232
Swedish Lutheran Church, 56

T

Team of the Week, 257
Tesone, Alex "Coach," 54, 191–92
Texas Flying Queens, 73
Thompson, Allen, 66, 78, 88, 91, 104, 115, 118, 129, 131, 133, 135, 141, 152, 158, 169, 176, 180, 188, 190, 199, 213, 216–17, 229, 243, 253, 255–56, 265, 286, 293
Thompson, Delbert, 154
Thompson, Jessie, 138
Thornton, Wilbur, 74
Tigers, 294
Timms, Paul, 265
tip-in, 166
track, 25, 216, 220, 310
Tri-Valley, 244, 252
Troutman, Arthur, 112, 114, 119, 205-08, 210, 212–213
Tway, Gary, 134, 136, 315
typing, 49, 113, 128

U

Uhrich, Bill, 14
Ulibarri, George, 41
"Unchained Melody," 182
United Brethren Church, 28
University of Denver, 72, 317
University of San Francisco, 73
U.S. Rubber, 309
Utah State University, 72

V

valedictorian, 100, 314, 316
Vannest, Frank, 254
Virgin Mary, 56
Vogel, Barbara, 262
Vogel, Ronnie, 229–30, 244
Von Loh, Allen, 283
Von Loh, Willis, 283

W

Walter, Beverly Jane, 43
Warner, David, 314
Warner, Edwin, 87
Warnick, Reed, 179
Warriors, Frederick, 53, 191, 274
Washington Generals, 73
Washington Highway, 11, 247
Weber, Ronald "Weber," 20, 26–29, 32, 66–67, 71, 86, 89, 109, 134–35, 152, 154–55, 160–63, 232, 261, 277, 285, 314, 333–35
Weber, Roy, 26, 32
Weber, Vernon, 314
Weingardt, Rosemary, 213
Weingarth, Mary, 338
Weld County, 1, 8, 36
Western State College, 320
Wichita Vickers, 72
Widger, Vernon, 28, 32, 41, 89, 114, 152, 154, 261, 277
Wilde, Brandon de, 335
Wilkinson, Bud, 164
Williams Wayside Inn, 309
wing, 106, 122, 184, 200
Winkles, Bobby, 274
Winter, Jack, 179
Winters, Kenny, 329
Wizards, 86, 107–8
Wolverines, 282
Wooden, John, 197
WPA (Works Progress Administration), 2, 36
Wright, Colleen, 136, 142
Wright, Frank Lloyd, 317
Wright, Ted, 320